"*This is where you belong,*" *Kit rasped, his voice thick.*

Had he heard her thoughts?

"Kit," she breathed. With that she looked up at him, his eyes incandescent. His mouth descended upon hers, hungry, pleading. And she felt herself responding, that strange jolt she had experienced earlier at his mere touch threatened to consume her entire body.

It was as if they had always been together, Deanie and Kit. The magic that had brought them to each other seemed to fade in the overwhelming power of their passion.

His mouth was just as she imagined it would be, strong yet soft, demanding yet supple. She was lost in a spiral, whirling in his arms, both safe and terrified at the same time. She stepped back, gasping.

"Kit," she panted. "What are we going to do?"

His eyes were foggy, and again he reached for her, pulling her close. "I know not," he muttered. "Dear God, I know not."

PRAISE FOR *ASHTON'S BRIDE*

"Quite simply, a must-read. . . ."

—*Publishers Weekly*

"This is more than just a time-travel, it's about finding out where you belong. Lush descriptions, vivid characters, and strong emotional writing combine to make this an unforgettable novel."

—*Rendezvous*

"I was captivated from the very first page. *ASHTON'S BRIDE* is fabulous! Poignant, powerful, utterly compelling and so very heartwarming. Judy O'Brien is the most exciting—and most original—new voice to hit the romance scene in years!"

—Brenda Joyce, author of *The Game*

"This tender, funny love story will haunt me for a long time. . . . I feel as if I've discovered a rare and charming new treasure to add to my list of favorite authors. Ms. O'Brien's fresh and witty style tickled both my funny bone and my heartstrings."

—Teresa Medeiros, author of *A Whisper of Roses*

"Judith O'Brien makes you cry and she makes you laugh. *ASHTON'S BRIDE* is an utterly heartwarming love story with characters who will captivate you and leave you basking in a warm, magical glow."

—Dorothy Cannell, author of *Femmes Fatal*

"This is one new writer who has a whole new light on the art of writing. I enjoyed this book, and it was with real regret that I had to stop when the story ended. 5 Bells, NOT TO BE MISSED!!"

—"Bell, Book and Candle" book dealer

Books by Judith O'Brien

Rhapsody in Time
Ashton's Bride
Once Upon a Rose

Published by POCKET BOOKS

JUDITH O'BRIEN

ONCE UPON A ROSE

POCKET BOOKS
New York   London   Toronto   Sydney

This book is a work of fiction. Names, characters, places and incidents are products of the author's imagination or are used fictitiously. Any resemblance to actual events or locales or persons, living or dead, is entirely coincidental.

An *Original* Publication of POCKET BOOKS

A Pocket Star Book published by
POCKET BOOKS, a division of Simon & Schuster Inc.
1230 Avenue of the Americas, New York, NY 10020

Copyright © 1996 by Judith O'Brien

ISBN: 1-4165-0315-3

This Pocket Books paperback printing May 2004

10 9 8 7 6 5 4 3 2 1

POCKET STAR BOOKS and colophon are registered trademarks of Simon & Schuster Inc.

Front cover illustration by Darryl Zndek

Printed in the U.S.A.

Huge thank-yous to my agent, Meg Ruley, my editor, Linda Marrow, and associate editor, Kate Collins. You guys have been great!

This book is for Radney Foster, who has more editorial sense than a country music star ought to. Not only did he answer my often inane and frequently repeated questions with a patience bordering on sainthood, but he left me laughing in the process. Thanks, Radney, for your friendship.

Chapter 1

*T*HERE WAS A SOFT BREEZE SWIRLING AT HER SLIPPERED FEET, the wind gently snapping the thick velvet hem across her slender ankles. It was early spring, yet a crisp winter chill lingered. The afternoon sun was slowly sapping the bite from the damp air, paving the way for a glorious day, a welcome respite from England's frigid rains.

She adjusted herself on the ancient stone bench, trying to ignore the cold of the seat as it snaked across her too-straight back. Her gown, many layered and sumptuous, glinted in the sun, riots of gold encircling the blue velvet neckline. The sleeves, capped tightly over her shoulders, fanned into generous folds of gold brocade, intricate designs studded with freshwater pearls. At her delicate wrists were fine linen gathers, edged in gold thread.

In her hands was an inlaid lute, which she strummed with an absentminded grace. Yet it was her face, petite under a peaked headdress, that was most arresting.

Black lashes fluttered over her liquid brown eyes, casting a shadowy fringe over cheeks of creamy perfection. Her nose, small without being winsome, managed to indicate a genteel dignity, and her lips—full and moistened by a swift caress of her tongue—hovered on the edge of a smile. For all her grave beauty, there was a wisp of humor as fine and silky as the stray tendril of chestnut hair that had somehow escaped the confines of the rigid angular headpiece and now rested tentatively against her smooth neck.

A rustling in the dense shrubbery caught her attention, and her hand paused above the lute strings.

A gentleman emerged from a small break in the bushes, wearing a maroon doublet the color of fine claret. The ruffles of his white shirt skimmed the lines of his clean-shaven jaw. His hair was a pallid red, matched by red eyebrows and pale eyes. He bowed low to the seated lady, a sword jutting behind him as his legs crossed in courtly greeting.

"Milady." His voice was full, a startling contrast to his undecided features. "Your lord has returned."

The woman on the bench was about to respond, her lips parted to reveal brilliant white teeth, when another voice pierced the air.

"Cut!" snapped the director.

He turned to the young cameraman to make sure he had stopped shooting. Then he focused his full wrath on the actor in the claret-colored doublet. "For God's sake, Stan, you can do better than that."

Stan straightened, his face at once haughty and defensive. "My name is *Stanley.*" His tone was impeccably modulated. "I am a Shakspearian thespian, sir. I am not accustomed to appearing in . . ." He closed his eyes as if seeking the inner strength to find composure, stammering to continue.

"That's all right, honey," the woman with the lute prodded, grinning as she waved her hand. "You just aren't used to being in music videos, are you?"

The man nodded, his ruff bobbing with every swallow.

"Well Stan, let me tell you"—she stood up, placing the lute against the leg of the stone bench—"I'm not used to England, not one bit. So I guess you could say we're even, okay?" Her voice was a soothing lilt, unmistakably Southern, yet filled with gentle, honeyed warmth.

The actor relaxed a little and gratefully shook the hand she offered. "Miss Bailey," he said, his voice again full and deep enough to reach the last row in any theater. "I must tell you how much I enjoy your music. Your compositions are unique, no matter which artist performs them. I usually don't care for—well . . . I usually listen to music of a more classical nature. But Miss Bailey—"

"Please call me *Deanie.*" She shrugged in her easy manner.

"Yes, well—Miss Deanie, I believe you have a real gift. As I said, I usually don't listen to, uh . . ."

"Country music?" she offered, raising her dark eyebrows as she watched the actor grope for words.

"No, I don't. I usually find it too . . ."

"Twangy?" Her voice was unable to conceal a bubble of laughter, and the actor smiled and nodded. Even with the thick Nashville accent, there was a richness to the way she spoke, how she rounded the vowels and hardened the consonants, that was undeniably appealing.

Before the actor and Deanie could exchange any more words, the director was beside them, cracking a riding crop against his flattened palm. A middle-aged man with a thickening waist and thinning hair, he shot the Shakespearean actor what he hoped was a withering glance.

"You, Stan, may pick up your check for the day's work. You may also tell the other spear carriers to go home, or back to your castle, wherever you guys hang out."

Stan gave no indication he had heard the director. Instead, he raised Deanie's fingers to his lips and kissed the back of her hand as he executed a bow of serene poise.

"You are a most gracious lady, and I can only but wish that—"

The director's eyes flickered up from the clipboard a production assistant was holding before him. "Stan, just beat it. Vamoose. Get outta here."

The actor straightened and, after a curt nod, walked over to collect his paycheck with whatever dignity he could muster.

"Now Nathan," Deanie muttered, shaking her head, "that wasn't nice, not one bit." She glanced around her. "Hey, where did my cigarettes go?"

"You shouldn't smoke," Nathan responded. "It will ruin your voice. This is your big chance, kiddo. Reba dropped out, and the record label is allowing you to drop in. This isn't just a once-in-a-lifetime chance. It's a once-in-a-million-lifetimes chance."

"I know, Nathan," she replied softly. "I've been dreaming of a chance like this ever since I was a little kid. You know," she continued, as her voice took on a whimsical lilt, "this is sort of like an old movie, *A Star Is Born* or *42nd Street* or whatever. I've paid my dues. All those years of writing songs for other people. Now I'm getting a chance."

The director ignored her. "And about that actor, Deanie. You don't know what these Brits can be like." The director signed the paper with a decided flourish, then looked at Deanie, tapping the riding crop against the side of his jodhpurs. He had never been within a hundred yards of a horse in his life, yet he always directed his videos in Prussian equestrian regalia. That way he could imagine he was Erich von Stroheim directing *Greed,* instead of Nathan Burns directing another music video.

"These Shakespearean actors all want to be the next Olivier," he continued, eyeing Deanie with avunclar wisdom. "You've never been to England before?" In truth, the director had never been to England either, but he would rather be forced to ride a horse than admit the fact.

"Nope." Deanie sighed, stretching her arms over her head. The costume was more than uncomfortable; it was torture, especially for a woman who usually lived in jeans and sneakers.

The headdress alone was uniquely painful. To Deanie's eyes it looked like a small toolshed, with angled sides just like a Tennessee birdhouse. The rims were studded with cut-glass stones that were supposed to resemble rubies, but up close one could see the glue swirls and the little pencil marks made by the person who'd decorated the thing. In theory it was supposed to make Deanie look like the member of a midsixteenth-century court. Instead, she felt like a second-rate showgirl with a barn on her head. She had even decorated the sides of the headdress with the words "See Rock City" in masking tape, but nobody thought it was funny.

"What's the name of this place again?" Deanie yawned as she asked the question.

"England." The director looked off toward a white trailer parked in the distance.

"I know that, Nathan," she said, grinning. "I mean, what's the name of this house, or whatever it is."

"Oh. Hampton Court Palace. It was the home of Henry VIII." He swished the riding crop in the air like a sword. "Where do you suppose Bucky Lee has disappeared to? We're losing the light." He squinted into the sun, using his hands—the crop jutting into Deanie's face—to frame an imaginary scene.

Deanie brushed away the crop, glancing at the trailer and the magnificent plum-colored palace beyond. Bucky Lee Denton. If she never heard that man's name again, it would be way too soon.

A cigarette would be perfect right about now.

She reached behind her, adjusting the Velcro fastenings on her gown. Bucky Lee Denton. Who the hell was he to keep the whole crew waiting? They had spent the day preparing the scene, stalling with the British actors, shooting footage that would never be used out of sheer boredom.

All the while, Bucky Lee Denton, the newest sensation to come out of Nashville, was cloistered in his extra-wide trailer, sending his assistants out for more hair spray and diet cola.

Several months earlier a well-known music critic had dubbed Bucky Lee the "Denton Disease." Outraged, the country music community had rallied around Denton like a circle of covered wagons.

And then, one by one, they got to know him. His backstage temper tantrums and a particularly ugly run-in with a department-store Santa made front-page news, along with his scathing comments about other country music artists.

Unfortunately, Bucky Lee Denton's records were selling faster than waxed lightning. He was impossible to ignore, and even more impossible to like.

It was Bucky Lee Denton who had insisted this video be shot in England. He claimed it was his artistic vision of the song, a gentle pastoral English setting. But Deanie knew the only vision Bucky Lee had was of the long-limbed teenage supermodel he was following all over Europe like a lovesick puppy. And since Bucky Lee Denton was basically paying the electric bill over at Era Records, the executives were bumping heads in frantic efforts to make him happy. Even if it was at the expense of Deanie Bailey.

"Is he ready yet?" asked a bored but stunningly beautiful woman wearing a spandex leotard and a conical damsel-in-distress headpiece. The orange chiffon scarf attached to the tip of the cone flapped in the breeze like an airport wind sock.

The director smiled warmly. It had been his idea to pepper the video with Tudor Babes—or TBs, as everyone on the set now called them. "It's Monica, right?"

Tudor Babe shifted on her spike heels and threw a swift glance at Deanie. "Yeah, I'm Monica," she confirmed testily. "How come she gets to wear a dress?" A manicured thumb was aimed at Deanie.

"Ah. Because, my dear, she wrote the song and will perform it with Bucky Lee. She's the female element to our touching duet." The riding crop twitched with pleasure as Nathan Burns took a step toward the TB.

Deanie let out an exasperated sigh and shook her head. If the director's pattern was to remain consistent, the TB would soon be upgraded to a serving wench. The serving wench scene was scheduled to be shot the next day, with Deanie and Bucky Lee lip-synching while being fed peeled grapes. That is, if Bucky Lee could get his hair—or, more accurately, his hair weave—under control.

It was her song. She'd written the lyrics and the melody, a simple love song. But Bucky Lee had ruined everything. From the moment her manager had told her the good news—that Bucky Lee Denton wanted to record her song— the tune had left her hands, spiraling out of control until it reached this absurd point. The budget for this video was a tightly guarded secret, but it was generally acknowledged to make the Michael Jackson *Thriller* video seem like vacation slides.

At least she was allowed to be a part of this project. The last few times one of her songs had been made into a video, she had been firmly relegated to the sidelines, watching with clenched fists as other performers mouthed her words to her tunes.

There was a sudden commotion in the direction of the white trailer, and Deanie bit her lip, wondering if Bucky Lee was about to make an appearance. The director stopped tracing his crop along the outside of Monica's shapely leg and stared at the trailer. An expectant hush descended over the cast and crew. Coffee stirrers were stilled in foam cups. Scattered conversations were halted midsentence. Even the birds stopped their chirping. All eyes were on the trailer.

The door swung open with a vigorous punch, and out stepped Bucky Lee Denton.

From the top step of his trailer he surveyed the scene,

master of all before him. His stance of comfortable arrogance proclaimed his confidence. He alone was the reason
they were all gathered in England, why the cast and crew
had been flown in from Los Angeles and New York and
Nashville. In his trademark red T-shirt and black cowboy
hat, he was in total command.

But all Deanie could see was a rather short guy in an
oversized hat, looking more like Deputy Dawg than a real
cowboy. In one of the more unfortunate instances of timing
that seemed to dominate and shape Wilma Dean Bailey's
life, she began to giggle. In the vast silence of the sloping
lawn, her voice carried as if amplified a million times.
Before she could get herself under control, Bucky Lee
Denton's furious glare settled on her, and he cocked his
head slightly.

That did it. All she could think of was the old RCA
emblem depicting "His Master's Voice," a spotted dog
listening to a gramophone, head cocked exactly as was
Bucky Lee's cowboy-hatted head. Deanie didn't just giggle,
she didn't just laugh. Wilma Dean Bailey, in that gentle
English backdrop, howled. Once she began she was incapable of stopping, and the laughter tumbled from her, speed-
ing beyond her control.

She looked down at her feet, trying to curb her hilarity,
taking deep breaths, but her feet reminded her of his
cowboy boots and the five-inch lifts he tucked into the soles.
So she tried to concentrate on her fingers, but that merely
caused her to recall Bucky Lee's one attempt to play the
guitar and the sour chords that rang from his prop instrument between takes.

Through her tears she could see the horrified glances of
the crew members Ping-Ponging between Deanie and Bucky
Lee. Then she heard a terrible, now-familiar sound: the
slamming of a trailer door. This time it left the aluminum
steps rattling, and a potted mum spilled off the top landing.
Everyone knew exactly what that meant: Bucky Lee Denton

would not make another appearance until the next day. If at all.

Suddenly it wasn't so funny anymore. She wiped under her eyes, where tears had dampened her mascara to the consistency of molten asphalt, and assumed the most contrite expression she could manage.

"Goddammit, Deanie!" bellowed the director. "How the hell could you do that?"

All eyes were now fixed on Deanie in her rayon Tudor gown with Velcro fastenings and plastic-seed pearls and birdhouse headdress. She swallowed. "I'm sorry," she whispered, her voice raspy with laughter and guilt.

No one responded. As the cast wandered off to collect their paychecks and the crew went through the motions of striking the set for the day, Deanie knew she was once again the victim of her lifelong curse.

Bad timing.

Wilma Dean Bailey's very existence was a virtual synonym for rotten timing. For instance, the name "Wilma Dean" was a bit of quixotic whimsy on her mother's part. As groping teenagers, Lorna Dune and Dickie Bailey made an early exit from the film *Splendor in the Grass* to get married. By the standards of Winslow, Kentucky, they had demonstrated tremendous restraint.

Ten months later their daughter was born, and Lorna named the dark-haired infant "Wilma Dean," after the character portrayed by Natalie Wood in the movie.

It wasn't until several years later, when the film was finally aired on television, that Lorna saw the entire movie. Much to her openmouthed shock, the Wilma Dean in the movie suffers a nervous breakdown and ends up in a mental institution.

But it was too late to change Deanie's name. The precocious tot was already scribbling it on every wall and overdue bill she could get a crayon on. Lorna was, of course, concerned about the eventual psychological ramifications of naming a child after a suicidal heroine, so she kept her daughter away from any and all Natalie Wood films, including *Miracle on 34th Street* and *Scudda Hoo! Scudda Hay!* Besides, Lorna rationalized, the Deanie in *Splendor in the Grass* ends up okay. Warren Beatty marries another woman. So what?

About this time Lorna made another unfortunate discovery. Her husband, Dickie Bailey, whose all-night revels with fellow good ol' boys had earned him a slew of randy nicknames, finally decided he was not cut out for marriage and fatherhood. Within a week he was gone. Lorna never did find out what had happened to her ex-husband. Their contact ceased with the signing of the final divorce papers.

Years later she saw an "Oprah" show on bigamists. One guest, an overweight shoe salesman sporting a limp string tie and exaggerated sideburns, looked suspiciously like Dickie Bailey, but Lorna could never be sure.

With steel determination and hard work, Lorna managed to scrape together enough money to leave their rural Kentucky home for Nashville. All she wanted was a chance to begin afresh, to raise her daughter away from the backhanded whispers of Winslow. Even worse were the pitying stares of other women, the mutters of "Poor Lorna, can't hold on to a man." She'd had enough.

In Nashville she found a job as a truck-stop waitress. The hours were grueling but the tips were usually good, and Lorna found happiness in the anonymity of the place. Even the regulars only passed through twice a month. It was well worth the occasional painful pinch from an amorous trucker.

Little Wilma Dean, meanwhile, grew from a giggling child to a woman of startling beauty. By the time her daughter reached high school, Lorna, alarmed by the way the customers would grin at her daughter while dripping grits in the lap of their jeans, had banished her from the truckstop.

The irony that her daughter bore an uncanny resemblance to Natalie Wood was not lost on Lorna.

"Why, ain't she the spitting image of that gal from *Rebel Without a Cause?*" gasped a beefy trucker with a paper napkin tucked into his red flannel shirt.

"Who?" inquired a doe-eyed Deanie as her mother shoved her through the restaurant door.

"Never mind," spat Lorna, glaring at the customer.

No one was really surprised when Deanie was elected homecoming queen her senior year in high school. Although she was, in the buffered words of a guidance counselor, "no student," Deanie was easily the most popular girl in her class. Not only was she the best cheerleader for the state's worst football team, she was also the president of the choral society and had the lead part in the school's production of *Annie Get Your Gun.*

What did surprise folks was the freak hailstorm that hit Nashville the day of the homecoming parade, tearing the corrugated roof off the gym and ending all hopes of Deanie receiving the ceremonial five-and-dime crown. Graduation came and went with all the pomp and celebration of a used-tire sale. Once again, bad timing and Wilma Dean Bailey were inexorably linked.

With her diploma in hand, Deanie began searching for a job, only to discover that businesses were less than thrilled at the prospect of hiring an uncrowned homecoming queen who could carry a tune. By the end of the summer, Deanie had finally found a job. Like her mother, Deanie became a waitress. Only Deanie, as if to prove her independence, worked at a Krispy Kream doughnut shop.

A crucial revelation hit Deanie that first fall after high school. She felt something vital was missing from her life, an emptiness that left her feeling incomplete. After ticking off the possibilities on her fingers, she realized that what was lacking was music.

For as long as she could remember, she had been involved in chorus classes or school-based musicals. As her interest in music grew, her voice, always pleasant, mellowed into a rich instrument of unexpected depth. When she sang, she wasn't just Deanie Bailey; she could imagine being anyone in the world. For her, music was magic. Her voice alone had never let her down; it was the one thing she could always count on.

Lorna, noticing her daughter's interest yet not quite understanding it, even gave her a guitar from the Sears catalog for her sixteenth birthday, and Deanie became good enough to accompany the chorus and strum along at school assemblies.

Deanie, who had lived a life free from the shackles of ambition, suddenly knew what she wanted to become. With the tenacity of a spawning salmon, Deanie set about becoming the next Patsy Cline.

She told no one at the Krispy Kream about her aspiration, only her mother and a friend from high school who had become a receptionist at a new company, Era Records. Her mother treated her announcement as seriously as she had taken previous proclaimations from her daughter.

When Deanie was eight, she decided she wanted to be a princess. "Fine, dear," a weary Lorna mumbled.

When she was eleven, she wanted to become an Olympic figure skater. "Very good, honey," Lorna replied.

Now Deanie wanted to become a country singer, and Lorna patted her daughter's head and asked her to bring home two dozen assorted doughnuts as a treat for the other truck-stop waitresses.

About that time, Deanie realized that just mouthing other people's songs was no longer enough. Although she could put tremulous emotion behind most tunes, it was really just musical play-acting. It didn't feel absolutely right.

Most country songs didn't fit her personality, as she couldn't identify with the raw emotions. Sure, she had faced rough times with her mom, but they had faced them together. Never had she been truly frightened or threatened or depressed. Since she'd never had a dog, she had never even experienced a dog's death, nor his running away or chewing a favorite slipper. She'd never once owned a pickup truck.

Above all, she had never been in love. As a whole, the life experiences of Wilma Dean Bailey were not the stuff of great songs.

But that didn't stop Deanie. Her first efforts were laughably awful, about wayward men and forgiving women. She borrowed from her mother's life, but it didn't ring true. Then she tried lyrics about Paris and grand romances, two more adventures she had yet to experience, although "gay Paree" did rhyme rather nicely with "his dungarees."

One evening, while soaking her throbbing feet in a tub of Epsom salts, she heard a radio interview with a country songwriter.

"You have to write what you know, what you're familiar with, what touches your heart," the writer stated. "Otherwise you won't believe it and, more important, other people won't believe it."

Without bothering to dry her feet, Deanie hopped out of the tub and grabbed her guitar. In about an hour she had written a song about a former beauty queen working in a doughnut shop. Even after playing and replaying the song into a tape recorder, she felt an unfamiliar thrill rush through her.

"This is it," she marveled aloud. "This is how it's done."

After that, songs came easily and quickly, usually when she was at work, cleaning the coffee machine or waiting for a customer to decide between the chocolate frosteds or the sugar-coated bismarks. Although she still had to experience the fodder of most country songs, Deanie had discovered she possessed a unique ability to convey lyrics. Phrases would come to her, snatches of offhanded comments. The speaker would leave, toting the white pastry bag, forgetting all about the conversation overheard by the eager young woman behind the counter.

By keeping her mouth shut and her ears open at work, she

heard enough from the customers and the other waitresses to fill a dozen lifetimes of country songs. Everyone had a story to tell, and Deanie added her own words and imagination to spin their tales.

She became a voracious reader of country music publications, and for the first time she regretted not taking her school years more seriously. There was so much she didn't understand about the business, phrases that meant nothing to her but seemed to be of great importance to those in the music industry.

She never came to work without a tape of her latest composition in the pocket of her apron, on the off chance that someone might want to hear her songs. One afternoon two long-haired men came to her counter discussing a recording session. Deanie was awestruck by their easy music banter.

"I write songs," she blurted.

The other waitresses rolled their eyes at Deanie, and she felt a furious blush creep up from the neckline of her starched gingham uniform.

One of the men raised a graying eyebrow. "Oh yeah?" He crooked a finger, and she leaned over the counter. "I'll give you some advice, doll," he whispered.

He then offered a suggestion that was nothing more than a very Southern variation of the age-old casting couch. Deanie was stunned, certain that she had not heard the man correctly.

In a voice loud enough to be heard across the shop, he repeated his lewd proposition. Her eyes held his as she reached behind for a fresh pot of coffee, smiled at him, and poured the scalding brew over his hand that rested on the counter.

The man howled in pain, but Deanie maintained an expression of serenity and informed him that refills were on the house.

As he ran to the bathroom, muttering oaths and shaking his hand in the air—a futile attempt to cool it off—his companion grimaced apologetically and took one of her tapes. He promised to get back to her within a week with an honest appraisal of her work.

As the first week stretched on into the second and third and still she'd had no word, she realized it was useless. She had no way to contact him anyway, since she didn't even know his name. She chalked it up to experience, but the exquisitely close brush with the music world had made her more determined than ever.

Then her friend, the record-company receptionist, convinced a low-rung executive to grant Deanie a five-minute interview. She called in sick at the Krispy Kream, terrified at the prospect of crossing the threshold of Era Records smelling like a glazed doughnut.

Dazzled by the feel of plush, unstained carpet under her feet, awed by the glossy photographs of stars and near-stars lining the hallway, Deanie followed her friend to the executive's tiny, windowless office.

He was young but prematurely bald, which gave him an aura of intelligence he did not deserve. He listened politely to her tape, cutting each song off after fifteen seconds. Finally he leaned back in his vinyl swivel chair, his fingertips steepled together in a practiced gesture.

"Well well, Jeanie . . ." he began.

"Deanie," she corrected, with the most submissive smile she could manage.

"Deanie? Oh, well," he frowned before clearing his throat. "Where are you presently employed?"

She swallowed before answering. "At the Krispy Kream."

"Ah. I see. Well, Jeanie, I suggest you hold onto that job and keep on working—" He was interrupted by the bleep of his telephone and gave her a dismissive nod. She snatched up her tape and left as quickly as possible, her cheeks burning with anger and humiliation.

Three weeks later, as she was closing up the shop, she heard a car radio blaring from the parking lot. It was the new single from Vic Jenkens, the country crooner with matinee-idol looks and a smooth-as-molasses voice. Deanie paused, a wet, coffee-stained rag clutched in her hand as she wiped down the counter.

Vic Jenkens was singing her song.

The rag flopped to the linoleum floor. She blinked, dumbfounded at hearing the words she'd penned while sitting on her own bed coming from a car radio. From Vic Jenkens's voice—*her* words set to *her* tune created on *her* Sears guitar.

The car either closed its door or left the parking lot, she never knew. All she was sure of was that her song had faded, leaving her under the humming fluorescent lights of the empty Krispy Kream.

How did it happen? Her mind whirled as she stumbled into the parking lot, her sweater askew, her white-soled shoes crunching the gravel. Her hands trembled as she fumbled for her car keys, numbly recalling that they were in her apron pocket.

Her apron pocket. Then it came back to her: The song Vic Jenkens had recorded was on the tape she had given those Music Row guys, the friend of the man she had spilled coffee on. They had stolen her song.

Her first thought was to call up a radio station—any radio station—and proclaim herself to be the composer of the new Vic Jenkens hit. Clearly someone had laid claim to the song, or she would have heard from his manager or the record company. She had devoured enough fan magazines to have a vague idea how those things worked.

But it would have been absurd, a ranting Krispy Kream waitress calling a radio station at midnight announcing that Vic Jenkens had stolen her song. Unwelcome images flooded into her mind, of people who claimed to have been kidnapped by aliens or of diehard Elvis sighters. She suddenly envisioned herself being interviewed on television, in her Krispy Kream gingham and ruffled apron, the mandatory hairnet glimmering under the TV lights, trays of doughnuts stacked behind her. She would look like a crazy woman.

With no proof to offer, no evidence other than her word against theirs, Deanie would be better off claiming to be Bigfoot's love child. By the time she climbed into her bed, she was convinced she had best let the whole thing go. This was an important lesson, she muttered to the foam pillow. Never again would she be so stupid. Never again would she be so trusting.

By the next morning she was feeling better, even a little pleased. The song had been good enough for those guys to steal. Deanie decided she must be on the right track.

Within three weeks, the song was hailed as the most brilliant of Vic Jenkens's career. It was everywhere, not only blasting from car windows, but at the mall and in the Krispy Kream and on television. Everyone seemed to be humming Deanie's tune. Even at the Piggly Wiggly, the damn song wafted over the poultry case.

Just when Deanie thought she would explode, the impossible happened: Vic Jenkens himself strolled into the Krispy Kream.

Deanie and the other waitresses knew something was up when his "people," vicious-looking men with walkie talkies and professional sneers, entered ahead of the star. Then came the photographers, giddy as prom queens with cold duck, clicking away as Vic Jenkens opened the clearly marked Krispy Kream door and feigned an expression of surprise.

Something about the absurdity of the situation struck Deanie as riotously funny. She began to giggle, squinting against the flashing lights, ignoring the hush of the other waitresses and the surly glares from Jenkens's people.

Vic Jenkens immediately spun to face her, cool fury evident in his eyes. Deanie swallowed, a smile still on her face. He was much better looking in real life than in print.

"What you laughing at, girl?" His voice was deep, and

although he was not speaking above a conversational tone, it silenced the whole store.

She cleared her throat and pointed to herself, her eyes questioning and innocent.

Jenkens's expression softened, and he rubbed a hand over his carefully whisker-roughened jaw, his gaze raking Deanie with undisguised enjoyment. The star liked what he was seeing.

"What were you laughing at?" This time there was a hint of amusement in his voice.

"Oh, um . . ." She shifted in her sensible shoes and patted her hair under the hairnet. "It's just that you looked so surprised by those guys," she said, motioning to the photographers. "And, well, I mean . . . this was more planned than most weddings I've been to."

At once he grinned, an engaging, soul-melting and practiced smile. Deanie, beaming, returned the smile.

And so began one of Nashville's and eventually—thanks to supermarket tabloid coverage—the nation's favorite oddball romances. Vic Jenkens took the adorable waitress out to dinner that evening, and from then on they were a couple. Vic Jenkens, that newly reinstated good ol' boy, and his salt-of-the-earth woman became a publicist's dream.

And Vic discovered an untapped resource of songs. On their first date she explained the story of how she'd written his current hit. Instead of laughing, he actually believed her, and he called his manager right then from his car phone. Deanie was not only paid for the song but was told she'd receive royalties if Vic ever recorded another of her tunes. She sent him more tapes the next day, and by the time he went back on the road, her songs were included in his concerts.

Wilma Dean Bailey had finally made it in Nashville, but not at all the way she had envisioned it. It was stardust, yes. But it was secondhand stardust, shrugged from the broad and well-connected shoulders of Vic Jenkens.

Soon into the relationship Deanie felt a vague uneasiness

growing in the pit of her stomach. She did not want to depend on a man—any man—for her identity. People were kind to her now, strangers smiled, but it was for all the wrong reasons. She had seen firsthand what dependence on a man could cost a woman. Every time she needed a reminder, a swift glance at her rail-thin, overworked mother usually did the trick. Somehow, Deanie would emerge from Vic's ever-looming shadow.

She held on to her Krispy Kream job, in spite of her growing bank account. As other waitresses came and went, Deanie remained, pouring coffee and selling doughnuts to Vic's fans who waited in the shop in vain hopes that their star would visit. He never did. But the prospect of seeing him kept crullers and jelly-filleds moving faster than a brakeless truck down a mountain.

The romance, such as it was, suited Vic's agenda perfectly, stilling rumors that he had gone Hollywood and left the real South behind. With Deanie occasionally on his fringed arm, the press could cluck approvingly at his success, give his records more airplay, make his videos even more appealing. Who could begrudge such a nice guy?

He was shrewd enough to keep in constant touch with Deanie, even when his touring schedule took him across the country. Sometimes he asked her to play her new songs over the telephone. Other times he would have his manager shuttle her most recent tape to his hotel on the road. The manager even made sure she had plenty of top-quality recording cassettes to use on the new machine Vic had given her for her twentieth birthday.

"It's like giving a baseball bat to Grandma," Lorna muttered after Deanie showed her the new equipment.

"What?" Deanie snapped.

"You know what I mean. The gift is for himself, baby. He's giving himself a bunch of songs for the price of one fancy-looking machine. That's all."

Deanie tried to ignore her mother's comment, but at night, after late conversations with Vic, Lorna's words came back to her. Every time she decided to break away on her own, he would come back with flowers and a hang-dog expression. She couldn't stand the thought of making anyone unhappy.

Theirs was a curious relationship. Deanie never did get over feeling like an outsider, as if some secret joke were being shared by all of Vic's friends, and she was never told the punch line.

She tried to talk herself into falling in love with Vic, but the best she could manage was a detached admiration for his singing voice. She did fall in love with the way he wrapped his voice around her songs, wringing from them all the emotion she had ever managed to instill. And she was truly flattered that he was showing her so much attention. Yet something wasn't quite right.

Through reading the music industry trade publications, she knew that most labels were favoring singers who performed their own material. The days of the singer as a mere interpreter of another writer's songs seemed to be fading; the hot stars all wrote their own stuff. She could sometimes see greedy appreciation of her work in Vic's bluer-than-blue eyes, and he would nod in subdued acknowledgment. But he never came right out and praised her. He always seemed to be doing her a favor by even listening to her meager efforts, much less recording her songs.

Vic also suggested she smoke cigarettes to calm her nerves, to sooth her growing suspicions of his motives. He assured her that most of the truly successful Nashville names were two-pack-a-day smokers, and that nonsmokers were even considered outsiders. Against her better judgment and to keep his nagging at bay, she began to smoke. Only after she had become hooked did she realize he'd probably harbored an unconscious—or perhaps even conscious—desire to see her voice ruined. She was never able to completely quit, but she did manage to cut down to a few precious cigarettes a day.

Deanie was not stupid. After the initial enchantment of dating a star dwindled into a dull routine, she realized how he had been using her.

It had taken one brief conversation to point her toward reality.

On one of the increasingly rare evenings they spent together, she decided to make a clean break. The speech was beautifully set in her mind.

After a candlelight dinner, he turned his eyes toward her—the same eyes that had been used so effectively in his last video. He told her, with wrenching honesty, how much music meant to him, how his granddaddy Jenkens had taught him to play the guitar and sing, how they used to huddle together and listen as their voices blended with the crackling hum of summer cicadas. His granddaddy was gone now, he said, his voice rife with emotion. He'd give his last Grammy to speak but one more time to his granddaddy, to thank him for the miraculous gift of music.

She reached up and touched his face, and he smiled.

Wilma Dean Bailey did not tell Vic Jenkens what was on her mind that night. He had shown her a side she'd never seen, had never imagined existed. He was vulnerable. He needed her.

Two days later she was brushing her teeth. The television was on in her bedroom, the cheerful postdawn sounds of "Good Morning America" filtering through the din of running water. Then she heard another voice, familiar, cajoling. In a daze, she stepped into the bedroom, still blotting toothpaste foam from her mouth.

There, hunched in a chair across from Joan Lunden, was Vic Jenkens. She had almost forgotten about this interview, the reason he had caught the red-eye to New York the night before.

"It was my great granddaddy Jenkens . . ." His voice broke, and he turned his soulful eyes on Joan Lunden, who was on the verge of tears herself.

Vic hadn't been talking to her the other night, opening up and trusting her with fragile emotions. Vic Jenkens had been rehearsing.

It was suddenly all clear to her: how he had been wooing not Deanie but her songs, how he had managed to keep her ability so well hidden from everyone but his manager.

With a new determination, Deanie made two vows to herself. One, she would never allow her work to be performed by another artist unless she specifically approved. And two, she would never, ever, trust another man.

It had taken her seven years to get this chance, to sing one of her own songs with a hot star like Bucky Lee Denton. Only her mother knew what the journey had cost, how agonizing some of the decisions had been along the way. She was still virtually unknown to the public, to all but the few who would slavishly read song credits, or watch the songwriters awkwardly accepting awards at some of the televised ceremonies.

Deanie Bailey was unknown but, she hoped, not for long. She had waited for this moment, worked and sweated and lost sleep and prayed to be given a single opportunity to prove herself.

A momentary rush of fear had jolted through her when she first learned that Bucky Lee would sing the duet with her, but she managed to push it aside. As her mother bid her a tearful goodbye at the airport, Deanie thought of all she was leaving behind, all that lay ahead.

Nothing could stand in the way of her dreams now. Except for Bucky Lee Denton.

Chapter 2

IF THERE WAS ONE INVALUABLE LESSON DEANIE HAD LEARNED during her years of songwriting success in the country music industry, it was when to make herself scarce. As the irritated, jet-lagged, and exhausted crew struck the video set, Deanie grabbed a bottle of Coke and a package of dry-roasted peanuts and slinked surreptitiously into the background.

Not that it was easy to slink anywhere in her costume. It was stiff, uncomfortable, and about the ugliest thing Deanie had laid eyes on since her mother picked out the dress for her first Country Music Association Award ceremony. The headdress felt like a vise on her temples. She would have gladly removed it, but the damn thing was held on with so many pins and clips it would have taken Houdini to unbolt it. As it was, she didn't want to risk the ire of the costume director, who had spent the past three hours sewing rhinestones onto a velvet doublet that Bucky Lee Denton now refused to wear.

They were losing the light anyway. Even if a miracle

occurred and Bucky Lee emerged from his trailer ready to work, the sun was sinking, as if it too wished no further association with Deanie or the video.

Deanie tried to smile at a trio of departing Tudor Babes, but they managed to avoid her gaze. Wisely, she decided not to bum a cigarette from a large man in overalls wielding a hammer.

Funny, she mused. Even in England, Nashville's male-dominated network was in full force. Everyone was mad at *her,* not Bucky Lee, who was the real cause of the aggravation. She had established herself as a solid songwriter, an up-and-coming performer, yet all it took was one flash-in-the-pan guy like Bucky Lee Denton to make her feel about as welcome as a hornets' nest at a picnic.

The grounds of the palace were lovely, although she preferred a less-clipped, more haphazard look to a garden. The flower beds were subdued, as if daring a stray bloom to rear its undesirable head. Every flower was in its assigned place, every shrub carefully pruned into submission, the approved rounded shape. It was beautiful in an artificial, plastic fashion.

The ninety-pence guidebook she had flipped through during one of the interminable breaks highlighted the garden and told the illustrious history of the grounds. The age and splendor of the palace at Hampton Court was mind-boggling to Deanie, who paced across the lawn, eyes glued to the booklet, still clutching the Coke bottle.

Gripping the guidebook between her teeth, she funneled the peanuts into the bottle, an old Southern trick. No matter what she was doing, whatever her state of mind, the sight of cola bubbling to a head with salty peanuts could always make her feel immeasurably better, like a bouquet during a snowstorm. The best part came last, when she could eat the sweet, soggy peanuts at the bottom of the bottle. Pure bliss.

Finally she glanced up and took an unbroken look at the grounds, at the palace in the distance. An odd feeling flowed over her, a sense of historical smallness in the face of such grandeur. This was the very soil tilled by the feet of monarchs and cardinals before anyone had ever heard of Nashville or Tennessee, when the United States was still the uncharted wilds of America. Had one of Henry VIII's wives ever stood on the exact spot, the same eerie glow of the setting sun making the horizon a pastel smudge?

With another sip of soda, slightly salty now, she looked about the grounds, barely aware of the roar of a jet circling overhead. This was a timeless moment, far removed from the pettiness of a video schedule. She felt very alone, a faraway sense of isolation from the rest of her world.

"It's a rather romantic place, is it not?"

Deanie turned to see a dapper gentleman of about fifty, glancing in the same direction she was. "I apologize," he added hastily. "I did not mean to startle you."

"Heck, you didn't startle me." She smiled.

"I live close by, you see," he returned the smile. He was English, of course, with a neatly trimmed beard peppered with gray. "I saw all the commotion, the trailers and lorries and show people. I do love having a look at the workings of a film." He slipped his hands into the well-worn pockets of his tweed jacket. "I saw them film *Anne of the Thousand Days* years ago, with Richard Burton."

"That must have been neat." Deanie's eyes widened in interest. "What did he look like?"

"He was rather plain, actually. But his wife at the time was Elizabeth Taylor, and she was spectacular. She watched him, and everyone else watched her."

The man suddenly jumped. "Do forgive me. My manners have been appalling." He extended a bony hand. "My name is Neville Williamson, and I'm afraid I'm a somewhat pathetic example of British hospitality. I do hope my fellow countrymen have demonstrated better style."

"Nice to meet you. I'm Deanie Bailey."

"Pleasure," he responded crisply. "Are you enjoying your visit so far? I suppose it's hardly a holiday to be working."

"To tell you the truth, Mr. Williamson—"

"*Neville,* please."

"*Neville,* then. Well, it's just beautiful here. All we've done so far is wait around, but I'll tell you, this sure is a pretty place to wait around in."

He laughed. "It is indeed. My parents fell in love here, in fact."

"Really?"

"Really. She had been engaged to another pilot, a chap in the Royal Air Force during the war. Well, he was missing and presumed dead. My father was a close friend of the missing pilot, and he decided to comfort his poor fiancée. Next thing they knew, they were in love—a grand passion, it seems. They waited a year to get married, and I was born right before the war ended. So you see, this has always been one of my family's favorite spots."

"And the other man never did show up?" Deanie swept a strand of hair from her forehead.

"Sadly, no. But they named me after him. My first name is his surname, you see. He was an only son, and they wanted the name to continue."

Deanie whistled through her teeth. "I love your phrase, 'a grand passion.' That would sure make a dandy song. Could I use it?"

"Excuse me?" He seemed genuinely perplexed.

"I write songs, and that story would make a terrific song. Would your parents mind if I use it?"

"No—well, I mean, they're gone now. It wouldn't hurt anyone, and it might be rather nice to have their story immortalized in song."

"*A grand passion,*" she repeated, testing the sound. "It sure is a great story. I just hope I can do it justice."

"Well, I must be off," he said after a few comfortable moments. "My wife makes a splendid tea every afternoon at this time. If I'm late, she eats all my favorite scones herself. Beastly woman." It was said with such affection that Deanie realized it was Neville himself who was anxious to get to his tea.

"It was wonderful meeting you," she said, waving goodbye.

"The pleasure was mine." Before he left he paused. "It just came to me! Who you resemble, that is. At first I thought you looked rather like Miss Taylor, when she was here watching Richard Burton. But it just occurred to me that you bear a spectacular resemblance to Natalie Wood. Have you ever been told that?"

Deanie winked. "Once or twice. But I thank you."

She smiled, and he gave a brisk wave before walking away. He sure was a nice old guy, she thought.

Alone once more, she returned her attention to the guidebook, increasingly aware of her vast ignorance. She had felt strangely compelled to write her name in the booklet, a gesture of ownership she rarely bothered with. This was her book. The thought of someone else walking away with it bothered her somehow.

Scanning the pages, she bit her lip as she came across unfamiliar phrases such as "barber surgeon" and "liturgical reformation" and terms she could only guess were Latin. It was the same feeling she'd had when she first read the show business trade papers so many years earlier. There was a realm of knowledge she never imagined existed. A whole universe had prevailed happily without her.

Something in the guidebook caught her eye, tearing her away from her musings. It was a stark black-and-white photograph of a massive hedge. Leaning closer into the book, hastily reaching up to push her tilting headdress back into place, Deanie read about a miraculous maze on the grounds, one so ornate that people were lost in it for hours. It warned tourists to avoid the maze if they had theater tickets that evening.

Deanie grinned. The warning may have been tongue-in-cheek, but the effect on her was instantaneous. She didn't just have theater tickets for that evening; she was to appear at Wembley Stadium to sing the duet with Bucky Lee Denton during his concert. Her manager would have a fit, while Nathan Burns, who was filming the concert for an upcoming video, would pull out what little hair was remaining on his head. To enter the maze at this hour would be more than irresponsible. It would be sheer folly, a career risk few stars would even contemplate.

It was absolutely irresistible.

According to the map, Deanie was within yards of the maze, and as she walked in what she hoped was the right direction, she continued to scan the booklet. The maze was almost as old as the palace itself, the guidebook cooed. It had been created for Henry VIII's second wife, Anne Boleyn, to remind her of the maze at her childhood home of Hever Castle. It had taken decades for the hedges to become truly inaccessible, and by that time both Anne and Henry had returned to dust.

Deanie peered over the guidebook, and at once she spotted the maze. Its rusty turnstile was chained, with a hand-lettered sign propped on top of the lock with a single word: "Closed."

How could it be closed?

With a swift glance over one shoulder to assure herself she was alone, she squeezed between the edge of the metal turnstile and the rough hedge. Luckily, she had spent her childhood gaining free access to amusement parks and fairs, and her slender build could still wiggle through small spaces.

The inside of the maze was something of a disappointment, although Deanie wasn't sure what she had been expecting. There were corridors of shrubbery, green and twisting, jutting off in unexpected directions. She wandered the maze, pausing to touch the knotty, gnarled branches. They were thick and coarse, roughened by centuries of rain and sunshine and snow.

Suddenly Deanie stopped, unable to walk any farther. The sun was about to set, and she glanced about at the incandescent last light, the final golden explosion before the day became dusk.

Something was wrong.

She held out her hand to steady herself, grasping a hoary shrub, ignoring the slivers of wood and bark that cut into her skin. The booklet fell to her feet, and she gasped for breath, momentarily blinded by the sun reflecting off the soda bottle. It hit the bottle at odd, sharp angles, glinting blue, so vibrant she was forced to close her eyes.

One thought penetrated her consciousness: earthquake. Who else but Wilma Dean Bailey would get caught in a British earthquake?

The vibration became more intense now, a deep baritone rumbling that seemed to ripple the very ground, defying the solid feel of the earth. Her whole arm began to shake violently, just her arm, unable to release the soda bottle. In the midst of the quake she opened her eyes and heard a hissing noise, like droplets of water on a hot frying pan. The rest of her cola evaporated, and the peanuts hopped at the bottom of the bottle like Mexican jumping beans.

There was one final roar, a terrible, almost human scream. White-blue lines bounced off the cola bottle, enveloping her in a pulsating prism. Then all was silent.

Her breath came in harsh, ragged gasps, and the soda bottle, suddenly hot to the touch, came crashing to the ground. A small puff of dirt rose as it landed without shattering. Her hands were trembling, and she instinctively clutched her throat, feeling the frantic pounding of her heart, every beat ringing in her ears.

She took a few deep breaths, trying to get her terror under control. And when she found her voice, it wasn't to scream but to laugh at herself. She slumped against a bush, its tender branches giving way under the weight of her back. Her eyes darted to the bottle, and she reached over gingerly to pick it up.

The peanuts were blackened and smoking.

Deanie inhaled the scent of the burned peanuts, as if proving to herself they were really scorched. She hadn't imagined it, whatever had just happened.

"I must have been hit by lightning," she marveled aloud, her voice tense and high pitched.

She closed her eyes for a moment and leaned back against the comforting embrace of the shrub. There was something wrong, something that didn't seem right. What could it be . . .

The bush.

Her eyes flew open and she spun around, ignoring the headdress as it drooped forward. Instead of a mammoth, ancient shrub, there was a young hedge, only just reaching over her head. Its branches were slender and smooth, its buds full and pale green.

All of the bushes were new. Everywhere she looked, she saw fresh young plants and could smell the unmistakable scent of soil mingled with manure.

"How now, art thou foe or friend of the king's?"

Deanie gasped, startled by the sudden intrusion. She hadn't heard anyone approach. Her first thought was of the kindly Mr. Williamson. Perhaps he had returned to take her to tea. Perhaps he had come to see if she was badly shaken in the earthquake. She turned in the direction of the rich, masculine voice.

It was not Mr. Williamson.

She was stunned by what she saw. It wasn't that he was inordinately tall, or bulging with muscles. The man before her had a magnetic presence, an aura that jolted her every bit as much as his unexpected voice.

He was an actor, of course. An extra in the video, judging from the costume he wore. Unlike Stanley and the other Shakespearean actors, this guy's outfit was less flamboyant: just a black velvet doublet and hose with a full white shirt underneath. At his left side was an elegant scabbard, black as the doublet, with the ornately carved hilt of a fake sword just visible under the folds of his costume. There were no gaudy paste-jewels, no fancy gold thread. But his stockings seemed a little baggy.

Deanie breathed a sigh of relief and smiled. "Hey," she

said, her voice still betraying uncertainty. "That was some earthquake. Did Nathan send you to fetch me? You're one of the actors, right? I think you can collect your paycheck."

The man, his gaze steady, drew the sword.

"How now? Be thou a friend of the king's?" His manner was terse, and his teeth, very white, remained clenched as he spoke.

"Me? Heck no. I'm a little young to have known the King personally, although I've seen some of his later stuff. You know, the Vegas recordings, when he wore those white jumpsuits and aviator sunglasses."

Now that her initial fear had vanished, she was able to properly appraise the actor, and she decided he had most certainly picked the right profession.

He stood about six feet tall, perhaps a little less, but his bearing seemed to voraciously consume the surrounding space. His hair was close to Deanie's in color and thickness, a rich mahogany. There was a decided curl to it, and the ends rested lightly against his expansive shoulders.

Yet it was his face, more specifically his eyes, that gripped her attention. They were a strange shade of hazel, dark brown circling the irises, and they seemed to see through her, with a sharp intelligence that made Deanie feel uncomfortable.

His face was lean, almost gaunt, with hollows in the cheeks and a very slight cleft in his chin. His forehead, high and smooth, was free of the creases that were at the corners of his eyes and bracketed his mouth.

His mouth. Even as he spoke, she pulled her gaze from his eyes to his mouth, a mesmerizing study in contrasts. The upper lip was rather thin, but the lower lip was full and generous, hinting at a hidden sensuality that his brusque manner so effectively masked.

He had spoken, and she realized she hadn't heard a word he said. She cleared her throat. "Excuse me?"

A look of irritation passed over his features. "Canst thou not hear? I quoth, how now——"

"Brown cow?" she replied.

His eyebrows, unexpectedly lush on a face so free of any other excess, rose slightly, briefly marring the smooth forehead with lines. His sword was still pointed at her, but he seemed to have forgotten it.

Deanie reached out and pushed the sword away. The moment she touched the blade, the flesh on her palm exploded in pain.

"Hey, what are you doing!" she cried, withdrawing her hand as tears flooded her eyes. "Y'all aren't supposed to use real swords." Her voice broke as she examined the gash, several inches long and bleeding freely.

From the corner of her eye Deanie saw him make a sweeping motion with his arm and heard the metallic sound of the sword slipping into its sheath, an exasperated sigh escaping his mouth. He stepped toward her and tenderly cupped her wounded hand in his.

The last thing on her mind was her hand as she felt his warm breath on her cheek. "Doth thou know not of weaponry?" Now his voice was soft, as if soothing a frightened child.

Deanie stared at his hand, surprised at how such rough, callused fingers could bring such comfort. His scent tingled her senses, musky and spicy, unlike any bottled fragrance.

"Your aftershave," she whispered. "It sure isn't Brut."

He turned his eyes to hers. Even in the encroaching darkness, they were even more extraordinary than from a distance. She could see the distinct flecks of sea green and sable brown.

"I apologize, my lady, if thou doth think me a brute."

With that he ripped the left cuff of his shirt, several inches of snowy-white fabric that extended from the close black velvet sleeve, and fashioned a makeshift bandage.

"Awe," Deanie said, smiling, "you didn't have to go and wreck your costume." He made no notice of her comment, intent on tying the bandage over her palm. "You know,"

Deanie added, uncomfortable with the silence and his nearness, "that's a dandy outfit."

His eyes flashed to hers, and she sniffed once, the tears evaporated. "I mean, it's sort of like one Wynonna has." She caught herself. "I mean, not that you look like a girl, nothing like that. It's just the black velvet and the white, well, you know . . ." Her voice trailed off and he stepped back, as if seeing her for the first time.

Deanie licked her lips, her mouth suddenly gone dry. "Why do you speak all backwards like? I mean, stuff like 'from where art thou' and all that?"

There was a small pause before he spoke again. "From where art thou?" he repeated.

She closed her eyes, trying to form a reply. At last she took a deep breath and opened them. "Nashville from am I," she answered triumphantly.

For the first time he smiled at her, an expression that transformed his entire face. The hollows of his cheeks became elongated dimples, and the lines around his eyes crinkled. Instead of looking menacing, although admittedly attractive, he was accessible and easy. Deanie felt a strange, roller-coaster tumble in her stomach.

He reached for her soda bottle and examined it, the grin still on his handsome face. "Nashville," he repeated, although from his lips the word sounded exotic and foreign. He was so close that she could see the separate strands of his hair, some very dark and coarse, others burnished golden by the sun, and a very few gray. Only up close were the gray hairs visible.

His eyes met hers. "Tell me again of your king." This time his voice was expressionless, and his thumb traced over some writing on the glass. It was the copyright label and the date the product had been bottled.

"Well, he's dead, of course."

That caused a reaction. The man stiffened, as if not believing her.

"Hey, are you all right?" The smile faded from Deanie's face as she realized he seemed to be ill. A sheen of perspiration formed on his forehead, reflecting the fading light, and Deanie touched his arm.

He jumped, as if surprised she was still there. With admirable aplomb he recovered and pushed his palm over his forehead, absentmindedly wiping the perspiration on the shoulder of his doublet.

"Please, tell me again of your king's . . . glasses." He seemed to struggle for the words.

"Those ugly aviator things?"

"Aviator," he breathed. "Aviator."

She was about to suggest they go to the medical van, the emergency vehicle insurance companies demand be present at all location shoots. But before she could speak, she heard the sound of men's voices shouting into the night, footsteps crunching on the gravel.

The actor seemed to snap out of his daze. He turned to face her, his expression once again clear and direct.

"I am Christopher Neville, duke of Hamilton," he rasped. The intensity in his eyes, his searing gaze, prompted Deanie to step back, but he gripped her upper arm painfully, pulling her closer. "You are my cousin. Remember that. You are my cousin, and you are from—"

"Hey, let me go!"

"You are my cousin," he repeated more emphatically. For a moment he seemed to be thinking out loud. "I must somehow explain your speech." A flicker of amusement laced his words as he pronounced, "You have just arrived from Wales."

"You're crazy," she gasped, genuinely alarmed.

Instead of becoming enraged, or at least insulted, she saw his teeth flash white, a smile in the darkness.

"No." She could hear the delighted satisfaction in his voice. He grabbed the cola bottle and lobbed it into the bushes, where it would be out of sight. "You, my dear, are addled. Your family has just sent you here in hopes of finding you a husband, and you will remain with me at Court until—"

"You just littered," she snapped accusingly. "Do you know what the fine for littering a landmark is?"

"Hamilton! Art thou within?" The call came from just beyond the shrubs.

"What is it with you people?" Deanie asked. "This backwards talk is driving me nuts."

Christopher Neville, duke of Hamilton, stared at her face for a moment, not answering. With a thumb, he gently tilted her face toward him. "Art thou painted?"

"Huh?"

"Thy face. Be that paint?" He lifted the remaining cuff on his other sleeve and, without waiting for a reply, scrubbed her face.

"Hamilton!" This time the cry was more insistent.

"Aye, within." he responded, removing the last traces of mascara and lipstick from her face.

Deanie, who had been too stunned to respond, was suddenly infuriated.

"Hey, you!" she shouted to the unseen voices. "There's a nut job in here—one of those damned actors Nathan hired. Get me out of here!"

There were muffled sounds of men conferring, and then, in the final light of dusk, Wilma Dean Bailey came face-to-face with the rest of the mad acting troupe. The man in front was older than the rest, perhaps in his fifties or sixties, and he carried what looked like an overgrown baseball bat. Again, there was some sort of shuffling as a new person entered the maze with a similar bat, but this one was on fire.

"Someone, quick!" Deanie cried. "Get the extinguisher!"

But all they did was light the old guy's bat. At that point she realized these were torches, like at a pep rally. Even in the flickering darkness, the men saw her blush furiously.

"Gentlemen," said Christopher Neville in a voice smooth enough to announce a game show. "May it please you, this is my dear cousin."

Deanie waved a weak greeting, still mortified by her gaffe. How was she to know they actually meant to carry flaming sticks?

"Hey," she said. "I'm Deanie Bailey."

The older man with the torch held it to her face, and she flinched, but she had the good grace not to back away. The poor guy was probably a fan.

"Dean of the Bailey?" His voice was incredulous. She could see him more clearly now, and he sure was an ugly old coot. His teeth were yellowed or missing altogether, and his eyes were beady and black, peering suspiciously over a large, thin nose. Even though he was lacking in the looks department, he wore a lavish, fur-lined robe and a strange dark velvet hat. All of the men were dressed in garish costumes, and someone—Deanie wasn't sure who—needed a bath. Badly.

"My cousin," Christopher repeated, smiling, "hath but just arrived from Wales." He then turned to the old man with the torch. "Cousin, may I introduce Thomas Howard, third duke of Norfolk."

"Hey, Tom." Deanie smiled. Christopher Neville winced.

"Nay, coz," again he was speaking with his teeth clenched. "His name be not—"

But Deanie tried to soothe the old guy herself. "Oh, sorry. Howard, is it?" Another strained silence. "Howie?"

The pressure on her arm, where Christopher Neville was twisting her, caused her last words to dissolve into a howl of pain.

"My cousin hath of late been ill with the brain fever," Neville said quickly. At that the men stepped back. "Thank the Almighty, in His Magnificence my cousin hath been spared, but the plague hath left her mind simple and childlike."

The men exchanged glances while Deanie held her tongue. This Christopher Neville seemed to think it was important to play this little game. She wondered if they were dangerously—even criminally—insane. Like everyone in the industry, Deanie knew the mental toll a life in show business could exact, especially a failed life in show business. From the smell of the actors, they were none too successful. She was wary, but she felt sorry for them and decided to play along. Given a choice between the aromatic actors with yellow teeth and the dashingly insane Christopher Neville, she would stick with Neville.

"Hamilton," the older man said at last. "The king doth require your company at his board. There is to be music this eventide, for His Majesty doth wish to forget the Cleves union. Wilt though come, sir?" There was something to his speech, a cruel inflection, that made Deanie scoot even closer to Neville.

"Yeah. I come anon." He rubbed her back briefly, and with all the strangeness that had just transpired, Deanie felt a rush of gratitude. "Cousin?" He crooked a powerful arm in her direction. After only a slight hesitation, she slipped her arm through his.

Thomas Howard's shifting eyes fixed on the bloody cloth wrapped around her hand. "A mishap, dear cousin?" He accentuated the last word.

"Ah, yeah," Neville answered, without missing a beat. "My dear cousin, overjoyed by the meadows, so gentle from the Welsh rocks, rode my mare this noon without her gloves. Her tender hands, I fear, were bitten by the reins."

"Right," she mumbled.

They were exiting the maze, but there were no turnstiles or painted signs to proclaim it "closed." Gone were the camera reflectors and the trailers; every piece of video equipment had vanished, along with the parking lot and the highway that had snaked beyond the maze. There were no London lights in the distance, illuminating the horizon.

Even in the moonlight, she could see nothing but the eerily lit palace. The serpentine chimneys that had earlier been free-standing, their buildings long gone, were now attached to the palace, odd brick spirals spewing black smoke. The palace looked like a sprawling medieval village, roofs at haphazard levels, gargoyles perched atop one of the slate flats. Some rooms were dark, others glowed with what could only be torch- or candlelight, flickering softly in the blackness.

Beyond the palace were hills and scrubby trees, and on a distant rise she could see the ghost of a cottage with a thatched roof.

The grass beneath her feet was lumpy and uneven, not the smooth, mechanically cut lawn she had walked over earlier. Her slippered foot stepped into something soft, and she realized the grounds were covered in animal droppings. Clumps of earth were tossed everywhere, as if a pack of grazing cattle or sheep had spent the past season frolicking on the lawn.

Christopher Neville held her tightly as she felt herself sway. Into her ear, so softly only she alone could hear, he whispered, "Welcome to 1540, sweet cousin."

Chapter 3

*D*EANIE HAD LOST THE POWER OF SPEECH. EVEN HAD SHE BEEN able to muster a voice above a squeak, there was nothing for her to say, no words that could possibly convey the magnitude of what had happened.

Christopher Neville was not insane. Deanie knew he had spoken the truth. Somehow, in defiance of every bit of rationality, and mocking the established laws of physics, she had just been thrown back to the year 1540.

It wasn't just the appearance of the men or the way they spoke. Nor was it the landscape details—the chopped-up lawn and the young bushes in the maze and the vanished parking lot—that convinced her.

Instead it was something indefinable, an elusive quality to the very air surrounding her, that told her she was more than four centuries from home. The atmosphere was thick, an almost suffocating heaviness when she breathed.

She stared straight ahead at the reddish brick palace they were approaching, her sense of smell assaulted by dozens of odors she had never before experienced. There was a pungent fragrance wafting from the chimneys, sticky-sweet and smoky, with the bitter stench of singed hair. Another scent, like that of damp animals, seemed to emanate from the men with Thomas Howard, and she realized it was their clothing. The furs and woolens reeked atrociously in the murky closeness of the evening.

Christopher Neville was speaking to her, his voice low and intimate. The harsh angles of his face lent him an almost savage countenance, yet his tone conveyed nothing but kindness. "You may call me *Kit,* which is the name used by those who know me best, including the king. You must know of my history, or 'twill arouse suspicions most vile. Canst thou hear me?"

Deanie turned to him, and something in her expression caused him to halt, pulling her to an abrupt stop. Without taking his extraordinary eyes from hers, he called to the other men.

"Gentlemen, please convey to His Majesty my eagerness to share his board, yet my gentle cousin is most over-wrought at appearing before her most gracious king. 'Twill take but a moment to allay her fears."

There was a murmuring of assent, and the men shuffled off, their broad-toed slippers crunching on the pebbled walk.

Christopher led her along a vine-covered wall to a bench set in an alcove. Deanie vaguely remembered the stone bench, weathered by pollution-drenched rains and smoothed by centuries of use, covered with the open cosmetic bag of the makeup artist hired by Nathan. Now it was new, the edges of the stone sharp, the floral design of the legs clear and fresh.

Her knees gave way just as he eased her onto the bench, and a powerful hand steadied her at the small of her back. Settling beside her, his heavily muscled thigh resting against her trembling knee, he watched her eyes, brown and large.

In dim profile, he took in her features: the small nose and softly sculpted cheekbones, eyelashes so thick they cast a shadow even in the faint light from the palace. A strand of shoulder-length hair, dark silk with a gentle wave, fell against her throat, and he resisted the urge to brush it with his fingertips. She seemed too delicate, too fragile to be of this world, a gossamer angel from above.

"How the hell did this happen?" she hissed, at once shattering his fantasy. His mouth betrayed the barest of smiles, a flicker of amusement at the ferocity of her voice.

"Oh, this is funny, is it?" There was a sharp anger reflected in her eyes. Gone was the lost, doelike bewilderment of a few moments earlier. "I have a show to do, Mr. Kit—which, by the way, is the most sissified name I've heard since Johnny Cash sang about a boy named Sue—and, well, this is not funny. Not one bit." Her voice began to waver from defiance to uncertainty, and she swallowed. "Oh," she said, a tiny cry. "Oh . . . how?"

With a roughened index finger, he tilted her face toward him, and he could see for the first time the sprinkling of freckles across the bridge of her nose.

"I know not," he said at last, and as her eyes narrowed in irritation, he repeated himself. "I do not know."

For a long moment she remained very still, then her shoulders slumped and her hands fell into her lap. "Oh," she said again. The bluster had once again vanished from her voice.

Christopher Neville glanced down at her. She seemed achingly vulnerable. Deliberately, with slow, gentle movements, he wrapped a hand over one of her small, cold fists.

"There is something about this maze," he said calmly. "It hath . . . has . . . properties, I understand not. I believe it to be magical, supernatural."

"In other words," and there was a small smile in her voice, "you know not."

"Aye." He chuckled, a warm, resonant sound.

She suddenly straightened. "You don't seem surprised. Have other people come through there?"

From the palace came strains of music: the full tones of a

hide-covered drum, high-pitched flutes, and a richly timbred lute. Laughter pierced the music, and the sounds of metal clanking on a stone floor. Somewhere within the brick walls, a dog barked.

Kit stood up and offered his arm. "The king awaits." His strong features tightened into an enigmatic smile. Deanie secured the bandage on her hand and rose to her feet. He took her hand and placed it on his forearm. She clung to him, leaning close to his body. For the time being, Christopher Neville, duke of Hamilton, was literally her only friend on earth.

The great hall was gleaming under the torches and candles big around as small trees. The uneven light cast looming shadows, leaving the corners dark while the center of the room glowed with fiery warmth. There were long planks covered with golden-hued pitchers and round loaves of bread. Food was being heaped generously onto rough trenchers and more elegant bowls and plates by young boys barely out of childhood, all bobbing and serving with humble efficency.

In spite of the fires and torches, it was damp in the hall, a bone-chilling dankness that seemed to permeate every square inch of the vast room. The very walls, of stone and wood, radiated chilled moisture. It was more comfortable outside than within.

Men and women swathed in richly colored fabrics were seated at the trestle tables, hoisting goblets dripping with wine or ale, laughing riotously among themselves. Above the din, in a loft jutting high over the hall, were musicians clothed in green-and-white tunics, playing song after song without rest.

It was a scene of organized chaos: great joints of meat and more dainty platters being raised over hatted and elaborately dressed heads, dogs roaming the hall at will, grateful to receive bones tossed by smiling gentlemen. One woman with very black teeth threw back her head and laughed raucously, while her companion flicked some sort of dried fruit into her mouth. Another man speared a piece of bread with a small jeweled dagger, using the weapon as a fork.

Deanie tried to flee, but Kit held her firmly, propelling her toward a raised dais where the most enormous man she had ever seen was pounding his fist on the table. Everything about him was oversized and exaggerated, as if he had been inflated to make everyone else seem trivial by comparison.

Thomas Howard, the duke of Norfolk, was at the large man's right, speaking furiously, his lips moving with frenzied speed. The big man seemed to ignore Norfolk, intent as he was on making the most noise possible by slamming his jewel-covered hand on the table. His clothing, sumptuous beyond anything Deanie could imagine, was studded with gems and gold brocade, adorning a burgundy doublet slashed in a geometric pattern so that the white of his underblouse could gleam through. Upon his head was a round hat, feathered at the brim, with clusters of pearls that quivered as he roared approval at a twirling dancer.

The man's face was extraordinary, covered with a brilliant close-cropped red beard, and a surprisingly small mouth under the fleshy nose. His eyes, beneath thin reddish brows, were tiny and heavy lidded, fringed by lashes so fair they seemed nonexistent. Draped behind him was a massive tapestry depicting a joust and a galloping herd of unicorns, and on the table was another tapestry, but Deanie could not identify the pattern. The raised table was the only one in the hall with any covering; the rest were bare wood.

Kit was speaking to her, his voice low. With the commotion surrounding them, she missed most of his words. He was giving her some information on his background: that he had risen from the rank of squire to duke in less than ten years, that he had become a favorite jousting partner of the king's. He also enjoyed the royal sport of tennis and often joined the king in the music salon.

Deanie nodded, watching as a dignified gentleman bowed to the large man, snapped out a massive square of linen, and tied it biblike around the man's neck.

She began to giggle as they paused, her arm still looped through his. "It's like all-you-can-eat night at the Sizzler's," she whispered to Kit, who only frowned in response.

"Hold your tongue, Mistress Deanie," he warned. "Should the king require speech of thee, be brief. Say nothing above the barest of revelations."

Deanie again nodded her understanding, staring in amazement as the large man lifted what appeared to be the entire leg of some animal to his face, and he launched into the joint with tiny yellowed teeth and pulled off an enormous mouthful of flesh. There was a smattering of applause and he grinned, chewing openmouthed, dribbling slightly in his gusto.

The large man, Deanie realized, her stomach doing a queasy flip, was King Henry VIII. This was not some dinner-theater production or an elaborately presented theme park. This was the real thing, complete with flea-bitten dogs and wine-soaked rushes on the floor.

They had reached the dais, and Kit seated them at one end of the tapestry-covered board. Immediately, young serving boys appeared, clanking metal plates and pouring thick wine into ornately carved goblets.

She watched the glint of light bounce off her goblet for a moment, trying to overcome a sudden urge to become ill. The odors, overpowering in the garden, were oppressive in the moist warmth of the hall. Everywhere she turned her head, new and evil fragrances threatened her unsteady stomach. Each dish carried its own spicy or pungent or greasy smell. The serving boys, some with food-spattered clothing, leaned close enough for her to distinguish the pastry bearers from the meat bearers by their stench alone.

Deanie decided to breathe through her mouth, but even that offered little relief. She peeked into her goblet. Red wine, heavy and sweet, rose to the brim, swirls of sediment floating on the surface.

"I hate to be difficult," she said, leaning toward Kit's ear and conscious of his leg pressed against hers on the bench, "but may I please have some water?"

"No," he replied, and he returned the greeting of a red-nosed man in a funny blue cap.

"No?"

"Cousin, the water is unsafe in England," he said at last, as if repeating the most obvious of facts. "Be it from the Thames or from a well, 'tis most foul and carries disease. Use it only for bathing, and then at your own peril."

"Oh," she murmured. "That explains why everyone smells so . . ." She stopped as Kit grinned, the hollows in his cheeks again becoming elongated dimples. "Not you, of course," she added hastily. "Everyone else is a little, eh, well . . ."

"Overripe?" he suggested.

She returned the smile, her nausea forgotten, and was struck by a sudden, irrational desire to touch his face, to feel the cleft of his chin or trace the contour of his face. Was his skin smooth or scratchy where a shadow of whiskers made it vaguely darker? Then she looked into his eyes, the strange pale irises rimmed by black, the ebony lashes. The smile gradually faded from his face as he met her own unwavering gaze.

"Why are you being so nice to me?" Her voice sounded as tremulous as her knees felt.

At once his eyes slid from hers, and he cast his eyes downward. In profile his features were sharp, his nose almost hawklike. The effect was one of unmistakable masculinity. He didn't answer for a moment. Then he spoke: "Because I know how it feels to be an outsider."

Although his accent was still thick with the strange British intonations, his words were almost normal to her ears.

"Kit! Hath thou no greeting for thy blessed sovereign?" The king's voice boomed over the dais. At once Kit stood up, his simply-cut doublet contrasting favorably with the gaudy fur- and feather-trimmed clothing of the other men. He bowed at the waist, then turned to Deanie.

"Rise, cousin," he whispered, lifting Deanie to her feet. Mechanically, she followed him to the king. Kit bowed again, one arm folded by his side, the other outstretched before him. Deanie did the same.

There was a muffled silence in the hall. All eyes were focused on her.

Suddenly the large man exploded with laughter. "Excellent, mistress!" he shouted, clapping his greasy hands. "Thou art most adept in the art of mimicry. Why, my fool Will Somers shall be in peril of losing his position!"

Everyone in the hall applauded and laughed with the king, although Deanie couldn't see what was so funny. Kit was fighting back a smile, and he cupped his hand under her elbow.

"If it doth please Your Majesty, this is my cousin, Mistress Deanie, newly arrived from Wales."

The King nodded. Without warning he stood up, leaned over the board, and kissed her squarely on the lips. He tasted of oily wine, his beard well lubricated with flecks of animal fat. She was about to wipe her mouth, but Kit, as if sensing her intent, gripped her hand.

"Forgive my poor cousin," he said. "She is but a weak woman, and Your Majesty's great honor doth render her mute." He shot her a warning glance, and Deanie bristled.

"Hey, I can so talk—"

Kit yanked her hand, and she was silenced. "Your Majesty," he continued, "if thou doth permit me, I will speak plainly. My cousin hath but recently been taken with a brain fever, and—"

The king backed away, a look of horror passing over his swollen features as he wiped his mouth with the back of a beefy, bejeweled hand. "A brain fever?"

"You may be of good ease, Your Majesty. The fever 'twas not of a virulent sort. Indeed, it cometh from a mighty blow to her head."

"Ah! Very well, my good fellow Kit." Relief was evident in his piggy black eyes. Again he grinned a greasy smile, hungry and lascivious. Deanie squirmed under his slow perusal, acutely aware of the cheapness of her clothes, the false luster of the plastic seed pearls, the itchy Velcro fastenings.

The king, a massive bib still tucked into the neck of his doublet, strode around the dais, stopping in front of Kit and Deanie. His colossal legs, large as tree trunks and covered with gold-colored hose, were planted solidly apart, arms akimbo, in a stance of entrenched power. Suddenly he clamped Kit on the back with such force it would cause most men to stumble. Kit stood as firm as his sovereign.

"Doth she desire a position at court?"

Kit pulled Deanie closer to his side. "'Twould be an honor of which she dares not dream, Your Highness. I would be forever in your debt."

"Excellent! 'Tis done then." The king laughed once more, his eyes raking her with obvious pleasure. "She be not right in the head, faithful Kit? Excellent! She shall favor the court with her grace and attend on the Flanders Mare. Ha! At last these royal eyes will have their fill of womanly beauty."

An unreadable expression passed over Kit's features, hard and almost defiant. In an instant, he was smiling again at the king, and Henry marched back to his board. Deanie and Kit were dismissed as the king waved to a serving boy with a pitcher of spiced wine.

Kit led Deanie back to their place at the far end of the dais, threading past a pair of brightly garbed jugglers and a dozen servers bearing meats, pastries, dressed birds, and bread.

"You are to be a lady-in-waiting to Queen Anne," he whispered into her ear after they were again seated. "'Tis a great honor, Mistress Deanie. But be aware, the king doth seek means to find another queen. Do not ally yourself too closely with the present queen, lest you suffer a like fate."

"You mean he wants to dump her?" Deanie asked, incredulous.

"In a manner of speaking, yes."

"Why? What has she done?"

Kit took a swallow of wine before answering. "His Majesty sayeth the queen doth stink." He held the goblet to his lips, muffling his words, so that Deanie alone could hear him.

"He should talk," she grumbled.

Only by the shaking of his broad shoulders, quaked by silent laughter, could Deanie know he had heard her.

The banquet passed in a lavish blur, course after course placed before her glazed eyes. Some of the dishes, such as savory meat pie made of wild boar and a whole fish covered with herbs, seemed more edible than others. Then there were dishes that ranged from strange to disgusting: platters of sharp-smelling pigs' feet, tiny headless birds served with their claws intact to keep them balanced on the plate.

The longer Deanie sat at the table, the more undeniable her journey seemed. The smells and sounds and startling colors pressed into her mind with ceaseless intensity. She was actually in 1540, in the court of one of the most feared monarchs in history.

Every time she felt herself panic, she would notice Kit, the solid feel of his leg against hers, his strong hand on her wrist emphasizing a point. His steady stream of conversation helped her remain calm, kept her from fleeing the hall in confusion and terror.

Finally she began to speak, blinking at each new sight. The sound of her own inane chatter seemed the only thing she could control.

"You know," she said to Kit, eating another small hunk of brown bread—the only food she felt brave enough to try—"I once had a date with a guy who loved to hunt. He picked me up in this old truck and made me sit on a burlap bag filled with dead ducks. I mean, all these plates of dead birds just reminded me of the Dead Duck Date."

"Dead Duck Date?"

She nodded, swallowing the piece of bread. "All I could think about were the little duck beaks poking me. I haven't been able to eat duck since then. The more a meal looks like what it was when it was alive, the less inclined I am to eat it, if you know what I mean. Give me chicken nuggets or a hamburger any time."

He smiled briefly, as if aware that what she had just said was meant to provoke an amused response, though not quite sure why. After another sip of wine, he leveled his gaze at her. "Hath you any accomplishments?"

"What do you mean?" She adjusted the ridiculous headdress, which was listing to the right.

"Canst thou ply a skillful needle, or argue theology, or make music?"

"Oh." She grew thoughtful. "I can sew. I used to make all of my own clothes in high school." His face brightened, and suddenly she wanted very much to please him. "But I need a sewing machine," she added quietly. "I can't sew worth a darn by hand." Then she smiled. "Hey, get it? 'Can't sew worth a darn.' It's sort of a bad pun."

"Yes. I see." He contemplated the designs on his goblet.

"Hey, but I can sing."

Kit's eyebrows arched. "Canst thou?" His voice was dubious.

"Of course. And I can write songs. That's why I'm here—in England, I mean. I'm a pretty big deal back home. Well, I hope to be, at least after the duet with Bucky Lee Denton hits the airwaves. As a writer, I've won three CMA awards and two Grammys, all for other people's songs, of course. Some of the big names, you know." She took a deep breath and continued: "And guess what? I've even played at the

Grand Ol' Opry, but I'm not a member. At least not yet. I was just a guest." Deanie beamed. "Does that answer your question?"

Kit, his face a mask of utter bewilderment, rubbed his chin pensively. "I fear, Mistress Deanie, I recall not the question."

Deanie's shoulders sagged. "Oh. You're not impressed." She shook her head, careful of the headdress. "I can sing," she said at last in a small voice.

"Ah, excellent!" Then the smile vanished from his voice, and he paused before continuing. "I need to ask of you . . . something of great importance." He cleared his throat, his eyes fixed upon her face with unnerving intensity. "The present queen be not of England born. She speaketh High Dutch."

"So?" Deanie shrugged.

He spoke deliberately. "Doth thou speak a Germanic language?"

"Me? No way José." She giggled. "I took a year of Spanish in high school, and all that did was help me order at the Taco Bell. I don't know anyone who took German. It's too hard."

There was still a palatable tension in him; one of his hands was clenched in a fist of such force that his knuckles were white. "Tell me," he said, trying to sound casual, but his voice was tight as his posture, "doth—do many people speak German in your time? Is it an international language?"

Deanie was mystified by his passion. "No. I mean, I guess the Germans do, but they usually stay in Germany. We only get a few tourists from there, at least in Nashville. You can always spot the Germans: They wear baggy shorts and black socks with sandals. Why do you ask?"

For a moment he remained motionless, **staring** straight ahead but clearly not seeing what was before him. A muscle leaped convulsively in his jaw. His fist remained clenched.

"Thank God," he said at last, his words an explosive sigh.

He seemed to relax a little, still oblivious to his surroundings. "All these years, I've wondered. Thank God."

He bowed his head as if in prayer, resting his forehead on the palm of his hand. Then he straightened, his eyes once again clear, and smiled at Deanie. She realized it was the first true smile she had seen from him, free of turmoil, free of tension. His teeth were very white, but one bottom tooth was crooked, a little out of line with the perfection of the surrounding teeth.

Something about that one imperfect tooth stirred an untried emotion deep within her, and she was unable to breathe. She clamped her hands together, resisting the urge to run her thumb over the fullness of his bottom lip. Her palms were damp and cold, and all she could do was stare at him.

"Art thou ill?" There was concern in his voice, tempered by a new-found lightness.

"Nope." Her reply was a dry croak. *A tooth,* she thought, her hands still pressed together. *I think I am falling in love with a crooked tooth.*

Just then a slender woman in a deep green gown and an angular headpiece curtsied before Kit. He smiled at the woman.

"Ah, very good, Mistress Cecily. This is my cousin, Mistress Deanie Bailey, who is to be a maid of the queen's household. Deanie, this is Mistress Cecily, daughter of the Lady Sellers and sister of Elizabeth Garrison, much beloved lady-in-waiting to our departed Queen Jane, mother of our most exalted prince of Wales." At the mention of Queen Jane, both Kit and the young woman made hasty signs of the cross. "Now she awaits Queen Anne."

Deanie smiled at Mistress Cecily, then turned to Kit. "So, what's she waiting for?"

Kit exchanged bewildered shrugs with Mistress Anne. "What dost thou mean, cousin?"

"You just said you're all waiting on the Queen. Well, what's holding her up, and when does she get here?"

"Ah . . ." Kit cleared his throat, and Mistress Cecily flushed crimson, glancing to her side as if wondering who else may have heard what Deanie had just said. "Doth thou recall not what I sayeth earlier? About the king?"

There had been so much information thrown at her in the past few hours that Deanie had to close her eyes for a moment, struggling to recall what Kit had mentioned. At once she remembered: that the king was not pleased with his new queen and would soon be seeking another wife.

"Oh, I get it." She leaned forward, and both Kit and Mistress Cecily moved closer. "So she's not here? The queen, I mean." Kit nodded once. From the corner of his eye he saw Thomas Howard watching the three huddled together, an appraising glare on his lined face.

"He must really hate her," Deanie mumbled, feeling sorry for an unwanted queen she'd never even met.

Kit suddenly rose to his feet, pulling Deanie with him. His hand was strong and sure on her elbow. "Mistress Cecily will show thee to thy quarters, cousin. Thou hath had a most unusual day and should be in bed anon."

At the other end of the dais the king stood up, clapping his hands in time with a group of musicians who had just begun to play. Deanie had barely noticed the music. Kit gave her arm a brief but reassuring squeeze before he handed her over to Mistress Cecily.

"Good night, coz," he whispered, his mouth so close to her ear she could feel a strange, tingling vibration.

She gave him an uncertain smile as Mistress Cecily pulled her through an arched door to the left of the dais. Deanie had one final glimpse of Christopher Neville, duke of Hamilton, as he turned toward a group of laughing women, his handsome face reflecting pure delight in their company. He did not look back at Deanie.

As if reading her thoughts, Mistress Cecily chuckled at Deanie when they entered the long corridor. "Your dear cousin hath won the heart of every lady at court, be they maid or married."

Deanie did not reply. They walked down the hall, through a labyrinth of polished wood floors and lush tapestries. Away from Kit, she felt lost and frightened, swallowing against a rising knot in her throat. This was real. She was actually here, with people who had been dead for more than four hundred years. The young woman holding her hand was dead. The king of England was dead.

Christopher Neville was dead.

Mistress Cecily giggled. "I fear the duke hath won the heart of his cousin as well," she said lightly.

Again, Deanie said nothing. But as they entered a small, almost bare chamber far from the din of the great hall, Deanie turned to her companion. With a very tight smile, she said, "I fear you are right, Cecily."

It wasn't the clock radio that woke her the next morning, nor the familiar smell of coffee, nor a wake-up call from the front desk. In her nether-sleep she had half expected to be back at the Dorchester Hotel, in her own suite, with the surly figure of Nathan Burns pacing the carpet and bemoaning his film career that never was.

Instead, she awoke to a sharp kick from a hairy leg.

With a gasp she sat up, clutching a linen nightshift under her chin. The thick red curtains on the bed sealed off all but a slender shaft of sunlight. Even with that tiny ray, she could see who was in bed with her. To the right was Mistress Cecily Garrison, her back turned to Deanie, her knees tucked against her curled body. To the left was a complete stranger, a large woman with dark hair who was snoring like a longshoreman.

Yesterday had not been a dream.

"Holy cow, I'm really here." Her voice sounded strange, abnormally loud against the silence of the bedchamber. Trying her best not to wake Mistress Cecily or the slumbering newcomer, Deanie slipped through the slight opening in the bed drapes, closing the fabric as soon as she was on the other side.

The floor was cold against her bare feet, and her first instinct was to return to the bed. Just as she was about to throw the curtains back to enter, she heard a snort from within. Somehow, that single sleepy wheeze changed her direction. Rubbing her eyes, she took a deep breath and faced the room.

It seemed even smaller than it had the night before, when, under the glowing light of three candles, Mistress Cecily had handed her a nightgown. Deanie had managed to hide her surprise at the sleeping arrangements; she hadn't expected to share a room, much less a bed, with another person. The new woman must have arrived after Deanie had fallen asleep. There was something disconcerting about waking up in bed with a complete stranger, especially a complete stranger of the same sex with hairy legs and an apparent adenoid condition.

Tentatively, she took in the details of the room, her arms crossed protectively under her breasts. The furnishings were spare: just a leather-back chair, a massive dome-topped trunk, and a couple of small tables bearing black-wicked beige candles. The leaded windows distorted the light, their thick, uneven panes covered with bubbles and swirls. On one wall was a rug, rich with burgundies and royal blues, and another held an immense fireplace, cold now but still smelling of burned wood and smoke. There were no protective screens or shields to keep sparking embers from leaping into the center of the room.

In the corner was another small table with a pitcher of water, and Deanie dipped her hands into the water and splashed her face, reaching for a small square of off-white cloth folded beside the water. It was scratchy and not very absorbent, but she scrubbed her face dry the best she could. The water was bracingly cold. Although Deanie was thirsty, the stagnant odor kept her from drinking.

She also recalled Kit's warning not to drink the water.

Kit.

Pausing as she refolded the cloth, she wondered if she had

dreamed Kit or if he was as real as the rest of this world. Had she imagined his magnificent eyes, the curl at the ends of his hair, the one crooked white tooth?

There was a soft knock on the door, and she jumped. Calming herself, she walked to the heavy door, not wanting to wake up Mistress Cecily and the stranger. She slowly turned the latch and opened the door.

"Deanie?" It was Kit.

She swung the door wider, unable to hide her excitement at seeing him. In the full light of day he was even more striking than by torchlight. He wore what appeared to be the same doublet and hose, but the shirt was fresh, a brilliant white, with full cuffs tied at the wrist and a starched collar tied at the throat. His hair was more unruly, the curls damp and tight against the vast shoulders. The black-enameled sword and sheath were on his left side, and in his right hand was a cloth bundle.

"Hey." She smiled. He peered over her shoulder, raising one full eyebrow in a silent question.

"They're still asleep," she whispered. Then she moved closer. "Who's the gal with the hairy legs and big snore?"

His burst of laughter seemed to explode in the silence of the corridor. Holding a finger to his lips to silence him, she tried to keep herself from laughing out loud as well. He cleared his throat and spoke into her ear. "That would be the Lady Mary Douglass," he answered in a low voice.

She nodded, again returning her gaze to his face. His eyes were remarkable this morning, clear and direct, the blend of greens and browns glimmering in the sunlight.

"I brought thee food, to break the fast." He held up the bundle.

"In here?"

"Nay, out of doors. The day brings fine weather."

"A picnic!" she squealed; then, remembering the other women, she cringed and looked over her shoulder. "But I don't know where my clothes are," she hissed, pointing to the nightshift.

"Be there a casket within?"

"A casket? I sure as hell hope not." Then she remembered the dome-lidded trunk. "Oh, you mean the trunk."

He nodded, and she crept over to the trunk and lifted the heavy top. Her clothes, carefully folded, were right below a large red gown she assumed belonged to Mary Douglass. Stepping behind the bed, where she'd be hidden by the curtains, she dressed swiftly, pulling the dress over her head and slipping on the soft ballet shoes. She was about to leave the cursed headdress but decided to take it along with her, in case she needed it.

Kit was astonished to see her reappear so quickly, completely dressed. "How didst thou manage to beclothe thyself?"

Running her hand through her hair like a comb, she grinned. "Velcro."

"Velcro?"

Turning her back to him, she reached behind and pulled apart the top fastening. The squares made a ripping sound, and she pressed them back together.

"'Tis most marvelous," he murmured. His warm breath on the back of her bare neck was extraordinarily unsettling. She swallowed against the shiver that ran through her.

She faced him, and for a moment they were both silent. His eyes swept her, drinking in each detail: the freshness of her complexion, the thick silken beauty of her hair. She was about to speak when he grasped her hand. "Art thou hungry?" His voice was husky, and he nodded once, although she hadn't replied, and led her to an airy courtyard.

From inside the king's chamber, he stared down at the Cloister Green Court. His chubby hand, with rings that grew ever tighter, rested against the cool stone ledge.

It was late morning, and still the duke of Hamilton was entertaining his Welsh cousin. He watched in fascination as the pair ate bread and cheese and drank of the small ale from coarse mugs. There was an animation most strange about the duke this morn. The king then watched the way the sun sparkled in the cousin's hair. It was shorn above the shoulders, and the king wondered if she had of late been cloistered in a convent.

He had noticed her the night before, had watched her from his place at the banquet. She was indeed a beauty. Just then she laughed and turned toward the duke, and he returned the smile.

The king swore under his breath. His leg was paining him. The royal physician, Dr. Butts, had lanced the wound, yet still it refused to heal, robbing him of his vigor and youth. He was once Bluff King Hal, the pride of Europe. He could tire a dozen horses on a single day's hunt, leaving his men panting in wonderment at their sovereign's superb physical condition. Bluff King Hal, the princely scholar, the very ideal of manly beauty.

Ten years before Mistress Deanie would have been fawning over him, those brown eyes flashing at Henry the man, not Henry the king. Ten years and four wives ago he would have had her, taken her of her own will, then tired of her.

Now he was saddled with the Flanders Mare, his Teutonic bride with whom he was to sire a second son, a duke of York to assure the Tudor line. Not only was the begetting of a son crucial to the realm, it was vital to a man who had thus far sired but three living children, two of them unneeded females.

In truth, he had not been able to perform the deed with his German wife. He recalled her sagging breasts and foul breath on their wedding night, and in his fury he kicked the limb of a fine inlaid Italian table. It was his bad leg, and the ulcer throbbed in protest, making him explode in a series of oaths. As a king, he had married for the good of England. But as a man, he wanted her gone from his life.

A new bride.

For the first time since that dismal January day when he

saw the horror who was to be his wife, Henry felt the stirrings of hope. He watched Mistress Deanie and Kit, the easy grace of his kinsman as he helped her to her feet.

The duke of Hamilton was a good man, one of his favorites. No other member of the King's Privy Council could match Hamilton for sport or conversation. His brilliant mind and bold military daring had more than once put down a rebellion on the Scots border. Surely he would help his King secure a more suitable bride. The Cleves union had been a diplomatic one, not a love match. He was becoming a laughingstock, his virility in question, his very manhood mocked. With his domestic life in order, he could be the sovereign he had always dreamed of becoming, the magnificent leader he could have become had his beloved wife Jane not succumbed after the birth of Prince Edward.

It was Henry's turn now.

"Cromwell!" He shouted to his chief minister. Cromwell had done this to him, arranged the union with the Cleves hag, shoved him into this most unsavory marriage. Cromwell would soon be gone. But first he would make Cromwell suffer as he had, to know the hourly torment of a hell on earth.

"Cromwell!" he again bellowed.

The door flew open and Thomas Cromwell entered, his blunt features reddened by the run to the king's chamber, his flowing cloak hanging askew from a golden chain secured at his squat throat.

"Your Highness." He bowed low, still puffing.

"Two things, Cromwell." The king did not face him, his eyes still on the striking couple in the courtyard. "One, get rid of Queen Anne as soon as possible. We care not how 'tis done, be it annulment or trial. Two, we are to be free to wed a new bride by midsummer."

Cromwell stammered an answer: about his treatment of the queen prompting a war, of the diplomatic disasters that would be caused by an end to this marriage. But the king did not listen. From his opulent chamber, he was watching the way the light from the sun caught Mistress Deanie's smile, and he wondered what it would be like to kiss those sweet lips in his marriage bed and to sire at last a duke of York.

Chapter 4

"*N*OTHING LIKE A BREWSKY FOR BREAKFAST." DEANIE
sighed, shaking the crumbs from her full skirt. "I feel as if
I've been on the road with Aerosmith in the seventies. What
I could really use is a cigarette and a cup of coffee."

"I know I shall regret this," Kit said with a chuckle as he
brushed grass from the back of her gown, "but could you
please explain the meaning of what thou quoth?"

Their hands almost touched as she looked up at him.
With only a small hesitation, she spoke. "Well, *brewsky* is
just an American bowling-alley term for ale, and *Aerosmith*
is the name of a group of music makers, sort of wandering
minstrels."

"Aerosmith." He paused, as if deciding whether or not to
continue, then smiled. "And the others?"

"Hmm." She bit a fingernail, trying to come up with an
explanation of *coffee* and *cigarettes.* "Okay," she said at last,
not noticing Kit's barely curbed amusement, *"coffee* is a
drink made from coffee beans. It's boiled, and the drink is
served hot, sometimes with milk and sugar. I like mine

black, which means without anything added. And it doesn't really taste that great, but it smells wonderful."

"If the flavor be not to thy liking, why doth thou drink the brew?"

"Easy. It's full of something called *caffeine.*"

His eyebrows rose in bewilderment. "A small calf?"

"No!" For the first time since he met her in the maze, she laughed, a genuine, infectious giggle. Unable to hide his delight at her reaction, he too began to laugh.

With a deep, bracing breath, she continued: "Caffeine is sort of a potion, I suppose. It makes you feel wide awake even when you're absolutely exhausted."

"Ah. Most fascinating. We unenlightened Englishmen simply sleep when exhaustion settles. Now, what of the other item you spoke of. Be that a potion as well?"

"Cigarettes? No." She cleared her throat, trying to squelch her urge for nicotine. "Cigarettes are made from plant leaves."

"And then boiled and swallowed?"

"Nope. The leaves are dried, then chopped up and wrapped in paper."

He ran a hand through his hair, making the already tousled locks even more unruly. "Dried leaves wrapped in paper? Paper is a most precious commodity, Deanie. What then?"

"Now, this is going to sound crazy, Kit."

"I think not. What could be madder than swallowing a bitter bean stock to keep sleep at bay?"

"Well . . ." Suddenly she turned to him. "How did you know coffee was bitter?"

He crossed his arms, a small smile betraying nothing. "Quoth thee that some people add sugar and milk. Why else would a personage mix sugar and milk, unless 'twas a potion most bitter?"

"Oh," she said uncertainly, and he gestured for her to continue. "Well, with cigarettes you take a little tube of dried leaves and paper, and you set one end of it on fire."

"I see," he said with a shrug. "A cigarette shall be a torch?"

"Not exactly. You put it in your mouth."

Kit said nothing, but his eyes narrowed, and he slowly returned his attention to cleaning up the remains of the picnic. "A jest at my expense."

"No, seriously! I'm not kidding, Kit. You put the end that's not on fire in your mouth, and you suck it in."

"And your mouth becomes an inferno?"

"No. It really tastes good—the smoke, I mean. You breathe it in. But it's not good for you."

"Deanie," he said slowly, "once a small fire overtook my home. A young page was caught within, and I returned to pull the boy to safety. I too swallowed smoke. It did not taste 'good,' as you say. Should you offer me a burning torch to put within my mouth, my answer would be to send you off, away from bed hangings and kindling."

"Well, it's true. And after years of everyone smoking . . ."

"Smoking?"

"Yeah, that's what they call it. After years of everyone smoking, some big government doctors discovered that it is bad for your health to smoke."

"Ah. How sagacious your surgeons must be." Kit shot her a grin as he unceremoniously picked up the picnic cloth, mugs, jugs, and half-eaten rounds of bread jumbling together.

During their meal he had been acutely aware of the piercing gaze from the royal chambers above. Had he known they would become the focus of the king's appraising stare, he would have chosen another courtyard for their meal. Any courtyard, or just beyond the moat; even the tilting yard would have been more comfortable. Kit had seen that intense stare before, and the memory left him uneasy.

He turned toward Deanie, who had suddenly become very quiet. She had chatted like a magpie as they broke the fast. Now she was looking at the center of the courtyard, a strange expression on her face.

"Where's the fountain?"

"The fountain?"

The headdress was dangling from her hand, forgotten for the moment. A bird suddenly flitted from one of the newly planted shrubs, trilling in contentment. The Cloister Green was serene in the morning, a silent place to think and converse. The arched-brick walkway echoed the hollow footsteps of busy courtiers or servants, who could rarely pause to savor the quadrangle.

"I just remembered," she continued, her voice wavering. "I took a tour of this place before we began shooting."

"Ah. Thou wast here on a hunting excursion?"

"No. We were shooting a music video, a film to go with my song with Bucky Lee Denton." She took a deep breath before going on. A light breeze rustled her hair, and she impatiently swept it from her eyes. "There was a fountain here. A major fountain, Kit. I think it was designed by someone named after a bird."

"A bird?" He tried to hide his smile by making a strong fist and drawing it to his mouth, as if in deep thought. "Perhaps 'twas a Master Robin, or a Sir Peacock."

"No. But it was old, Kit. I mean, it was really old, and it's not here yet." The headdress slipped from her hand. *"I'm really here. I'm here. What am I going to do?"*

Without hesitating, Kit dropped the breakfast bundle and gently grasped her shoulders. "Deanie, sweet, listen to me." She turned her eyes to his, and before speaking he cast a swift glance toward the large windows of the royal apartments. The king was no longer watching them.

She blinked against the force of his scrutiny. "You are here. You must understand what I am saying, or you may find yourself in serious trouble." His accent, undeniably British, was lighter, less bent by the odd Tudor intonations. "You are in a time and place you know not of. They play by different rules; everything is dictated by arcane custom and superstition."

"Everyone here should be dead," she muttered to herself. He tilted her face toward his, running a finger along the line of her jaw.

"Not you," she added. "Oh Kit. I didn't mean that you should be dead."

His face was unreadable. She would have thought he hadn't heard her, but there was an almost incandescent glint in his eyes. "I should be dead," he said at last. "But I am not."

"No. I mean everyone else here." She spoke quickly, wanting to rid the strange, haunted expression from his face. "The king. He should be dead."

Kit's eyes snapped to hers, clear now. Gone was the vague uncertainty she had seen for such a brief moment. "Nay. Speak not of such things. Just listen. 'Tis treason to even imagine the king's death, or the death of the prince of Wales. Should an enemy hear your idle words, 'twould immediately be brought to the king's ears."

"What are you talking about? How the hell could I have an enemy when I only got here yesterday? Sure, there are a few label executives in Nashville who would probably like to see me brought down a peg or two, not to mention Vic Jenkens and Bucky Lee Denton, but here?"

"More so than you know." His voice was tender. "This court, 'tis a viperous place fraught with jealousy. And a fair maid such as thyself, well . . ." His speech became halting. "I will be by your side as much as possible, as much as my duties allow. When I cannot be with you, try not to bring overmuch attention to thyself."

She remained silent for a moment. From a distance, she heard the laughter of a group of men, the neighing of a horse. A pair of serving maids scurried across the stone walkway, a large wooden bucket balanced between them. One of the women, with a white bonnet tied under her chin, looked swiftly at Kit, then away, to the giggles of her companion.

"Why are you being so nice to me?" Deanie's voice was taut as Kit's grip on her shoulders loosened. His thumbs rotated lazily on her arms, soothing the spot where his hands had grasped her so harshly.

His hair caught the sun's reflection, and she was aware again of how potent he was, how very masculine. He wasn't simply handsome, for in truth his features were too harsh. His nose, in profile, was too hawkish, his eyes too penetrating. Yet, taken together, with the sublimely luxurious mouth, he was the most breathtaking man she had ever seen.

"Why am I kind to you? You have asked me that before." He cleared his throat. "I have no family here," he said at last. "You remind me of my sister."

That was not what she'd had in mind. She smiled anyway, feeling a deep warmth course through her body. "Thank you. I think."

He gave her a quick wink and then crouched to swoop up her headdress and the remains of the breakfast in one hand. His sword jutted out as he bent over, and she wondered if he was ever without it. Perhaps at night. In bed. By himself . . .

"Now cousin," he said, taking her hand, "let us see about getting rid of thy clothing."

"What?"

He laughed. "Thou art a lady-in-waiting to the queen, and gowns are needed. There is a Master Locke, who designs gowns for all, nobility and royalty alike. We shall see to it anon."

"Oh."

Together they left the courtyard. From another window, Thomas Cromwell watched the interplay between the two, tapping his fingernail lightly upon the glass, thinking of his next move.

* * *

Mistress Cecily Garrison could not hide her fascination with Deanie's costume.

Unlike customary gowns, a white linen undersmock topped by a second layer with the surgown on top, Deanie's was all of one piece. Small strips of white cloth appeared, at first glance, to be an undersmock, but they were false. The bodice of the gown was a single layer, cuffs and collar sewn on with glossy thread. The petticoat visible from under her hem was also but a paltry few inches of cloth. The fabric was of an inferior quality, poorly sewn. Her slippers were already wearing thin at the soles, with a strange band stretching across the instep.

She had been so astounded by the Velcro fastenings, she had confided to Kit that Deanie's clothing may possess magical powers. He had laughed, raising her hand to his lips and causing Mistress Cecily to blush tremulously.

"Ah, fair Cecily," he whispered. "'Tis simply a Welsh fashion."

"She sayeth the bewitching lacings be called *Velcro.*" Mistress Cecily hoped the duke would not notice how damp her palms had become. She had never been this close to him, although she had indeed tried to gain his attention many times.

"Yeah, 'tis true enough. A *Velcro* is a Welsh rodent, a vermin of unusual ferosity with prickly skin."

After that Mistress Cecily left Deanie's clothing alone, never commenting on the strange fabric or the odd design. Instead, she helped Kit procure a wardrobe for Deanie, including a reed-and-canvas corset, some quilted under-garments to keep her skin from rubbing against the bindings, sleeves that could be worn with two new brocade bodices, and several round, wimplelike headdresses called French hoods. They had long folds of cloth hanging down the back called *lapets,* which could be left alone or pinned neatly to the side of the headdress.

Deanie had been helpless at first, not understanding how

the clothes were to be worn. They were all separate, reassembled and tied together before each wearing. There were holes in the corset, which wasn't nearly as uncomfortable as she had feared. The holes were to tie layers of starched petticoats in place. Mistress Cecily, eager to impress Kit, assisted happily, clarifying the finer points of fashion that Deanie's remote Welsh upbringing had caused her to miss.

Two details of court clothing fascinated Deanie. One was the long train of cloth that dragged behind every female of rank. Kit explained that only women of substantial means could afford such a luxury of swirling cloth about on the floor.

"Are you a man of means, Kit?" Deanie asked, practicing the current court posture and walk. Every step involved kicking out to clear the cloth from treading feet, causing the hips to sway. Kit had been watching her appreciatively, enjoying her surprising ability to mimic the other court ladies precisely, down to the haughty carriage of the head and the stiff, straight spine.

"What was the question?" He crossed his arms and stepped back, neatly missing her blue velvet train.

"I asked if you are a man of means. I mean, you must have some money to afford all these clothes for me." She tossed a handful of cloth to her other hand, and walked back across the room.

"I have funds enough, from Manor Hamilton, my estate, and from other sources. Very nicely turned, Deanie."

Another thing that startled Deanie was the complete lack of underwear other than the smock and a pair of linen hose. She had expected drawstring drawers, perhaps even bloomers. But even the finest of ladies wore absolutely nothing else under their skirts. It took some getting used to, and she was in constant terror of pulling her train too high or of falling down a flight of stairs.

"In truth," Mistress Cecily confided, "that is exactly what

most gentlemen of the court are waiting for. They pray for a misstep, and position themselves thusly, to gain the best view."

Suddenly court did not seem so very foreign after all.

Mary Douglass, Deanie's other bedmate, remained stubbornly sullen, glaring at Deanie from under stubby lashes. Cecily said that Mary, like so many other women at court, had fallen prey to her cousin Kit's charms. Although, she hastened to add, "he hath done nothing to encourage the chit."

Deanie sympathized with Mary. She too felt a giddy delight when in Kit's presence, a euphoria at just being by his side. And while part of her reveled in the new, strange feelings, another part warned her of the dangers of falling for a man like Kit. Now was not the time to become so vulnerable. Her own pathetic track record demonstrated how unreliable the male sex could be.

In spite of the turbulence of her new life—learning the ways of the royal court, adjusting to a foreign way of speaking, eating peculiar foods, and comprehending that she would probably never see her mother or her home again—Deanie had one constant and exquisite thought. Before she fell asleep each night, wedged between two unbathed women with hairy legs, she remembered that in the morning she would see a smile of dazzling whiteness with a slightly crooked tooth at the bottom.

The duke of Hamilton was not easily impressed.

Nevertheless, watching the facility with which Deanie memorized names and titles and positions at court, the correct forms of address and deference, gave him an unfamiliar sense of pride.

"It's nothing, really, Kit," she said late one afternoon, reaching back to loosen one of her laces. They ran on either side of her gown, and Kit had told her the clergy called the side lacings the "Gateways to Hell." "I've done so many Nashville parties and concerts, I can do this kind of stuff in my sleep. I can tell you every producer's name, his label, his wife or girlfriend or boyfriend's name, the kind of car they drive, and where they go to church. All that information comes in handy."

"'Twas years before I could master a quarter of the titles. Here, let me help you." He guided her to a massive chest of drawers standing in a corridor. With experienced fingers, he let out the lacings, careful to fasten them again. "Is that better?"

She sighed. "It sure is. If I could only get rid of this damned corset."

"Alas, cousin, I do not decree the fashion."

Closing her eyes, she took a deep breath and rubbed the back of her neck with her hand, still bandaged from when she'd touched his sword. He watched the rise and fall of her breasts beneath the gown of dark green velvet. The embroidered corset top peeked from above the bodice, and the sleeves, tied at the shoulders, had matching blue embroidery. Upon her head was a French hood, the lappets flowing down her back. It was a simple style that only a woman of rare beauty could wear. Deanie was such a woman.

"I don't know about you, but these dogs are barking." She opened her eyes, her lips curving into a soft smile.

"Dogs? I hear no hounds."

"No, I mean my feet hurt. These stone floors are about as comfortable as asphalt in July."

A group of courtiers swept past, intent on their private conversation. Deanie was still astonished how crowded Hampton Court was. Every threshold marked a favorite lounging spot, each chair held at least one courtier eager to curry favor.

And it was a motley crowd indeed, with dignitaries speaking every strange language imaginable, cloaked in their native clothes, sweeping through the airy hallways of Hampton. One man in particular struck Deanie as an oddball: a square-jawed fellow with an angular beard and Moe Howard haircut. His clothes, though made of a fine fabric, were always covered with drips and smears of brilliant-colored paint, fiery reds and rich blues and dulcet yellows. The man's eyes had a wild, ever-shifting expression. He was also the only courtier Kit seemed to actively dislike.

"He is admired greatly by the king for his artistic skills, although I trust him not," Kit said, pulling Deanie from the man's path as he charged down the hallway toward the royal chapel. "He is German, a painter. Hans Holbein by name."

"Has he ever painted you?" Deanie asked, watching the man stop abruptly, throw his hands into the air, and run back through the door he had just come from, again narrowly missing Deanie with his gesticulating arms.

"No," he replied, irritation evident in his voice. "I could not tolerate his guttural ramblings whilst he worked."

She looked down at her hands, twirling one thumb over the other. "Oh. I guess I must sound awful to you, the twang and all," she murmured.

She had not been fishing for compliments, and wasn't even sure Kit had heard her, when she felt one of his powerful arms glide about her shoulder. "Nay, Deanie. To me, your voice is like music."

Her eyes met his, questioning, wondering if he was making fun of her. Before she could speak, he kissed her forehead. "Let me show you the music salon," he said softly. "Perhaps you may enjoy some of the instruments."

He guided her through the corridor, his hand on the small of her back. Both nodded at passing courtiers, Kit providing a running commentary.

"Lady Cowen hath a most profond affection for her stud master. . . . That gentleman in the soiled buskins? Ah, he is Sir William Wade, known for his peculiar penchant for plundering table linens. He was once discovered without so much as a stitch of clothing, rolling the laundresses' basket. Yonder lay a massive wardrobe of cherry wood, twice pilfered by servants. 'Tis a problem to find manservants of honorable character."

"Wow. Even here, I suppose good help's hard to find."

"Exactly." Kit smiled, allowing her to enter the room first.

It took a moment for her eyes to adjust from the sun-drenched corridor to the darker, wood-paneled room. And when she did, she gasped.

In every corner, upon every table and chair, were musical instruments. She glanced toward the heavy russet drapes covering the window.

"To give the musical tones a more pleasant sound," Kit answered her unspoken question. With reverence, she touched the closest instrument. It was large and stringed, shaped like a swollen gourd. The neck was bent back. It gave the appearance of a rounded woman gazing at the sky.

"A lute," he said. "That one belongs to the king's lutinest, Phillipe Van Wilder."

"I know. I played a fake one during the video shoot, but it was nothing like this. Nothing at all."

There were keyboard instruments. Kit identified each one as she reached it. "A clavichord. Spinnet. Organ." Some had black keys, one was a double keyboard. All were ornately carved, covered with gilt or romantic paintings of angels or the Virgin Mary. Returning to the stringed instruments, she continued touching them, not actually picking them up. These were museum pieces.

"Mandolin, lyre," he continued. And then she saw it.

"Guitar," they said in unison.

It was smaller and more narrow than the type she was used to, but the shape was unmistakable. "Oh, Kit," she breathed.

"Would you like to play?"

She leaned closer, not daring to touch it yet. "Holy cow!" She whistled. "How many strings does this thing have?"

"The usual—five pairs. A total of ten."

"A ten-string guitar?" She straightened, wiping her palms on her skirt. "Man, I'd love to see Lee Roy Parnell get his hands on this guitar."

"Why don't you play?"

Deanie shrugged. "I don't know. This thing's probably worth a fortune."

"No. 'Tis worth a few shillings. At least, that is what I paid for it."

"It's yours?"

He nodded, handing the instrument to her. The back was an incredible design of geometric cubes, three dimensional in appearance. The neck was fretted—as far as she could tell with the same number of frets as on a modern guitar. The head was bent back at a graceful angle, as if in repose and listening to chords played on its strings.

Kit strode to a corner and returned with an ornately carved chair of dark wood with a high back and no arms. There were faces all over the chair, weird gargoylelike leers and grins. "Geeze," she muttered. Even through the wooden corset and layers of undergarments, she could feel the sharp bumps and indentations of the wood. "Haven't y'all ever heard of a nice, smooth-backed chair?"

"In a royal household?" Kit looked offended. "Never!"

Settling the guitar on her lap, she savored the weight of the instrument, the satiny feel of the varnished wood. "This is gorgeous, Kit. Where did you get it?"

"From a Spanish trader, a gentleman who provided the late Queen Katherine with many of her goods." He made the sign of the cross at the former Queen's name.

After some slight hesitation, she began strumming the instrument. The tone was sonorous and rich, surprisingly deep considering the smallish size of the guitar. Just as she was about to play another chord, a sharp pain stung her injured hand.

Kit knew immediately what had caused her to stop. "Your wound," he said softly. "I am so sorry, Deanie. Please, let me have a look at it."

He examined the palm of her hand, intent on the cut from his sword. "I think it will heal nicely if you just keep it clean. Don't muck it up with any of those balms or salves of the court physicians. They mean well, but God only knows what the ingredients are. Eye of newt, most probably."

Her eyes met his, a strange expression on her face. "Be there something wrong?" he asked.

Withdrawing her hand, she rested it on the neck of the guitar. "Just now, Kit, you sounded different. I mean, you didn't use those confounded *thees* and *thous* and talk backwards."

"I know. I am trying to mimic your speech patterns, so you can understand me more clearly." He took the guitar away and placed it against a wall. "I speak several languages, Deanie. Yours is most strange, but easily learned."

"Oh." She stood up, smoothing the folds of her gown. "It must be like speaking pig latin: sort of familiar, but not. Right?"

"Thou cannot be serious. Pigs can speak Latin in your time?"

Deanie chuckled, looping her arm through his. "Never mind, Kit. I'm starving. Do you suppose we can get something to eat? Preferably something without a head or feet?"

"I believe I saw some bread and cheese beyond the larder. Would that satisfy thy hunger? Or does cheese speak in your time as well?"

Laughing, they left in search of lunch.

Chapter 5

FINALLY, AFTER MORE THAN A WEEK SPENT LIVING AT THE court of Henry VIII, Deanie was to meet the queen.

There was an extraordinary frenzy of activity about the palace. Tapestries were beaten and rehung, panels of richly carved roses—the Tudor rose—were polished to a lustrous gleam. Flower garlands were laid over every mantle and doorway, accompanied by a furious sweeping of the hallways and chambers and brick-vaulted passageways. Fresh rushes were scattered on the floor of the great hall, over those drenched in wine, food, and dog urine. A new crop of ladies-in-waiting, from the queen's native duchy of Cleves, arrived overnight to prepare the way for the bride.

To everyone who had witnessed the barely restrained fury of the king, it was clear that he was not looking forward to his wife's arrival. He lashed out with increasing frequency at his closest ministers, especially Thomas Cromwell, who, in a surprise move that stunned the court, had just been elevated to the rank of earl of Essex.

The king had taken to physically hitting his newest earl,

slapping and kicking him like an ill-used cur. Embarrassed witnesses told of the king whacking Cromwell's shoulders and head, and of Cromwell ducking sheepishly back to his own quarters after such beatings.

"Why did the King make Cromwell an earl if he hates him so much?" Deanie asked as they sat in what had become their favorite spot, the Cloister Green courtyard. Others stayed away because of the king's apartments, and the excellent view the royal eyes had of the yard. Kit and Deanie felt it was worth the privacy, gambling against the off chance the king would be watching.

Her gown, of deep blue velvet with a low, square neckline, bordered with tiny flowers of black-and-red embroidery, fanned out behind her where she sat on the grass. She shifted, the tightly laced corset pinching her sides, trying to get comfortable. It was a losing battle. The queen was to arrive at any moment, and Deanie, along with the rest of the ladies-in-waiting, had to be ready. She lifted a finger to scratch under the rounded headpiece, a French hood studded with pearls, showing a crown of dazzling dark hair parted down the middle.

The shortness of her hair, concealed under the headpiece, had elicited comments from Mistress Cecily Garrison and Mary Douglass. Both women assumed Deanie had been in a convent, for only nuns wore their hair shorn. Most ladies never cut their hair, letting it flow well past their waists when free from the confining headdresses.

Kit, again coming to Deanie's rescue, had heard the gossip and neatly put an end to it by mentioning how distressed she had been when her hair fell out during her illness. The court ladies, and even some of the men, felt a surge of sympathy for the lovely young maid who had survived the throws of brain fever. Instead of making her an oddity, her shoulder-length hair made her an object of compassion. And Kit and Deanie relished his terrible pun: that poor Mistress Deanie had been "distressed" at being "detressed."

Kit chewed on a piece of grass in the courtyard, watching Deanie in her fruitless effort to get comfortable, tugging on the knotted laces of her bodice, running a finger under the square neckline to loosen it. He grinned, the blade of grass tilting up with the motion.

"Well?" she asked again, a little breathless from her exertions.

From his expression, the sharp angles of his face augmented by his smirk, she knew he hadn't paid attention to her. But she couldn't even pretend to be annoyed. She too had found it increasingly difficult to follow his words. Instead, she would notice the way the sunshine played off his hair, or how the dimples in those lean and severe cheeks would appear just before he smiled. His doublet, of dark gray velvet, was of the simple style he preferred, with a narrow collar at the throat. The sleeves were slashed to reveal the white shirt, tied at the wrists and collar. His hose showed his legs, thick with muscles, the ever-present sword sheathed in black enamel resting on his thigh.

Leaning on his elbow, he plucked the grass from his teeth, the tip chewed flat. It reminded Deanie of a cigarette, and she swallowed against the craving for nicotine that had been plaguing her for a week.

"What did you ask?" His tone was insolent, a grin behind the voice.

"Me?"

He nodded, absentmindedly brushing a small clump of dirt from her hem. They had rarely touched each other, except for his offering of a courtly arm or her tapping his hand in excitement as they spoke. The single exception was when he kissed her forehead, a lapse in his customary control. Yet a tension ran between them, a strange awareness of each other that seemed to expand and intensify with each passing day. It was as if they were in ceaseless physical contact, alert to each other's every move. When he entered a room, she knew before looking up that he was there. When she retired with the other ladies of the court, he could feel her absence without being told she was gone.

Deanie closed her eyes to remember her question, knowing she could not possibly gather her thoughts with his face so close, every detail becoming so familiar, so fascinating. She would never grow tired of watching him.

As her eyes shut, her fine brows furrowed in thought, she missed the sudden gentleness in his expression. The harsh lines seemed to vanish as he studied her face, drinking in each feature: the light blue veins on her eyelids, the tiny freckles on her nose. He thought of the way her eyes would widen, brown and luminous, whenever he supplied her with yet another aspect of court life.

She was vulnerable here, away from all with which she was familiar. For the first time since he had arrived at court ten years earlier, he felt overwhelmingly protective of another human being. Before he'd been unattached, unencumbered by the gentle strings of affection. His duty was to the king and to the families who called Manor Hamilton home. No other thoughts had softly plagued his sleep. No radiant smile had rewarded his smallest of gestures.

Now there was Deanie.

Everything about her was enchanting. The dichotomy of the dark-haired beauty was enthralling to him, a strength mingled with delicacy, a determination touched by uncertainty.

Perhaps she trusted him simply because he alone knew of her past, where she came from, of the miraculous journey that had led her to England, to 1540 . . . to him.

It would mean nothing if he could not protect her from physical danger, from the very real perils of the court: the petty jealousies, the power-hungry courtiers who would ruthlessly destroy a life simply to enjoy more useless luxury.

Sitting before him, she closed her eyes, as unaware of the menace swirling about her as she was of his own open expression. He realized with a jolt that he loved her. His breath caught in his throat as he mentally articulated the concept.

I love her.

Before he could ponder the revelation, make sense of the rush of emotions pounding through his veins, she opened her eyes, beaming.

"I remember! I was about to ask you why the king made Cromwell the earl of Essex when he clearly can't stand the guy."

Kit blinked, as if startled, and rolled over on his back. He closed his eyes against the sun. Against Deanie.

He paused before he could answer, breathing heavily as if he had just run a great distance. Deanie watched his broad chest rise and fall, the unfamiliar look of confusion on his face. Kit, who seemed to know all there was to know about everything, suddenly looked as lost as a little boy at a state fair.

He took one deep lungful of air, and once again his face wore the usual controlled, composed expression.

"I believe he maketh Cromwell an earl so that his fall, when it occurs—and mark my words, it will," he said, raising an eyebrow to Deanie, "will be all the more dramatic and devastating because of the height."

"You mean," she said softly, "he's setting him up just to knock him over?"

He nodded once, and Deanie whistled through her teeth.

Kit could not help but smile at himself, at the inevitable parallel his words had just drawn. Like poor beleaguered Cromwell, Kit wondered if he had unwittingly set himself up for a colossal fall.

They lined the Great Hall, all the ladies and gentlemen of the court. Off the hall, on the domestic side of Hampton, the massive kitchen and all its wings—including the larder, dry-fish room, spicery, pastry room, and the buttery—lay in pristine order. The hundreds of servants stood in neat, motionless rows, as still and solemn as the scoured pots and neatly arranged spoons, awaiting inspection from the queen. Her jewel-studded slippers might not pad beyond the great hall, but, just in case, every attendant was scrubbed and ready.

King Henry held Anne of Cleves at a formal distance, more regal than was absolutely necessary. His face did not betray his distaste, for above all, Henry took enormous pride in his ability to perform his royal duty with unfailing elegance and dignity. When he glanced at his bride, which he did as infrequently as possible, his pursed lips would twitch under the reddish mustache, and the great beard would tighten, as if the king were making a superhuman effort not to be ill.

Deanie was in the low curtsy she had been practicing with another new lady-in-waiting, a chirpy, plump teenager named Katherine Howard. Deanie had been stunned to learn that Mistress Katherine, who reminded Deanie of a typical school cheerleader, was the niece of Thomas Howard, the creepy man who had been in the maze when she first met Kit. It seemed impossible that bubbly Katherine was in any way related to Norfolk, who had made clear his disapproval of Deanie by making peculiar huffing noises whenever he passed.

Her eyes were lowered, just as Kit had instructed. She was not to look up until the queen addressed her directly. Deanie could not see her yet; she was lingering over each and every member of the court. The hall was stifling in the unusual afternoon heat, made all the more uncomfortable by the layers of heavy clothing. The windows were sealed against the threat of fresh air. She tried to take a deep breath, but the corset bound her ribs and the breath was stopped short.

I'm going to faint, she thought with alarm.

Kit stood directly behind her, bowing low along with all the other titled peers. Deanie, as a new lady-in-waiting as well as his cousin, was allowed the privilege of standing with their ranks. He saw her shoulders begin to slump forward, and very quietly, without disturbing the sword at his side or elbowing a grizzled duke standing barely a foot away, he reached toward her and firmly gripped her waist.

She didn't jump at the sudden sensation of a pair of strong hands bracing her. It was as if she had been expecting his help. He steadied her for a few moments, her full weight in his grasp. He knew that if he let her go she would tumble to the ground.

He also knew how completely she trusted him.

It was the longest physical contact they had ever enjoyed, had ever allowed. The queen was approaching more quickly now, nodding to her ladies, graciously bestowing smiles upon her subjects.

Deanie let the corner of her voluminous skirt fall and caressed one of his hard hands, giving a soft squeeze. He smiled, understanding her signal. With a returning press, he withdrew his grasp. The bones in her hand had felt fine and delicate in his, gentle hands to be cherished.

Warmth flooded Deanie's face, a tenderness that threatened to bring a tear to her eye. And then, too late, she realized the queen was before her.

Snapping back to reality, Deanie tried frantically to recall what she was to do next. Damn! They had practiced just that morning, Deanie and Mary and Cecily and Katherine.

Then it came to her: She was to sink deeper into a curtsy. In her haste, she'd forgotten that she had let go of a corner of her gown to touch Kit's hand. The toe of her slipper caught the hem of her skirt, and in the blink of an eye, Deanie plopped unceremoniously to the ground.

For a moment all was quiet, as a stunned, startled hush fell over the entire hall. One lady allowed a soft gasp to escape her mouth. Someone—probably Thomas Howard— snorted in disgust.

Kit stepped forward to help her rise, placing a foot on the swirling train of her gown. Muttering apologies to the king and queen, he lifted her halfway to a standing position, when suddenly the material he was unwittingly standing on began to rise with its wearer. Both Deanie and Kit slammed to the ground, his sword clattering beside them.

Deanie scrambled to stand, leaning on Kit's shoulder for leverage. With a dazed Kit still on her skirts, there was no hope.

Suddenly a single booming laugh filled the hall. Henry, his face flushed with glee, threw back his head, pounded his hands together, and roared with genuine, unaffected laughter.

"By God," he shouted, the peers beginning to smile among themselves, relieved at their sovereign's delight. "'tis the best jest we have seen in years! Ha! Mistress Deanie and Hamilton, we most heartily thank ye!"

The king then dissolved into a fit of hilarity, tears streaming down his massive face, his bejeweled doublet shaking with unrestrained glee.

At last Deanie and Kit were able to stand and face the queen.

She was not at all what Deanie had expected. Instead of some foreign, exotic beast, Anne of Cleves—in spite of her strangely shaped headdress and high-necked gown, thick with gold thread and belted under ample breasts—was one of the most friendly, unabashedly kind-looking people Deanie had ever seen. She was certainly not attractive. Her nose was large and crooked, her skin slightly pockmarked, and her eyebrows, heavily plucked, rested over droopy eyes.

But then she giggled, an infectious, girlish laugh, and clasped Deanie's hand.

"Mistress Deanie," she said in her ponderous accent. "I too must give thee thanks for making my most gracious husband happy."

Kit hastened to explain that his cousin was very new to the court and had yet to learn its ways. He apologized, bending over her hand, causing the queen, like every other female, to blush with pleasure at his charms.

The king was still howling with laughter. The queen, before continuing the reception, whispered into Deanie's ear: "I hope, Mistress Deanie, that since we are both so very new at this court, we shall become special friends." Then she left to conclude her royal progress.

Deanie, still startled by what had happened, felt herself smile. She liked the queen, no matter what the king or even Kit felt about her.

Another thought crossed her mind: Even in a world of mucky, foul smells, Anne of Cleves sure did stink.

One of the king's ministers was not in the Great Hall. His absence was a glaring omission, one the king had specifically planned, one the king particularly relished.

Thomas Cromwell paced in his chamber, ignoring the plush, fur-trimmed collar that tickled his cheek. Downstairs the queen was receiving the other peers. Cromwell, as the newly titled earl of Essex, should have been there, beside Norfolk and Suffolk and Hamilton. Instead, the king had ordered Cromwell to work on the annulment proceedings, even as the queen, oblivious to her impending fate, played the role of genteel consort.

It mattered not that the workings of England could grind to a halt at the king's every whim and fancy, that a fine day could find the king and his Privy Council galloping the countryside in search of a beast to slay for mere sport.

Cromwell was not to be allowed the honor of receiving the very woman he had made queen.

The quill in his hand snapped in two. Cromwell knew what the king's conduct toward him meant; he could read the ominous writing on the stone wall. He had seen his sovereign act this way before; his once-blazing enthusiasm for a subject could pivot overnight into deadly, sometimes irrational hatred.

It had been that way for Anne Boleyn, another woman Cromwell had made queen. She had once been the center of the king's universe; then, within hours it seemed, Henry told of his loathing, how she had bewitched him, how the very sight of the woman he once adored made him physically ill.

Like the quill in his hand, Anne Boleyn had ended in two pieces, her dark head separated from her slender body by the executioner's sword. At the time, members of the court had remarked on the king's marvelous kindness in hiring an expensive but expert swordsman from France to make his former wife's death swifter, and presumably less painful, than it would have been had he relied on a native headsman with a dull, thick English ax. Nobody dared to mention that Henry had already procured a divorce from Anne Boleyn. He had been free to marry again, free of his second wife. Her death had been a stroke of malevolent spite from an enraged sovereign.

Others had been executed, good men, great men. There were too many to count now: Thomas More and Bishop Fisher and Lord Rochford. Like a spoiled child grown weary of a shiny new trinket, Henry would toss aside men, turning his back on those who had served him most faithfully.

Cromwell knew the pattern. He had assisted the king on countless occasions, winning a conviction of treason here, usurping a peer's land and worldly goods there, always expeditious in condemming last week's favorite to the Tower.

And soon it would be Cromwell himself.

It was no fault of his that reports of the Cleves woman had been grossly inaccurate. His own ministers had attested to her beauty and wit, that she would be in every way a most perfect wife for the great Harry of England. If anyone was to blame for the deception it was that German artist Holbein, whose magnificent portrait of the sister of the duke of Cleves that had whet the king's considerable appetite in the first place.

But the king became infuriated when Cromwell suggested that the culpability lay with the painter.

"He is an artist, Cromwell," the king sneered. "I, above all, understand the artistic mind. 'Tis no fault of his." Unspoken, but implied by the king's glare, were the words "How canst thou, naught but a blacksmithy's son, know of art and beauty?"

Cromwell had arranged the marriage, and now the king would find the means with which to make him pay.

In his mind he envisioned the reception below, the bobbing ladies and bowing gentlemen, the eyes meeting in silent awareness that Thomas Cromwell, the earl of Essex, was absent. It would begin now, his slide to ruin.

Who would take his place? The duke of Norfolk, Thomas Howard, would be eager as a puppy to please the king. He had managed to extricate himself from that disastrous niece of his, Anne Boleyn, by becoming her most vocal detractor once he saw the king had tired of her. By licking the king's boots, Norfolk was again in favor, backed by Catholics alarmed by Cromwell's dissolution of the monasteries.

The king had been happy enough to take the riches of the dissolved monasteries. His lavish court had all but bankrupted England, and someone had to pay. The monies had replenished the royal coffers. Now the king blamed Cromwell. The Catholics blamed Cromwell as well, and they heaped on added reproach by throwing in Anne of Cleves, a follower of the heretic Martin Luther. Never mind that she had played the part of dutiful Catholic since arriving in England.

Cromwell alone would be blamed, accused, and condemned.

Now Norfolk was pushing another niece—how many did he have?—toward the king in hopes of securing permanent favor. Katherine Howard was but fifteen, pretty enough in a plump, sluttish way. He was right, that Norfolk. Whoever supplied the king with an antidote to the Cleves woman would reign supreme at court, topped only by the king himself.

His fist came down on a stack of parchments, documents

drawn up by his clerks to win an annulment. Once that was achieved, Cromwell's time would be up.

Unless . . .

He recalled a few days earlier, in the king's chambers, the expression on Henry's face as he looked upon the new woman, that cousin of Hamilton's, the wench from Wales. The royal countenance had been hungry, lascivious. She was indeed extraordinary in appearance. The king liked women of spirit, with flashes of wit, women who could amuse his regal humor. He professed to love virtue in a woman, although what he really loved was gaiety and vivacity.

Hope began to blossom in Cromwell.

He would control Hamilton's cousin, present her to the king as a precious jewel on black velvet. It may actually work to his advantage, the Cleves union, for the king would be so eager to rinse the bitter taste of Anne from his mouth that any dainty tidbit would be all the more delectable.

What was her name? Ah, Mistress Deanie Bailey. A common name, but it would be regal enough once she shared the king's bed.

Now it would be a game. Cromwell loved games; the higher the stakes, the greater his triumph. Mistress Deanie would be his pawn in this tournament of chess; Norfolk had Katherine Howard. And whoever captured the king would win.

There was only one slight problem: Christopher Neville, the duke of Hamilton. He seemed inordinately fond of Mistress Deanie, above the realm of mere cousins. If indeed she was his cousin. The king was attached to Hamilton, which might pose another obstacle.

Cromwell's face folded into a smile of anticipation. One way or another, the gallant Hamilton would be removed. It mattered not how, just as long as Cromwell had a clear shot at the Bailey wench. Hamilton was bright, more clever than most of the courtiers. It would take an even more clever man to best him, to win this ultimate tournament. Cromwell loved games, adored gambles. Whoever lost this game would surely forfeit his life.

Thomas Cromwell, the earl of Essex, was again on familiar ground.

Deanie tried to hide her yawn, turning her head slightly and placing a hand over her mouth. Even the three-legged juggling black bear, fascinating at first, now seemed old and dull. The trainer, cloaked in absurd patched hose and a red stocking cap with bells on the tip, tried to amuse the audience with a limp backflip. But he missed and slammed into Lady Alison Conyngham, who shrieked in horror. Deanie would have smiled at that bit of slapstick humor, but she was numb with exhausted boredom.

Kit, of course, saw her stifled yawn, even as he was engaged in a discussion of jousting techniques with Charles Brandon, the duke of Suffolk. Poor Suffolk. He was a good enough fellow, Kit supposed, watching the once-handsome face betray a life of increasingly rich food and drink and increasingly less physical activity. Kit glanced down at his own hand, not realizing until then he had been tapping a finger impatiently. He stopped, not wishing to insult Suffolk. But he was still restless. The trestle table seemed to sway under the weight of the food piled on plates of silver and gold, goblets of wine, and leather-covered tankards of ale.

The banquet, which had begun in the late afternoon, showed no signs of ending. The Hampton Court clock struck eight times, each ring echoing its melancholy chime.

Everyone knew why the king was so reluctant to disperse the crowd. That would mean that he had to be alone with his queen, the woman chatting happily by his side in High Dutch and halting English, blissfully unaware of the terrible plans the king was at that very moment orchestrating. If she was lucky, it would be an annulment and disgrace. If not, well . . . For her sake, everyone in the hall hoped it wouldn't come to that. She had shown herself to be a pleasant enough woman; there was no malice in those eyes of dung brown, not a sliver of ambition in her friendly nod.

Kit was sharply aware of every move Deanie made, of every gesture, of every morsel of food she took and every comment she made to Mistress Cecily or Katherine Howard.

Charles Brandon was slamming his hand on the table, forcing Kit's attention back to his dull, stale tale of a tournament a decade and a half old. Poor Suffolk. When into his cups, as he was tonight, he became a cloddish boor. Even hangers-on eager to ingratiate themselves in the royal ranks found him difficult to tolerate; the same jousting tales were recited over and over, every detail becoming just slightly inflated with each go-round. He pounded his fist on the table, causing filled goblets of wine to spill their contents like so much blood. Without turning his head, Kit knew that Suffolk's imaginary opponent had just been vanquished by one of his self-proclaimed brilliant maneuvers.

In his youth Suffolk had wielded more charm—and eventually more power—than anyone else at court. The king had even forgiven him for eloping with Princess Mary Tudor, the king's own widowed sister. Now, like his sovereign, Suffolk rode tournaments only in his memory, wooed the fair ladies only in his heavy dreams.

With a muffled sigh Kit shifted on the bench. Deanie leaned toward Kit's ear, whispering softly. "Isn't that the same story he told on Monday?" she hissed. "The one where he manages to single-handedly defeat the French knight with the lion on his shield?"

Suffolk again pummeled the table, and a small fleck of spittle escaped the corner of his mouth. "Hamilton! Listen to me!" he demanded. "Now, Sir Jean de Coeur Lyon galloped upon his mighty stallion. But I, Charles Brandon, duke of Suffolk, was prepared to fight. . . ."

"God help us, Deanie," Kit murmured. "'Tis the long version."

"What say you?" barked Suffolk.

Instinctively, Deanie slid her hand upon Kit's thigh. "Oh, my Lord Suffolk," she purred. "My cousin asked me to pass the roast venison. Your tale has us all enthralled, and I did not hear him. Please—I mean, *pray* continue."

Kit's hand folded over hers and he nodded, unable to speak for fear of laughing out loud. Deanie's face remained serene as she raised her eyebrows, urging Suffolk to continue, which he did with renewed gusto.

"As I was saying . . ." he droned.

A large platter of venison, complete with hoof, was plopped before them. In surprise, she backed against Kit and her hand tightened in his grip. She almost laughed, but the warmth and solid feel of his hand stopped her. Slowly she turned her eyes to his, the constant sound of Suffolk's voice a blurred hum in the background.

All of the Great Hall seemed to dissolve as her palm turned up in his. A jolt ran through her arm, a mild tingling sensation. From Kit's sudden stillness, she knew he felt it too. He stared ahead for a moment, then he faced Deanie.

He was so close that she could smell him, a marvelous fragrance of leather and grass and a unique, masculine scent, primitive and undeniable. Her eyes took him in; she wanted every detail etched forever in her memory: the stray lock of hair that fell over his forehead, the cleft in his chin, the slight shadow of new whiskers, the solid angles of his face. Above all, his eyes—the strange, shining luster of greens and ambers, reflecting almost black in the flickering light of torches and candles.

Her breath stopped short when she saw his expression. The unwavering fervor was almost frightening and she would have backed away, but she felt utterly compelled to return the gaze. She realized that she had indeed forgotten to breathe, and when she opened her mouth, a squeaky hiccup escaped.

It was loud enough to cause Suffolk to pause. "God's blood, what was that, eh?" Only the vaguest of smiles lifted the corners of Kit's mouth.

Katherine Howard giggled into her napkin when Deanie hiccuped a second time, and Mistress Cecily handed her a full goblet of warm spiced wine.

"Perhaps some fresh air?" Kit's voice was tight, and Deanie nodded, scrambling over the bench as he helped her to her feet. They walked slowly past the watching room off the great hall. Deanie, who usually paused to admire the wool-and-silk tapestry of "The Romance of the Rose," glided by as if it didn't exist.

Both were unaware of the stares that followed them. Thomas Howard pretending to listen to an Italian diplomat, followed their every move with his lips thinned in concentration. His hand rose slowly to touch a jewel on his cloak, as if to reassure himself it was still there.

The king, reaching for a honeyed almond, smiled to himself. Mistress Deanie, her back straight, her carriage graceful, her face more lovely than a fresh rose, was leaving the hall with Hamilton. His small eyes glimmered with a shrewd and knowing intelligence. Soon she would be leaving the hall on the arm of her king. Soon she would be his.

The cool night air caressed their faces as they stopped in the courtyard. The music of the minstrels seemed far away; the laughing and table-pounding of the banquet wafted from the leaded windows as if from a great distance, distorted and muffled.

Kit turned to face Deanie, the yard illuminated by blazing torches within. For a long moment they simply stared at each other, her hiccups forgotten. He drew his hand deliberately to her face and, with exquisite tenderness, brushed her silken cheek with his hard knuckles. "I've been wanting to do that," he said hoarsely.

His features were partially shadowed, and she reached up to touch his hair. It was coarse and thick, just as she had imagined it would be. The ends curled in her fingers, springing back when her thumb pressed them down. Her hand slid to his face. She slowly ran a trembling finger along the side of his lean cheeks, the hollow beside his mouth. And then she did what she had dreamed of ever since she first saw him: She stroked the fullness of his bottom lip.

At once his arms closed around her in an embrace of stunning urgency. Ignoring the awkward tilt of her rounded headpiece, she wrapped her arms about his slender waist in response. Her eyes closed as if trying to block out everything but the sensation of being so close. Beneath his velvet doublet she heard the strong pounding of his heart.

This is where I belong, she thought. Of all the strange events that had brought her to him, everything now made perfect sense. This one embrace made it all clear to her, and for the moment, they were the only two beings who mattered. She felt her knees give out, and he held her more tightly as she reached up and gripped his shoulders. The muscles under his clothing shifted, heavy and solid.

"This is where you belong," he rasped, his voice thick.

Had he heard her thoughts?

"Kit," she breathed. With that she looked up at him, his eyes incandescent. His mouth descended upon hers, hungry, pleading. And she felt herself responding; that strange jolt she had experienced earlier at his mere touch threatened to consume her entire body.

His mouth was just as she'd imagined it would be: strong yet soft, demanding yet supple. She was lost in a spiral, whirling in his arms, both safe and terrified at the same time. She stepped back, gasping.

"Kit," she panted. "What are we going to do?"

His eyes were foggy, and again he reached for her, pulling her close. "I know not," he muttered. "Dear God, I know not."

But they both knew.

It was sheer madness, utter folly—yet utterly right. She was no longer able to stand, and he was no longer able to support her weight. It was as if all strength and wisdom had fled him at the same time. As her knees collapsed he eased her gently to the ground, and somehow their lips were again joined, touching at first—lightly, delicately, then fiercely passionate, grinding together as if the world were melting.

His hands caressed her leg through the velvet, then inched up the gown until the hem was clenched in his fist. She felt the cool night air, the prickly smooth grass at once on her thigh. And then she felt his hand, the hand she knew so very well.

Her back arched, bringing her even closer to him, and deep in the back of his throat she heard a low groan.

"Deanie."

"Oh, please," she whispered.

He hesitated a brief moment, and in that instant she clung to his body with unnatural ferocity, ignoring her headdress as it tumbled beneath her.

"Kit."

With the sound of his name on her lips, any chance of control vanished.

All she wanted was to be close to him, to feel his powerful body next to hers. Every other desire was tossed to oblivion.

"My Lord Hamilton!" The shout came from one of the king's young pages.

For a moment they remained very still, the silence broken only by their ragged breathing.

"Quickly," he rasped, pulling her as he rose to his feet. He was slightly unsteady, his hands still trembling as he began to adjust her skirts.

Still dazed, she could only blink as he hastily replaced her headpiece and tucked a stray strand of hair into place.

"Deanie." His voice seemed to come from a great distance.

Before he could speak again, the sound of footsteps in the courtyard echoed harshly in their ears.

"My Lord Hamilton," repeated the page as he emerged from behind a hedge. "There you are! And Mistress Bailey! The king doth require your presence within! Pray come! He desires to hear my lady's music."

"Bad timing," she murmured, her voice shaky.

He took a deep breath. "Later we must speak." He placed her hand through his arm.

"When?" she whispered as the page approached.

Kit did not address her. Instead he nodded toward the page. "Tell the king we will be within presently, as Mistress Deanie catches her breath."

"My Lord." The page bowed, then left the courtyard.

"Later we will speak," he repeated. "But now the king awaits."

They began to walk toward the great hall, both lost in their own thoughts. "Kit, I just realized I don't know where you live. I mean, you don't just hang out at court all the time, do you?"

He smiled. "After what just very nearly occurred, you want to know where I live?"

She nodded. "Do you have your own home, or do you just follow the king?"

"Nay, Deanie, I have my own estate, called Manor Hamilton. It's a smallish place compared to the royal palaces, but large enough, with servants and pages aplenty."

"Does your sister live there?"

He stopped, a strange cast to his eyes. "Why ask you of my sister?"

"Because you said I reminded you of her," she answered, perplexed.

"My sister is not alive." He looked down at her, and his eyes again softened. "Come. The king awaits."

"I'm sorry," she stammered at last.

But he said nothing as he led her back into the great hall.

Then she stopped. "My God, Kit," she whispered. "I need a second." She swallowed and closed her eyes. "I'm about to play a gig for the king of England."

The king clapped his hands as they entered. "Ah! Mistress Deanie! My lutist Van Wilder doth praise your skill on the guitar. Let us hear thee." The queen smiled and nodded, as if happy to see attention diverted from herself but unsure of precisely what the king was saying.

Van Wilder, his glinting doublet garish under a red satin cloak, handed her Kit's guitar.

She had to concentrate, she told herself. This was a show. Never mind what had happened in the courtyard.

There was a murmur of conversation as she refused the chair he offered and looped the guitar over her shoulders. She had fashioned a makeshift strap out of an embroidered kirtle, and she winked at Katherine Howard's expression of shock.

With a casual shrug, she tossed the three-foot train of her blue velvet gown over her right shoulder. There was a collective gasp from the women, which Deanie carefully ignored.

"Good evening, ladies and gentleman," she began, the practiced words of her opening banter. "Oh, and king and queen." She did a swift curtsy, and the royal couple acknowledged her with regal nods.

"Hope y'all have enjoyed the show so far." What was she saying? How could she call a troupe of mummers and a wrestling bear an opening act? Kit made a motion as if to come to her side, and she shot him a smile.

This was the one thing she *could* do. For once, since landing in the maze, she was not in need of Kit. She was not waiting to be rescued.

Most of the audience were intoxicated. This was the dinner theater from hell, she thought, the artificial smile still on her face. Once she had played a little honky-tonk in west Texas. There was chicken wire strung across the stage to keep the audience from throwing bottles at the performers. The place was so dangerous, she had used the phone with her back pressed against the wall, watching every patron like the potential felons they were.

All in all, she wished she were back in west Texas.

Swallowing once, she cleared her throat, finding the

familiar chords on the slender neck of the strange little guitar. Without any further banter, she launched into the old standby of every female country singer unsure of the crowd: a medley of Patsy Cline hits. From "I Fall to Pieces" and "Crazy" to "Walkin' After Midnight" and finally "Sweet Dreams (of You)."

At first she was tentative, unsure of her voice and the guitar in the vastness of the hammer-beam ceilinged hall. After four bars she realized the acoustics of the hall were spectacular; and her voice was rich and mellow, rising above the openmouthed audience.

The more she played, the more the songs carried her away, and she began to stroll, making eye contact with her audience. Some stared at her with their eyes comically wide, while others squinted in bafflement.

Damn, she thought. *I'm good.*

The audience remained silent. Her mind whirled, trying to think of a logical reason. Perhaps since they had never heard the tunes before, there wasn't that spark of recognition and fond memory that usually prompted the most inebriated listener to leap to unsteady feet after the medley.

So without waiting for more humiliating silence, she embarked on a tune that would be a number-one crossover hit for another singer in about four hundred and fifty years. It was her own composition, a rocking ballad titled "A Strong Man's Weakness." Sure, whenever she imagined her own concert, she saved the number for later in the show. But with this audience, she wasn't sure how much of a show there would be. The bear and his colorfully dressed trainer were waiting for a sign to reenter.

Their immobility bothered her the most. Like the seasoned small-club performer she was, she'd be damned if she'd let them get away with it. The eye-contact trick wasn't working, so she had to grind harder. Strolling from table to table, she reached over a platter of oysters and plucked the broad-brimmed velvet hat from the duke of Suffolk. Stunned at first, he began to smile groggily at the absurdity of the moment, pleased by the attention. Before he could comment, she grabbed another hat, this one belonging to an elderly man in somber garb.

Unfortunately, the old guy was the new bishop of Winchester. But he was game, and he soon began to nod his now-naked head in time to her music. The next hat was Norfolk's. Deanie decided to skip him altogether. She also passed over women, knowing from painful experience how difficult the headpieces were to fasten to the hair.

Their hats piled up on the edge of the table, she kept moving, kicking the hem of her gown out of her path each time she changed direction.

She was aware that her voice was unusual to their ears. From what she had heard—placid women strumming limply on lutes, seated delicately on a heavy chair—they were accustomed to high-pitched, Deanna Durbin–type voices. But Deanie's voice was rich and deep and confident.

Deanie also noticed that she sounded smoother than before and attributed the change to her not smoking cigarettes. High notes she had been forced to fudge back in Nashville, by shifting into a lower register, now came easily, soaring as she bent into the final syllable.

She could usually gauge an audience easily. This crowd was different. The hatless ones seemed pleased, but others remained perfectly still. At different times throughout her performance, an intrepid drummer in the minstrels' gallery tried valiantly to play along, only to peter out into an uncertain tee-tum. A single wooden recorder tooted once before warbling into oblivion with the drum.

The song ended, guitar strings vibrating the last resonant chord. And then there was the sound of one clap, strong and slow at first. The clapping grew faster and more furious. Deanie, blinking in astonishment at the bold clapper, turned toward the source of the solitary applause.

The king of England.

Chapter 6

TAKING A CUE FROM THEIR SOVEREIGN, OTHERS IN THE HALL began to clap, some stomping approval, a few clanging pewter-and-silver goblets on the thick table boards like an inmate uprising at Leavenworth. A large hound, who had unceremoniously chewed his rear leg for fleas during her entire performance, shrugged from the hall, clearly annoyed by the commotion.

Deanie was uncertain how to respond. With a swift curtsy and a mumbled "y'all have been a great audience," she began to back away. The guitar dangled from its strap, bumping her hip with every step.

The king rose to his feet, a strangely animated look on his mammoth face. He lifted one beefy hand into the air, silencing the hall. He walked around the dais, passing a stupefied Norfolk and a benevolently smiling Queen Anne, her oblong headpiece shadowing her eyes.

Kit began to move protectively toward Deanie, his wary hazel eyes fixed upon the king. Few noticed that his right hand was poised over the hilt of his sword. The voiceless, expectant tension had all eyes riveted on Deanie, her own stance uncertain as she stepped slowly toward Kit.

Henry's height, well over six foot two, and his enormous gold-clothed girth reminded her of an oversized Christmas tree, garishly decked by zealous children with more humor than taste. She averted her stare from the gem-studded codpiece poking from the lavish folds of his doublet skirt.

The king shook his head, clicking his tongue as he approached. His small mouth compressed into a compact pucker. She slammed into Kit's side, and both of them ignored her awkwardness when she stumbled on his foot, her gown causing her to slide along his leg. With nowhere else to go, she stood stockstill, unsure and more than a little alarmed. Could the king kill her? Behead her for not performing to his imperial satisfaction? She had heard of acts dying on stage but never being executed.

"Mistress Deanie," the monarch whispered, his booming voice subdued and almost meek. He stopped several feet short of Deanie, and from the corner of her eye she saw Kit, solid and motionless as a stone wall.

Forcing herself to look directly at the king's face, she felt her jaw drop in astonishment.

The king of England had tears in his eyes.

"Never—" His voice broke as he pulled her hand to meet his lips. "Never hath we heard such music, such poetry. Never. So simply wrought, yeah, so elegant." He brushed his damp mouth and crumb-dusted beard across the back of her hand. "Thou hath moved the royal heart with thy Welsh songs."

With a brief squeeze of her hand, he bowed to her. Deanie grinned. Suddenly she liked the king. Heck, he was just another fan.

Tilting her eyes to Kit, hoping to see grudging admiration on his face, perhaps even the glazed adulation of a newly won Wilma Dean Bailey enthusiast, she saw instead a flash of vexation. She had seen such a reaction before: in Vic Jenkens, in Bucky Lee Denton. It was something more than simple jealousy. They were threatened by her, as if her ability to create and perform music somehow detracted from their own talents. Vic and Bucky Lee did not like to share the spotlight with anyone, much less a woman. Deanie was momentarily stunned to realize that Kit was no different from the others.

An irrational, childish impulse overtook her. How Kit must envy her, the skill she displayed on his guitar. He must play himself, but she had never heard him. He was probably no good at it, the jerk. Now he was ticked off at someone showing him up, especially in front of the entire court and the king.

With calculated coyness, she turned her most dazzling smile on the monarch, the same smile she used at award ceremonies and press conferences. She was well aware that the king prized perfect teeth. Three months of extensive dental work had given her a smile brilliant enough to light up any video. Adding a dash of Tudor flourish, she curtsied low and gazed adoringly at Henry.

She completely ignored Kit.

The king's expression changed. For a few moments his face was blank with confusion, then something in his tiny eyes seemed to ignite. His whole body stiffened.

"Mistress Deanie," he said gruffly. "It would be our greatest pleasure to visit thee in thine own chambers."

Deanie was about to turn to Kit in bewilderment. Why was the king asking permission to wander about in his own palace? He had said "we," so she assumed he would take the queen as well.

Just before she raised a questioning eyebrow to Kit, she remembered her anger. He stood completely motionless, and she knew he'd heard every word the king had just uttered. Good, she thought. Not for nothing was she a top performer in Nashville. Okay, maybe not exactly top, but close enough. Perhaps she was far away from home, but no man—not even Christopher Neville, the duke of Hamilton—could hold her down.

"Your Majesty," she replied, not daring to glance at the king's face, "you are welcome at any time."

Before she could speak another word, the king was clapping his hands, motioning to the minstrels. "A galliard! A galliard!"

The hall was suddenly a bevy of activity, with serving boys shooing away dogs, the musicians scurrying into place in the gallery. The king winked once at Deanie and returned to his place on the trestled dais, a decided spring in the royal step. The ulcered leg was forgotten. The last two decades seemed to have melted away from the king.

Courtiers could not help but notice that for the first time in recent memory, Bluff King Hal had returned.

The ladies and gentlemen left their benches, some still chewing the remains of the banquet, others grabbing a quick swallow of wine. On the center floor they formed two straight lines, the men facing the women. Deanie wanted to see the dance, which was beginning to resemble her high school square-dancing lessons. She whirled to face Kit, smiling in anticipation. He grabbed her upper arm.

"Hey, what do you think you're doing?" she shrieked in protest, startled by how painful his grasp was even through three heavy layers of fabric.

He did not answer. With a single swift motion, he pulled the guitar from her shoulders and handed it to a passing carver, who stood momentarily baffled, juggling a large platter of half-eaten venison, a heavy gold knife, and the instrument. Then Kit dragged her through a passage to the courtyard, the exact spot where they had shared a sublime interlude less than thirty minutes before. By the time he let go of her arm, her surprise had become fury.

Without speaking a word, she turned on her heels to leave.

"Hold," he ordered. She stopped, her rigid back toward him. He was close enough that she could hear him breathing, even over the music and laughter inside.

She glanced down at her clenched fists, the sumptuous

fabric covering her wrists, delicate lace trimmed in black. Then her eyes blurred with tears, hot and heavy. A knot formed in her throat, and although she tried to swallow it, it remained painfully in place.

"You're just like the others," she murmured, unaware that she had spoken aloud. The hurt was too deep for her to care, and she began to pluck unmercifully at the lace cuffs, unraveling the fine needlework, not caring as she shredded the fragile material.

"Deanie." He reached for her shoulder. This time his touch was gentle, the anger in his voice diffused. She did not pull away; she no longer had the energy.

"You're just jealous." She sighed. "I've seen it before, Kit."

"Canst thou not," he began, taut with swelling rage. He took a ragged breath and started over. "Listen to me. Follow my words." Lifting her chin, he saw the tears and, with a thumb, wiped them away. "In short, Deanie, you have just agreed to become the king's mistress."

"What?" All traces of self-pity vanished. "You must be joking, Kit. The old guy just wants to bring his wife over to—"

"His wife? When did he make mention of his wife?"

She rolled her eyes, shaking her head in exasperation. "He said 'we would like to visit,' or something like that. He's bringing someone, at any rate. He won't be alone."

"Deanie." Kit held both shoulders now, forcing her to face him directly. "He employed the royal 'we.' Hath thou . . . have you not heard of it?"

A slow dawning closed over her expression. "Oh."

"Yeah. Oh."

For a moment they were silent. Then she brightened, almost enjoying the still-thunderous expression on his face. He wasn't angry at her talent, jealous of her ability to entertain. He was merely concerned for her reputation.

"Hey, Kit. It's no big deal. I'll just apologize to the king, you know. Let him down gently. And then . . ."

"Nay."

"Nay?"

As if exerting supreme control, he closed his eyes and let out a deep breath. "The entire court saw the exchange," he said softly. "Did you not espy Norfolk's expression? God's blood, Deanie." The hazel eyes opened, then softened as he saw her bafflement. "Let me speak plainly: The king has asked you to become his mistress. You have accepted."

She was about to speak when he held up a hand to stem her flow of denials. "Listen to me." At last she nodded, and he continued. "Before the entire court you have accepted. Now you must understand something. The king will not tolerate being made a fool. He can bear petty uprisings, foreign invasions, even stupidity on the part of his ministers. But he will never allow anyone—especially a woman—to make him appear buffoonish."

"Awe, come on, Kit. It's not that serious, just a little misunderstanding."

Kit made a fist, as if willing her by force to understand him, then let it fall between them. "Deanie," he said, his voice rough with meaning, "another woman quoth like words to me. She too was confident, and waxed happy that what had transpired between the king and herself was 'just a little misunderstanding.'"

Deanie grinned. "Oh? Who was that?"

"Her name," Kit said sharply, "was Anne Boleyn."

By the time Deanie returned to her chambers, exhausted and stunned by what Kit had told her, she was eager to share the problem with Cecily Garrison. As both the sister and daughter of longstanding courtiers, she would certainly know if there were any way out of the situation. Perhaps Kit was just overreacting, jumping to conclusions because he had seen the king behave harshly with other women.

But Cecily, and all traces of her, had vanished. Nor was sulky Mary Douglass anywhere to be seen. In an over-crowded palace, with well-bred courtiers and eager wannabes taking up every inch of surplus space, Deanie suddenly had her own room.

For a moment she knew blind panic, a clawing fear that Henry would bound into the room at any moment, his glittering codpiece dangling before her eyes. Gripping the mahogany post of the bed, she leaned her forehead against the carved wood, aware of the sharp edges biting into her skin. Somehow, the physical pain calmed her, made her acutely aware of her surroundings.

All was quiet. She could no longer hear the raucous clatter of the banquet below, the broken conversations of lovers escaping into the courtyard. She let go of the bed and reached for a muslin-covered bolster, hugging it close to her.

She needed to find Kit.

Placing her chin on top of the bolster, she sat stiffly on the bed. Her clothing made it impossible to get comfortable, but she didn't care. She had to get out of here, out of this palace. Kit had been right: The court was governed by rules beyond her comprehension. Arbitrary laws of behavior were set in stone. She was only now beginning to understand what a dangerous game she had been playing.

There was a soft knock on the door, and she jumped. Could it be the king? She stood up, the bolster rolling off her lap and onto the thickly planked floor. Perhaps if she didn't answer, whoever it was would go away.

There was another knock, more insistent this time.

"Mistress Deanie?" whispered a soft voice. It was Cecily Garrison. She swiftly unlatched the door, and Cecily slipped into the room.

Instead of simply chattering away, as she usually did, Cecily sunk into a low curtsy.

"What are you doing?" Deanie asked incredulously, pulling Cecily to her feet. Cecily kept her head bowed, not meeting Deanie's eyes.

"We are to depart next morn to Richmond, mistress,"

Cecily said. "I am to help you, should you require anything."

"What? Cecily, what's going on here?" Deanie felt the fear return in an awful rush.

Finally Cecily looked directly at Deanie. "Oh, Mistress Deanie, 'tis a great honor to bed the king."

"No way!"

Cecily continued, her expression one of respectful admiration. "The king is England itself. What England wishes, her humble subjects must be only too joyous to deliver. Let me assist you with your stays and laces, milady."

Without further instruction, Cecily began unfastening Deanie's headdress and unlacing the ties down her back. Numbly, Deanie submitted, noting how Cecily averted her eyes from Deanie's nearly naked body. Once she was free of the confining clothes and alone, she could somehow reach Kit. He was on the palace grounds. He would know what to do. Perhaps she could return to the maze and travel back to her own time with Kit. Perhaps . . .

"Mistress Deanie, wilt thou require anything else?"

She glanced at Cecily, a fleeting thought of asking for help in an escape plan. That wouldn't be fair. Cecily had no notion of how Deanie truly felt, deeming it a high honor to be chosen by the king. Everyone here was of the same mind, except for Kit. He alone knew what she was getting herself into, the torment she would endure. He had tried to warn her, but her stubborn, stupid arrogance made her turn on him like a German shepherd in a junkyard.

"No, Cecily." She faked a smile.

Cecily backed out of the room, as if Deanie had just been coronated.

Alone once more, wearing nothing but the loosely flowing white nightshift, Deanie slumped into the bed. She stared at the flickering candle, watching the beige wax drip hot and thick. She had to think, find a way to leave before she was confronted by Henry.

There was another knock on the door. Deanie, lost in her dismal thoughts, combed her fingers through her hair. "Come in, Cecily," she said distractedly.

The door opened, and a man wearing a dark green velvet cloak and a black hat with a turned-up brim entered. Deanie pulled the coverlet to her chin as he walked boldly to her side.

"Mistress Deanie," he said, bowing low.

She knew who he was, although they had yet to be formally introduced. Thomas Cromwell, the newly created earl of Essex, stood in her bedroom, a small grin twisting his fleshy lips.

"What are you doing here, Mr. Cromwell?" His eyes darkened at her use of 'mister' in his name. "Is the king coming?" Her voice was small, and she swallowed.

"Nay, milady. But if thou playest correctly, the king shall indeed make this chamber his own."

He leaned close enough for her to smell his breath, moldy and corrupt. Although his words were simple, there was an unmistakable sense of menace behind his manner. Perhaps in the light of day he would take more care to polish his demeanor. But now, in the dank hours of night, before a new member of the court, there was no reason to smooth his coarse edges.

Deanie pressed her back against the headboard of the bed, clutching the bolster and the coverlet against her bare neck. Cromwell smiled once more.

"Now, Mistress Deanie, some questions to pave the way for a smooth transition. Art thou of the Catholic faith?"

"No," she gasped, wondering why a fully clothed earl would wish to discuss religion at this peculiar hour.

"Nay?" His beady eyes caught the glint of the bedside candle. In the massive fireplace, a log crackled, and a sprinkle of red ash puffed into the air. The night was cold for late spring, and she suddenly felt a chill trace the length of her spine.

Cromwell continued, his voice neutral. "Thou hath been

absent from the daily Mass. Good. Art thou then a follower of Luther?"

"No. I mean, are you talking about the bad guy Lex Luthor? In the Superman comics?" Her voice had reached a high pitch, and she realized she was beginning to babble. "Oh, of course you aren't. What the hell am I thinking of." Her palms were damp. "Why are you asking me these questions?"

Calmly, he repeated the question: "Art thou a follower of Luther?"

Her mind whirled, trying desperately to recall what Kit had told her about religion in the court. She had been staring at his eyes, wondering how a man of such potent masculinity could have such dark lashes. He had been emphatic, she remembered. But she also recalled how close he had been, how she had averted her eyes from his face, only to be drawn to his hands, the veins on the top, the spray of black hairs just visible beneath his full cuffs.

What had he said?

Cromwell remained silent, patiently awaiting her response. She had the uneasy feeling that he would wait as long as it took for her answer, ever quiet and composed, whether it took her a month or a minute to speak. He folded his hands, and she noticed how thick and stubby they were, with a heavy gold ring on one finger. She glanced up at his face, a flat monkey face, the wide gap between his two front teeth.

"Well?" he prodded. "Art thou a Protestant?"

That sounded right. Growing up, her mother had never been able to take Deanie to church, since Sundays were always big-business days at the truck stop. She assumed she was a Baptist, since everyone else she knew was. Whenever she attended services with a friend, it was always at a Baptist church.

"Baptist is Protestant, right?"

For once Cromwell looked befuddled. "Mistress Deanie, it matters not that thou was baptized. What matters is—"

He was interrupted by shouts outside her door and a scuffling sound. She had been unaware of anyone else in the hallway. At once the heavy door swung open, and a gentle beam of light from the hall torches lit her room.

"Sir!" A breathless young man, his soiled leather jerkin askew, threw a pleading glance toward Cromwell, completely ignoring Deanie. "The duke, he—"

From behind, a powerful hand pulled the young man back into the corridor. Deanie recognized the fleeting sleeve, the mighty hand.

"Kit?" she said softly. Then she hopped out of bed, heedless of the cold floor and the swift perusal Cromwell gave her barely clothed form. "Kit!"

With a casual motion, Cromwell grasped the neck of her gown and twisted it, stopping not only her cry but her ability to breathe. Her hands flew to her throat, clawing uselessly in the air.

The corner of his mouth twitched slightly, as if aware that it would be terribly bad taste to smile but unable to entirely mask his pleasure.

"The duke may enter," Cromwell announced grandly. The grunts and shuffles in the hallway ceased.

Deanie saw Kit enter the room, blood on his forehead and the front of his doublet torn. The backs of her knees began to buckle as Cromwell held firm his grip.

"You will tell the king nothing of this," Cromwell said softly, his gaze never leaving Deanie's desperate face. Kit did not answer. Instead, he charged toward her.

From behind she saw a heavy iron staff, with a blade as wicked as an ax, with red tassels near the head. With the last of her ebbing strength she tried to warn Kit, gesturing with her hands of the danger behind. But her hand movements were indecipherable.

In a crazy blur she saw the staff swing up, gathering momentum, then slice down with an awful thud on Kit's shoulder. For a horrifying moment she thought the man had hit Kit on the head, but at the last instant he swerved.

Cromwell loosened his hold on her and she gasped, her chest heaving for air, as Kit crumpled to the ground. The staff was again raised. As Kit shook his head and began to push himself up, Cromwell nodded to his henchman, the go-ahead to strike again.

"No!" she croaked, her voice barely audible. Cromwell paused, stopping the staff-wielding henchman with an understated shrug.

"You will tell the king nothing of this," Cromwell repeated. Deanie nodded in frantic agreement. With that he let go of her gown, and she stumbled over to Kit.

At first she couldn't see his face; his thick curls of black hair tumbled forward, obscuring his expression. She knelt beside him, gingerly placing her hand on his upper arm. His breathing was loud and ragged, and for a moment she thought he was going to be ill. With the blow he had just taken, she was astounded he was still conscious. Only tremendous physical strength and willpower was preventing him from slipping into senselessness.

Before he looked up, his hand, strong and sure, clamped over her wrist, as if assuring her all would be well. Then his head snapped up, his eyes to hers, and her breath caught in her throat. Never had she seen a look of such unwavering intensity. It was clearly costing him a great deal to focus. Behind the searing gaze was a slight cloudiness. He closed his eyes tightly and shook his head once more. Again he looked at her, the incandescent hazel depths clear of all fog.

He stood up quickly in a forceful rolling motion, pulling Deanie with him. Only she noticed the slight unsteadiness in his stance. The gash on his forehead, the fresh blood seeping through the crook of his neck where he had just been hit, and another slash on his arm told her what a beating he had withstood before he even reached her chamber.

She had a strange feeling in the pit of her stomach, a sticky-sick feeling of tumbling in air. She drew in a shaky breath, and his solid arm closed protectively around her shoulders.

He loved her.

No other man had ever so much as crossed a street for her. No other man had offered a hand unless it would directly benefit him. But Christopher Neville, the duke of Hamilton, had just endured a physical beating to get to her.

"Oh!" Her voice was a small cry, and she turned her face toward his chest, savoring his fragrance, his unyielding energy. His other arm pulled her closer, encircling her in his warmth.

Her hair fell over her face, and Kit saw her neck, white and fragile and vulnerable, the angry red line where Cromwell had gripped her. He felt her burrow closer, her hands pressing him to his side, as if she wanted to be as close as possible.

"How very charming," drawled Cromwell. He motioned for his men to leave the room, all except the large man with the staff. They did as they were ordered.

"Now," he began, as the huge door closed soundlessly, "shall we discuss the future?"

Deanie ignored Cromwell and looked up at Kit. Her hair cascaded like chestnut silk from her face, her eyes large and liquid brown. "I want to be with you," she whispered. "I want to go with you, wherever you go. I don't care, Kit. I just want to be with you."

He ran a finger along the side of her face and was about to speak when Cromwell laughed.

"Mistress Deanie, thou hath attracted the king's eye. Follow me, and all of England shall soon call thee queen."

She blinked. "But I don't want to be—"

"Ignore my words," said Cromwell, his voice lowered, "and thou shall burn as a heretic."

"Thou art mad," snarled Kit. "A desperate, pathetic man who will soon attend the block. Thou hath lost all reason."

"Nay, Duke. Hath Mistress Deanie been once to the Holy Mass? Or followed the king in prayer?" Cromwell spoke easily. "As for thee, Duke, will you enjoy a charge of treason? 'Twill be treason to sample property of the king, to cuckold the royal stud. Ah, how easily treason will be proved. To have that handsome head mounted upon a rusty pike at Traitor's Gate, rotting for all of London to see. Will the ladies find thee so handsome then, Duke?"

"No!" Deanie felt her knees wobble. Her throat, still raw from Cromwell's hold, was thick with rising bile. She didn't care about the threats to herself, but his description of what would happen to Kit was so vivid, so appallingly real. "No. Please. I'll do anything."

"Deanie, he's bluffing." Kit glared at Cromwell.

"Am I?"

Without waiting for a reply, Cromwell lifted a single stubby finger to the man with the staff. Immediately the staff came crashing down on Kit's shoulder, in the exact spot on which it had landed before. A low moan escaped his lips, and Deanie felt his full weight go limp, then slump to the ground.

"Kit!" She knelt beside him, her hands trembling with panic. His head was at an awkward angle, and for a moment she thought his neck had been broken. Gripping his wrist, she found a pulse, weak but steady. "Kit," she repeated in a whisper.

"Now, Mistress Deanie," Cromwell continued as if nothing had occurred, "shall we discuss the future?"

They would kill him, she realized. If she did not play along with this madman, Kit was as good as dead. Swallowing hard, she faced Cromwell, her hand still clamping Kit's wrist, the pulsing beat giving her strength.

When she spoke, her voice was flat and emotionless. "Yes, Mr. Cromwell. Anything you wish."

Chapter 7

THE SUN BEAT HARSHLY ON HER FACE, CAUSING HER TO BLINK against the heat and glare. Deanie shifted in the saddle, an absurd device that felt more like an instrument of torture than an aid to female riders, the jutting pummel under her knee meant to hold her uncomfortably in place. Although she had been horseback riding dozens of times, she had never been forced to ride sidesaddle, wearing over ten pounds of clothing and a wooden corset.

She wiped the perspiration from her upper lip, silently cursing the tightly laced sleeves. Although it wasn't hot—not the humid warmth Deanie was accustomed to—she felt as if she had been placed in an oven. Her clothing felt dirty and four sizes too small, her throat was scratchy and raw.

Cecily Garrison rode on her right, and to her left was Katherine Howard. To the casual observer, the women presented a fetching sight; three ladies-in-waiting on the royal caravan to Richmond palace, a few miles closer to London. They took the Thames-side road, winding and twisting as the whims of the river directed them.

Unlike the rest of the courtiers, Deanie wasn't concerned with what sort of image she projected. She had not slept the night before and had not been able to eat for fear she would become ill.

Her horse stumbled over a log, but Deanie barely noticed. Her sudden grip was more reflex than a desire to prevent any mishap. She didn't really care one way or another. Her senses were numbed. Everything seemed distorted and harsh; the pungent odor of the horses, Katherine Howard's incessant giggles, the shouts of servants and courtiers along the stone- and mud-covered path. The only thing she was achingly aware of was that every hoofbeat took her farther from Kit.

Kit.

Was he even alive? Cromwell had assured her that he was, yet she had little faith in the man's word. She closed her eyes, trying to rid her mind of the last glimpse she'd had of him, being dragged from her chambers the night before. The clumsy henchman had bumped into the threshold, slamming Kit's lolling head against the stone and wood, but Kit had made no sound, no noise at all. The elongated pool of blood left on her floor had been the only evidence of his presence.

Everyone else in the caravan was buzzing about Queen Anne, also left behind at Hampton, last seen waving rather forlornly from under the clock tower. She had tried valiantly to follow the train as far as the bridge over Hampton's moat, but she had been humiliatingly guided back by Thomas Howard, the duke of Norfolk.

Kit.

He had fought for her, had beaten his way to her chamber door. There was so much unfinished business, so much she wanted to tell him. He didn't even know her shoe size, or that she was allergic to shellfish. And there was so much basic information she didn't know about him. When was his birthday, and how old was he? Did he prefer blue or green, and what was his mother like?

Her horse again pitched forward, this time tripping over a burlap cloth, muddied and twisted into a knotted pile.

She had sold her soul to Cromwell. To spare Kit's life she had agreed to his demands, to play the role of mistress to the King, to even become Queen, all the while securing for Cromwell his old position as the king's most trusted adviser. She must turn her back on Kit, allow no hint of Cromwell's threats to plague his ambitions.

Perhaps she should just slip under her horse, allow herself to be trampled by dozens of well-equipped horses and carts filled with the royal furniture, gold plate and napery. She might be better off dead than have to follow Cromwell's hideous orders. But if she were dead, she could not help Kit. She would never see him again. It was better to have a shred of hope than to give up altogether.

With a deep breath she craned her neck and looked behind, hoping against all reason to catch sight of Kit riding to her rescue. He would be on a large black horse, his full cloak billowing behind, his hair tangled by the wind. But of course he was not there. Only other chattering courtiers, nodding and smiling and tossing coins to the ragged peasants lining the road.

Kit.

Was he being cared for? The entire court had believed Cromwell's tale: that Kit had been stricken with a sudden illness. It was a vague story, but the court—and especially the scourge-obsessed King Henry—had been willing to accept the account. Deanie's own wan appearance lent authority to the story. Her cousin the duke was to recover at Hampton, cared for by the queen's foreign staff and a few members of the regular Hampton crew. The king and his court would travel to Richmond as planned, his people and servants by land, the king in the well-appointed royal barge.

Cromwell was nowhere to be seen in the caravan. But in her mind he was everywhere, lurking in the shadows, grinning from the darkness. He had been triumphant the night before, standing in her chamber as if it were his own.

With Kit gone, she had been alone—more alone than she had ever been in her life.

"So, Mistress Deanie," Cromwell had uttered smoothly. He snapped his squat fingers and pointed to the pool of Kit's blood, and a young boy appeared silently and blotted the stain. Cromwell continued speaking to her, but she was unable to follow his words, watching in sick horror as the boy scrubbed the floor with blood-soaked rags, never meeting her eyes.

The boy left, and Deanie blinked at Cromwell. "And then, Mistress Deanie," he concluded after a strangely theatrical pause, "thou may have the satisfaction of preserving the Duke of Hamilton's life."

At that her eyes snapped to his face. He sighed like an indulgent uncle. "Lest there be any misunderstanding, I shall repeat. Do as I say. When the king casts his eye upon a maiden"—he looked her up and down—"or whatever, she can scarce disregard his will. You shall be his, Mistress Deanie. Thou hath a brace of choices: to capitulate unwillingly, and hear of the duke of Hamilton's death, unfortunate and tortuous. Or you may follow my instructions. Do as I command. Come to the king when he beckons—not before. Let him believe he is the mighty conqueror; welcome him with your soft arms open wide. Thou shall become his mistress, perhaps even the queen. And sing high my praises. In short, secure my good favor in the king's grace, and we shall all profit. Turn away from my good counsel, and thou shall go to thy grave knowing that stubborn pride and girlish whims caused the agony and death of a favored duke. And your grave will not be long in waiting; a charge of heresy shall be made against thy person. Disobey me, and a heretic's death shall be your ultimate reward."

Deanie tried to recall what she had said to Cromwell, but she could not remember her exact words. It didn't really matter. She had agreed to follow Cromwell's commands. She had no other choice.

The earl of Essex had added another caveat: Should she tell the king what had transpired, or should the king hear through the court gossips—and here Cromwell had folded his hands under the fur cuffs as he spoke—the duke of Hamilton would meet with an untimely and painful end. Everyone already believed he was ill. No one would be surprised by his sudden death. Of course the king would be saddened, but then he would find another favorite, another virile young man through whom he could relive his lost youth.

In the distance ahead Deanie could see the stragglers in the first cluster of the royal caravan, the way-pavers, the warners who informed all ahead, from Hampton to Richmond, of the king's imminent arrival. Then came the second wave, the peers and other courtiers, a veritable moving banquet of wine and sweetmeats and chatter. Finally, bringing up the rear, were the carters and the household staff, the cooks and pages and keepers.

And somewhere behind those, following the last cow being led by a cheeseman's son, was Kit, left with a dishonored queen and her skeleton staff of foreigners. And of course half a dozen of Cromwell's minions, ready to convince the duke of the wisdom of Cromwell's plan.

Deanie wiped the perspiration from her upper lip again. When Katherine Howard offered her a skin filled with spiced wine, she declined. She knew she would not be able to keep a single swallow down. But instead of confessing to the fear gnawing the pit of her stomach, she shot Katherine one of her brilliant smiles.

Just as Cromwell had instructed.

The odor was unbearable. It was a potent stench of unwashed bodies and grease and spices, some overly sweet, others bitter and foul.

There was a hand on his forehead, gentle, soothing. In the back of his mind he thought of Deanie. What had happened? He could see her face, the luminous eyes, the red mark where Cromwell had hurt her. Damn it, he hadn't brought any of his own men. What folly had overtaken him to confront Cromwell without assistance?

But of course he hadn't known the depths of Cromwell's plans, the extent of his desperation. Deanie had been out of his sight for no more than twenty minutes when he realized they would have to leave, to flee England if they were to have any chance of a life together. After that night, it was already too late for them. The king had set his sights on Deanie. Once the royal mind was made up, there was no changing it. He had broken with the Church in Rome for the sake of a woman. No, it was time for them to leave. Perhaps go to Calais or Madrid.

Where was Deanie? He tried to curb his anger, furious at his own foolish actions. Since arriving at court he had never taken a rash step. Every move he made, every syllable uttered had been carefully considered. Never had he let down his guard. Even with women—especially with women—he had been cautious, watching his intake of wine, circumspect in the most intimate of situations.

He heard a moan, and he wondered if the noise had come from his own throat. He tried to move his head but was stopped by a bolt of pain, crackling, exploding, more intense than any in his memory.

The soothing hands were still there. They were not Deanie's. These hands were larger; Deanie's were small. Delicate.

Then he was flying.

In his mind he could see the ground below: farms and stone fences and lone horses and cattle grazing. It was a timeless scene of the English countryside, quiet and simple.

Then he saw iron tracks and a puffing locomotive. From above he could hear only the roaring sputter of his own engine and the wind. Down through the clouds, tiny as a child's toy, the train was chugging away, filled with children fleeing the dangers of war. The smallest refugees, forced to leave their mums and dads. Then he saw the distant smoke of London, the dome of St. Paul's Cathedral. Big Ben. Landmarks, landmarks. If he could see them, so could the enemy.

Training. They had been training for the mission—how to keep the enemy from shopping at Harrod's, his fellow Royal Air Force pilots had all dubbed it. How to keep Herr Himmler from taking in a show at the Gaiety. They had laughed, smiling at each other over those precious few cigarettes. Then they were told how to get home, how to refuel. The last part was a formality, a bit of comfort for the green ones who still thought there was a chance of returning alive. They had yet to experience empty chairs at the officers' mess, belongings hurridly bundled off before evening. The odds were hopelessly, ridiculously against them, but they paraded about the barracks with all the dash and swagger of a Gilbert and Sullivan officer.

The mission was nothing short of suicide. Kill the enemy, kill themselves. Perhaps save England.

This was his last sortie, after a summer and autumn of being on alert twelve hours, sometimes fifteen a day. In August he had flown seven sorties in a single day. Number seven, a lucky number. One last twenty-four-hour furlough.

He borrowed another chap's motorcycle—what was his name? They had read history together at Oxford. Took his motorcycle, even his goggles, and rode, driving the rickety cycle, heedless of the shameful waste of petrol.

Where was he? In the air he would know. On the ground, with all the signs and markers plucked from the soil to confuse marauding Germans, he was lost. Then he saw the chimneys of Hampton and wandered there, goggles in hand, to the maze. Wandered for hours, it seemed, clutching the leather and glass goggles, knowing what the next hours would most likely bring.

Above, he heard the familiar buzz of planes, the exploding shells falling outside of London. He had flown over Berlin, just as the Germans now circled over London.

There was a heavy feeling in his stomach. Not fear,

exactly; just a swelling knowledge that he was breathing his last. He'd had that feeling before, of course. Before every sortie there was a sharpening of his senses, a keen awareness that made every movement exaggerated and uncomfortable.

This time it was different, more intense. Before he had been too exhausted to mentally calculate his odds, flying by instinct alone, shooting an enemy plane by swooping down from the clouds. Dorniers and Heinkels, the plodding but effective German bombers. Earlier in the summer it had been Stukas, but the Germans realized how slow they were, how easy for a new RAF pilot to cut his teeth on.

Everything seemed to happen in slow motion, every movement etched with prickly detail. Yet the hours had raced by with stunning speed. This time it was different.

He took note of his every gesture. When he stopped to tie his shoe in the maze, he wondered if this knot would be his last. He stretched his fatigued arms over his head and stood looking at the old yew bushes. Reaching in his breast pocket for the last of his cigarettes, he could feel his own heart beating steadily. How odd, he thought, that the steady beat would be stilled. It hardly seemed possible.

He checked his watch. It was time to get back, time to prepare for this last mission. If all went well, he would survive to train the next crop of pilots. He had already been uncommonly lucky. Number seven in a single day.

Then the strange, pulsating beam of light, blue and effulgent, bounced off the goggles. The rumbling roared like a hundred bombers, a sickly tremor of the very earth. In his surprise, his mind spun the possibilities. Did the enemy possess an earthquake machine, the product of a twisted Nazi mind?

Diabolical. Dastardly. Once he had been close enough to a Messerschmitt escort plane to see the pilot. Their eyes locked at five thousand feet in the air, and they shared an instant of recognition. There was intelligence in the Luftwaffe pilot's eyes, a glint of humor. It hit him heavily, like a low blow: This man was just like him. University educated. Joined the local flying club as a lark. In another time, another year, they would be friends.

Now they were meeting at five thousand feet, and in an instant he had shot down his German doppelgänger, blinking as the Messerschmitt spiraled into flames, the wind shrieking against the wings like hell's banshee.

Far away he heard a groan. His? Then a woman's voice, deep and guttural.

German. The enemy.

Name, rank, serial number. Name, rank, serial number. All he had to say, all they could make him say. Goddamn Hitler. Goddamn Nazis. Wish to God the Yanks would join in. Wish to God his Spitfire would hold up.

Name, rank, serial number.

"Neville, Christopher. Captain. Royal Air Force, nineteen-forty." That was the year, not his serial number. What was his serial number? "Fifteen forty," he mumbled. No. That was the year, not his serial number. Then his voice faded out. He tried to ask where he was. Had his plane gone down behind enemy lines?

The German woman was speaking. Goddamn Nazi. Goddamn Hitler. Where was Deanie?

Then all vanished into black velvet nothingness.

Chapter 8

THE TWISTING FOUR MILES FROM HAMPTON COURT TO RICH-
mond palace passed with inane languor. It seemed to take
hours. Without a watch, Deanie had no idea how much
time had actually passed. She supposed she was probably
hungry but wasn't sure. Her whole body seemed anesthe-
tized, emotionless.

Even in her detached state of mind, she was aware of the
magnificence of the countryside. Richmond Park was a
startling combination of wildly lush forest and carefully
pruned gardens. From the corner of her eye she caught sight
of a long-limbed stag leaping over a hedge, its graceful
movements unnoticed by anyone else in the caravan.

Katherine and Cecily were discussing men, whispering
from beneath their cupped hands like a couple of students
in gym class.

"Thomas Culpepper? Nay, I like him not," hissed Cecily
Garrison. "He thinks too highly of his own charms."

Katherine Howard nodded eagerly. "What you say, 'tis
true. But surely his face is worth looking upon if his

character can be forgotten. Yet in my mind no man can compare with the duke of Hamilton." Cecily tried to shush her friend, but Katherine was oblivious to the hint, happily reveling in her own fantasies. "I do hope he recovers from his illness soon, Mistress Cecily," she continued, her vapid eyes glazed with her own thoughts. "Is there another man so handsome or pleasingly mannered? Ah, and so manly too. Not foppish, like so many of the young bucks of the court."

Finally she noticed the strained silence and, blinking, turned to Cecily, who was now glaring in anger. With an embarrassed swallow, Katherine turned to Deanie.

"Pray forgive my prattle about your cousin, Mistress Deanie. He is a respected peer, and deserveth not to be named with the base-born Culpepper."

Deanie, her face a ghastly white, simply nodded and turned away. Her orders from Cromwell had been clear. But how on earth would she manage to carry them out?

Just then they turned into the gates of Richmond palace. Straightening in the saddle, wondering if her leg would be permanently hooked in the position, she strained to see the palace itself.

Why hadn't Nathan Burns picked this as the sight of the video? It was also of brick, with chimneys and smoke stacks, but this palace was more manageable. About a third the size of Hampton, it resembled a private college rather than a royal residence.

They rode into a quadrangle, stableboys and servants rushing from every corner to assist the ladies in dismounting, steadying a few of the more inebriated men. The moment her foot touched the cobbled ground, Deanie had but one thought.

She had to get back to Kit. Somehow, as soon as possible.

"Mistress Deanie." A beefy hand grasped her own, and she peered into the bloodshot eyes of Charles Brandon, the duke of Suffolk.

"Thank you," she murmured. She was about to back away when she paused. "My Lord," she produced one of her best smiles, and Suffolk lapped it up, his eyes atwinkle with some secret thought she did not wish to discover. He bowed.

"Is Cromwell, the earl of Essex, within?" Deanie tried to sound casual, but something in her voice made Suffolk straighten. His eyes were now keen, appraising. She had to be careful.

"Cromwell? Nay. The king this morn hath sent Cromwell on a journey of state business. May I be of service?"

She didn't wait for him to complete his offer. "He's gone? He's not here or at Hampton?" Oh please, she prayed. Let it be true.

A stableboy took the reins of her horse. She watched him go through a gate, noting where the stables were, then turned back to Suffolk, who was watching her with an intelligence she did not think he was capable of.

"And the king?" Her voice was strained.

"He waits within, attended by the royal surgeon. The journey pained his leg, and he may rest."

An idea formed in Deanie's mind, and she almost smiled at the thought. She would faint. She would fake an illness, which would buy her precious time.

"My Lord," she said weakly, willing her hand to tremble as she grasped Suffolk's sleeve. It was not difficult: She *was* terrified. Should this fail, she would place Kit—and herself—in even greater danger. "I fear I am unwell."

With those words, Mistress Deanie Bailey swooned into the brocaded arms of the duke of Suffolk. In the commotion that followed—the ordering of a litter to carry her within, sobbing Katherine Howard attesting to how unwell she had seemed during the ride from Hampton—no one noticed the slight smile animating Suffolk's mustache.

The king peered over his physician's shoulder, anxious for the task to be completed.

"We bid you haste, Dr. Butts." He gritted his teeth against the pain as the cloth covering his leg was pulled back, making the ulcerating sore throb. The physical discomfort was nothing new. But His Majesty's light mood was.

Dr. Butts took a deep breath through his mouth, trying to avoid the stench of the festering thigh, and changed the dressing as swiftly as possible. He certainly did not wish to bait the king's well-known temper.

"Your Majesty, 'twill be but a moment."

His hands flew deftly over the large royal limb, noting that the wound was unchanged. No worse, but certainly no better than the day before. Would it ever heal? It had already plagued the king for years, ever since that jousting incident. It was a miracle that the king had survived. Nobody realized how severe the injury had been, how deeply the opponent's lance had cut into the king's thigh. Only the fevers that followed, the recurring bouts of delirium, had revealed the true nature of the injury. The best of modern medicine had been employed, from leeches and bleeding to exotic ointments and fervent prayer. Nothing had helped. The wound remained unhealed.

The king grunted, whether in impatience or pain, the physician was not willing to hazard a guess.

There was a knock on the door. "Your Majesty?"

The king smiled, recognizing the voice. "Come in, Suffolk, come in."

The door swung open, and Charles Brandon entered. "Your Majesty." He bowed.

Henry gestured him to rise. "Come come, Suffolk. Hath she arrived?" He was as eager as a small child.

"Yes, Your Majesty." Suffolk straightened. "She hath arrived, and betimes fainted."

"Fainted?"

"Yes." Suffolk was unable to keep the laughter from his voice. "She fainted into my arms, Your Majesty."

"God's blood, Charles. It's not amusing." Henry slapped Dr. Butts on the back. "Enough. Be gone." The physician, noting the irritation in the king's tone, was only too happy to flee.

"Think thee she has the same malady as her cousin, Hamilton?" The king sat heavily on his chair, kicking the footstool away with his good leg. The footstool skidded across the floor, tipping on its side when it hit the heavy oak-paneled wall.

"I know not, Your Highness. She rests in chambers across the yard."

"Aye," the king spat. "And we would much prefer she do anything but rest in this very chamber." A harsh grunt escaped his mouth, and he balled his hand into a fist. Then he too smiled. "Fainted," he mumbled.

"Dead away, Your Majesty," Suffolk confirmed.

"Ha! Another jest, eh, Suffolk?" The king reached for a gold dish filled with peaches, silently offering one to Suffolk, who shook his head. "Any word on Hamilton?" The king took a bite of the fruit, a river of juice winding through his russet beard. "'Twill be most dull without him at our board."

"Mistress Katherine Howard quoth he is yet unwell, Your Majesty."

"Katherine Howard, eh?" The king shifted his bulk in the chair. "Make sure the Howard wench is seated at our board, eh, Suffolk? With Hamilton ill and Mistress Deanie in a swoon, 'twill be the very devil to find amusement."

Suffolk bowed low again and took his leave. Something was afoot, and before he dared mention it to the king, he was bound to discover exactly what it was.

It was well past midnight. There was a clock somewhere nearby, not a massive one like at Hampton, but smaller. The "ping" was light, delicate.

Deanie was fully clothed. She didn't dare risk undressing, for fear she would not be able to clothe herself again. Time after time that evening she had been forced to turn away well-meaning servants and Mistress Cecily and Katherine, all solicitous, all wanting to make her more comfortable, all hoping she would be well enough to dine with the king. When it was apparent she had no intention of leaving her heavily furnished room, a silver tray filled with delicacies was delivered to her door.

Across the courtyard she caught fleeting sights of the king. Once she peeked out the window, only to meet the royal gaze. He had been spying on her, and when he saw her face, he jumped back as quickly as she did.

As spacious as her room was, she longed for Hampton. Not only did she miss Kit, she missed the few privies there, closets with drains to run sewage to the river. Here there were no such luxuries.

It was time, just after midnight. She had to leave now, while all was quiet and before Cromwell returned. The low-ceilinged chamber felt safe and solid as she stepped noiselessly to the door. She didn't dare bring a candle, as that would be asking for attention.

The door creaked as she opened it, and she paused, holding her breath. She had to get to the stables to find a horse; then she could ride back to Hampton. All she had to do was follow the Thames downstream, and she would be there in a couple of hours. She would check on Kit, make sure he was being treated well, then ride back to Richmond before daybreak.

She almost stepped right in front of a servant. Pressing herself into an arched doorway, she remained motionless until the figure had retreated through another hallway. Her cloak, dark and sumptuous, rustled as she walked. It had seemed such a clever idea to wear the damask hooded cloak. But now it sounded as loud as a car alarm.

Outside, she crept through the courtyard, hugging the brick walls. She could see candles flickering in some windows. Her slippers padded silently over the cobblestones. Just around the corner she could hear the whinnies and snorts of horses in the stables.

The stables were illuminated by large torches on the walls. Again she paused before entering, hoping none of the horses made a noise as she passed.

Crouching, she crept along the stalls, keeping low so the horses didn't see her. She looked for the mare she'd ridden earlier, a docile beast named Fancy. It would be easier just to walk to Hampton, but she didn't have the time to get there and back before sunrise without a horse.

In the third stall to the end she saw Fancy, a burlap blanket over her back. The latch squeaked.

"Fancy," she whispered, reaching up to rub the mare's velvety nose. "Are you up to a quick ride back to Hampton?"

A large figure suddenly emerged from the shadows. "Again, Mistress Deanie, I ask, doth thou require my service?" Charles Brandon, wearing the same colorful brocade doublet as earlier, clamped a hand over her wrist.

She jumped at the sound of his voice, her eyes wide. How could she explain her presence in the stables?

He continued, his voice even: "I could not but note how you found the direction of the stables most fascinating, even as a swoon overtook thee. How fare thee now, mistress?"

"Um, hello." She smiled, too perky for the hour and circumstances. "I'm doing much better, thank you. I just thought I'd check on the horse. She seemed a little, uh, under the weather."

"I see." Suffolk released her wrist. "'Twould seem, mistress, you confuse the facts. 'Twas thee, not the mare, who fell into a swoon this day."

Deanie cleared her throat and pulled the cloak tighter about her shoulders.

"Let me speak plain," he said. "Why art thou here?" She was about to answer, but he held up one of his large hands. "Play not the innocent. I heard your words: Thou art bound for Hampton."

Deanie remained very still but then slumped against the side of the stall, a very twentieth-century curse escaping her lips. Suffolk smiled. "That is better. Honest, at the very least. Tell me, mistress."

At once she was exhausted, and she rubbed her eyes. "I'm worried about Kit. He's ill, and I was going to ride back to see him for a few minutes. Just a few minutes, I swear. I was hoping to get back here by sunrise, so nobody would even know I had gone."

"I see," Suffolk said. His eyes raked over her, the fatigue so evident. "What manner of illness doth plague the duke?"

The horse began to prance in place. Before Deanie could answer, Suffolk opened the stall door and pushed her away from Fancy's clopping hooves. Once outside, he folded his arms. "Let me ask another question: Doth Cromwell have anything to do with Hamilton's malady?"

Deanie's eyes snapped to his. She was about to deny it when something in Suffolk's expression made her stop. There was no way for her to lie to this man, who seemed to see straight through her. Instead of saying a word, she simply nodded once.

Suffolk stiffened. "Damnation," he spat. "I feared as much."

He paced away from her, his back stiff. "He is a knave, that Cromwell. The king allowed him much, because there was naught Cromwell would not do for His Majesty. Power corrupts."

"And absolute power corrupts absolutely," Deanie mumbled.

Suffolk turned, his eyes again sharp. "Thou art right. However did you know?"

"Oh, I think it was a question on *Jeopardy!*"

For the first time, confusion clouded his brow. Then he reached for her arm. "Art thou in jeopardy?"

She nodded. "Will you help me get to Kit?"

"Nay. Not without more information. Why doth Cromwell risk all to harm Hamilton? Surely he knows the duke is a favorite of the king's."

She hesitated. How could she be sure Suffolk wasn't working for Cromwell?

"Tell me all now," he said softly. "Or I will go to the king in a thrice."

"No!" She lowered her voice. "No, please." There was no choice now, no choice but to take a chance and trust Suffolk. "Cromwell wants me to become the king's mistress. He even wants me to become the next queen. The whole time I am to get Cromwell back in favor with the king. If I don't agree, he'll kill Kit."

"But I thought . . ." Suffolk began, shaking his head. "What of the other night, the exchange between His Highness and thee? Was that not an agreement?"

"No, no. I misunderstood. You see, where I come from—"

"Wales?" Suffolk offered.

"Yeah, sure. Wales. Anyway, I didn't understand what I was doing. It was a mixup."

Suffolk crossed his arms again. "But for any woman, 'twould be the greatest of honors to be a companion of the king's."

"No!"

Suffolk said nothing. The horses were becoming restless with the sound of people in the stable, and she heard hooves kicking against the stalls. "Tell me," he said at last. "Doth thou love another?"

"Yes." Her voice was very small.

"The duke of Hamilton?" he added.

"Yes," she whispered.

There was a long moment, and neither said a word. Then Suffolk clutched her arm. She gasped, realizing he was probably taking her straight to the king.

Instead, he pulled her from the stables, away from the palace. "Where are you taking me?" she panted, stumbling as Suffolk led her into the woods.

"There would not be time by horse to get to Hampton

and back," he hissed. "The roads are dangerous. Vile persons would hurt thee."

"What?"

"Boat. We will travel by boat, Mistress Deanie. Be quick."

He moved with a speed and agility she did not think was possible. Kit had told her that Suffolk had been the greatest jouster in his day, the most able horseman, the only courtier to rival the king in athletic ability. As he guided her through the woods, his feet moving with amazing speed, his vast body suddenly light and youthful, she believed the stories.

They reached the Thames, and he gave a boatswain a handful of coins and helped her into a rickety boat. By the time she had caught her breath, they were well on their way back to Hampton, Suffolk puffing as they pushed the boat forward with a long pole.

"Why are you helping me?" she asked, remembering that she had asked similar words of Kit.

For a while Suffolk said nothing. She assumed he hadn't heard her, so laboriously was he propelling the boat.

"Did you know I was married to the king's sister?" His voice came from the darkness. She shook her head, but he did not see her. The outlines of trees seemed to fly by in the night as they glided down the Thames. "I was sent to get Mary, sent to Paris to collect her after her husband, the king of France, had died. He was a bitter old man." Suffolk laughed. "Old man—he was of an age with me now. Mary was beautiful, the fairest maiden at court before she became queen of France. I was to escort her home to yet another arranged marriage, another diplomatic contract. She sobbed on my shoulder and confessed her love for me."

"So did you take her home? I mean, did she have to marry someone else first?" Deanie had forgotten for the moment her own problems.

"Nay. We were married in Paris, in 1514."

Deanie sighed, leaning back against the boat. "How romantic."

"Yes. It was. The king forgave us then, for he too was a young blood like myself. I fear I was not a good husband to Mary. I was too young, too full of fire. I was not faithful, but she was a good wife. We were married until her death seven years ago this June. She was unhappy, Mary. But gad, as a girl, she was a beauty. Her hair dark as midnight, her eyes sparkled."

Deanie closed her eyes, imagining the obese Henry as a dashing young prince and the bloated Suffolk as his handsome companion. Both had loved fiercely. How exciting it must have been, two rogues, strutting in their power and glory.

"Mistress Deanie?" Suffolk's voice startled her.

"Humm?"

His voice was dry. "She looked like you. My Mary, she looked like you."

The remainder of the journey passed in silence. Only the water sounds, gentle droplets as they sliced through the river, echoed in the night.

Deanie stood beyond the moat of Hampton, staring up at the colossal palace. Resisting the urge to go back to the boat where Suffolk was waiting, she loosened the hood from her cloak, letting her hair hang freely to her shoulders. She peered beyond the small bridge.

It was not a real moat, this little stream surrounding the building. It had been created by the original builder of Hampton, Cardinal Wolsey, who fancied the romance and beauty of a moat.

A guard appeared from the side of the building.

"Ho! Who goes?"

Deanie guessed that without the king in residence, security would be rather lax. Perhaps the king secretly hoped that invaders would storm the palace and kidnap Queen Anne, thus making his own dilemma a great deal easier to resolve.

She cleared her throat. "It's me, Mistress Deanie Bailey. I have come to see my cousin, the duke of Hamilton." To her own ears, she sounded incredibly stupid, appearing at three in the morning at the foot of a moat.

The guard grasped a torch and approached her cautiously, squinting as he observed her features by the orange glow of the flame. But he didn't ask any further questions. "Come with me," he muttered, and she could smell the heavy odor of wine on his breath.

He led her through the first three courtyards, not saying a word. She began to panic, wanting desperately to ask him how Kit was, yet afraid of the answer.

"Through there, to the left. The queen has been caring for him," he said, leaving her to find her own way.

There were far fewer torches on the walls, evidence of the king's strange sense of frugality. The halls were silent, and to the left of the hall she found a door partially ajar.

Slowly, she entered. In the center of a small room, illuminated only by a single candle, she saw a figure lying motionless on a bed.

"Kit?"

There was no response. Beside the bed was a chair, and she shrugged out of her cloak and sat down, the legs of the chair scraping on the ground. Reaching for the candle, she held it up to the person's face.

It was Kit, lying so still she thought he might be dead.

With a trembling hand she touched his forehead, hot and dry to the touch. His dark hair was disheveled, lying in a haphazard tumble about the pillow. The gash on his forehead had been cleaned, or at least wiped. Drawing her finger along his lean cheek, she could feel the heat rise even above the growth of whiskers.

"Kit, it's me. Deanie," she whispered, hoping her voice didn't sound as frightened as she felt. There was no reaction.

A peculiar fragrance wafted through the room, musky and pungent. Distractedly, she glanced around the room but couldn't find the source. She returned her gaze to Kit, touching a strand of his hair. His doublet had been removed. All she could see beneath the coverlet was his shirt, streaked with blood and dirt.

"I'm here, Kit." She leaned close, speaking into his ear. The strange aroma was more powerful now. She sniffed and realized it was coming from his shirt. Gingerly she untied the laces at his throat, watching his chest rise and fall with swift, shallow breaths.

Suddenly she felt awkward and embarrassed, unlacing his clothing as he lay unconscious. His chest was broad and muscular, as she already knew from their embraces. What she wasn't expecting was chest hair, curly and black, covering the upper portion of his torso. She touched it and quickly pulled back. This wasn't right, it was indecent. Yet she could not help but enjoy the feel of him, the strength that radiated from him even when he slept.

Then she saw the wound.

She clamped her hand over her mouth to keep from crying out. At the crook of his neck, where Cromwell's man had struck him twice with a steel-headed staff, was a large, gaping wound. It looked as if his collarbone had been broken, and his right shoulder was at an unnatural angle. Dried blood caked in black splotches surrounded the area, with jagged raw edges revealing bits of cloth stuck to the wound.

The odd odor was caused by some sort of salve smeared all over his shoulder, glistening in the candlelight. Careful not to disturb the wound, she swiped at a smear with a fingertip. Up close it was speckled and filthy. Perhaps it had been the work of Cromwell, a poison to finish him off.

She reached behind for her cloak and gently dabbed away whatever she could of the salve. Some was too deeply entrenched in the wound for her to remove without hurting him further. The light was poor, and she wasn't sure if she had wiped enough. There was a bowl of stagnant water on a table, but she didn't want to risk using water unless it had been boiled.

Her gaze returned to his face. Those strong features, so

vulnerable, filled her with a surge of determination. She had felt curiously indecisive before. Now she had a definite goal: to get him well. She leaned over, staring at his face up close, and kissed him on the cheek. The whiskers were scratchy, his skin was unnaturally hot, but it felt right.

Time was meaningless as she sat with him, murmuring soft words, stroking his hair. Once she saw his throat work, as if he would speak, but he remained silent.

She had never taken care of anything important. Now she was needed to save the life of the most wonderful man she had ever met.

She would do it.

From the window, she could see a soft lightening of the sky; it was a gentle gray rather than the pitch-black of earlier.

Suffolk leaned into the room. She hadn't heard his footsteps, yet she didn't jump when she heard his voice.

"Mistress Deanie," he said, walking to the bed. "We should go anon. As it is we shall not make first daybreak." He looked down at Kit, at the wound on his shoulder.

"Damnation." He felt Kit's forehead. "He burns with fever."

"I know," she said quietly, her eyes never leaving Kit's face. His left hand lay next to hers, and she raised it to her lips, pressing it to the side of her face.

And very softly, his fingers caressed her cheek, briefly, tenderly.

"I know," she whispered, her voice broken. "You can't talk, but you know I'm here. I'm not leaving, Kit. I won't go away."

Suffolk slowly backed out of the room. "I go forth, Mistress Deanie." His voice was rough. "Bid me luck, for betwixt here and Richmond I must concoct the tale of my life for both the king and Cromwell."

"Mistress Deanie, Mistress Deanie."

She was on the edge of a dream, a deep, solid sleep. A

voice was calling her in the distance, strangely accented. She was slumped forward, leaning against a bed, propped in a chair. For a moment she thought she had fallen asleep in her hotel room. On television was an old Elke Sommer film, her clear German accent making everyone else sound dull and ordinary.

"Mistress Deanie, pray awaken," the voice pleaded.

With a jolt she opened her eyes, realizing where she was. Queen Anne of Cleves, the fourth wife of Henry VIII, was nudging her shoulder, uncertain and hesitant.

"Your Majesty," Deanie gasped, rising lopsidedly to her feet and simultaneously trying to curtsy without dropping Kit's hand.

Queen Anne made a dismissive gesture and motioned for Deanie to again take her chair. "The duke: He fares better this morning?" The queen was outlandishly garbed in gold brocade and gemstones, her face framed by an angular headdress shaped like a kite.

Deanie looked down. He seemed the same; his unnatural pallor was more apparant in the even light of morning.

"My own physician from Cleves hath tended him." The queen reached over and touched Kit's head. Deanie held her breath, overpowered by the queen's aroma. "Is good. The fever lessens," she concluded with a brisk nod.

"He's been looked at by a physician, Your Majesty?"

"Ya. His bone here," she said, gesturing to his collarbone, "hath been split. Then goes it down, and hurt the air going in and out. My own Dr. Cornelius make the balm for the wound." Queen Anne seemed enormously proud of herself.

"Oh. Thank you." Deanie watched Kit as his head turned slightly on the pillow. She was about to ask what the ointment was made of, afraid of the answer, when the Queen glanced about the room.

"We are alone?" she whispered, checking under the bed with a sweep of her foot. Her heavy gown prevented her from bending down.

Deanie nodded, and the queen pulled another chair, one she hadn't seen the night before, next to Deanie's.

"Englebert bade them leave, but I fear they return."

"Englebert?" Deanie asked, completely confused.

"My man, Englebert. From Cleves, when I was girl." She leveled her hand to the height of about four feet. Deanie wasn't sure if the height represented Anne as a girl or Englebert as a man. "They quoth to him they stay, but Englebert, he say no. They no stay."

Deanie was about to ask what the queen was talking about, when the information dawned on her. "Cromwell's men?" She lowered her voice. "Were they Cromwell's men?"

The queen nodded eagerly. "They say, 'We stay.' Engelbert know them from when we come first here. He know they men of Cromwell, not men of king. He say, 'We tell king now.' And Cromwell men leave."

Deanie rubbed her thumb over the top of Kit's hand, thinking. The hand was strong and sure. "Your Majesty," she whispered, "that Englebert—he's one smart cookie. If I were you, I'd keep him around."

"Ja," she responded, the word coming out as *ya.* "Englebert is cookie."

Deanie glanced up, inches away from the earnest face of the queen. The royal bride was looking at Kit with un-abashed concern. Her broad, flat hand skimmed his forehead. "Fever is less?"

"I think so," Deanie agreed. "I hope so."

"Dr. Cornelius come soon for to bleed him."

"No"—Deanie tried to keep her voice even—"I really don't think that's such a hot idea. I was just thinking of boiling some water with some bandages in it and changing those filthy rags on his arm."

The queen clicked her tongue. "Dr. Cornelius know about all things physick. He say bleed the duke. He send for best barbers to bleed duke."

"Barbers?" Deanie straightened. "You know, those

whiskers on Kit must be really uncomfortable. Maybe they can shave them off. That would give them something to do and make everyone happy. Right?"

The queen gave her a dubious look. "Dr. Cornelius say we bleed duke."

"I say we shave his whiskers. I'll make a deal with you, Your Highness. Give me five minutes alone with the barbers and I'll convince them to shave Kit instead of bleeding him. Okay?"

The queen's eyes narrowed, but her lips curved into a grin. "Okay."

Deanie, her smile still in place, returned her full attention to Kit. The queen, however, folded her hands and spent the next half hour practicing the words *okay* and *cookie*.

He was dreaming again.

That was the only explanation. He took a deep breath, swallowing against the pain. His head hurt, his shoulder hurt, his entire body felt as if it had been pushed through a sieve.

The guttural conversations were still floating over his head. This time there was another voice, gentle, an edge of laughter to the tone. Yet she wasn't laughing. The accent was American, unmistakably Yankee. Not Yankee. It was an accent from the American South. Harsher than Vivian Leigh's vowels in her new movie, *Gone with the Wind*. He remembered seeing Miss Leigh on stage, all those plays. They called her the "fame in a night" girl. She was lovely, with large hands. Big hands for such a slight woman.

The hands on his face were light, delicate. There was a whisper. "I'm not going away, Kit. I know you can hear me, and I'm not leaving you." Did he imagine feeling a soft face wet with tears? Was she crying for him?

Deanie. Of course. How could he forget?

He took another deep breath and could hear the air come in. It sounded like a terribly large amount of air, but he still needed more. He couldn't seem to take in enough air.

There was another set of hands on his face, these hard and masculine. There was something familiar about the scraping he felt, then he realized he was being shaved. He tried to speak, to form words to say "I don't need a shave— I need more air!" but he could not.

Something else was happening. He could hear Deanie's voice with a cajoling tone. He tried to open his eyes, but they remained closed.

"I promise." There was a laugh in her voice, and he could imagine her smile, those eyes. God, how he wanted to see her.

"Okay, come over here," she was saying. He heard the uncertain shuffle of feet on the floor. They were following her to another part of the room, away from his bed.

For a while he heard nothing. There was a sloshing sound of water in a bowl, the grate of a chair on the floor. And nothing.

"Ouch!" she shouted.

He had to help her. What were the barbarians doing?

Another female voice said, "Okay!"

With a supreme effort, he opened his eyes. It took a moment to focus, and the world tilted crazily out of control before he could see. From his barely opened eyes, he saw Deanie surrounded by half a dozen barber-surgeons. They huddled about her, their cloaks forming a tent, nodding in serious but muted conversation. One of them was wielding a large curved knife with a beefy hand, and he had Deanie's long and slender bare leg in the other.

It looked like a scene of pagan animal sacrifice. He tried to get enough breath to shout, to give her a chance to escape, when suddenly he saw her toss back her head and laugh.

"No, I'm not kidding." She smiled. "Where I come from, all the ladies shave their legs. You have no idea how great it feels."

The Cleves queen nodded. "Okay. The men say they no bleed duke, you keep your bargain. Okay?"

There was relief in her voice now as Kit shut his eyes.

"Great. Just leave him alone, and I'll let them shave my legs whenever they want to."

Part of him wanted to laugh at this outrageous woman who had struck such a deal with members of the barber-surgeon guild. The sheer audacity of her idea delighted him.

Another part of him, where his emotions were raw with turmoil, wanted to weep.

Instead, he slept.

Chapter 9

W HAT MEAN YOU, SHE IS GONE?" THE KING DEMANDED, ALL traces of his recent good humor vanished.

Charles Brandon, the duke of Suffolk, paused for a moment before elaborating. Judging from the shade of crimson now flaming the royal visage, he knew King Henry was more upset by the absence of a comely woman than angry at an errant subject.

"Your Highness, she feared bearing disease to her most gracious king. After swooning here at Richmond, her first thought upon awakening was of her king's own health. She bid me help her swiftly back to Hampton, where she could both tend her cousin and keep Your Majesty from harm."

A low growl escaped the king's throat as he looked down at his finely jeweled doublet. He had worn it for her, for Mistress Deanie. Now she was gone. His first instinct was to kick a dog, but there were none about to kick. He stood with his legs planted apart, his mighty arms akimbo, as if reassuring himself and Suffolk of his imperial power.

Suffolk's words then edged their way into his mind. "She

was concerned about our health, then." He made it a proclamation, to allow Suffolk no chance of changing the story.

"Verily she was," he confirmed. "I did see Hamilton with mine own eyes, Your Highness, and his sickness seems not of the infectious sort."

The king nodded once, brisk steps striding to the window. His broad back to Suffolk, he bounced on the balls of his feet with surprising buoyancy for a man of his girth.

"What manner of illness, then, keeps Hamilton away? He is a hearty sort. Never have I seen him bend to injury or disease." The king's tone was light yet probing. Suffolk realized the king suspected something other than the usual plague or sweating sickness.

Suffolk had long before ceased being amazed by his king's ability to decipher a situation. For all his good-fellow pats on the back and displays of pomp, King Henry was a shrewd judge of character. He could size up a man's worth with the briefest of conversations, and once his decision was made, only rarely could it be altered. Unless, of course, changing his mind would benefit his cause, whatever it may be. At the moment, Henry's cause was to find a new wife. Suffolk, from a lifetime of hard-won experience, knew that nothing could dissuade Henry from his path.

"I left Hampton early this morn, Your Highness, ere the house began to stir. I know not what the doctors say and judge myself not amongst their ilk." Suffolk kept his voice even, carefully choosing his words. "All I know is that Mistress Deanie is in excellent health now, and the swoon of yesterday was perchance from the lengthy journey in the high heat of the noon sun. Mistress Deanie's concerns are for her king and for her cousin."

"In that order?" Henry inquired.

"I believe so, Sire," Suffolk said calmly. He wanted to tell Henry of Cromwell's part in Hamilton's illness, but to do so would also require explaining the exact relationship between Mistress Deanie and Hamilton. Perhaps the king could tolerate the news later, once his infatuation with Mistress Deanie had faded. Perhaps then he could explain, gently, tastefully. Not now.

Henry turned to face Suffolk, about to speak again, when the chamber door flew open. Cromwell, covered in spattered mud and dust from his journey, swept into the room. His black cloak billowed behind as he made a low bow. "Your Highness," he mumbled, only just then noticing the presence of Suffolk. Cromwell nodded once to Suffolk, his thick eyebrows dotted with flecks of soil. "Suffolk." It was less a greeting than an observation.

Suffolk maintained a bland expression, biting back the urge to accuse Cromwell, right before the king, of ordering Hamilton's brutal beating and blackmailing Mistress Deanie. Instead, he gave a curt nod. "Essex."

The king crossed his arms. "I did not hear you knock to gain entry, Essex."

For a fleeting moment, a rare uncertainy crossed Cromwell's broad features, a slight look of confusion. In eight years he had simply entered the king's chamber, especially when bearing urgent matters of state. Now he was reprimanded, dressed down like a common scullery maid, for behaving as was his custom.

"I wished not to delay the good news, Your Highness," he announced with more confidence than he felt. What did the king know? There was something about his stance, his unwavering glare, that alarmed Cromwell. "All three bishops—Winchester, Durham, and York—agree there is much cause for annulment. God is withholding His blessings from this marriage, and the king must be free to choose a wife more of his liking, a wife to bear fruit, for the good of the realm."

Instead of the jovial bearhug or slap on the back he had been expecting, even preparing for, the king said nothing.

"We go tonight to Hampton." Henry seemed to be speaking to Suffolk, but his eyes never left Cromwell's face.

"Hampton, Your Highness?" Cromwell's tone was incredulous. "Why, we left Hampton but yesterday."

"Very good, Essex." There was an unpleasant chord to the king's voice. "I see your travels have done nothing to weaken your mental capabilities. We left Hampton but yesterday, and tonight we return."

Cromwell's lips tightened as he bowed once more. "Excellent, Your Highness. I shall order the household staff to—"

"No." The king spoke without moving. "You need not bother, Essex. I believe the duke of Norfolk can handle the arrangements."

"Norfolk? But Sire, it has always been my duty to discharge this task." Cromwell swallowed. "Norfolk knows not how it is done."

"Norfolk can handle the arrangements." The king's voice was low but unmistakably firm.

Beneath the cloak, Cromwell's hand clenched into a fist. The ruby ring on his index finger bit into his skin, leaving an indentation he did not feel.

"Your Majesty." Cromwell bowed again, backing from the room, feeling the heat of Henry's and Suffolk's stares. He would not leave this way, cowed by the king and his smirking duke. "Oh, Sire." Cromwell's head snapped up, his face stretching into an intimate, knowing grin. Often he had spoken to the king thus, friend to friend. "And how is Mistress Deanie? Is she pleasing to the royal palate?"

The king's face remained impassive, and Suffolk spoke: "You know not what happened, then? Last night I did bear Mistress Deanie back to Hampton, so she could care for her cousin Hamilton."

"Hamilton?" Cromwell's voice warbled in a shrill pitch before he could control it. "The duke of Hamilton is not here at Richmond? I knew not he was ill."

"We did not say he was ill, Essex." Suffolk clasped his hands behind his back in an effort to keep them from closing about Cromwell's fat neck.

Cromwell's small eyes shifted before he responded. "'Twas but a deduction, Suffolk. You said Mistress Deanie was attending her cousin. Logic led me to believe he was ill."

"Good day, Essex," the king said without his usual warmth.

Reining in his escalating rage—fury at his own men, Hamilton, and above all, that Bailey wench—Cromwell thundered from the chamber. Someone was going to pay for this humiliation, he vowed. He would see a head tumble, and what amusement it would provide! Someone was going to bitterly regret playing Thomas Cromwell, earl of Essex, for the fool.

"My fool, my fool!" Queen Anne clapped her hands in delight as the young man tumbled. The bells on his toes and clipped to his floppy red hat jingled as he rolled into a standing position, arms spread wide to receive his applause. The queen laughed merrily and turned to Deanie, who sat quietly at her feet.

They were in the queen's chamber, playing an interminable game called Blank Dice and watching a tumbler who would have been given the hook on "The Gong Show." All Deanie could think about was Kit, still unconscious below in the small, stifling room. Dr. Cornelius had ordered her from Kit's side, promising to tend to the duke with his own hands.

That's what had her so worried.

"My fool, he is okay, no?" The queen was trying her best to amuse Deanie, to keep her mind off Kit.

"Yes, Your Majesty." Deanie tried to smile. "He's a regular laugh riot."

The queen raised her plucked eyebrows and giggled. "A *laugh riot?* I shall recall that phrase. It is to my liking. A laugh riot."

Englebert, the queen's footman, stepped forward, bearing

a silver tray filled with tiny cakes. The queen took a handful, then gestured to Deanie. "You have not ate a little even all the day long," she urged. "You have some of these. My cook make special."

Englebert pushed the tray under Deanie's nose, and she closed her eyes in an effort not to be sick. "No, thank you. They smell delicious, though. Sort of like doughnuts."

"Doo-nots?" The queen was intrigued. "What be those?"

"Oh, little pieces of fried dough. I used to sell them in Nashville."

Englebert seemed as intrigued as the queen. Only after she had gently steered the platter from beneath her face did Englebert nod once and back away.

The queen's footman was a short, bullet-headed man of middle age and unnaturally black hair. He moved in a perpetual stoop, yet even in that stance he seemed to serve no one unless he truly desired the duty. His devotion to Queen Anne was unquestionable. Since Queen Anne had made her friendship with Deanie so obvious, Englebert looked upon her with rare favor.

"Maybe you show cook how to make *doo-nuts,* okay?" The queen gave Deanie a look of such earnestness that she could not help but smile in return.

"Okay," she said, her voice thick with exhaustion and worry.

The tumbler rolled at their feet. He began to tug at Deanie's skirt, making exaggerated faces like a monkey. The queen thought his antics hilarious, and even Englebert began to grin.

Encouraged, the tumbler pushed harder at Deanie's knee. She swallowed against the tears suddenly pricking her eyes. All she wanted was to return to Kit, to sit by his bed even though he was insensible to her presence. Instead she was forced to endure the horrid little tumbler, his ridiculous bells ringing with every tip of his round head.

The corners of his lips turned down, and his face puckered into a pathetic expression that exactly mirrored Deanie's feelings. The queen clapped in delight, turning to Deanie to share the fun.

At once the queen stopped clapping. "Enough." She turned to the tumbler, who shrugged and rolled away, tucking himself under a table.

Deanie could only stare at her own hands, clenched atop the sumptuous velvet gown.

"You go back to your cousin," the queen said. "You know where from here he is?"

Deanie blinked, confused by the queen's odd phrasing. Then she realized she was being dismissed, allowed to return downstairs. A feeling of gratitude washed over her. Impulsively, she grasped the queen's large hand and kissed it.

"Thank you," she whispered. Then she stood up, but before she left the queen's chamber she sank into a low curtsy. For the first time the bow was real, not a pretend imitation of court manners.

Deanie walked swiftly to the door, again making a deep curtsy before she left. A gentle smile spread across the queen's face. It transformed her from a plain woman to one of unique comeliness. She was not beautiful; instead she wore an expression of welcome kindness.

As Deanie's long train disappeared into the corridor, the queen turned to Englebert. "Mistress Deanie, she is one okay cookie." Then she clapped once for the tumbler to begin again.

Deanie's eyes took a moment to adjust to the darkness of the room. Although she could not see precisely where the bed was, she knew Kit was there. She could feel him, his presence, his very being.

The doctor had passed her in the hallway, his lined face grave. Dr. Cornelius spoke better English than the rest of Queen Anne's household, but he was still hard to understand.

"The duke is better, mistress," he intoned. "Much because of my ointment, I suspect. It is the ground bee wings that help the most. How came he by the wounds?"

Deanie didn't answer him. "Thank you, Doctor," she mumbled, brushing past him in her haste to see Kit. She felt the doctor's eyes on her back, realizing how strange she must look without a headdress, her hair falling free and unadorned to her shoulders.

She closed the door to Kit's room behind her, leaning against the heavy wood, gathering her thoughts. From the odor she knew the doctor had applied more of the foul salve. She had suspected he would. In the corner of the room she had folded clean strips of cloth.

The laundress had thought her mad, asking to boil bandages as if they were to be used in a broth. The queen, however, had given Deanie permission to ask what she wished of the household. They would do whatever she requested to aid in her cousin the duke's recovery.

Opening the heavy drapery covering the single window, she let a ray of sunlight into the room so she could see Kit. She stood for a moment, staring at his impassive form on the bed.

Although he was still unnaturally pale, an aura of power somehow emanated from him. Even asleep, he seemed bold and undeniably masculine. She stooped and gathered the clean cloth strips, careful not to make too much noise as she returned to his side. The chair she had occupied earlier was still in place, by the right side of the bed.

His forehead felt cooler to the touch, his cheeks already scratchy with a new growth of dark whiskers. By the bed was a pitcher of water—also boiled by the perplexed staff. She dipped a corner of the cloth into the water and eased open the drawstring on his linen shirt. Very gently, she cleansed the area of the new layer of salve, the cloth becoming thick with the speckled ointment as she worked.

Her hands moved mechanically. She felt strangely detached, watching them go through the motions of pressing the cloth against Kit's muscular shoulder, then dipping fresh cloth into the water and repeating the gesture. There was something familiar about the movements, and she stared at her hands as she worked.

Then she remembered.

Her mother. When she was eight and ill with the chicken pox, her mother had sat by her bed just like this, pressing cool cloths dipped in pink calamine lotion against the itchy rash. Her hands, in that shaft of light, looked exactly like her mother's. Why hadn't she ever noticed it before?

She heard a woman sob, and for a moment she was startled. It was her own voice, she realized. Carefully, she completed the task of caring for Kit, patting the wound dry and covering it with his white shirt. But she couldn't stop crying; her weeping almost choked her as she succumbed to the misery.

She cried for Kit, she cried for herself, she cried for her mother.

There was a hollow ache of emptiness, a strange knowledge that she would never again return home to all that was familiar. Balling her hands into fists, she buried her face in the coverlet by Kit's side, as if reassured by his warmth and closeness. Her sobs came out in broken, jerky breaths, leaving her drained and limp.

Then she felt a hand, large and warm, on her shoulder. "Shush," said a male voice, rough and dry. The hand continued to rub her shoulder, although she could feel the hand tremble, a weak, shaky gesture.

"Kit?" She looked up, almost afraid she had imagined it. She sniffed, and his eyes opened very slightly, his parched lips formed into a narrow smile. His hand remained on her shoulder, motionless, as if forgotten.

"Oh, Kit," she said softly. Only then did she know how terrified she had been that he would never wake up. The fear had been there all along, looming over every other thought. He still looked like hell, but at least he was conscious. "Are you all right?"

It was a stupid question, she realized immediately. He remained very still for a long moment, and she clasped the hand he had put on her shoulder between her own two hands. Then, very slowly, he made a motion with that hand: his fingers curved into a fist, and his thumb went into the air in the old unmistakable thumbs-up gesture.

"Can I get you anything?"

Almost imperceptibly, he shook his head. With a great effort he opened his eyes, oddly incandescent in the light. "Cromwell?"

"He went away, some trip for the king. Suffolk knows everything, Kit. He helped me get back here to you." She brushed a thatch of hair from his forehead. "Your fever's down."

He did not reply, but his eyes closed again in exhaustion. She reached for a fresh cloth, dipped it in cool water, and touched it to his dry lips.

"We need to talk," he said.

"Not now, Kit. You need rest." She slipped her hand into his, surprised by the strength when he closed his fingers over hers.

"Soon," he murmured. "Soon." Then he was asleep.

At once she was exhausted, her own eyelids heavy. Yawning, she rested her head against his side, their hands still entwined. For the first time in days, she slept a peaceful, contented slumber.

The queen peered from her window, the remains of her meal still on the tray. In the courtyard below she saw two couriers dismount from their horses, their Tudor green-and-white tunics proclaiming them messengers of the king.

Several minutes later Englebert entered the queen's chamber. "The king, he returns within the hour, Your Majesty."

"He's coming back?"

"Yes." Englebert couldn't hide his excitement. Perhaps the king's sudden return would portend good news for his mistress. Perhaps the big English sovereign would finally see Queen Anne as the jewel all of Cleves knew her to be.

The queen smiled. "Very well, Englebert. We shall be ready to greet His Highness."

Englebert knew exactly what to do, and he left the room with a low bow. There was much to be made ready in an hour, and already he was listing the chores in his mind. On his way to the kitchen, an order to Scholsenberg the cook on his lips, he was haulted by a young page.

"Mr. Englebert," the youth said, his pale face betraying worry. "There are half a dozen members of the barber-surgeon guild beyond the moat. They say they come to attend Mistress Deanie, sir. Other members of their guild bade them come here. What shall I tell them?"

"Mistress Deanie?" Englebert waved the boy off. "Be gone for now, young man. The king arrives within the hour."

"The barbers are most insistent, sir." The boy bit back the urge to cry.

"Then let them in to Mistress Deanie. She is with the duke below."

The boy nodded and ran to inform the restless guild members of Mistress Deanie's whereabouts. By the time he reached them they had grown in number to nine, and the boy wondered why on earth Mistress Deanie had need of half the barber-surgeons in the county.

With his good arm, he tried to pull her closer, inhaling the fresh scent of her hair. She sighed in her sleep and stretched alongside him on the small bed. Even in slumber she moved from his wounded shoulder, resting her head against the other shoulder. The pain of her movement had awakened him, but he was glad to be alert, relieved to find her here.

Kit lifted his head and scanned the room. His head throbbed with the motion, and he took a deep breath to squelch the nausea. He was unfamiliar with this room. From the angle of the light falling from the window, as well as the tiny dimensions of the room, he supposed it was one of the lower chambers used for servants. Good. It would be easier for them to leave unseen from this location than from his usual chamber above, in the thick of palace activity.

He glanced down at Deanie, her face drawn even in sleep. He almost loosened the ties at the sides of her bodice to make her more comfortable but felt the canvas corset underneath. There would be no use in unlacing the ties, for the corset would remain tight. Instead, he kissed her forehead and closed his eyes.

Just as drowsiness was about to overtake him, the clattering of boots in the hallway forced his eyes open. He felt Deanie stiffen, and he closed his arm about her more tightly.

"Kit?" she whispered, unable to mask the terror in her voice.

"Be still," he said, his voice still rough and dry. His lips touched her forehead, and she seemed to relax a little.

The door banged open. Even in the single shaft of light, they both recognized the bulky form of Thomas Cromwell.

In a single movement the earl of Essex threw the draperies open, causing Deanie and Kit to squint against the sun.

"You defied me." Cromwell spat with ragged fury. "Both of you defied me. Now you shall pay the price."

With that the henchman who had wielded the staff against Kit's shoulder entered the chamber, his face registering excitement rather than anger.

Kit began to rise, but Deanie sat up first. "We did not defy you, Mr. Cromwell," she began. "I just wanted to make sure Kit was being cared for. I will return to Richmond with you, if that's what you want."

"You fool!" he hissed. "The king arrives here soon. He will be most grieved to learn of the duke's death, yet Mistress Deanie will be a balm to his pained soul."

"You're the fool," Deanie replied coolly. Kit, who had been about to speak, turned in astonishment. Her voice was almost unrecognizable, with a hardness he would never have believed her capable of. "Do you think I will become the king's mistress without Kit alive and well? Forget it. If you so much as touch him, you can find the king another woman."

"Then you shall die as well." Cromwell's voice was firm; only his eyes, flickering once to Kit, showed a hint of uncertainty.

"Fine." She shrugged, rising to her feet.

"No!" Kit propped himself up on one elbow, his lips white with pain. "Let her be, Cromwell. Do what you will with me, but touch her not."

"If anything happens to you, Kit, I don't give a damn about myself."

"This is madness." Cromwell turned from the two to his henchman, his finger beginning to rise in a command, when the hallway was filled with the clattering of footsteps. At once a young page peered in the doorway.

"Mistress Deanie? I have over a dozen barber-surgeons without, all here at your bidding. Shall I send them in?"

"A dozen?" Cromwell's small eyes darted to the boy.

"Well, sir, a few more just joined them. Word has spread, sir, that Mistress Deanie has frequent need of barber-surgeons, and throughout England they come to Hampton. I know not why, but more are coming by the hour."

"Oh, send them in!" Deanie's knees gave way as she sat on the edge of Kit's bed. She grasped his hand, and only by the cold and damp feel of her hand did he realize how frightened she had been.

Cromwell and his man backed away, forced from the room by a strange assortment of men, of all ages and sizes, all carrying satchels.

"This is not over," mumbled Cromwell.

But Deanie did not hear him. She was already selecting the barber-surgeons to shave her legs for the second time in less than twelve hours.

Chapter 10

DEANIE NARROWLY AVOIDED A HEAD-ON COLLISION WITH THE queen's tumbler as she slid into the great hall, her slippers still damp from the eighteen barber-surgeons who had just taken turns shaving her legs. Her skin was stinging. One of the barbers had been mortified when he accidentally nicked her leg, and yet another barber was sulking below, muttering bitter words about arriving too late to have a turn.

When it was announced that the king had arrived, Deanie ran from the room at full tilt. Her last glimpse of Kit had been of him offering the disappointed barber a chance to shave his legs, which the man failed to find amusing.

She took her place beside a giggling Katherine Howard and Cecily Garrison, sinking into the deepest curtsy her much-abused legs would allow. Deanie refused to think about what might have happened had Cromwell not been interrupted by the eager barbers. She glanced up to see Cromwell glaring at her from across the hall. Norfolk and Suffolk stood just behind the king, Norfolk somber and dreary, Suffolk smiling. His eyes lit upon Deanie, and he raised a questioning eyebrow. She nodded once, with a brief smile, and he seemed satisfied. Just before she turned her gaze downward, Suffolk winked at her.

The queen greeted her subjects with regal grace, moving elegantly alongside her husband. Unlike Deanie and the Englishwomen, the queen wore a skirt that was rounded at the hem, free of the treacherous three-foot trains that threatened to hobble Deanie at every turn. Deanie had been so impressed with the queen's managable skirts that she had ordered a similar style from the court clothier, Mr. Locke. Although Locke had been surprised by her request—most of the other courtiers had been snickering about the queen's unfashionably foreign gowns—he reluctantly agreed. Within the week, Deanie too would be able to glide through the room without kicking out her skirts at each direction change.

The king peered over the elegant heads, as if searching for someone. He was massively resplendent in his bejeweled doublet, brilliant tufts of fine white linen peeking from the embroidered slashes in the fabric. His wife followed his gaze with palpable reverence, and more than a little fear. Deanie longed to take the queen's hand, to reassure her that all would be well in this strange land. Deanie, above all, felt the same trepidation about the unpredictable court. Both were at the whim of a mercurial-tempered monarch and his jostling noblemen.

"Ah! There she is." The king threaded his bulk nimbly through the crowd to Deanie. The queen hastened to follow, her face partially hidden by her headpiece and demiveil. Henry's burly hand, his nails cleanly squared, reached out to Deanie. She had no choice but to take it.

"Mistress Deanie." For the first time she noticed how rich his voice was, redolent with mellow tones. "We are most concerned with the health of our most favored subject, the duke of Hamilton. How does he fare?"

There was nothing suggestive or lecherous about the

king's question. Deanie sensed genuine worry. For once the royal eyes did not flit up and down her figure as he spoke.

"Much better, Your Highness," she replied. "I must thank the queen for her wonderful care of Kit—I mean, the duke. She sent her own physician to him, and sat by his bedside until I could return."

Deanie kept her head bent, not wishing to see the king's displeasure as she praised the queen. But Deanie felt it necessary. The king had no idea what kind of a woman fate and diplomacy had gifted him with.

Slowly, she raised her eyes. The king wore an expression of mild befuddlement. "The queen? She nursed Hamilton?"

"Yes, Your Majesty," Deanie hastened to add. "The queen has been most kind to both myself and the duke." Deanie wanted to elaborate, but she instinctively knew he was not ready to hear such lavish commendation. Perhaps the king could only tolerate a little of Queen Anne's praise at a time.

The king frowned, and his black gaze slid to his wife. "We are most pleased," he announced to everyone in the hall, to Anne in particular. "We are most pleased indeed," he repeated. "I will visit Hamilton anon." Then he patted Deanie's hand and rejoined his wife.

Even from across the vast hall, Deanie could feel the hatred blazing from Cromwell.

She had waited long enough.

That blasted bell-jingled clown of the queen's was tumbling across the floor, much to the rapture of his audience. Deanie ground her teeth, wondering when she could at last leave the hall for Kit's room below. Finally she was given the subtle nod from the queen. She could leave.

She raced through the corridors again, much the way she had run hours earlier when she had heard of the king's arrival. Her slippers skidded on the corners, and she bunched her gown in a handful between her legs to get to Kit as soon as possible.

Grabbing the archway of a door to prevent herself from slamming into a wall, she turned down the hallway. Still breathless, and puffing a wisp of hair away from her eyes, she entered Kit's room.

"Whew!" she said, breathing hard and slamming the door closed. "Talk about a bunch of stiff shirts. Or should I say stiff doublets."

The room was brighter than before, illuminated by at least a dozen thick yellow candles. Then she saw Kit.

"Hey." She grinned, pleased beyond all reason he was sitting up. "Did the barbers finally leave you alone?"

"Indeed, they have left us all alone, Mistress Deanie." The sonorous voice came from King Henry, who was seated in the same chair she had earlier abandoned.

"Your Majesty," she curtsied, flustered by the unexpected presence of the king. She had seen him retire, leaving the Great Hall with a simple nod to his bowing subjects, and had assumed he was going to his own chambers.

"Please, Mistress Deanie. No fanfare." The king gestured to the other chair. "We are amongst friends."

With only slight hesitation, she ducked into the chair, her hands folded primly on top of her lap. The three of them looked at each other, sharing a sudden awkward silence as Deanie struggled for something to say.

"How are you feeling?" she asked Kit. Simultaneously, Kit spoke: "I'm feeling much better."

The king chuckled. "Mistress Deanie, can you hand us that piece of paper by your foot?"

Perplexed, she glanced down. Beside the leg of her chair was a sheet of beige parchment, folded into an oblong shape. She reached down and passed it to the king.

"Your Majesty, I do not think . . ." Kit began. He had a strange tone to his voice, beyond the exhaustion of the injury and illness. Her eyes snapped to his, a questioning frown on her face.

"Nonsense, Kit." The King laughed. "Has your cousin seen the trick? Mistres Deanie, this is most cunning. Show us again how it works. The duke can always find means of amusing us. Show us, Kit."

He passed the parchment to Kit. For a moment Kit did nothing but lean back against the pillow and close his eyes. Suddenly Deanie was alarmed.

"Kit, are you feeling ill?" She reached out her hand to touch his forehead, but his skin was cool.

"Show us the trick," the king repeated, the note of impatience unmistakable.

Taking a deep breath, Kit opened his eyes and stared at her for a few moments. He did not smile, but the hollows of his cheeks seemed to deepen, as if he were under a great strain. Then, without tearing his gaze from hers, he began to fold the paper, again and again, into slender triangles.

"Ha! Now make it fly, Kit!" The king seemed like a child, his fat hands clapping together in delight. "What do you call it again? What was the word, Kit?"

With a single motion, Kit launched the paper into the air. It soared above the bed, then looped down into Deanie's lap. She stared at it, not believing, her hands trembling.

"It is called, Your Highness," Kit said, his voice flat, "an aeroplane."

"Yes!" Henry thundered. "An *aero-plane!* Most ingenious."

For a moment Deanie thought she was going to be ill. The color drained from her face, leaving her a deathly white. The only sound she could hear was the fierce pounding of her heart.

"Mistress Deanie, fear not," said the king, noting her sudden pallor. "This is not black magic or sorcery. The Duke knows many feats of engineering, unparalleled in the world of science."

"A paper airplane," she said numbly.

The sound of a knock on the door pierced the air. One of the senior butlers entered the room, his face grave. "Your Highness." He bowed. "The earl of Essex requests your attention. It is a matter of the utmost importance, Sire."

"Cromwell has sent for us?" The king was astounded, the paper airplane forgotten. "By God, I shall see him fall." Gone was the jovial monarch. The king in his fury rose to his feet, oblivious to Kit and Deanie, and strode from the room in two great bounds. The manservant, cowering at the king's heels, followed him through the door.

Deanie was staring straight ahead, her mind reeling.

"I was going to tell you, Deanie," Kit said gently. She did not respond, and he continued: "I was born in 1917, in Kent. My father was killed in the Great War, so my mother raised myself and my older sister, Caroline. Are you listening?"

She swallowed. He reached over to her, and blindly she took his hand. She was still trembling.

"How did you get here?" Her voice was strangely hollow.

"Through the maze. Deanie, there is something about the maze—it is a portal of sorts. I've been trying to get back to my own time. Every chance I get while I'm here at Hampton, I enter the maze, hoping to find the portal once more. When I met you I was trying to find my way back home."

With a deep breath she looked at him. "What year are you from?"

His callused fingers folded over hers. "I came here in 1940, and I've been in this time for ten years."

Slowly, he drew her toward him, his good arm encircling her as she reached his side. Mechanically, she leaned against him, her arms folded against herself as if for protection. For a long time she said nothing and simply closed her eyes, her head tucked against his chest. He stroked her hair with a soothing, hypnotic rhythm.

"How did it happen to you?" Her voice sounded more even.

Her head rose slightly as he took a deep breath. "I was a pilot in the RAF, the Royal Air Force. I was to fly my last sortie, to keep the damn Luftwaffe from invading England. We were waiting for you Yanks to join us. You did, right?"

"Yes," she murmured against his shirt. "But I was no whiz in history."

"History?" She felt him smile. "Gad, but I feel old. Hitler lost, right?"

"Oh, sure. He shot himself in a bunker at the end. He was a real nut by then."

"He was always a nut." Kit looked up at the ceiling, the flickering shapes made by the candles against the wood. "Do you recall what year the war ended in?"

Deanie thought for a moment. Kit's hand tightened into a fist before she answered. "It was 1945. There were all these fifty-year celebrations when I left."

"My God!" Kit's arm tensed. "How did we survive? We were about done in by 1940."

They remained silent, each lost in thought.

"You were a pilot?" Deanie's question jarred the quiet.

He nodded.

"That must have been scary as all get-out."

At first she thought he hadn't heard her. Finally he spoke, his voice was rough and low. "By the time I came here, most of my chums were gone. Chaps I'd gone to university with, good men all. I don't know why I survived, why I lived and they didn't. I still miss them. They haven't been born yet, and I miss them." He cleared his throat, and she remained silent. "That's why it was relatively easy for me when I came here. A joust is nothing compared with a duel in the sky. I suppose I attracted the king's attention because my style was even more reckless and foolhardy than his own."

Deanie raised a hand to her eyes and rubbed them, as if trying to massage sense into her jumbled thoughts. "I knew you were different from the rest," she said at last. "Right from the first, you accepted my story of where I came from. Now it makes sense—at least the reason you were so kind to me."

"If I was kind, it was because I understood what you were experiencing."

"Oh."

He smiled. "At first, Deanie, that was the reason. Almost immediately, it came to me that I—well, I had grown fond of you."

She tilted her head up, her lips brushing along his jaw. "Really?" she asked, trying to keep the pleading tone from her voice.

He turned his face to hers, and she closed her eyes, eager for the feel of his mouth against hers. Instead, he dropped a distracted kiss on her forehead. "Tell me, what happened exactly when you came here through the maze?"

Startled, she opened her eyes and glared at him. "I thought I told you everything."

"From the beginning, Deanie. Maybe we can figure out how to get back." His tone was eager, full of hope.

"Okay . . . let me see. We were filming a music video, and I entered the maze."

"It was spring for you, but I came here on September 11, 1940." His brow creased in thought. "Perhaps the sun is the same distance from the earth in spring as it is in the autumn. About what time was it?"

"Close to sunset. We were about to quit for the day, because we had already lost the best light."

"The same with me," he said, his hand stroking her hair again. "It was time for me to leave for my mission, and the sun reflected off a pair of goggles in my hand."

"And I was carrying the soda bottle," she added excitedly. "Did it make blue-white lines, like a triangle?"

"Exactly! It was a prism, but it seemed to be almost alive."

"I wonder if we go back there at sunset, whether the same thing could happen again."

"You came in spring, I arrived in the autumn." He spoke softly, as if thinking aloud. "If there is some significance in the time of the year, the placement of the sun, we can only hope to catch the same alignment."

"Then we need to hurry, Kit. It will be summer soon. If

we miss it now, we might have to wait until fall to try again."

"We can't wait," he warned. "The whole court will be on its ear by then, and we may not survive."

Deanie raised her head. "It might work, you know."

"But if it does, we have no guarantee that we would land in our time. I came from 1940, you are from a half century later. God only knows what year we would emerge."

"Maybe we should just stay here," she wondered quietly.

"Oh, hell," he muttered. "Cromwell's out to kill us, the king wants to make you his mistress, and at any moment either of us can contract the plague or be charged with witchcraft." He glanced down at his shoulder, which was beginning to throb with molten pain. "We have to leave England, Deanie. We cannot stay here—it has become far too dangerous. Perhaps you should flee to Spain alone. I could join you—"

"No," she said with finality. "I will stay with you, Kit." He did not respond, and she suddenly felt embarrassed. "After all, you have been so, um, helpful. It would be rotten for me to duck out on you now."

"You needn't stay from a sense of obligation." His voice was tight. "You are not required to pay me back."

He had become still, no longer stroking her hair. The arm about her shoulders was tense, as if he was reluctant to touch her.

She swallowed and looked down at her hand, her palm resting on his chest. Her fingertips were still callused from years of playing the guitar, yet she was exquisitely sensitive to his every movement. He seemed to stop breathing. Beneath her hand she could feel his heart beating heavily, painfully.

An overwhelming ache welled up within her throat, theatening to choke her with its intensity. Why was she acting like this? Why was she being so dishonest with Kit, with herself?

"Kit," she whispered, her voice wavering, "I lied."

She felt him glimpse down at her, but he couldn't see her face. "What did you lie about?" He spoke softly, his breath ruffling her hair.

"I lied because I didn't tell you the truth."

He sighed, a little of the tension flowing from him. "That is the usual definition of a lie, Deanie. What did you lie about?"

Turning her face toward his chest, she inhaled the familiar scent of him, the feel of his shirt and the muscles of his chest, allowing his warmth to give her the courage to speak. "I don't want to leave without you because I love you."

For a moment they both remained motionless. Deanie cringed, waiting for him to push her away—or worse, to laugh. Her hand clutched his shirt, gripping with all her might against whatever his reaction would be. Every second seemed exaggerated, a slow-motion agony of waiting.

Slowly, hesitantly, she allowed herself to look up. His lips were tight, the hollows of his cheeks prominent, causing his face to take on a harsh, fierce appearance. His eyes gazed straight ahead, a burnished sheen reflected in the clear depths. She thought perhaps he had not heard what she said, and for a fleeting instant she was relieved. Then she saw him blink.

A single tear escaped from his right eye.

It traced a path across his lean cheekbone, and as he turned toward her, it slid onto her hand.

His words flowed as a single breath. "My God, Deanie. How I love you."

With that his mouth was crushed against hers, and she felt his hand fan out against her back. Startled, dizzy with a strange warmth that seemed to spiral through her abdomen, she relaxed against him.

His mouth, those lips she had dreamed of touching since first she saw him, pressed against hers with a sweet, firm need. He shifted, putting most of his weight on his uninjured shoulder, and as he moved her tongue grazed his teeth. Through her exploding haze of passion she could feel the single crooked tooth, the gleaming imperfection that had haunted her every moment.

He pulled away and stared at her. A strand of her hair fell across her face, and he gently pushed it back. "Deanie," he said softly.

She opened her eyes, glazed with desire, unseeing.

"Deanie, we can't."

He too was breathing hard, and a glimmer of perspiration dotted his forehead.

"What?" she answered groggily.

He groaned, pulling her against him again. She reached up to kiss his glorious mouth once more, and he laughed.

"Deanie, at any moment either the king or Cromwell may enter unannounced." He swallowed.

That stopped her, and she was unable to repress an involuntary shiver. His hand caressed her arm.

"It just doesn't seem important now, Kit. Cromwell and all those guys seem so very far away."

"That's a dangerous way of thinking." His eyes slid to hers.

"I just want to stay here forever." She sighed, a slight smile on her lips.

"Please listen to me. Now, more than ever, we must decide what we are going to do. Perhaps we should escape tonight. If we flee to Manor Hamilton, we could buy ourselves some time. I have men there, servants who are loyal to me."

"Are you well enough to travel?" Deanie cast a worried glance at his shoulder, and when she saw it she immediately jumped off the bed and reached for a clean cloth. Their embrace had caused the wound to start bleeding again.

"I'm fine." His good arm remained in the open position, where she had just been, but he too frowned when he saw the shoulder. "Damn."

She dipped the cloth into the water and pressed it against the wound to stem the bleeding. "How far away is Manor Hamilton?"

"About fifty miles," he admitted.

"Great. How will we get there? Fly in one of your paper airplanes?"

He grinned. "If you only knew how marvelous it sounds to hear you say *airplanes*. Ouch."

"Sorry."

Then he stopped smiling. "You must leave first, Deanie. I can't travel just yet. It would be folly to attempt a journey of such length with this blasted shoulder."

"No." She refolded the damp cloth. "I don't want to be separated from you."

"Nor I from you. But it may be our only way out, barring the maze. And that may very well fail."

"I just have this awful feeling that if we are separated we may never get back together."

He thought for a moment. "I believe Suffolk knows a duke in Spain, and I am acquainted with some diplomats from Queen Katherine's court who have returned to Spain. I wouldn't want to slow you down, and with me bleeding all over the continent we couldn't get far enough to be safe."

Their eyes met as she took his hand. "I will not leave you behind," she said with determination. "I think we should give the maze a try. It seems to me we ought to be able to get a round-trip fare out of those old bushes."

He smiled, and Deanie felt herself swallow hard. Even injured and recovering from illness, he was absolutely devastating. His voice was rich, compelling. "The maze it is, then."

"Do you think the soda bottle's still there?"

"I would think so. Hardly anyone goes there since Anne Boleyn was beheaded—it's thought to be bewitched."

"And it is." With a sigh she looked down at their entwined hands. They seemed to fit together perfectly. "What if we do end up in some strange time?"

"Frankly, Deanie, we'd be better off almost anywhere else. My guess is that we can only go forward, since the maze is just a decade old now. When I arrived it was new. As long as we move ahead, all should be well."

"What if we can't find the bottle? Do you still have the goggles?"

"Ah. The goggles. Of course I still have them—back at Manor Hamilton. For years I carried them with me, stepping into the maze every chance I got, but nothing ever happened. I kept on returning, with or without the goggles. Force of habit, I imagine. Maybe I didn't want to leave badly enough until now."

She stiffened. "Holy cow, Kit! If someone else finds that bottle before us, we may never be able to get out of here."

"That thought crossed my mind."

"I should go right now, with a candle—"

"No, Deanie, not now. You would be too noticeable with a candle. Besides, you couldn't see well enough. Why don't you wait until morning?"

"Morning will be even worse. The servants are up and about at dawn, including the gardeners."

"Then wait until tomorrow afternoon, and I'll go with you. We can say we are perambulating for my health or some such nonsense."

She was about to argue, to mention that he might not be well enough to go out tomorrow, or the next day, and that every minute lost offered another passerby the chance to stumble upon the bottle. Instead, she just nodded. "Fine," she said, avoiding his gaze.

There was a strong knock on the door. "Come in," Kit answered, giving Deanie's hand a quick squeeze before returning it to her lap.

A large woman entered, garbed in a rough pleated skirt and a Germanic headdress peaked at the top. "Mistress Deanie? The queen bids you good night, and I am to see you to your chambers."

Deanie stood up. "Thank you, Mother Lowe." She turned to Kit. "Have you met the queen's head of the ladies-in-waiting?"

He shook his head, astonished by the size of the woman.

Mother Lowe nodded curtly and muttered, "Ya, Duke," before she turned to the door.

"Believe it or not, she's shy," confided Deanie in response to Kit's raised eyebrows.

There were mumblings outside the room, all in German. Englebert entered.

"Sir," he said, bowing to Kit, "we have placed four of our guards from Cleves outside your chamber for your comfort. We do not want barbers to come at night, no?"

Deanie smiled at Englebert. "Thank you," she whispered warmly, giving him a swift hug. In return he blushed.

"Will you be okay?" Deanie asked Kit. There was so much more she wanted to say, so much had happened in the past few hours. But between Mother Lowe and Englebert and the guards, it was impossible. She was being forced to leave, and they would have no more time alone. At least not tonight.

His unwavering gaze caught hers. Somehow, with just his eyes—reflecting dark green in the candlelight—he conveyed every emotion she herself was feeling. Her breath halted in her throat, and she placed her hand instinctively over her heart.

At the exact same moment, Kit raised his own hand and rested it over his heart.

"Mistress Deanie?" Mother Lowe loomed in the threshold, and Deanie backed away.

"Good night," she said softly, her voice betraying her shattering love.

"Good night," he returned, his voice echoing a promise, a pledge.

And with that Mother Lowe pulled a shaken Deanie up to the safe quarters of the other ladies-in-waiting.

Something woke him.

Perhaps it was all the spiced wine he had consumed or the extra helping of dove pie. More than likely it was his seething anger. He would not allow them to carry out their vile plans. It was unthinkable.

He threw open the heavy draperies on his bed. It was cold this night, and his fire had been allowed to dwindle into glowing embers. His feet—noble feet—felt the chill as they touched the floor.

He walked to the window. Not that he was expecting to see anything, not at this hour. Just as he was about to go back to bed, the room lit only by the vague moon, something caught his eye.

By God, there was someone in the maze!

He could see a flickering light, a candle wavering. Whoever it was must be very close to the ground, perhaps on hands and knees.

He threw on his surcloak, which had been resting on a chair by the window, and walked as quietly as possible out toward the maze. Doors that never squeaked seemed to be in need of oil this evening, planks that were ever silent now seemed to announce his every movement.

Finally he reached the back garden, creeping along the grass to avoid crunching the pebbles.

As he got closer, he heard a voice coming from the maze.

"Come on, come on. I know you're in here."

Ah! Mistress Deanie!

His first instinct was to push through the yew shrubs to confront her, but he quickly tossed that thought aside. Perhaps he could learn more by just watching her.

She was rummaging with great intent, and he was nearly consumed by curiosity.

"Yes!" Mistress Deanie hissed, delight evident in her voice.

She immediately snuffed the candle, and he watched as she scurried back to the palace. It was impossible to determine what she was carrying.

Silently, he entered the maze himself, feeling a path to where Mistress Deanie had been. Nothing. He suddenly realized the idiocy of his impulsive trip outside. It was cold, and he was barefoot—his tender feet assaulted by every rock and slip of sharp stone. Besides, he was almost blind in the dim light.

Harrumphing at himself, he turned to leave when his foot slid on something. He reached down and picked up some papers.

Shoving them into his cloak, he ran back to his chamber as quietly as possible. Breathing hard, he closed his door and lit a taper on the last glow of the fire.

He pulled out the papers and gasped. What was this? What manner of witchcraft?

The papers, slick and smooth as glass, were bound together. Upon each page were paintings, paintings of such fine quality he felt he could reach out and enter the work.

There were printed words, strange and even, unlike anything he had ever seen, and he owned over a dozen books. Holding the candle, he read what he could.

It was all about the court, about Henry and his wives.

Then he almost cried out, for there was a portrait of himself! He was to begin sitting for the painting this week; Holbein had completed the rough sketches. But here it was, completed, filled in with lush colors.

Further in the book were paintings of court women, some identified as Henry's wives. But they were not his wives!

His hands trembling, he saw his name with a date—a date in the near future. Was someone wishing him dead?

And then he saw something that made him nearly cry out in fear. Toward the back of the book was a painting of the king. He was old and bloated, and the date was 1547.

Someone was practicing witchcraft and predicting the death of the king.

He flipped the book over and looked at the cover. The words were strange and unfamiliar.

A Tourist's Guide to Hampton Court Palace.

His palms sweating, he shoved the booklet under his mattress.

Mistress Deanie had placed the booklet there, he was sure

of it. Not only was she guilty of witchcraft, she was guilty of a far greater sin: high treason.

He pulled the drapes on his bed shut, wondering what could be done with this new information. By dawn his pulse had slowed, and on his face was a confident smile.

Before breaking the fast, he had decided how to use his new information. Very soon the entire court—perhaps even the king—would bend to his every whim.

At last he would secure his rightful, God-given place in the realm.

Chapter *11*

*I*T WAS HOPELESS.

There was no way for Deanie to hide the cola bottle long enough to reach Kit's chambers. It was too large to slip under her belt or tuck within the embroidered false sleeve of her gown. She tried to fold it under the flowing lappets of a gable headpiece, but one glimpse of herself in the distorted, speckled mirror caused her to yank it off in disgust. The sight of a lady-in-waiting sporting a headdress plumed with a Coke bottle was more bizarre than anything Andy Warhol could have dreamed up.

So she settled on carrying the bottle in the open. Her first thought was to fill it up with ale and hope no one noticed her strutting through the palace corridors with an open bottle of beer.

She nixed that idea because the dried-up, blackened peanuts still rattled in the bottom. Although she was fairly certain the nuts had nothing to do with her passage through time—and as far as she knew Kit did not travel with his goggles full of peanuts—she didn't want to alter the bottle for fear it might upset a delicate balance.

It was a glance outside the window, the spring sun beaming on the garden, that gave her the inspiration she'd been seeking. She simply walked decorously through the grounds, nodding gently at the passing courtiers, and grabbed stems of roses as soon as they passed. By the time her stroll was completed, there were so many brilliant-hued flowers rioting from the innocuous bottle that no one noticed the plain glass carafe.

She had kept her possession of the bottle a secret from Kit for four days, watching as he recovered from the wounds and fever. Like a tethered puppy, he wanted nothing more than to leave his chamber, and only the combined efforts of Suffolk and Englebert and the queen and, above all, Mother Lowe, kept him in the room.

By her third day he paced the chamber restlessly, vowing to get past the Germanic guards and mumbling disjointed curses about their parentage. Deanie used every ounce of charm to cajole and reason with him, urging him to stay in place until he had recovered.

"You think you've had a rough time?" She had finally lost the frayed remains of her temper. Hands on hips, she cornered Kit, who had been forcing open the window in hopes of escaping to the garden.

"I've had my legs shaved a dozen times, come to fisticuffs with the laundress who refused to bring your bandages to a complete boil, and been forced to block Dr. Cornelius from bleeding you every chance he gets. Humor me, Kit. Hang around here just a couple more days—or at least until you can jump out of the window without hurting something."

He glared before finally laughing and agreeing with her logic.

For days she resisted the urge to run to him, to whoop with joy over her triumph of retrieving the missing soda bottle. Besides waiting for Kit to recover, she had two other reasons for waiting.

The first reason for her sedate manner was that she was once again housed in the wing with the other ladies-in-waiting. She had been given the same room as before, the same room in which Cromwell had made his threats and wounded Kit. There was no physical evidence of that mayhem. Still, the very motion of entering the chamber caused her stomach to tighten with apprehension, making it impossible for her to forget what danger they still faced.

The second reason for her hesitation was that Kit would be furious with her for risking everything to find the bottle on her own. Even as she searched in the dark, she realized the stupidity of her actions. She just wanted to find the damn thing so they could get on with their plans. Without the bottle, their most likely escape route was blocked.

As she toted the flowers to Kit's room, she felt as if she held the very key to their future together.

She was prepared to find him awake, perhaps being shaved by a new flock of barbers. Even the sight of him still asleep, allowing his exhausted and battered body some much-needed rest, would not have alarmed her.

The last thing she expected was to find him gone, vanished as if he had never set foot in the small chamber.

The bottle nearly slipped from her hands when she realized he was not there.

"Kit?" she whispered, as if in a hospital ward. There was no answer. The guards from the night before were also missing. The only items in the stark room were the few furnishings: the small bed, two chairs, a table. The cloth bandages and her boiled water were nowhere to be seen.

Gripping the bottle harder, she tried to control her fear. There was probably a perfectly logical explanation for his absence. Maybe he was having breakfast with Suffolk or the King. Perhaps Mother Lowe, whom she had seen twice that morning, had decided to change his room.

But wouldn't Mother Lowe have mentioned something to Deanie? She'd had ample opportunity, and her English wasn't *that* bad.

A more likely scenario crept into her mind. Cromwell. She could almost feel the heat of his anger, the rage he struggled to contain in the great hall. He had men who would do anything for a coin. They relied on his commands and power, not on their own tattered conscience.

Kit was a strong man, but he was not yet recovered from his beating.

"Kit?" There was still no answer.

She walked calmly from the room, her head erect. She would not run, she would not scream his name.

With her knees growing ever more unsteady, she glided through the halls, peering into each room as she passed. There were over a thousand rooms at Hampton, and she vowed to search each one until she found Kit.

She walked for almost an hour, her anxiety mounting by the minute. The rest of the court seemed to be enjoying the grounds, and she could hear occasional snatches of laughter from the gardens and the tilting yard as she passed.

The roses were pressed so close to her body they began to wilt from the heat. Feeling light-headed, she recalled that she hadn't eaten since the previous day. Her plan had been to have breakfast with Kit.

She was walking in circles now, not really seeing into the chambers as she passed. Finally she went outside, hoping to find Englebert or Mother Lowe or someone who could tell her where Kit was.

A large circle of courtiers stood in the tilting yard, chatting among themselves, occasionally erupting into spontaneous applause. There was a metallic clanking sound from within the crowd, and she recognized the noise as swords clashing.

As she approached, the circle opened to let her in. A few of the women stared at Deanie, her face ashen, carrying a large armful of limp flowers.

"Hamilton, your cousin approaches. It seems she has been busy plundering the gardens of their every bloom!"

The voice belonged to Charles Brandon, the duke of

Suffolk. In the center of the circular audience were several young men engaged in a show of swordsmanship.

One of them—using his left arm—was Kit.

He handed Suffolk his sword and walked immediately to her side. He appeared to be disarmingly healthy, wearing nothing but a loose-fitting shirt and hose. Even in her relief, Deanie saw the hungry stares from some of the women.

"Cousin, for me!" Kit said as he reached her side, gesturing to the bouquet. Many of the courtiers laughed and returned to their conversations, or watched young Surrey begin to battle Brandon.

"Where the hell have you been?" Kit demanded as he placed a brotherly arm about her shoulder. He glared down at her, a brilliant smile fixed on his face, his eyes flashing dangerously. "Goddamnit, Deanie, I've looked everywhere for you. Don't you ever disappear like that again."

"Where have *I* been?" she repeated incredulously. "I've only been searching through that entire stupid castle for you. When you weren't in your room, I thought something had happened to you. Oh, Kit." Her voice broke, and through his anger he realized how frantic she looked, the way she hugged the soggy flowers to her chest.

With a swift glance around to make sure they were not being watched too closely, he guided her behind a hedge. There she fell against him, suddenly unable to support herself.

"Where did you go?" she asked against his shirt.

"Englebert woke me early this morning. He said he saw Cromwell conferring with some of his men and thought it might be a good idea for me to switch to another room. I thought he would have told you."

She shook her head, her feeling of dread just now beginning to ebb. "No. I'm glad he didn't, because one of Cromwell's guys might have followed me to you." She backed away, a small smile playing at her lips. "You were right, by the way. These roses *are* for you."

She handed them to him, and he was about to speak when he realized what the container was. "How did you . . ."

"Don't ask." She pushed them into his grip.

"Did anyone see you?"

"No. I went the other night—don't get mad. It was about three in the morning, and I put out the candle as soon as I found it. Did you know it gets dark at that hour? I almost walked into the brick wall about a dozen times."

"I should be furious with you," he said, his hand closing around the bottle. "But I'm so damned relieved to see you. When Suffolk pressed me into one of his impromptu tournaments, I could hardly refuse. He had a very good point: It's not safe to be out of sight for long in this court."

Her hand swept a thatch of hair from his forehead. "How are you feeling? I can't believe you're up."

"I feel like hell," he admitted. Only then did she notice that behind the apparently healthy glow his skin bore a chalky whiteness. The lines beside his mouth and radiating from the corners of his eyes seemed deeper. "I couldn't stand being in that room one more day. Besides, I believe I'm on the mend."

"Thanks to Dr. Cornelius and his magic ointment?"

"No." He had stopped smiling. "Thanks to Wilma Dean Bailey and her magic love."

The abrupt change in his tone took her by surprise. She raised her hand to her mouth. He gazed over her head, wary of curious courtiers. They were alone. Setting the bottle on the grass by the concealing shrub, he drew her to him, enfolding her in his arms. Although they ached from the punishing swordplay, her very nearness seemed to soothe away the pain.

"Shall we try it tonight, at sundown?" His breath ruffled her hair as he spoke.

"Maybe later," she murmured, her eyes closed in a dreamy haze.

"Later? But we need—" His sudden laugh startled her. "Deanie, I mean, shall we try the *maze* later, not, well . . ."

Her face flushed and he nodded, unable to answer. Pressing closer, her arms closed about his waist. She linked her hands tightly behind him, as if preparing to be wrenched away.

Kit rested his chin on her head, inhaling the fragrance of her hair. His eyes remained watchful as he listened for the telltale rustle that would signal an intruder into the boundaries of their private world.

"It has to work, it just has to," she said at last, her lips moving against his chest.

He said nothing, and she pulled back slightly and looked up. His fierce stare was fixed beyond her, his expression hooded and unreadable. He swallowed and his eyes shifted to hers. At once his face softened, melting into a gentle smile.

"We'd best rejoin the fray," he murmured, bending down to pick up the bottle. He held it up to the light, the flower petals fluttering to the ground as it moved. "Should I be unable to speak with you, perhaps we should agree on a time to meet in the maze. How does six o'clock this afternoon sound?"

Deanie tried unsuccessfully to repress a shiver.

"Are you cold?" he asked, offering her his arm.

"Yes." Her voice was subdued. "I've been cold since I got here."

"Ah. There's a very good explanation for that." They emerged from behind the hedge, the sun barely warming the air. He spoke quietly, leaning toward her. "We are in the tail end of an ice age."

"You're kidding."

"No. It's a good ten or twelve degrees colder now than it was in the twentieth century. Haven't you noticed?"

"I just thought it was all the palace creeps that made me feel so chilly."

He grinned. "Well, they surely don't help."

The duke of Suffolk waved from where yet more courtiers

had gathered. "Hamilton, there you are. Come try your arm with Surrey."

Kit held up a hand, indicating he would be right there. "Six o'clock?" His gaze held hers.

"Six o'clock," she confirmed.

"Hamilton!" He looked up just as Surrey tossed his sword, and he caught it with his left hand.

With his right he passed Deanie the flowers and cola bottle. He brushed the back of his hand along the curve of her cheek. "Take care until six," he mumbled, then turned to join the men.

"Of the bottle?" she asked, watching his broad back as he walked away. His dark curls barely reached the collar of the white shirt. He halted and very slowly turned to face her.

"No." His shrouded expression revealed nothing. "Take care of yourself, Deanie. Take care of yourself."

With that he hefted the sword in the unfamiliar hand and left her wondering what on earth his strange tone could have meant.

The king was doing everything in his considerable power to impress Mistress Deanie in the music salon.

"Ah, the clavichord," he announced as he stretched his great hands with a delicate flourish. He began one of his favorite tunes, each note vibrating in the air. He hazarded a peek at Mistress Deanie, who sat stiffly on the window seat, the gypsy guitar of Hamilton's resting as if forgotten in her lap.

God's blood, but she was lovely! Her hair had much red in its chestnut hues. The setting sun seemed to cause her thick tresses to glow with warmth. She had a most distracting habit of looking out the window, and the king was determined to force her complete attention on his princely prowess.

She had come willingly enough after the noon meal. Of course she sat with her cousin Hamilton at her side, and they seemed to enjoy each other's familiar company the way close family members often do. When the meal ended Hamilton seemed reluctant to leave her, even as the ladies retired to their own chambers.

"Is it to your liking, mistress?" The king played the last few bars of the music.

"Excuse me?" She seemed startled by his voice.

The king pursed his lips, trying to control his impatience. His red beard had been trimmed earlier by one of the scores of barbers that seemed to overrun Hampton of late. One had snipped at his thinning hair, then frowned and put a plumed round hat on his head like a crown. The king was well aware of his encroaching baldness, and he resented a mere barber being privy to the knowledge.

"The music, Mistress Deanie," he repeated. "Is it to your liking?"

"It is just fine, Your Majesty."

The king squelched the urge to scowl. Instead, he gave her one of his most dazzling smiles. He was proud of his teeth; they were mostly intact, and not as badly discolored as those of most men his age.

The song ended, and the king looked down with approval at the glittering rings on his fingers. "It is a composition of my own making," he said.

"Really?" He had caught her attention now. "Why, it was wonderful, Your Highness."

"Yes, it is rather wonderful." He stood up and approached her. "Mistress Deanie, would you favor our ears with another of your own compositions?"

"Of course." She tried to smile. She had no idea of the exact time, but she knew it was rapidly nearing six o'clock. She would have to race to her room to retrieve the bottle before she could meet Kit in the maze. Her fingers faltered on the neck of the guitar, fumbling for a chord. She had no notion what she was going to play; she just wanted to make it short and fast.

"Mistress Deanie." The king's voice was unexpectedly

soft. "Is there something amiss? It does not escape our notice that you seem to be distracted."

Deanie strummed a sour chord on the small guitar and appraised her situation with the king. She immediately dismissed the idea of telling him everything, of Cromwell and his strong-arm tactics. Cromwell would merely lash out with more speed and ferocity, since he would have nothing else to lose.

Instead she chose her words carefully. "I fear, Your Highness, that I am not yet accustomed to the ways of the court. Everything is so unfamiliar, and I am afraid I will somehow offend a courtier—or worse, yourself."

The king relaxed, sitting alongside her on the window seat. The jewels on his round hat reflected the sun, its rays bent through heavy leaded panes.

"Did you know I wasn't supposed to ever become king?" The regal accent was gone from his voice, and he seemed more human, less overblown.

"Really?" She put down the guitar, suddenly interested in what he had to say.

A small laugh escaped his mouth, and he stretched his silk-hosed legs before him. A large red garter covered the spot where the ulcer ate at his limb. "I was merely the duke of York, the second son. My older brother, Arthur, now he was the true prince.

"What happened to him?"

Henry was more than a little surprised. Even in Wales, the story of his family was common knowledge. But he explained anyway. "Arthur was my father's favorite, named for the legendary king."

"Oh, I get it! King Arthur." Deanie's eyes, fringed with impossibly long black lashes, were completely focused on Henry. It was a sensation he found enormously enjoyable.

"Yes. Arthur was every inch England's fair prince. He was even wed to the fairest princess of Christendom: Katherine of Aragon, daughter of Ferdinand and Isabella."

"The guys who sent Christopher Columbus to the New World?"

Again, Henry laughed. "Indeed, the very ones. But only after my father, in one of his few instances of poor judgment, refused to finance the voyage. The explorer's brother, Bartholomew Columbus, came to England to beg funds from my father. It was not much he asked, but my father refused. He said it would not be profitable."

Deanie, forgetting she was with the king, whistled through her teeth. "Man, I'll bet he sure regretted that move."

"Not nearly as much as I regretted it. It is rather costly to finance a realm." His voice was light, and there was a distinct twinkle in his beady black eyes.

"I'll bet," she agreed. "But what happened to Arthur?"

"Ah. When he was a bridegroom of but fourteen tender years, he died."

"No! I'm sorry. Oh, that's terrible. Poor Katherine."

The king cleared his throat. "Well, Mistress Deanie, Katherine as a young woman was lovely. All of a sudden, I, simple Hal, was thrust into the position of prince of Wales. My poor father raced throughout Europe to gather the best tutors available. As the second son, you see, my education had been sadly lacking. Oh, it was suitable for a man of the Church, that bastion of second sons. But it was lacking for a king. Only by diligent study was I able to succeed."

"In other words, you had to cram?"

The king blinked, then nodded. "I suppose that is an apt phrase for the book-learning I experienced. *Cram.*" He flicked an invisible speck from the rich silk of his doublet. "One of my tutors was Katherine, widow of my brother, Arthur. And when my father died, I was eighteen. Katherine was twenty-three. So I married her."

"Wait a second—you married your dead brother's wife?"

"Yes. Much to my regret, for God did not bless us with a living son. We were punished, you see. Punished for defying

God's will. It is against theological teachings for a man to marry his brother's wife. The marriage was annulled."

"How sad."

The king frowned. "Yes. It was sad indeed."

Deanie sensed that she should change the topic. "So how on earth did you learn to become such a wonderful king?"

He seemed to expand within the confines of the immense doublet. "Ah. I believe God touched me with greatness."

Deanie bit her lip, well aware that he was not jesting. In the corner of the room she heard the ping of one of the king's many clocks.

"Oh, Your Highness," she said, counting the strokes. Six. It was six, and Kit was waiting in the maze.

The king gave her a lazy grin. "Yes." There had been passion in her voice, and he liked the husky tone.

"I must—" She stood up, an idea hitting her. "I must visit the privy," she whispered anxiously.

The king straightened. "By all means, Mistress. Leave at once." A look of royal distaste crossed his face. He did not like to think of women having bodily functions. It was most upsetting.

With a quick curtsy, his hand waving her on, she exited the music salon, propelling herself faster than the heavy skirts were ever meant to move.

The earl of Surrey, Norfolk's son, waited for Hamilton to pass.

It had been a day of humiliation for Surrey. He had called for swordplay with Hamilton, well aware that the man's shoulder had been severely wounded. He feigned surprise and concern, trying to console Hamilton when Suffolk, that bloated fool, told of the injury.

Just as he'd expected, Hamilton said he could fight with his left hand. The ladies almost fell into a swoon of delight, and Surrey ground his teeth in an effort not to shout, to curse Hamilton. Who was he, after all? Who knew of his parentage? He appeared every inch the product of nobility, but his title had been bestowed by the king.

Surrey stood straighter, hoping his nose was not overly red. Springtime always made him sneeze.

He was going to defeat Hamilton. Before the court, before his father and Suffolk. Above all, before the ladies. Somehow, even his obvious good breeding and noble manners did little to attract the fair sex. Hamilton, rough and less dignified, seemed to have his pick.

How had it happened? How had Hamilton, wielding his sword with his left arm instead of the right, managed to defeat him twice? His ears burned with humiliation. Some of the ladies had laughed. Hamilton had not, merely offered his hand after the final bout. He took it, of course. Had to. But he had wiped it as soon as Hamilton and Suffolk left for supper.

Hamilton.

Surrey jumped. Someone was approaching. Perhaps if he just slit Hamilton's throat, all would be well. No. Not yet. There were too many people who'd witnessed the mortifying defeat of Surrey not to cast vile suspicion upon his fine name should anything happen to Hamilton.

"Kit?"

It was Mistress Deanie. Surrey licked his lips. She was a beautiful wench. How would Hamilton feel if another man took her, had his way with her, then tossed her aside like so much rubbish? Ha. It would be good to see Hamilton suffer. It would be good to take Mistress Deanie.

His father couldn't abide her. Of course, his father wanted his slut of a cousin Katherine Howard to become the next queen, to raise them all above their present noble position. They had survived Anne Boleyn, his other sluttish cousin. They would survive Katherine.

"Kit?"

The luscious Mistress Deanie was but half a dozen yards away. He could grab her, touch her fair—

"Deanie!"

Hamilton, curse his eyes, rounded the corner. Surrey backed away. *Another time.* He smiled in promise. Before he left the gardens, he blew Deanie a silent kiss.

They entered the maze at a slow pace. Should anyone be watching from the palace or happen upon the couple, they would appear to be enjoying the waning minutes of daylight.

"Calmly," Kit warned as he felt her tense. The Lady Longley and a red-faced groomsman emerged from behind a bush. "Good eve, Lady Longley." Kit smiled. Deanie merely showed her teeth.

Lady Longley nodded and walked swiftly toward the palace, the groom chasing after her.

Once within the maze, Deanie handed Kit the bottle. She had removed the flowers. It seemed stark and bare, the blackened peanuts rolling at the bottom.

"It is almost time." He squinted toward the sun. "Was this about where you were?"

"I'm not sure."

"Well, this is where I was standing, facing over there." His hand sliced the air, strong, decisive. He turned to her. "Are you all right? You are wearing a rather greenish complexion." He lifted up her chin.

In the light his eyes were extraordinary, the greens and browns battling, creating the magnificent shade of hazel. She pulled her gaze away, trying to think. It was impossible with Kit so close.

"Something's wrong," she said at last.

He held the bottle above his head, testing. His other hand gripped her upper arm.

A single shaft of light hit the glass, bouncing off in a blue light.

"Deanie . . ." he began, holding her tighter.

Suddenly she reached up and pulled the bottle from his hand. The blue light vanished immediately.

"What are you doing!" he shouted.

She shook her arm free. "Something's wrong, Kit. This isn't right."

With an explosive sigh he tried to grab the bottle back, but she jumped out of reach. "Goddamnit, Deanie."

Her mind raced, and she covered her face with an unsteady hand, trying to come up with an explanation for what was wrong. Kit stood so close she could feel his warmth. She stepped back even more, needing to think clearly without the distraction of his presence.

It came to her. "Anne!" She gasped. An awful dizziness swept through her, and she couldn't seem to think clearly.

He caught her as she stumbled backward. "Deanie, look at me," he asked, his flash of anger gone.

The sun set with one final burst of light.

Kit led her to one of the stone benches in the maze, and she sat beside him, not daring to come in contact with his body. Taking a shaky breath, she faced him. "What happens to Queen Anne?"

"For God's sake, Deanie, don't do that to me again." It was then she realized how shaken he was, taking great gulps of air and shooting her irritated looks.

"What happens to Queen Anne?" she repeated, beginning to feel better by the moment.

"So you want a history lesson?" he snapped. "Deanie, don't you remember the old schoolyard chant?"

"What schoolyard chant?"

"About Henry and his six wives. My sister taught it to me, so I would remember the order in which they came. What kind of education did you have?"

"A very bad one. Just tell me, Kit: What happens to Anne?"

His hand reached down and folded over hers. "It goes 'Divorced, beheaded, died; divorced, beheaded, survived.'"

Deanie began to count on her fingers. "Could you repeat that?"

He did, and she stopped on her fourth finger.

"Kit, Anne is his fourth wife," she said quietly.

"Yes."

"Henry will divorce her."

Kit nodded. "Cromwell will arrange an annulment."

"It's up to Cromwell?"

Again he nodded. "Deanie, what's wrong?"

"Cromwell," she said at last. "If we leave, I don't think Anne will just be divorced. Now that we're here, everything is different. Cromwell is furious, Kit. What if we somehow have changed history? Even worse, he's scared to death. Couldn't you tell the other day in your room? The man's at a breaking point."

Kit remained silent, and she continued.

"If we leave, who do you think will bear the brunt of his rage? He needs someone to blame—you know that better than I do. He'll take it out on Anne. She'll be his logical target. He'll be backed into a corner and see Anne as the reason. He'll make sure she's beheaded. It will be our fault!"

He said nothing for a few moments, then he raised her hand to his lips, brushing her knuckles with a kiss. "You're right, Deanie. But in truth there's nothing we can do."

"We can't let that happen." She snatched her hand away, but the warmth of his lips still lingered.

"Deanie, we can't possibly attempt to change the workings of the court."

"Why not?"

"For Christ's sake, don't be such a Yank." He kicked a pebble, then turned to her. "This is not Boston in the eighteenth century. There is no concept of democratic justice here, no way to enlighten their narrow beliefs. For all our purposes, we are in the Middle Ages. People are burned for witchcraft and sorcery. And much as it hurts your American notion of equality, women rank somewhere between a decent plough horse and a sturdy pair of boots."

"But . . ."

"Use your eyes and ears, Deanie," he continued. "How

183

the hell can we save a queen who was destined to fail by either death or divorce the moment Henry laid eyes on her?"

"She saved your life."

He was about to speak but halted.

"You just don't like her because she has a German accent," Deanie hissed, her eyes radiating such fury he straightened.

"Deanie, you're getting hysterical."

"The Germans lost, Kit. They lost the Second World War and lost it big time." She swallowed, trying to get herself under control. "Anne is not a Nazi, she's just some poor woman from Cleves with an ambitious family. And she nursed you with her own hands, did her very best to see that you survived. And how are we going to thank her? By letting her die?"

In the silence he looked to the sky, wondering if he had, indeed, condemned Anne for the sins of her countrymen, distant relatives who would not be born for another three and a half centuries. In fact, Anne herself would have no children. She would leave no one to rise against England in the faraway future.

"The sun is gone," he said mildly. "We can do nothing more tonight."

"You are wrong, Kit." Now she placed her hand within his. His fingers automatically folded over hers. "We can do something tonight. One person is more powerful than Cromwell. Henry. Perhaps if he likes his wife even a little, he wouldn't go along with Cromwell's plans so easily."

"It matters not how insane Cromwell's plans are, how unnecessarily vindictive. I've seen the king agree with Cromwell's plots simply because they suit the king's own desires. Now Henry wants Anne gone, and the king has a remarkable ability to deny any culpability, at least to himself. It's useless, Deanie."

"Maybe," she began, "we can make sure Anne keeps her

head. After all," she said softly, "without her, you wouldn't have my heart."

"Unfair." He groaned. Then with a sigh, he stood up. "Mistress Deanie, do you wish us to play matchmaker between the king and his wife?"

She nodded eagerly and stood alongside him, their hands still clasped.

"God help me, I believe I'm going to live to regret this." Kit tossed the bottle into the air, catching it easily with one hand. And together they walked back to the palace, both lost in their own thoughts.

Chapter 12

THE KING WAS IN BUOYANT SPIRITS AT THE EVENING BOARD. His face, flushed with wine and good humor, radiated a peculiar excitement. All present benefited from his joyous mood, from the lowliest page to Thomas Howard, the duke of Norfolk, whom many in the hall failed to recognize. He was wearing a most unfamiliar disguise: a pleasant expression. Several commented behind concealing hands that Norfolk should pull out the camouflage for the next royal mask, for no one would guess that behind the anemic but genuine smile was the most noble duke of Norfolk.

Even the presence of Queen Anne didn't seem to disturb the king's air of joviality. She sat quietly, slipping tiny bits of food into her mouth and trying not to bring undue attention to herself.

Kit was exhausted, saying little and eating even less.

"You should go to bed," Deanie whispered as Charles Brandon once again retold the tale of the duke of Hamilton beating young Surrey in the tilting yard.

Kit acted as if his attention were riveted on Suffolk's

every word, but from the corner of his mouth he was able to speak to her. "Not tonight, with Cromwell perched like a bird of prey. And until the king retires, I must play the part of dutiful subject."

"I'm sure the king would understand. He saw with his own eyes how sick you've been. Come on, Kit. I'll stay here and distract their attention from your absence."

"That's the problem." He leaned close to her ear. "I fear leaving you with the king and Queen Anne. Lord only knows what plans you have fermenting in that mind of yours."

"How much trouble could I get into in a single evening?"

"Please, Deanie." A slight smile deepened his cheeks as his thumb rubbed the rim of his goblet. "It seems the king has ordered mummers for this evening. I can always take a nap then."

"They're that boring?"

He raised his eyebrows, nodding halfheartedly at a woman who sat on the other side of the room, staring at Kit with an intense expression on her face. "The mummers give new meaning to the word *dull.*"

"Who is she?" Deanie asked of the woman.

The torchlight reflected off his hair as he faced her. "Ah. I see your plan now: You are going to keep me awake by interrogation. I believe such treatment violates the rules of the Geneva Convention."

"Seriously, Kit. She looks as if she's about to devour you with her eyes."

"I wouldn't put it past her," he mumbled.

A strange feeling knotted Deanie's stomach, and she straightened her back. The woman was still watching Kit, her lips parted slightly. Deanie suddenly averted her eyes to her lap, glancing at the ornate tufted bodice of her gown, idly tracing an embroidered flower with a finger.

Other women had stared at Kit with the same expression, a hazy, wanton quality. Earlier she had failed to notice how many feminine eyes batted as he passed, how their faces became still when they caught his attention. She had been in such a whirl herself, with new sights and smells and sounds at every turn, that it had never occurred to her that he was the center of much of the court's focus.

Her hand crept up over her bodice, and she felt her flesh beneath the canvas corset, so familiar, so confoundedly ordinary. She imagined Kit speaking to Suffolk, describing her body as they thrust with swords.

"She brings new meaning to the word *dull*."

Suffolk would chuckle with understanding.

"Deanie, do you feel ill?"

Jolted, she flushed when she realized Kit had been speaking to her. Katherine Howard and Cecily Garrison exchanged puzzled shrugs across the table.

"Have you ever been in love before?" she blurted, trying to lower her voice.

A stupefied expression spread across his face as he took in her words. The question seemed to come from nowhere, and he shook his head slightly in astonishment, mystified by her train of thought. "Yes," he answered at last, returning his attention to the goblet.

It hit Deanie what that unpleasant knot in her stomach was: jealousy. Never before had she experienced the tug of genuine envy. Sure, she had watched with awe as other women soared to the top of the charts with their songs or conquered a restless audience with a perfect set. But it had never touched her private life, never entered her relationships with men.

She was jealous.

"Were you in love with that woman over there?" It was as if she could no longer control her words, she so desperately needed to know.

"With Bessie Carpenter?"

Unable to speak, she merely nodded.

"Good God, no."

A strange sense of relief uncoiled within her, and she took a deep breath.

"I don't believe I could truly love a woman from here, from all this." His hand made a dismissive gesture, as if flicking the court into oblivion like a pesky fly. "Their minds baffle me, with too many absolutes, too many ideas taken for granted that I could never accept. I would have to counterfeit a life for myself, to play an endless role."

Lost in his own thoughts, he continued as if Deanie wasn't there. "To a certain extent, I've had to do just that: to construct a background. The thought of falling in love with a woman and having to play that role twenty-four hours a day, each day of the year, is ˜overwhelming. Can you imagine the burden? Relentless, crushing . . ." She watched his jaw clench. "No, Deanie," he concluded. "I could never love one of these court ladies."

He gave her a vague, amused smile.

"Who was she, then?" She knew she should quit while she was ahead, but some inner demon was pushing her forward. "The woman you were in love with?"

Crossing his arms gingerly because of the tender right shoulder, he regarded her, appraising the look of eagerness on her face. "It was nothing, years ago. Certainly not a grand passion. More of a schoolboy crush, really."

Her mouth dropped involuntarily, and she closed it as soon as possible. Of course she had always heard rumors about British men, about those remote boys' boarding schools where that sort of thing went on. She had watched enough "Masterpiece Theatre" episodes to recognize his upper-crust accent. Still, she was taken off guard by his admission.

She sat straighter, trying to act as nonchalant as possible. "Oh, I see. What was his name?"

Kit turned to her, a look of total bewilderment on his face. "What was whose name?"

"The schoolboy you had a crush on."

For a moment he said nothing. Then a dawning understanding lit his gaze. "You mean you think I . . ."

"It's okay, Kit." She pressed a sympathetic hand upon his

forearm. "I'm in show business. That sort of thing goes on all the time."

"Deanie, I was engaged to be married once. We thought we were in love; she was my friend's younger sister. She was not, it seems, my one grand passion."

Something seemed familiar about the last phrase, but Deanie ignored it. For the next several moments the great hall of Hampton Court, presently occupied by the most resplendently powerful men in England, rang with the raucous timbre of the duke of Hamilton's laughter.

The idea was so simple, she was almost ashamed not to have come up with it before.

It was after Kit had stopped laughing, when he finally caught his breath and explained that he had been in love with the younger sister of one of his Oxford chums, that the notion came to her as swiftly and as powerfully as a summertime storm.

The queen's man Englebert, watching with wary glances as Cromwell slipped from the hall, had brought the queen a platter of sweets. The king had his back to her, raising a goblet of wine to Katherine Howard. Something caused him to spin about, to face Englebert. It was the fragrance of sweets. The king would toast Katherine Howard only after his craving for something sugary had been satisfied.

Doughnuts.

The king would go crazy over doughnuts. Deanie had a sudden vision of King Henry VIII stepping into a Krispy Kream, raising a chubby royal finger, and buying the entire stock. Glazed, chocolate frosteds, jelly-filleds, bismarks, crullers—the man would have a field day.

Deanie knew how to make doughnuts, and the king would love them. If the king received doughnuts from Queen Anne, his exuberance over every bite might very well spill over to her. She may not be able to win the king's heart, but she could most certainly lay claim to his stomach. And with Henry, both were equally vital to his happiness.

Surely he would not behead a source of doughnuts.

Just as Deanie was about to tell Kit of her plan, the mummers began to perform. The king had apparently signaled them to begin, although she had not seen him issue the command.

Unable to speak because of the floor show, Deanie watched the half dozen mummers go through their slow-motion routine, pausing as they fell into each pose. They wore brightly colored robes, all with face-concealing hoods. There seemed to be some order to what they were doing, although to Deanie they just seemed to be striking random positions.

She slid Kit a look of understanding and saw his lips tighten in an effort not to grin. The mime's old trick of the glass wall or the steps to the basement would be a welcome relief.

Then an even more brilliant idea came to her. While all eyes were focused on the mummers, she could sneak into the kitchen with Scholsenberg, Anne's cook, and explain how to make doughnuts. The basic dough was simple, and similar to the batter they already used. The king was in such a uniquely good mood, it would be a shame to pass up this chance. Who knew when the capricious royal temper would again be so accommodating?

She rose slowly to her feet, careful not to call attention to herself. Kit clamped a firm hand over her wrist and began to stand, but she shook her head and, with an embarrassed shrug, nodded toward the door leading down the hall to the privy.

As she left the feast alone, three alert sets of eyes scrutinized her every step.

One belonged to Kit. Another belonged to the king, who wondered why all women seemed to spend an inordinate amount of time traveling to and from the privy.

The third belonged to a gentleman of the court who deemed it his new duty to follow the Bailey wench wherever she might go. He was clever. While everyone else watched her departure, he crept in the opposite direction, slipping through the door on one side of the hall—by the king's watching chamber—while Mistress Bailey left through the main door.

No one noticed his quiet exit.

In three weeks since she'd arrived at Hampton, Deanie had finally learned not to instinctively reach for a light switch whenever she entered a room. Katherine Howard had once caught her groping along a wall, and she had blushed, explaining that in Wales even the finest paneling could not compare to the excellence of the royal walls.

Before three weeks ago, she had never paused to think of the difference that bright, even lighting made to a room. Without the luxury of a lightbulb, nighttime corridors and empty rooms become darkly mysterious, places where shadows flutter and flinch.

The minstrels below were playing an unfamiliar tune. Deanie supposed it was one of the king's more recent compositions. He had a fairly good ear, but he would never make it on Music Row. As she swept through the hallway, she had another mental image of Henry in twentieth-century Nashville, this time with a secondhand tape-recorder, his demo tapes being cut off by an impatient producer after fifteen seconds.

She could imagine his crimson-and-purple fury, ordering the offending producer to the block. Most producers would simply yawn and wish Henry good luck at another label.

That's when she realized she was lost.

Everything was suddenly silent; the minstrels had either stopped playing or she had gone beyond earshot. There were so many hundreds of rooms she had never been near, even during her quick pass-through searching for Kit, that she hadn't the faintest idea which wing she had entered.

Trying to squelch the sudden urge to yell for help, she backtracked to where she had just been and peeked through an open chamber door. Could she recall a room with a single torcher and a tapestry of St. Sebastian? Nothing seemed familiar.

Just as she began down the hall again, she had the distinct impression that she was being followed. She stopped short, but there were no other sounds. It was clearly just her imagination.

She turned down another hall and gasped, her hand flying to her throat. This particular hall was indeed familiar— from the original tour she took with the crew before the first day of shooting the video. The guide had said the hall was haunted by the ghost of a woman. Yet Deanie couldn't remember the ghost's name. Blast, why hadn't she paid more attention? For all she recollected, it could be Deanie herself who would haunt the corridor for the next five centuries.

Again she stopped, and this time there was a brief *whoosh* behind her. She *was* being followed.

"Hello?"

As soon as she spoke she realized how ridiculous she sounded. What did she expect, a ghost to step from the shadows and introduce itself? Or some evildoer to bow and explain why he was following her into the dark reaches of the palace?

Picking up her pace, she walked briskly toward yet another hallway, not even bothering to look into rooms as she passed. Her throat was parched with fright, but she ignored the discomfort. Behind her she felt someone else mirroring her every move, faster or slower as she made her way to a large double door.

Just before she was able to reach for a huge circular doorknob, a hand pressed over her mouth.

"Be still, mistress." The voice was unfamiliar. A man pinned her to his body, tall and thin against her shoulder blades.

With a sharp jab, she elbowed his side. He groaned but did not let her loose. Instead he tightened his grip. "That was not wise."

Her arms were now held back at a painful angle. She bit down on his hand with all her might. He spat out a startled curse, and she used his momentary shock to escape.

Taking two steps in blind, animal panic, she made for the large door just beyond her reach. She slammed the door behind her, her hands shaking, searching in the dim light for a lock. There was none.

Her pursuer yanked on the door from the other side. Using all her strength and the leverage of her weight, she kept the door pulled shut. With a frantic glance over her shoulder, she saw a tapestry-covered table and a high-backed chair. Upon the table was a single thick candle, its wax dripping freely over the needlework. The rest of the chamber was cloaked in shadows.

Stretching out her foot while still holding on to the doorknob, she pulled the chair to her side and jammed it at an angle beneath the doorknob. She knew it wouldn't hold for more than a few seconds and immediately dashed for the table, ducking under the tapestry and praying that it wasn't a chest of drawers—and that she didn't tip over the candle and set the whole palace ablaze. Although at that moment a roaring, out-of-control fire offered her more safety than cowering under a table in a dead-end room.

The table was, indeed, just a table, and there was plenty of room for her to hide. Just as she heard the chair crash to the planked floor, she pulled the train of her gown farther under the table and tried to still her ragged breathing.

"I know you are in here."

There was a triumphant sneer to his words. Deanie tried to identify her assailant but could not.

"Ah, methinks my beautious prey is hiding." He gave a sharp, unpleasant chuckle. "Perchance under the chair? No. No room there. I espy a table. The flame yet quivers atop, as if some unknown personage disturbed its glow."

Deanie was about to speak, to crawl out before he plunged a sword into the tapestry. Just as she pulled the tapestry aside, another voice pierced the air.

"Leave."

It was a single command, barked with authority.

"Who goes?" Her assailant's tone was unsure.

"Thomas Cromwell, earl of Essex." Deanie had known who the third person was before he identified himself. His voice was etched forever in her most vivid nightmares. "Be that young Surrey? Sheath your weapon, pup."

Deanie's mind reeled. Surrey? Henry Howard, Katherine's cousin and Norfolk's scrawny son? She sank against the wall, her hand over her mouth. Why would Surrey want to follow her?

"Cromwell." Surrey was growing bolder by the minute. "Are you again hiding in disgrace? The true peers are below, with the king."

"That explains your presence here then." Cromwell used the same mild tone he had used with Deanie.

"Why you upstart cur!" Surrey sputtered his anger. "You have nary a drop of noble blood in your coarse veins! You . . . you . . ."

"Yes, Surrey?" Cromwell paused. "Do I detect a slight impediment in your speech? Too much blue blood breeds imperfections. Such as your stuttering tongue. And your comical swordplay."

"No!"

"You may leave, Surrey. Now. Before I call for my men."

Deanie could imagine the mortified expression on the younger man's face.

"You will soon be felled, Cromwell," spat Surrey with a final rush of bravado. She then heard the heavy door open and slam shut. In his blast of shame, Surrey had forgotten Deanie, still huddled beneath the table.

She remained still, waiting for Cromwell to leave, hoping he had somehow remained ignorant of her presence. If the chamber was divided by a screen, or perhaps a small antechamber, Cromwell might believe the earlier scuffling to have been Surrey alone.

"You may come out now, Mistress Deanie."

Now real fear gripped her. Surrey was an unknown quantity. With Cromwell, she knew the danger she was in, the violence of which he was capable. He had already caused Kit's agonizing wound with the simple lift of a finger. She remained silent, the terror causing her limbs to stay motionless.

"Come come, mistress. You have nothing to fear."

"Yeah, right," she muttered aloud.

"I will repeat my request one more time. Remove yourself from this ridiculous position immediately. Or perhaps you would like one of my men to assist you."

In an instant she crawled from under the table, her headpiece catching on the leg, her knees tangling in the yards of fabric of both the tapestry and her gown. With an annoyed sigh, Cromwell held the tapestry still as she struggled to her feet.

For a moment they said nothing to each other. Deanie stared at him, aware how very vulnerable she was, and also aware how vulnerable Kit was down below. She hoped he hadn't noticed Cromwell's absence from the hall, silently prayed he was not at this very moment searching for her.

"What were you doing?" Cromwell asked simply.

Deanie blinked. The calm manner of his question both surprised and alarmed her.

"Excuse me?"

"There is a banquet below, as usual. The king is there, as usual." Cromwell straightened. "Lest you forget, we have a bargain, mistress. What are you doing creeping through the halls?"

Crossing her arms and stalling for time, she tried to think of an answer. Something that wouldn't lead to even more trouble for both herself and Kit. Then it hit her: the truth. There was nothing wrong with where she had been going, or why.

"I was trying to find the kitchen," she said at last.

"The kitchen?"

She nodded. "I know how to make something the king

would like. They're called doughnuts, and I'm sure he would love them."

"Where is Hamilton?"

"He's below, watching those awful mummers."

"And he allowed you to go unescorted into the kitchen?"

"No," she admitted, shaking her head. "He thinks I went to the privy. The idea just hit me downstairs. I saw the king turn his attention from Katherine Howard to a tray of sweets and realized how much the king would enjoy doughnuts. So I decided to sneak down to the kitchen to tell Scholsenberg all about—"

"Scholsenberg?"

"Oh, the queen's cook. Anyway, I just thought—"

Cromwell held up a hand to stop her. "I see." Slowly he turned his eyes to the single candle, one finger tapping in the air as if an entity of its own. He did not seem to be aware of Deanie. For the moment he was in a solitude imposed by his own thoughts.

Deanie did not like the silence. Cromwell's efficient mind, spinning mayhem with just such malignant concentration, had created far too many disasters.

"May I ask you a question?" Deanie rushed.

He seemed startled and fixed his attention on her face. With a brisk nod, he signaled her to speak.

"These last few days, well, you've pretty much left us alone. You almost killed Kit last week, but you've stayed clear since then."

There was no indication on Cromwell's bland, flat face that her words had penetrated. He continued staring at her before answering.

"Would you prefer I complete the task?" He spoke softly.

"No!" She gasped. "We just don't know what to expect, and it's driving us crazy."

Cromwell lunged toward Deanie, his black eyes glinting. She was about to scream when his arm glided past her and gripped the candle on the tapestry-covered table.

"Come here, mistress." For the first time there was no malice in his voice, no threat behind each syllable.

He led her to the back of the chamber. The candle cast a yellow circle of light on the furnishings as they walked. She realized she had stumbled upon his private chambers, his personal lair where he attended to business, both state and personal.

There was a massive desk covered with parchments. Holding the candle, not looking at her, he gestured toward the stacks of thick paper, the bottles of ink and bundle of quills. There was a heavy seal made of either brass or gold and a shaker. She knew the silver shaker was full of sand to blot ink dry.

"These documents will both annul the king's marriage and lead Queen Anne to the block. They are almost complete, lacking but a handful of easily purchased signatures."

Deanie was unable to speak, and Cromwell continued. "Within the past several days there had been a certain— well, thawing of the king's treatment of the queen. My men say it began when you told him how kind the queen had been to Hamilton, how she nursed him with her own hands."

"It's true."

"She is not becoming a demanding shrew, as Kathrine of Aragon and Anne Boleyn so foolishly became." Finally he looked at her. "I care not who is the queen, as long as the king is content and my own position is secure."

"You mean it doesn't matter whether it's Anne or Katherine Howard or me?" She tried to keep the excitement from her voice.

"Nay, I did not say that. Should Katherine Howard be mistress or queen, I shall be destroyed. And mark my words, I will take you and Hamilton and Queen Anne with me." He glared at her in the darkness. "If you can persuade the king to dislike the queen a little less, it will be well for all of us."

She was about to ask him another question, to explain what he meant, when he waved her off. "Go now. Go in haste and make the king a most pleasant treat."

Now was not the time to press the issue. She all but ran from the room, holding her train in one hand, the other stretched out in the pitch-black air, hoping to stop herself from colliding with a wall or a piece of furniture. Just before she reached the door, she halted.

"Excuse me, Mr. Cromwell?"

There was silence, then an irritated response. "Yes?"

"How do I get to the kitchen?"

A strange sound erupted from the direction of Cromwell. Deanie realized it was a laugh—a dry, humorless laugh. A shiver traced down her spine. Even while laughing, the man gave her the creeps. "Down the corridor, to the left. Follow the scent from there."

"Thank you," she hazarded.

There was no response. She ran from the earl of Essex as quickly as her feet could carry her.

Cecily Garrison returned to the Great Hall, pausing only to curtsy to her sovereign and his wife. She went directly to the duke of Hamilton, who was waiting for her report.

"Did you find her?"

Kit was uncharacteristically anxious. The same man who had coolly faced mortal danger in the skies over England, who had just that afternoon risked his well-deserved reputation as an unparalleled swordsman by engaging in a brutal match with Surrey—a lesser opponent but a healthy one—was showing distinct signs of worry. And the reason?

The failure of his cousin to return from the privy.

"Nay, I did not," she responded.

Kit began to rise, not bothering to be charming to Mistress Cecily or, for that matter, to anyone in the court. Just as he began to bolt to the passageway, his left hand hovering over the hilt of the sword, he slammed into the figure of a woman who seemed to appear out of nowhere.

"Kit!" she breathed.

"Deanie, for God's sake, where have you been?"

The mild commotion the pair created was quickly up-staged by the queen's tumbler, performing a duet with the three-legged brown bear.

With a firm grip he pulled her to their place on the bench. Once settled, she turned a dazzling smile on him. "You'll never guess what just happened!"

"I'll tell you." He spoke with his teeth clenched, the color on his face high. "I almost charged through the halls, sword drawn, searching for you. Didn't I ask you not to disappear again? Didn't I ask you, just this morning?" At last he took a deep breath and looked at her.

Her eyes grew large, her complete attention focused on him. All his anger seemed to evaporate as he took in the sight of her. He realized he was still clutching her arm, and with a gentle squeeze he released her.

"There is something white on your nose," he said softly, reaching out and brushing a dusting of powder from the bridge of her nose.

"Oh, that's flour." She rubbed the remaining flour from her nose, leaving it reddened. Kit could not help but smile.

"Look! Look at the king!" she whispered. She was about to tell him about her meeting with Cromwell but decided to wait until he had calmed down.

"Why?"

"Just watch."

On the dais, Englebert, bowing humbly, presented the king with a large golden platter filled with round clumps of pastry. The queen, peering nervously over his shoulder, saw the contents of the platter. For a moment her face was blank; then, as a slow smile eased her features, she turned her eyes to Deanie.

"What is this?" the king's voice boomed. Then he looked closer. His jeweled hand immediately grasped one of the objects. He sniffed it once like a suspicious dog, then took a large bite, his small teeth gnashing in mechanical speed.

Then the motions slowed, and across the hall Deanie held her breath, her hand closing over Kit's forearm.

The king turned to the queen, his mouth still full. "From you?" He pointed an accusing finger—the one not holding the pastry—at Queen Anne.

Her face momentarily fell, and she nodded. *"Ja.* They are called *doo-nuts."*

The king stared, still chewing furiously. And then he grinned, his red beard sticky with honey. "My queen! Excellent!" He reached for another glazed doughnut, gesturing for others to join him. Finally, like a precious gift, he offered the last one to Queen Anne.

Englebert beamed.

Kit began to laugh. "You made doughnuts for King Henry?"

Deanie nodded. "I wanted to make sugar-coated, but did you know they don't have regular sugar here? I had to use honey instead."

"You would fit right in with the NAAFI women." He chuckled, wrapping his arm briefly about her shoulders.

"The *what* women?"

He leaned closer. "They brought tea and biscuits to the pilots, ladies with aprons and those marvelous cigarettes."

"Like the USO," she murmured, enjoying the weight and warmth of his arm. "Wait a minute: You said *cigarettes.* Do you mean to tell me that you made me explain what they were, making me feel like an absolute idiot, and all along you used to smoke?"

He raised his lush eyebrows and grinned. "Like a chimney."

"Kit, tell me: When will I forget about cigarettes? I mean, if we end up here, or in a time without tobacco, when will I stop thinking about them?"

Just then Englebert passed a tray of doughnuts, and Kit took two, handing one to Deanie. "Please, Kit," she pleaded, kneading his sleeve. "When will I get over it?"

With deliberate languor he took a bite of a doughnut,

nodding in agreement with the king's appraisal. When he swallowed, his face became grave. "I'll tell you this much," he whispered. "The first ten years are the hardest."

Her face fell tragically. And for the second time that evening, the great hall was filled with the laughter of the duke of Hamilton.

Chapter 13

THE NEXT DAY KIT AND DEANIE WERE FORCED TO WAIT UNTIL long after the fast was broken to speak. The night before, she had been able to give him the gist of her exchange with Cromwell, noting the quietly puzzling change in his behavior.

"Now he's even more dangerous," Kit concluded. "He knows that if the king marries Katherine, he's finished."

"Why?" Deanie asked as they left the hall. Before speaking she made sure no one was listening, pressing against his arm as they walked. "She seems nice enough. No rocket scientist, but a sweet kid."

Kit laughed then. "The very idea of Katherine Howard as a scientist . . ." He shook his head. "But it's not Katherine who threatens Cromwell—it's her family. They're every bit as ambitious as your Wallis Simpson."

"I don't have a Wallis Simpson."

"You know, the divorced Yank who married our Edward." When she still seemed perplexed, he halted and coaxed her into a corner with a gentle nudge. "Please,

Deanie. Don't tell me you have no idea who I'm taking about."

"I have no idea who you're talking about," she confessed.

"The famous 'woman I love' speech?"

Deanie's face lit with understanding. "Oh, I *do* remember! There was a made-for-TV movie all about it. She was a Baltimore divorcee, and Edward abdicated the crown for her. It was wonderful! I think Jane Seymour played her in the movie."

"Jane Seymour?"

"Not the queen. This Jane was in James Bond films, then went on to become Dr. Quinn on television."

Kit shook his head and raked a hand through his hair before continuing. "Anyway, our little Katherine has a pushy uncle and an even more pushy flock of Catholic supporters. They're still smarting from Cromwell's dissolution of the monasteries. If Katherine becomes queen, as indeed she shall, Cromwell will be left alone, bearing the wrath of Henry and Norfolk and every Catholic in the land."

"Doesn't Cromwell have any supporters?"

Kit made a dismissive gesture with his hand. "He has never been known for his personal magnetism. Cromwell's biggest talent has been to make himself indispensable to the king, never trusting anyone else enough to share the power. At this point he's already alienated all his potential defenders. He's always acted alone and never bothered to build a political force behind him. It worked for a while, but . . ."

Kit stopped talking as Norfolk approached and acknowledged them with a curt nod. Now that the king had been taking an active interest in his niece, he seemed to expand within his office, gaining momentum with every leering twinkle the king bestowed upon Katherine.

Just as they were about to continue their discussion in the corridor, the evening ended abruptly with Deanie and the other ladies-in-waiting escorting Queen Anne to her bedchamber. There wasn't time for her to mention the run-in with Surrey.

She spent the next morning in a frustrating attempt to learn needlepoint from the wasp-tongued Mother Lowe. Meanwhile, Kit passed the hours with Suffolk and the other gentlemen, planning a tournament to celebrate the coming of summer. He found her in her chamber, back turned toward the door, dabbing her fingertips with a cloth. The halls were unusually silent. Most of the members of the court were admiring the king's new bowling alley below.

"It's raining," Kit announced from the doorway. His arm was raised over his head, gripping the archway with casual strength as he leaned into her room. The pain in his shoulder was still intense, but he was determined to defy it, refusing to admit to any limitations. "We have to wait until the weather clears before we can try the maze again."

"Good," Deanie said, her back turned toward Kit.

"Good?"

"That gives us more time to work with Queen Anne. After those papers Cromwell showed me, I hope we have weeks of rain. It's going to take a lot of time to ensure her safety, Kit."

"I thought you were pleased with how well the doughnuts worked," he said to her back.

"Six dozen doughnuts do not a marriage make."

Kit frowned. "What the hell is that supposed to mean?"

"It just means we need more time—lots of time to help the king appreciate his queen."

"We don't have a lot of time, love." He lowered his voice. "The longer we remain here, the more likely we are to be brought up on charges of witchcraft or treason."

"You've managed to avoid that problem nicely for more than a decade," she reasoned without facing him.

"That was before you arrived. On my own, I was fine. You're the wild card—everything's changed. What on earth are you doing?"

She paused and looked straight ahead. "Is it good or bad that everything's changed?"

"Mostly good." There was a smile in his voice. "Mostly wonderful; just those treason or witchcraft threats to make us skiddish."

"I wonder what would be worse," she mused. "I mean, between treason or witchcraft."

With a light chuckle he shifted his weight. "Given a choice, I believe I'd opt for witchcraft. You might get lucky and have your fire put out by rain. There's not much hope with being hanged, drawn, and quartered."

"All three?" She stiffened. "Isn't that overkill?"

"That's the general idea. Why, they make sure the poor sod is still awake to watch himself get disemboweled. Say, Deanie, what are you doing?"

Deanie turned and held up her left hand. Even from across the room he could see the tiny rivulets of blood.

"Good God, what happened?" He reached her side in a few long strides.

"I tried my hand at needlepoint." She sighed. "It looks so easy, Kit. The ladies just hanging around, chatting up a storm and sewing. But those needles are sharp, and Mother Lowe made me finish the sample."

As he examined her wounded fingertips, she reached for her small sample of needlework. With obvious disgust, she held it before his eyes.

"It's okay. You can laugh if you want," she muttered.

Kit transferred his attention to the little square of cloth. "Oh. Well. I say, Deanie, it's really very good. Jolly good indeed." He squinted, leaning closer, then averted his eyes, complete befuddlement apparent on his strong features.

"Do you know what it is?" A smile tugged at the corners of her mouth.

"What? Well of course I do. I'm not a complete idiot. Hmm, let me see." He focused again on her fingertips. "A little iodine would be welcome now."

"What is it?"

"Iodine? Why, it's an orange-colored medicine to kill germs."

"I know what iodine is, Kit. I'm asking if you know what my needlepoint is supposed to be."

"Oh, that."

She nodded solemnly.

"Well, let's just take another look, shall we?" His voice was artificially cheerful. "My, what colors! Really, it's quite astounding, Deanie. Look at your spectacular use of red."

"Red? I didn't use any red." Looking closer at the cloth, she bit the inside of her cheek to stop from giggling. "That's blood," she said finally. "Mother Lowe wouldn't let me use a thimble."

"Oh. I see. Well it works very well, doesn't it?"

"Never mind the colors, Kit. Tell me what it is."

"Come now, Deanie. Of course I know what it is."

"Then tell me," she insisted.

The dimples in his cheeks deepened in concentration. At once his expression brightened. "Why of course! It's a bug!"

She shook her head.

"A bird? Those are wings, are they not?"

Raising her eyebrows, she crossed her arms and tapped an impatient foot.

"You are not going to help me out, are you?"

Again she shook her head, this time unable to keep the mischievous grin from her face.

"Very well. It seems to be some creature from mythology, perhaps a phoenix rising from its ashes. No? Let me see. Hallo! Is that a man inside the neck of the creature?"

She nodded eagerly.

"Charades it is, then." Clearing his throat, he looked at Deanie, the expectant, eager smile on her face. And he realized what she had done.

"Deanie." His voice was suddenly rough as he turned the sample on its side. For a long moment he said nothing, just examined her clumsy attempt at needlepoint, the wild

207

shape with a lopsided hump on the top. His unwavering gaze slid to her face. "It's an aeroplane."

"Bingo."

He swallowed hard before he returned to the needlework, wondering why he felt a sudden ache in his throat. She had made it for him, for him alone. He tried to keep his tone easy, tried not to show how touched he was by the gesture. "What kind of plane is it?" His words sounded harsh and accusing, but Deanie didn't seem to mind.

"Oh, I don't know." She shrugged. "I sort of made it up. I mean, on the road I've seen tons of old war movies. It's hard to get right to sleep after a concert. So I just closed my eyes and tried to remember what the planes looked like in this old film with Dana Andrews. I kept on waiting for a woman to appear the first time I saw it, since I thought 'Dana' had to be a lady." Realizing she was chattering to cover his silence, she peered down at the cloth, suddenly embarrassed. "Do you like it?"

When she looked into his eyes, she caught a strange, unsettling flash before he spoke. "Yes," he said at last, pulling her slowly toward him with one arm, still examining the work in the other hand. "May I keep it?"

"Sure. I did it for you."

Unlacing the front tie of his black doublet, he slipped the piece within his full white shirt. The peculiar expression was still on his face.

"Deanie, was that one of our planes, or an enemy aircraft?"

Confused, she looked up at him as he led her through the door. "One of ours. Why?"

"Just wondering," he murmured, taking her hand. He paused, then drew her needle-pricked fingertips to his lips and pressed them with a warm kiss. "Now, are you *positive* we won the war?"

"Very funny," she whispered. But at that moment, the last thing either of them had on their minds was the war.

* * *

Queen Anne summoned Mistress Deanie to her chamber an hour before the evening meal was to be served. The rain still poured against the windows, making the palace seem more damp and chilly than usual.

"Mistress Deanie." The queen smiled as soon as Deanie curtsied. "Those *doo-nuts* last evening, I must say thank you for to bring them. The king, he sure thought they were okay."

Deanie raised her eyes and grinned. "He sure wolfed them down, didn't he, Your Majesty."

"I do believe he eat four or five in one wolf." The queen made a motion for Deanie to rise and gestured to a chair. "Come, sit. I need to chew off your ear."

"Excuse me?"

"I need to talk, to chew off your ear." Ignoring the bewildered frown on Deanie's face, the queen swept past her and returned with an official-looking parchment. For an awful moment Deanie thought Cromwell had served her with the orders of execution. She quickly dismissed the thought with a sigh of relief. The queen was preoccupied with something, but she did not seem to be in mortal fear.

"Read this, may it please you," the queen said, handing Deanie the paper.

It was written in a beautiful hand, one more legible than most of the samples she had seen since arriving in 1540. Deanie whistled through her teeth. "Very nice, Your Majesty. Whoever did this could work calligraphy at any gift shop or make a fortune writing names on diplomas."

The queen pointed with one flat-nailed finger. "Read it, please."

Deanie shrugged her shoulders once and began to read.

"Permit me to show, by this billet, the zeal with which I devote my respect to you as a queen, and my entire obedience to you as my mother. I am too young and feeble to have power to do more than felicitate you with all my heart in this commencement of your marriage. I

209

hope that Your Majesty will have as much goodwill for me as I have zeal for your service."

Perplexed, she looked up at the queen. "Wait a minute: I didn't know you had any kids," she said. "Whoever wrote this calls you his or her mother."

Queen Anne nodded. "'Tis my stepdaughter, the child of my husband, the king."

"Oh." Deanie frowned over the paper. "How old is she?"

"Six."

"What? You mean a kid of six wrote this herself?"

The queen gave a half smile. "She seems to be one smart cookie, no?"

Deanie nodded in agreement, her eyes again reading the princess' words. "Where is she?" she asked without looking up. "I haven't seen her at court. I haven't even seen the little prince. He's guarded like some sort of prisoner."

"He's the king's heir, next in line to the throne. The king must be careful with his only son."

"The princess is also the king's heir, Your Majesty. Why isn't she at court?"

The queen looked satisfied by her response. "That is what I am riled up about, mistress. Doesn't it seem to you that the little Princess Elizabeth should be here?"

The parchment rested in Deanie's lap. "Of course. Where is she?"

"Banished to another palace. The king seems to hate her and will not allow her to reside in his presence."

"Why on earth does he hate her? She's just a kid," Deanie mumbled. The image of an eager, bright six-year-old, unwanted by her father, flamed her own memories of childhood. "I'm a little hazy on all this, but who's her mother?"

The queen seemed taken aback. "Why, her mother was Anne Boleyn, executed over three years ago by the king."

"Holy cow! The kid was three years old when it happened."

With a wary glance toward the door, the queen crept over, peering down the outside hall before she closed it. She spoke in a hushed tone. "I showed the king this letter, hoping he would feel pity for his little kid. I even had my cook make some more *doo-nuts* before I spoke."

"So what happened?" Deanie's head was next to the queen's. Up close she was momentarily distracted by both her large pores and the now-familiar scent, thick and mucky but not as unpleasant as it used to seem.

"He became angry, Mistress Deanie. He swore some curses, I know not the meaning of some of the phrases. He told me to go hence, away from him, and that the mother of Princess Elizabeth was but a whore."

Deanie involuntarily flinched, imagining the king's rage. "So he won't allow her to join the rest of her family at court," she said quietly.

"No. He has further instructed me to give this letter to Cromwell, who is then to answer nay."

"Great. Cromwell would make any six-year-old girl one swell pen pal."

The queen seem surprised. "Think you that?"

"No, Your Majesty," Deanie said at last. "I think this is terrible." Glancing back at the paper, she noticed a tiny figure drawn in the corner. It was a little girl's sketch of a flower, so small it was easy to miss, a tentative plea for friendship from a lonely child.

"Has Cromwell seen this yet?" Deanie could imagine his glee, striking out at the innocent child of his tormentor.

"No. Mistress Deanie, I have no influence with the king. You do. Can you think of anything to help this poor little princess?"

Deanie clenched her hand over the letter, wondering if the kind queen, begging help for a child she had never met, knew of the danger she herself faced. There was something in the queen's dark eyes that made Deanie believe she was very much aware of the hazards of the court.

"Your Majesty, could you give me a little time to think?" She rubbed a hand over her forehead, trying to imagine what ideas Kit might have.

"But of course." The queen smiled and rose to her feet, gently lifting the letter from Deanie's lap. "Perhaps at the evening meal we may speak again."

Wearily, she nodded. As she left the queen's chamber, she wondered where she might find Kit. He would most certainly be able to come up with a brilliant plan.

"You promised her what?" Kit demanded, breathing hard after a fencing match. The tip of his foil rested on the ground next to her foot, and she backed away slightly. With a distracted hand he rubbed his sore shoulder.

"I just told her we would try to help," Deanie repeated. The sound of clashing metal echoed in the fencing chamber. In the far corner was Surrey, glaring at her from under a cumbersome screened helmet. His father insisted he wear the protection, much to his embarrassment. None of the accomplished swordsmen had requested a match with him, further fueling his fury.

"If the rains cease on the morrow, we must try to leave," he said in a soothing tone.

"No, Kit. I really want to stay here and help, now more than ever."

"Don't you understand? We have no choice." He took a deep breath and looked about the room. The ladies had just been admitted: a prime opportunity for the young men of the court to show off their athletic skills. The men were without their doublets, much to the titillated delight of the women.

Even in her concern for the princess, Deanie couldn't help but notice how superior Kit was to the rest of the gentlemen. Some were attractive, a few had rather nice physiques. But the duke of Hamilton, his handsome face flushed from exercise, the dark hair curled at the nape of his neck, was extraordinary.

"Please, Kit. You should see the letter. Honestly, it broke my heart."

"Your concern for others is admirable, love." He wiped a droplet of perspiration from his eyes. "Save some of that concern for us. Even as we stand here and talk, we are placing ourselves in peril. We will try to leave tomorrow, and then all of these intrigues will hopefully be distant history."

He turned and walked to a corner of the chamber, nodding to a cluster of ladies as he placed his foil in the rack on the wall. Arms folded, she followed him, trying to control her anger, ducking beneath an earl's raised foil as she crossed the floor.

"I don't care if you refuse to help me," she hissed into his ear. Startled, he turned, stunned by the unfamiliar vehemence in her voice. "You have no idea what it's like to know your own father doesn't give a hoot what happens to you, if you're sick or well or smart or stupid. You were a rich kid, with a stable family."

"My father was killed in the war when I was a child."

"I know, and that's awful, it really is. But at least he didn't leave on purpose, letting you spend the rest of your life wondering what you did wrong, what you could have possibly done to make him leave." The tears made her vision blurry, but she continued. "And at least you and I had our moms, and you had a sister. Who does Elizabeth have? She's all alone, all by herself, writing letters to strangers and asking them to be her mother. Oh, Kit. The poor kid."

"Perhaps the 'poor kid' needs to be treated thusly. She may not be a giddy child, but she will grow up to be a magnificent queen, one who will have the backbone to keep Spain at bay. Leave her alone, Deanie."

"Okay, so she'll be a magnificent queen," Deanie countered, her voice rising. "Maybe she'll be even more magnificent if she can have a happier childhood."

"And maybe her unhappy childhood is the key to a great

queen." Other courtiers had hushed, trying to make sense of the strange exchange between the two. But even the nearest gentleman could not make head nor tails of their conversation. All there knew, however, that they were witnessing a scene full of passion.

"I'd rather give the kid a hand," she spat. Then with a deep breath she continued, trying to calm herself. "Please, Kit."

"Deanie." His voice was rough as he put out a hand to steady her. "Love," he said softly, "helping Elizabeth won't do a jot for your own childhood."

Deanie stared ahead, not really seeing. "I don't know, Kit. Something about this letter has really gotten to me. Maybe . . ."

"Maybe what, Deanie?"

"Maybe I want a child of my own," she breathed. "A child of ours, who will never worry about where her parents are, or if they love her. I've never felt this, never."

Wordlessly, he brushed the tears from her cheeks, wanting very much to hold her but fully aware that the most proficient court gossips had already taken note of their conversation.

"If all goes well in the maze, we will have that chance. Only then. Otherwise, we will never have our turn."

"Kit, please. What if something happens to us in the maze, if we're separated or killed? We both know that's a very real possibility. And if that happens, what will we leave behind as a legacy? A recipe for doughnuts? A spectacular jousting record? That's not much, Kit. But if we can make a little girl happy, a future queen. And then also help a generous woman, someone who is just as out of place here at court as we are . . . Well, no matter what, we will have lived for something important."

For a long moment the only sounds were the echoes of clashing foils and the soft whispers of conversation. Finally a very small smile appeared on Kit's mouth. "All right, Deanie," he acquiesced. "I will make a deal with you. If it rains again tomorrow, or proves too cloudy to attempt the maze, we'll try to think of something to help little Elizabeth and the queen. But if it's sunny, we'll try to leave."

Through her sniffles and relief, she smiled and prayed for an English monsoon.

Neither Kit nor Deanie had noticed the growing smirk on the face of Henry Howard, the earl of Surrey.

Chapter 14

*T*HERE WERE RUMBLINGS AT COURT.

At first Deanie feared the news concerned Queen Anne and the much-anticipated annulment finally taking place. The corridors vibrated with a hushed excitement. The usual morning greetings seemed subdued and hesitant, as if by the very act of acknowledging another, one might miss the latest tidbit.

By ten the sun was rolling high above a cloudless sky. Usually such weather brought a frenzy of activity, of courtiers gathering in select groups to plan a day of splendid outdoor sport. But on this morning even the most restless court members lingered within, reluctant to leave the palace and its fluctuating rumors.

In the queen's chamber, it was clear that something was up. Deanie and the other women spoke of fashion, with Katherine Howard detailing the latest high neckline just beginning to emerge from Italy and France. She alone seemed oblivious to the unnatural pauses and distracted comments from the other women.

"And above all, 'tis most flattering to all figures, be they round or slim," she concluded. Then she stopped, her gaze rounding the circle. "However, a great deal of caution must be exerted."

All five of the ladies' heads, including that of the queen, snapped to attention. Their needles hovered in midair, waiting for Katherine to continue.

"Why is that, Mistress Katherine?" asked the queen, her voice dry and brittle.

"Because . . ." Katherine leaned forward, and Deanie held her breath. As the king's apparent confidante and Norfolk's niece, she could very well be the best source of information in the entire court.

Katherine yawned before she spoke, a languorous, unhurried stretch, giving all the women time to imagine the worst.

Finally Katherine was ready. "One must exercise caution, for the high collars may indeed become entangled with one's headdress." With that she nodded, satisfied that all had heard her statement.

"What?" Deanie asked, ignoring the needle that just plunged into her thumb.

"'Tis true. One must wear a bonnet, much as the gentlemen do. And be wary of all headdresses, be they gabled or of the French hood fashion."

Deanie's eyes met the queen's, and at once they began to giggle, joined shortly by Cecily Garrison and the others. Katherine Howard seemed perplexed.

"But it is serious," she began. "I have heard of many a lady caught by a troublesome headpiece, and once—"

Katherine halted when the door flew open. Englebert, his face pale, entered the room and bowed to his queen before handing her a note. Her eyes scanned the paper, and she too became pale.

"My ladies, I require some privacy, if that is okay," she mumbled. Deanie rose with the others and began collecting her needlework.

"Mistress Deanie, you please stay."

As the other ladies filed from the chamber, Deanie stood uneasily, brushing bits of clipped needlepoint thread from the front of her gown. The door closed, and from the hallway she could hear the whispering of the dismissed women.

The queen did not delay speaking. "Cromwell this morning was taken by water to the Tower."

Stunned, Deanie sank back into her chair without asking permission. "Is that good or bad?" she asked bluntly.

"I don't know," the queen muttered, the note from Englebert still in her hands. "Cromwell arranged my marriage. He made allowances for my foreign behavior and dress. I am far from my home, Mistress Deanie. You know how that feels. I am at the mercy of my husband."

"Maybe you should leave," Deanie said in a rush. "Maybe you should go home to Cleves as soon as possible. I'd be glad to help, and I'm sure Kit would do anything to—"

"No." She walked to an inlaid desk and allowed the parchment to flutter from her hands. "I am a married woman now. No matter what happens, I will not disgrace my brother by returning to Cleves."

"But what if things don't work out?"

"Don't work out? I know not what you can mean."

Clearing her throat, Deanie struggled for a diplomatic way of phrasing her thoughts. "Through no fault of your own, the king may wish another for his wife."

"Think me stupid?" the queen snapped. This was the first show of temper Deanie had seen from the serene Anne. "One day he wants you, one day he wants Katherine. Holy cow, Mistress Deanie, he has never wanted me, and for that I am mightily glad."

"You mean you don't mind not receiving the king's, eh, attentions?"

"Don't mind? Ha." She returned to Deanie's side and sat heavily in the chair next to hers. "I hear what happened to the ladies who received the king's attention. One grew older

than her years and died in exiled degradation, one got her head chopped off. The lucky one died in childbed. No. Let me stay queen, and let the king give his attentions to some other poor cookie."

"But Your Majesty, the king wishes a duke of York."

"So? I am not stopping him. I will have the duke of York, then he may go to another." She seemed satisfied.

Now Deanie was completely perplexed. "You mean you and the king have, well, you know?"

"I know what?"

"Well, let me think how to put this." Deanie glanced out the window, watching a bird on the sill. The sprightly figure of the tiny bird was distorted by the thick glass. "Is there a possibility that you may have a duke of York soon, Your Majesty? If that's the case, you can pretty much call the shots around here."

"If the king commands it, I shall have a duke of York soon."

"Pardon me, Your Highness, but it takes a little more than a royal command to produce a Duke of York."

The queen raised one of her plucked eyebrows. "Yes?"

Again Deanie cleared her throat. "What I'm asking is, uh, well . . . what happens at night between the two of you?"

"Oh, I see! It is quite pleasant, really. The king pats me on the shoulder, and says 'Good night.' "

"And then?"

"Why of course, I say back to him 'And good night to you, Your Grace.' "

"And then?"

"Well, it is the nighttime, and I go to sleep."

Deanie folded her hands. "But before you go to sleep, doesn't he sometimes, well, kiss you?"

The queen gave her a blank stare. "Why should he kiss me and keep me awake, when already it is time to sleep?"

"Holy cow, Your Majesty." She leaned forward. "Don't you know anything about the birds and the bees?"

"Of course I do, silly. They both fly in the air."

Just as an uncharacteristically speechless Deanie stammered for a response, there was another knock on the door. Englebert appeared, less ashen than before, yet still solemn.

"Your Highness, the dukes of Suffolk and Hamilton request an audience."

Deanie jumped to her feet. "Kit! Are you all right?"

"Deanie?"

The queen, unable to resist a smile at Deanie's sudden eagerness, nodded, and Englebert held the door wide. Kit emerged first, his face flushed and eyes bright, with more of a slide into the room than a stately entrance. Without thinking twice, Deanie ran to him and threw her arms about his waist.

With measured steps, the duke of Suffolk made his grand entry, sweeping into a low bow before the queen. From beneath his scraggly eyebrows his gaze found Kit and Deanie, a decided twinkle to his formal countenance.

All in the room watched the couple, the strange intensity as they seemed able to isolate themselves from the rest of the world. For a moment they said nothing to each other, her face buried against his doublet as his arms tightened round her shoulders. The queen saw the expression of relief on the duke's face. His eyes closed, as if the only sensation he wished to be aware of was the feel of the woman in his arms.

He pulled back, framing her face with his hands. His thumbs gently stroked her cheeks. "Have you heard?"

She nodded. "Cromwell's in the Tower. What does that mean for the rest of us?"

"If I may speak," said the duke of Suffolk. "That is precisely what we are trying to determine. Your Majesty, have you been in direct contact with either Norfolk or the king this day?"

"Nay. We have been closeted within since early this morn." The queen still gaped at the couple.

"It's a sunny day," Kit said softly to Deanie.

"I know." Both left their words hanging. Only they knew the significance of their exchange. "But with Cromwell in the Tower, Kit, aren't we all better off?"

"Not necessarily. For the moment he's too preoccupied with his own hide to worry about us. Others, however, can now focus their attention away from Cromwell. They're free to look elsewhere to threats real or imagined. I fear that may mean us." In spite of the dire meaning, he gave her a slight smile, and she caught a fleeting glimpse of his crooked bottom tooth.

Deanie reached up and touched his face, briefly, gently.

"I saw it all." His face became somber again. "I saw his humiliation. God knows I have never agreed with Cromwell's politics, but never have I seen a more piteous sight. Norfolk pushed him to the ground and snatched away one of his gold medallions. He proclaimed Cromwell guilty of treason—by which means I know not. Cromwell threw down his hat and asked if anyone else there saw him as a traitor."

Kit looked about the room, at the queen and Englebert and Suffolk before continuing, his hand reflexively tightening over Deanie's shoulder. "Norfolk said nothing, nor did any of us. But then Norfolk kicked Cromwell, kicked him hard and enjoyed it."

"Aye, that he did," confirmed Suffolk. "Of all, Hamilton, you should have reveled in Cromwell's downfall. You have borne the brunt of his anger these past weeks. All there knew 'twas Cromwell who did you such grievous harm. But you seemed ill at ease. In truth, I thought you might become ill."

"Never have I witnessed such brutality. All the peers gathered about him like hungry wolves, taking his garter and fur-trim cloak. All had called Cromwell a friend, had courted him for his power. It indeed made me ill to watch them turn on the man who walked as their equal for more than eight years. No one is safe. And where was the king?"

"Ah." Suffolk rocked on the balls of his feet as he spoke, as if chafing to get on to the next topic. "The king cannot bear to see suffering. It makes him weep like a woman, and he invariably rescinds whatever order caused a soul to suffer."

"What did they arrest him for?" Deanie's voice sounded shrill compared to the rich tones of Suffolk and Kit.

"No charges, Deanie," Kit answered. "The monstrous thing is that he was felled by his own creativity. He is being held by the Act of Attainder, the very device he invented to hold the old countess of Salisbury for so long. All of his worldly possessions, every house and inch of land, every plate and tapestry and inkwell, have been confiscated by the Crown. Cromwell has nothing to his name, nothing at all."

"Will there be a trial?" asked the queen. For a moment Kit looked surprised, since he had long before decided that the queen was hopelessly simple and would never manage to master the English language.

"Nay." Suffolk shook his head. "I doubt it, Your Majesty." Suffolk shot Kit a questioning glance, and Kit nodded once. "Your Majesty," continued Suffolk, "we believe the king has sent Cromwell to the Tower with more than just his rent clothing. We believe Cromwell has in his cell the final papers for an annulment. Forgive me, Your Majesty. But the king wishes to dissolve your marriage."

Instead of swooning or falling into a justifiable fit of tears, the queen merely straightened. At first Deanie wondered if she had understood Suffolk's words.

"What can I do?" she asked after a brief pause.

Englebert dashed to his queen's side, but she pushed him away. "Be gone, Englebert. I am fine, okay? But I ask of all you here, What can I do to save myself from the block?"

Deanie was torn between inching even closer to Kit and comforting the queen. With a gentle nudge in the small of her back, Kit prodded her to go to Anne. Instead of brushing Deanie aside, the queen clutched her hand.

"How can the king legally annul the marriage?" Deanie gave her hand a squeeze. "They are married by law. Everyone knows that."

"Indeed, Mistress Deanie, that is where the difficulty lay." Suffolk gave his hat a brisk flick to remove a small piece of dirt. "He may feel forced into a corner to come up with an excuse. And however ill used Cromwell is, he forges yet forward on the proceedings. God only knows what his state of mind will lead him to contrive. His only hope—and it is a slim one at that—is to successfully win for the king an annulment. I beg Your Majesty's forgiveness for speaking so directly."

"Nay, good Suffolk," the queen said softly. "'Tis you gathered here who are my true friends, not those who think to save me from harsh words, no matter how true those words may be."

Kit shifted uncomfortably as Deanie shot him a carefully subdued nod.

"Again, I ask of you, what should I do?"

"I believe the problems with both Queen Katherine and Anne Boleyn could have been avoided had they been more agreeable to the king's variable tempers," offered Kit delicately.

"Should the present queen bear a male heir, the king would no doubt change his mind," added Suffolk, speaking slowly.

"I fully intend to bear a duke of York soon," proclaimed Queen Anne, and Deanie winced.

"Well, we might have run into a little roadblock in that department." Deanie gave a helpless shrug toward Kit, who immediately understood her meaning.

"Do you mean to tell me . . ." he began.

"You've got it," she confirmed.

"What means this?" the duke of Suffolk waved his bonnet between Deanie and Kit.

"Mistress Deanie fears the king and queen may not be having, well . . ."

A dawning expression crossed Suffolk's reddened face. "Oh, well. Hum. Well."

"Exactly," confirmed Kit.

The queen, who had observed the entire conversation without joining in, narrowed her eyes. "Speak your words, please. I understand not all this forth and back."

"Does Your Majesty recall the discussion we were having before the dukes entered the room?"

"Indeed I do, Mistress Deanie. We were discussing the new collars from France, although in Cleves we have worn such collars for many years now."

"No, Your Grace," Deanie whispered into her ear. "The conversation about the birds and the bees."

"Oh, that." The queen was genuinely mystified.

Kit suddenly began to cough, and the duke of Suffolk stroked the plumes on his hat, staring at them as if they were the most fascinating object he had ever beheld. Even Englebert, until then so silent they had all but forgotten his presence, started to straighten chairs.

Then Kit stopped. "I believe we have hit upon the very device Cromwell and the king may seize for the annulment," he said, no longer uncomfortable. Suffolk's eyes snapped to Kit's, and he nodded slowly.

"But what can we do, Kit? How can this information help us?" As Deanie spoke, she walked to Kit's side. Without looking at her, his gaze still on Suffolk, he opened his arm to her, and she automatically ducked into its warmth.

"Maybe," she began tentatively, "it's not too late for them to have a happy marriage. Maybe if we show her how to please the king, you know. We can show her how to flirt and play the guitar and sing. And you, Kit, can show her all about hunting, and we can get her some new clothes, and then, well, just maybe they would be happy."

Suffolk gave Deanie a genuinely warm smile. "Alas, sweet Mistress Deanie, although your heart is full of good sentiments, I fear it is too late for such deeds. We have but small time before the king will make a move."

Kit felt Deanie shudder, and he pulled her closer before kissing the top of her head. "We should be gone now," he murmured.

"Do you mean *really* gone, or just gone for a little while?"

"Both. But for now, we will be gone but a few hours. Suffolk and I need to find out more." Under his breath he added, "I could never tolerate flying blind."

As Suffolk and Kit made their formal goodbyes, promising to get word to them as soon as they uncovered more news, Deanie felt a stab of fear in her stomach. "Kit." She reached out to him, not wanting to see him leave.

Instead of stopping, he merely smiled. "While we are gone, I believe you and the queen need to have a little talk."

"Oh hell," she mumbled, all trepidation at being separated from Kit momentarily forgotten.

"I do believe, love, that Suffolk and I have by far the easier task. We need merely seek out vital information." He gave her a swift wink. "You, however, must find means to impart some knowledge. Be delicate, Deanie."

With a final parting glance at the queen, whose bewildered face darted from Kit to Deanie, Kit and Suffolk left the chamber.

Just when they thought the dukes had left, Kit leaned again into the chamber. "Oh, and Deanie: Whatever you do, do not try to illustrate your talk with one of your needlepoint creations."

"Very funny," she murmured with a grin.

After the chamber door had closed for a final time, Deanie set about telling Anne of Cleves, the queen of England and wife of Henry Tudor, all about the facts of life.

"Say nothing. Just smile," Kit ordered, coming up from behind and hooking his arm through Deanie's.

"Geez, Kit. Don't do that again! You scared the daylights out of me," she gasped. They were on the palace grounds, milling about with all the rest of the court. Now that it had become common knowledge that Cromwell was in the Tower, the other peers felt comfortable enough to venture onto the manicured lawns to enjoy the unusually fine weather. They traveled in small groups, their heads bowed together as they discussed the dangerous atmosphere of the court.

Only after she had taken a few deep breaths to regain her composure did Deanie notice the strained expression on Kit's face. His strong profile seemed more harsh than usual in the brilliant sunlight, and he kept his gaze straight ahead rather than on Deanie.

"What's happening?"

"Smile as I speak," he instructed. She did so, and he continued. "We're leaving now, Deanie. We are going straight to the maze. The bottle's in my doublet."

"We can't, Kit. What about Anne and Princess Elizabeth? They both need our help." The artificial smile, forgotten for a moment, reappeared on her face.

"We will have to leave them to Suffolk, love. It appears our dear friend Norfolk has convinced the king that I too am guilty of treason." He nodded pleasantly to Lady Rochford as they passed. "By nightfall I may very well be sharing lodgings with Cromwell."

Only Kit's firm grasp kept her from stumbling. "Well, we can't have that," she chirped, and Kit glanced down and gave her a curt smile.

From the corner of her eye she saw a conspicuous group of four men. At first she thought they were yet another wave of barber-surgeons, seeking her out to shave her legs. Then she recognized them as Cromwell's henchmen, including the large one who had wielded the staff that wounded Kit.

"Kit," she began, her voice rising.

"I know. They've been following me all afternoon. Now that their former patron is in the Tower, they have managed to shift alliances. Mind your step." He guided her over a log bordering the path. He was taking them straight to the maze, not even bothering to follow the decorative walk. "They belong to Norfolk now."

"How on earth could they charge you with treason?"

He merely shook his head, then he folded a hand over the clenched fist resting on his arm. "You're really very good."

"Huh?"

"I never got the chance to tell you, Deanie. Your singing—it's really quite exhilarating. Very different, but quite marvelous nonetheless."

She blinked in confusion. "Thank you. Remind me to sign you up for my fan club when we get back home."

"May I also have your autograph?"

"We'll see." She smiled up at him, squinting against the glare of the sun.

Suddenly he slowed their pace, then stopped altogether, turning her toward him. "I need to tell you something," he said quietly, his eyes darting over her head to the burly quartet just beyond the path. "Should this not work, should we not make it together, you must try it alone."

She began to protest, but he silenced her by placing a gentle finger upon her lips. "I may have been here too long to ever return. Ten years—almost a third of my life has passed in this time. I may be too ensnared by all of this to ever leave. I speak the language, follow the custom without a second thought. At times I almost think as a Tudor man rather than as someone who once listened to jazz and flew an airplane."

"But . . ."

"No, listen." He swallowed, tracing the contours of her face with his unbroken stare. "You do not belong here. You're far too fresh and vital and young. Whatever happens when we enter the maze, know one thing: I love you, Deanie. I adore everything about you, and that can never change. If by chance I remain behind, take my love with you."

He took a deep, shuddering breath before he continued. "I will be dead, my love. Long dead, my body gone. But still I will love you. You will always be the one grand passion of my life. Remember that. Through the centuries I'll continue to love you, but you must find love in your own time, warm, breathing love."

"Kit," she whispered, unable to utter anything else.

"I almost fear I'm tempting fate. God help us both," he groaned, his mouth closing over hers.

They did not care that it was broad daylight, that the entire court was but a stone's throw away, or closer. His tongue plunged into hers as if he would consume her, and she responded, matching his rapture with her own.

With one swift motion, their mouths still locked in joyous union, he swept her into his arms, cradling her trembling body to his own. Thus joined, they entered the maze, oblivious to the stunned and giddy onlookers.

And not a single person dared to follow.

There were no words between them, just complete understanding. He lowered her tenderly to the ground, pulling away for but a moment to take in her features. Everyone else seemed to have dissolved, leaving them blissfully alone and unhurried.

Slowly his hands unlaced her stays, each tie falling limp between his fingers. When the bodice and skirts slipped away, followed by the undergown, he simply stared at her.

"I never knew such perfection," he uttered, more to himself than to her.

She felt no shame, no embarrassment at her nakedness. Instead his gaze warmed her with a welcome embrace like the morning sun—all consuming, full of simple enchantment.

He seemed to remove his own garments in one bold movement, the sword, forgotten for the moment, resting beneath the crumpled pile. She stared wantonly at his body, at the sheer male perfection now being offered to her. He was just as she imagined he would be, just as she knew he would be: finely muscled, strong yet lean. There were marks and scars on his arms and torso and thighs, slashes that had healed into light white lines or jagged trails. Instead of marring him, in her eyes they represented his life of physical hardship, the pain he had been forced to endure these past ten years.

Something about those healed wounds, as well as the recent one from Cromwell, moved her, and she felt her eyes prickle with the weight of tears. He had always seemed so very mighty and invincible, yet now she saw him as simply brave but vulnerable.

Tenderly she kissed the scar on his shoulder, then the one on his upper arm. He moaned softly, his hands raking through her hair.

There was not time for anything else, no sweet words or slow, delicious caresses. They were both aware, even in their haze, of the sun's movement, and they were drawn together as if by another force.

At once he was inside her, and they were transported for a blissful second to another place, where they were the solitary souls, and all else melted into oblivion.

They lay together, entwined in each other's arms.

Deanie was afraid to speak, for fear of breaking the magical rapture that seemed to wrap itself about them, sheltering them from the afternoon sun, protecting them from the unwelcome intrusion of others. Her head rested on his chest, rising and falling with every breath he took; her eyes were closed in drowsy contentment.

He inhaled deeply, his arm tightening about her, drawing her closer.

"It's time." His voice sounded odd to his own ears, and he felt her stiffen.

"No."

But she did not resist as he propped himself on one elbow. His eyes swept over her once more, and he ran a tender hand along her curves before he reached for her clothing. They dressed wordlessly. He pulled each layer of her gown into place, kissing the hollow of her throat as he laced the sides of her bodice. As she drew his billowy shirt over his head, she paused, savoring the feel and fragrance of his bare chest one last time.

When he closed his doublet, she saw him adjust a small piece of cloth between his shirt and doublet. He carefully fixed the square directly over his heart, and with a pang she realized it was the bit of needlework she had done for him.

Smiling, he held out his hand, and she slid her palm over his. The sun was about to set, and he held the bottle in the air.

A fine blue line began to pulsate from the glass, darting at an angle. Both held their breath as his arm began to vibrate, and she clung to him, her eyes closed.

And then it stopped.

"What the hell?" he began.

Immediately she stepped back. "What happened?"

"I don't know. It just stopped working." He turned the bottle over, hoping to again catch the glint of the sun. Nothing. The bottle remained stubbornly inactive.

"It worked before, just like that," she said. "Is that the way it worked with you and your goggles?"

"Exactly the way. But it continued."

"Right." She gave the bottle an accusing stare. "It worked before. What could be wrong?"

"Well, we may have missed the sun." She flushed, and he shook his head. "No, I don't mean today. We may be too far into spring for it to work."

"Oh crap," she muttered, and for the first time in hours they both laughed, uneasily, nervously.

When they caught their breath, he tapped the bottle. "Think, Deanie. What was different when you traveled here?"

They remained silent for a long while, each contemplating the details of their journey.

"The weather was about the same," she said at last.

"With me too."

"It was just about dusk." He nodded in affirmation. Suddenly he stood very still, and with questioning eyes she looked up at him.

"The planes," he said at last.

"What planes?"

He spoke quickly. "There were rumblings, flashes of light

from the bombs being dumped on London by the Luftwaffe. At first I thought I had been hit, Deanie. That's what I thought the flashes were, the rumbling."

"I thought it was an earthquake," she said in a rush. "There were flashes with me too."

Then she stopped. "Holy cow, Kit: the camera reflectors!"

"The what?"

"There were camera reflectors set up all over the lawn. With you there were flashes of light from nearby bombs. What if that's it? What if . . ."

"The instability," he finished. "The flashes, the bursts of light. Deanie, you're a genius!"

"So how can we replicate it?"

He said nothing at first, merely ran a finger over the bottle. "Let me think." Rubbing his hand wearily across his jaw, he continued staring at the bottle.

"Ho, Hamilton?" A familiar voice called from just beyond the maze.

"Suffolk, we're within," Kit's attention was still focused on the bottle when Suffolk, puffing with exertion, came into sight.

"The whole court is merrily discussing the pair of you," he mocked. "Some even situated themselves on the hill just yonder, vying for the most advantageous view. God's blood, Hamilton, what has gotten into you?"

"Quiet, Suffolk. I'm thinking."

"Perhaps you should have done that earlier, instead of . . . well, you know." He glanced at Deanie. "My apologies, mistress."

Deanie shrugged absentmindedly, her eyes still fixed on the soda bottle.

"By the by, mistress, what happened with the queen and your discussion? Methinks this afternoon's, eh, episode was but a demonstration for your lecture."

"Watch it, Suffolk," Kit warned, but Deanie merely chuckled.

"She did not believe me."

Kit's head snapped up. "She didn't believe you?" he repeated, a shadow of a smile creasing his face.

"Nope. She yelled 'God save me!' and 'Fie, begone!' and chased me out of her chamber. Last I heard poor Englebert was trying to calm her down."

A bark of laughter escaped Suffolk's throat, swelling into a fit of hysteria. Kit too began to laugh. "So she believes without question that her husband wishes an annulment, that she may very well be beheaded, yet she is unable to believe . . ." He was unable to continue as great waves of laughter overtook him.

"Awe, come on," she began, trying her hardest to resist their ebullience. But it was impossible, and they exited the maze laughing still, Kit in the middle with an arm about each of his companions, Deanie leaning against him, one hand clutching the soda bottle.

"Lady Longley, come look," cried a startled groomsman, "'Twas not just the two of them! The duke of Suffolk was within, all along!"

Lady Longley pushed the young man aside, looking with intense wonderment as Hamilton slapped the duke of Suffolk's back with good-humored delight and simultaneously planted a tender kiss upon Mistress Deanie's forehead.

"Well, well," she said, her voice suddenly gone husky. "It seems our handsome duke is far more fascinating than I ever imagined."

"And so is his cousin," echoed the groomsman, who received a sharp elbow in the ribs for his comment.

Chapter 15

*T*HE TENSION IN THE COURT SEEMED TO INCREASE WITH EACH passing hour. There was an unconvincing attempt on the part of every peer, page, and servant to pretend it was business as usual, that the king's sudden disappearance meant nothing at all. Yet all knew the dangers that twisted through the halls. This was the king's pattern, to evacuate the court whenever any less-than-pleasant event was to take place. He would order its execution, then leave as if he had no prior knowledge of the occurrence.

Cromwell was the new guest in the Tower. It was anyone's guess who would be the next to fall.

The morbidly curious could not help but light upon the duke of Hamilton. Norfolk and his minions fueled the reports, eagerly adding whatever morsel would cast weight to the rumors of the handsome duke's impending doom.

Hamilton played his part well enough, acting every inch the charming courtier at the evening meal. The only noticeable difference was his marked reluctance to be separated from his cousin, Mistress Deanie.

A few shrewd observers noticed the physical contact they seemed compelled to maintain constantly. When he spoke to another gentleman across the board, his arm remained firmly, boldly, about her shoulders. When Katherine Howard engaged them in light conversation, Mistress Deanie's hand rested lightly upon his thigh.

Some thought it was nothing more than the aftereffects of the now-celebrated frolic in the maze. Others saw something deeper, more poignant in the intensity of their closeness.

The meal ended, and the ladies-in-waiting gathered in a cluster about their queen. Anne seemed disturbed, her eyes following Kit and Deanie with a keen curiosity.

The duke of Suffolk at last rose to his feet, planting an amiable hand on Hamilton's shoulder before leaving the hall.

"Take care, friend," he muttered. He had remained unusually silent throught the meal, a different man from the gregarious merrymaker who could turn every occasion into his own drunken celebration. Tonight he sipped little from his goblet, ate even less.

Deanie approached the queen, her head bowed. "Your Majesty, may I remain a while longer with my cousin?"

The queen seemed to be weighing the matter, then she nodded once, as if indisposed to grant her servant's wish. The ladies removed themselves from the hall with grave dignity. Deanie caught the flicker of a smile from the queen before they swept through the arched doorway.

There were but a handful of people remaining in the hall as Kit reached for her hand. "So far, so good." He grinned.

"Maybe the rumors are all false," she said hopefully. "Norfolk seemed calm tonight, didn't he?"

He did not answer. "Let's go outside for some fresh air." The servants had commenced the frantic sweeping and cleaning of the hall, gathering pitchers and plates and shooing the dogs from underfoot.

The sky was beautifully clear, the stars adding eloquent

flashes of light to the lush hue. They said nothing in the darkness. It was a comfortable silence, brimming with words unspoken, sentiments raw with untried bounds.

She shifted her gaze to his profile, the sharp angles of his face stark even in the gentle blue illumination of the moon and stars. He did not seem aware of her watching him, lost in his own thoughts. Suddenly a small smile appeared, the lines at the corners of his eyes deepening.

"I want to fly again," he whispered.

For a few moments she simply concentrated on his features, the way the night bathed his face in its tender glow. Slowly, without breaking the spell, she leaned her head against his shoulder. And together they stood beneath the timeless stars, dreaming of a future they hoped would be theirs.

It was just after midnight when the duke of Hamilton walked alone through the proud halls of Hampton Court Palace. Deanie was safely in her chamber, the snores of the other ladies-in-waiting testifying to an uneventful evening.

He had handed her the soda bottle, staring at her face as if committing every feature to memory.

"Good night." His voice was tight.

Later she wondered why they didn't speak more, why they didn't flee to some distant shore. She was acutely aware of every sound and sensation, the dampness of the corridor, the crackle of a wall torch. A lock of dark hair tumbled over his forehead, but she didn't brush it aside. She felt as if a heavy weight pressed upon her chest.

"Good night," she responded, mechanical, hollow. Her fingertips brushed the warmth of his hand as she took the bottle.

And then he left, placing distance between them with his sure, clean strides. She wanted to call out, to stop him for just one more touch, one more word.

He too wanted to halt, to stay the night beside her. To be by her side, to know she was there.

The footsteps behind him were silent. Even if the men had not been commanded to take extra care, Kit would never have heard the warning sounds through his own churning thoughts.

And when the club came down, ushering him into darkness, he wasn't surprised, just strangely empty.

For God's sake, why hadn't they talked more when they had the chance?

The moment she awoke, after a brief, fitful sleep, she knew what had happened.

She paced in her chamber, fully dressed since a little after five in the morning. Just before eight a note from the queen was delivered.

"The Duke of Hamilton was last night taken to the Tower. AC."

A handful of words. Nothing violent, a simple statement of fact. No surprises.

"The Duke of Hamilton was last night taken to the Tower. AC."

They had expected this, even last night under the traitorous luster of the stars. He had known then, and so had she.

Deanie rushed to the queen's chamber. Englebert let her in immediately, without his usual formal protocol. The queen sat by the window, looking out upon the garden.

"It is so very pretty, the flowers and the green, Mistress Deanie." She sighed. "Yet it covers terrible things."

"Please, tell me what happened, Your Majesty."

"The duke last night was set upon by four men. Some people saw it, but who exactly saw I know not. He was hit from behind, over the head with a *whack.*"

Deanie sank into a chair, her face betraying numb disbelief.

"Shall I continue?" The queen spoke in a softer tone. Deanie stared straight ahead for a few moments, her eyes glazed and unseeing, before she nodded for the queen to go on.

"We have been told the duke then fell and was carried away by the men. He never uttered a single word. Englebert believes the duke did not wish to have any more company in the Tower and feared very much the thought of you being taken."

"Has anyone seen Norfolk?" It was painful to speak.

"Yes, and this is the strangest thing of all: Norfolk seemed surprised. He knew not the duke was to be taken, not so soon."

Deanie rubbed her hand over her eyes. "Does anyone know what Kit's been charged with?"

The queen hesitated before answering. "The word is that the duke is accused of conspiring with Cromwell."

"What?" Deanie straightened, the numbness beginning to ebb. "You know that's crazy, Your Majesty."

"I know, that's what I tell Englebert, but he says people talked of how he refused to beat Cromwell, even when given the chance. They say 'twas most strange and unnatural for a man who was said to have been harmed by another man not to wish him great harm in turn."

"Great. So he's locked in the Tower for the grand crime of failing to beat a defenseless man." Deanie stood up abruptly, folding her hands. "Will there be a trial?"

"No. No trial, Mistress Deanie. He will suffer the same fate as Cromwell."

"Not if I can help it," she said. "Where is the king?"

The queen shrugged. "No one tells me where the king is, but some say he is at Richmond." Then she gave Deanie a pointed stare, as if observing her for the very first time.

"Mistress Deanie, I heard about you and the duke in the maze."

Deanie flushed, trying to think of something to say, but the queen continued as if she had been discussing the weather. "I also watched you two last evening at the meal, the manner in which you spoke and conversed. I must apologize."

"Excuse me?"

"Yesterday, I did not believe what you told me, of the bees and the birds. But I think about it, mistress. Holy cow, I think all night about it, and now I do believe you."

Deanie smiled, an expression that didn't seem to fuse with the way she was feeling. "Your Majesty, I would never kid about something like that."

The queen returned the smile, and she crooked her finger for Deanie to come closer. "Now I am truly glad not to have attracted the king's attentions," she mumbled into Deanie's ear.

The king rubbed his hands together in anticipation.

Thomas Howard, the duke of Norfolk, knew precisely what his sovereign was thinking of. His niece Katherine waited below, clothed in the newest designs from Mr. Locke. He had spared no expense, enveloping her in the richest clothing his beleaguered finances would allow. He had considered the velvet and silks an investment, for if Katherine could indeed snare the king, the Howard family would once again rank supreme.

This time, with pliable Katherine instead of willful Anne Boleyn, Norfolk himself could orchestrate the outcome. Katherine was not intelligent or overly educated; indeed, she was barely able to read or write. But Katherine knew how to entice a man, especially a grossly obese monarch who had grown more difficult to please with every added year and pound.

The king was grooming himself like a peacock. Norfolk watched him preen with all the deliberate satisfaction of a young stud. What did he see in the mirror? Surely not the image the world viewed as Henry of England.

Norfolk knew, as did all the other successful courtiers, that the key to preserving one's career was to maintain the king's own illusions. To Henry, he was still the youthful prince, the pride of Europe, unrivaled in athletic skills, learning, and manly beauty. In short, the ideal prince, fit for any story book or young girl's dreams.

Norfolk cleared his throat, a bid to gain the king's attention. The king seemed not to notice, intent as he was on his own reflection. He held only a hand mirror now; no longer did he wish to seek his full form in the unforgiving glass of a long mirror.

"Your Highness," began Norfolk. The king simply raised one nearly transparent red eyebrow in acknowledgment. Norfolk took it as a sign to continue. But the king spoke instead.

"How is the temperament at Hampton?"

"Your Highness?"

"After Cromwell's arrest," the king said irritably. He hated that about Norfolk, his stubborn inability to follow Henry's lightning-swift subject changes. One thing about Cromwell: He could always anticipate the king's fluctuations. Norfolk was confoundedly deliberate and plodding. He elaborated. "Cromwell was arrested yesterday, Norfolk. You were at Hampton when it happened, and perhaps you may illuminate us as to the court reaction."

"Oh, I see," mumbled Norfolk. "In truth, Cromwell's arrest was no great surprise, Your Majesty. Many who had watched the low-born cur had expected, even anticipated his eventual stumble."

"Was there great sadness?" The king wanted to know, to gauge when best to return. He wished to avoid the unpleasant scene of Cromwell's arrest, but he was already chafing at Richmond. Hampton Court was by far his favorite home.

"Nay, no sadness for Cromwell." Norfolk spoke carefully, as he had practiced during the barge ride to Richmond. He kept his voice neutral. "I will confess, however, that there was a great deal of surprise over the sudden arrest of Hamilton."

The king frowned, setting the mirror to rest in his ample satin lap. "Hamilton? Never did I order the arrest of Hamilton. There must be some mistake. You must have heard the facts awry."

Norfolk tensed. This is what he had feared. Of course he

wanted Hamilton out of the way, but it was too early in the plan. Hamilton was yet too popular, and his sudden and unexpected arrest would only garner more supporters. Then the duke's cousin would come into play, and the king's eyes would rest favorably on her exquisite figure. Damnation. Katherine was too plump and too insipid to keep the royal attention if Mistress Deanie should become available.

Damnation.

"We like Hamilton," muttered the king. "He is in truth one of my favorites." His small eyes lit momentarily on the dour form of Norfolk before he continued. "Someone else has abducted him, and I mean to find out whom. They shall pay dearly. If they harm Hamilton, they shall forfeit their life."

Norfolk hoped to keep his face bland, but he flinched at the king's tone. When he spoke thusly, low and calm, he was far more dangerous than when he ranted and roared.

"I will seek whatever answers you shall require, Your Majesty."

Henry tapped his finger on the now-forgotten glass. "How fares Mistress Deanie?"

"Your Highness?"

The king did not repeat his question. "Send her here at once, Norfolk. I wish her in my presence on the morrow."

"But Your Majesty." Norfolk smiled, spreading his hands in a gesture of reasoning supplication. "Below waits an eager young maid, hoping to make her most beloved king the merriest sovereign in Christendom."

"Then we shall allow her the opportunity," the king said mildly, rising to his feet with a grunt. "And I shall expect Mistress Deanie at Richmond on the morrow."

Norfolk knew he had just been dismissed. Frantically, he grasped for something to add, some slender straw by which he could alter the king's mind, cause him to forget Mistress Deanie.

"Your Majesty, may I say—"

"Good day, Norfolk."

The duke bowed and left the royal chambers, silently cursing whoever it was who had stolen the duke of Hamilton.

The last thing Norfolk could afford, other than more lavish clothes for his dim-witted niece, was an unexpected loose end.

He was growing accustomed to waking in unfamiliar surroundings with a headache severe enough to rouse the dead.

Kit opened his eyes, for a moment thinking he had gone blind. He could not see his own hand, or the room in which he was imprisoned. Then he saw a flash of light from a distance of a dozen feet, a slender shaft from under a door.

There was a strangely familiar fragrance, of must and damp and soil, and he determined he was below ground.

Wouldn't they keep him above ground in the Tower?

Slowly he sat up, holding a hand over the top of his head as if it would split in two. With a thick breath he paused, elbows resting on his knees, head in his hands, willing the throbbing pain to cease.

For a long time he remained in the position, his eyes closed even though he was in almost complete darkness. The lump on his head was achingly tender, yet he knew the injury was not serious.

Then he thought of Deanie.

He hoped it was a brilliantly sunny day, that she would enter the maze and return to her own time. Would she remember him? Perhaps her memory of their weeks together would be erased. In a way he hoped so, for it would be easier if she did not remember him.

"Please don't forget me," he murmured, startled by the sound of his own voice. Had he said that?

He took a deep breath and wondered what was happening to him. Not the sudden captivity, not the confounding events at court. He had faced far worse in this time, had come up against political intrigue and savage actions with almost tiresome regularity. The Kit of the past ten years was a man of unthinking action, of knee-jerk response.

And last night, when confronted by men who took him, he capitulated as meekly as a lamb. Two months ago such a response would have unthinkable. Two months ago he would have struck back at his assailants with unwavering ferocity.

Two months ago he was not in love.

He bit out a curse in the darkness, his head pounding. He was thinking too much, pondering his every action in terms of its effect on Deanie. In this court, that was more than perilous. It was well nigh suicidal.

Yet he had no other choice. One rash gesture or word could mean death for either of them. All of the mechanisms he had developed in a decade of living at court were meaningless. Suddenly he was exhausted, tired of playing a role he had never before bothered to question. And he had Deanie to consider now.

Again, he tried his voice. "Hello?" It echoed against the moist stone walls. He could smell their wetness, slick and slimy. Was *hello* a word in 1540? His mind was not functioning; he seemed to forget all the details of living in this time.

He had nothing to lose by calling out again.

"Hello?" His voice was stronger now. "Am I in the Tower of London?" The question seemed ridiculous, but he needed to know the answer.

From the other side of a thick door he could hear a clattering sound.

"Good morn', Duke," replied a cheerful man. "I 'ave food, sir. Close yer eyes and I'll shove it on through. We don't want the light hurting your head now."

"Where am I?"

"Mind, 'ere it comes." The door shot open, but before Kit could push his way through, it slammed shut again.

He blinked at the sight before him. There was a tray piled with covered dishes, and a single candle still flickering from the journey to his cell. From the scent he could tell it was a veritable feast: meats and pastries and a round loaf of bread jutting from beneath a linen cloth. There was also a large jug of wine. Clearly his captors had no wish to starve him. If this tray were any indication, they may wish to give him an advanced case of gout.

He wasn't hungry, but he ate from habit. As he shifted, he realized his sword was still by his side. What sort of prison was this, where they gave the prisoner lavish meals and allowed him to keep his weapons?

The food was, as he expected, delicious. The roast chicken was prepared exactly as he preferred it, with a crust of herbs and salt. The wine, too, was excellent, good enough to be poured without the spices that masked the flavor of an inferior beverage.

When he had finished, he stretched on the cot. The candle still illuminated the cell, but it didn't seem to be a prison at all. Indeed, it looked more like the cellar of some great house or estate.

"Hello?" he shouted once more.

"Was your meal good, Duke?" The cheerful voice had returned.

"Yes, it was," Kit replied, feeling very much as if he were speaking to a waiter in one of London's better prewar restaurants. "Where am I?"

"Never worry, Duke. You are safe as safe can be 'ere."

"This is not the Tower," he said, a statement rather than a question.

The response was a short bark of a laugh.

"May I send a note to someone?"

"Well now, that depends." The unseen man was clearly thinking. "Give it a try. It cannot 'urt."

Several minutes later the door opened, but Kit remained calmly seated on the cot. Until he knew exactly where he was, he would not make any attempt at escape. He wasn't concerned with his own fate, but he did not want repercussions from a rash act to harm Deanie.

The solicitous man pushed a quill, several sheets of parchment, and a small bottle of ink under the door.

"Candle 'olding up, Duke?"

"Yes, it is," Kit answered, pulling the light toward him. "Thank you."

After thinking for a few moments, Kit began writing a note to Suffolk. He would not risk Deanie.

Suffolk,

I seem to be held by persons unknown, in a place as yet unknown. Forgive me for asking of you a great favor. Could you help Mistress Deanie with a strange endeavor? She has need of someone to light small bundles of gunpowder about the maze at Hampton. Think me not insane. She alone will know what to do within the maze.

Should she remain at court, please take care of her until such time as I am able to attend to her myself. Should fate dictate otherwise, and I am not able to return, use any monies from my own estate to help her.

Finally, let her know I am well cared for at the present time, and love her above all else.

I thank you, my good Friend.

Hamilton

When he had completed the note, he pushed it through the door.

"Who does this note go to, Duke?"

Kit had clearly addressed the letter; he realized the guard could not read. "It is to go to Charles Brandon, the duke of Suffolk."

There was a pause before he replied, "I will see what I can do, Duke."

"Thank you," he said. Suddenly his head began to ache once more, and he closed his eyes, exhausted, hoping the note would somehow reach Suffolk, and that Deanie could somehow reach her own time.

Chapter 16

THE DUKE OF NORFOLK GLARED SULLENLY AS MISTRESS Deanie was led into the courtyard at Richmond. He stood at an angle, so if by chance she should look up she would not see his visage in the window.

She had been allowed the extraordinary privilege of making the journey from Hampton Court in the royal barge. The little fool did not realize the meaning of the gesture. Only the king's closest, most intimate friends were blessed with a ride on the royal barge, the sumptuous floating palace that Henry used with princely delight. Her common backside rested against tufted velvet, her plebeian feet trod the rich carpet.

Norfolk had yet to be invited upon the royal barge.

He hated the Bailey wench, despised the way she smiled at Suffolk, the bloated idiot. He held her hand with courtly pride, as if she were the queen of Sheba. His insipid niece would not compare favorably with Mistress Deanie's dark, slender beauty, set off this day by the deep crimson of her gown.

And then, unexpectedly, he grinned.

Mistress Deanie, who would soon be trotted before the king like a prize filly, was clothed in the plain manner of homely Queen Anne. Indeed, her red velvet gown was remarkably similar to the one worn by Anne in the disastrous Holbein portrait that had so misled the king. Although she wore a French hood instead of the clumsy gabled piece of the Cleves mare, there was no train to swirl behind in luxurious folds, no fitted bodice to entice a manly eye.

The king, upon seeing Mistress Deanie, would first lose his appetite for the wench, and then, with thrilling predictability, lose his majestic temper.

The duke left his excellent view by the window. He was unwilling to risk missing what promised to be a most amusing scene.

Suffolk held Deanie's hand as they strolled regally through the courtyard. Both were aware of Norfolk, who mistakenly thought he was hidden by the glare of the thick, uneven glass. He was wrong.

"Why in God's name are you attired thusly?" Suffolk asked, a smile pasted upon his face. He had been at court long enough to have mastered the ability to speak without altering his diplomatic expression.

"What's wrong with how I'm dressed?"

"Do not act the innocent, my dear. You are wearing a gown of unfortunate Germanic tailoring. The king will not be pleased. Mind your step."

Deanie did not reply. From the moment Suffolk helped her off the barge she had been conscious of being followed by unseen eyes. The courtyard was strangely silent, yet she felt the heat of curious, hidden stares.

"Kit's in the Tower," she whispered. "I'm going to get him out."

Suffolk halted momentarily, then continued as usual. "My dear, just how do you propose to release him from the Tower?"

"I'm going to do some big-time royal rear-end kissing."
She smiled, nodding to a page who emerged from the side
entrance. A moment later the duke of Norfolk walked
steadily from the main arched door, his hands folded within
the large fur cuffs of his robe. His clothing, always of
superior quality, had become even more opulent in the past
few weeks.

"Ah, Suffolk and Mistress Deanie." Norfolk stood as if he
alone were the master of the palace. "Allow me to—"

"Suffolk!" The unmistakable boom of the king's voice
seemed to rattle the windows and bricks. "Mistress
Deanie!" He walked with an awkward gate, a slight wince
when he placed his enormous weight on the leg with the
ulcerated thigh. His white satin hose bore an embroidered
garter to cover the many layers of bandages, and he wore a
large amount of cologne to mask the wound's foul odor.

He stopped cold, and the cheerful expression on his
swollen features became hard and unyielding. "What are
you wearing?" His voice became a growl.

"How generous of you to notice, Your Highness." Suffolk
bowed at the waist. "By God, it's been years since you've
found me in the very least bit attractive."

The king's tiny eyes, glinting like black pellets, flicked to
Suffolk. Norfolk, watching from several feet away, was
unable to resist the quiver of a thin smile.

Then, to everyone's astonishment—including the
king's—Henry began to laugh. "Charles, you mule! Now
that the ladies don't find you irresistible, you seek approval
of your old friend? Ha!" His well-stuffed doublet rolled with
his chortle. The smile faded from Norfolk's face.

"Mistress Deanie, now I am able to see how the gown
should truly be worn, and it is indeed a gratifying vision.
Now come within. We shall have food and drink and merry
times."

"Your Majesty." Norfolk's tone was brisk. "My niece
Katherine shall join you."

"Fine, fine," the king answered distractedly, turning his

back on Norfolk. As Suffolk, Mistress Deanie, and the gaily dressed king entered the palace, Norfolk watched with bitter hatred.

He vowed, for the tenth time that day, to become the most powerful man in England.

It was his duty. He alone, through the grace of God, was worthy.

The king seemed oblivious to the strained tension in the chamber. He was delighted to be once again in amusing company, for Richmond was dull indeed compared to the lavish routine of Hampton. Richmond still bore the severe lines of his dour, disapproving father, a man of little humor and even less thirst for the worldly pleasures of life.

The twenty-foot ceilings were inlaid with Henry's initials entwined by a Tudor rose. More than once Deanie looked up and counted the panels, reminding herself of when she used to count the accoustical tiles in her dentist's office.

Katherine Howard giggled incessantly, speaking rapidly and leaning in a conspiratorial fashion toward the king. He nodded, flattered by the way her plump hand concealed her meaningless words from the others. Norfolk seemed on the verge of interrupting her, alarmed by how base her behavior seemed even to his own encouraging eyes. The king seemed not to notice.

"Mistress Deanie." The king spoke over Katherine's voice, but she did not seem to be distressed. "How fares your cousin, Hamilton?"

Completely taken aback—she had just counted the forty-eighth ceiling panel—Deanie tried to gauge if the king were playing one of his cruel games. She shot a glance at Suffolk, and he too seemed startled by the question.

"Thank you for asking, Your Majesty. When I last saw him two days ago, he seemed to be well." She added a neutral smile and shifted against the carvings on the high-backed chair.

"Do we know where he is?" The king stroked his beard in thought, his eyes never leaving Deanie's face.

From the corner of her eye she saw Suffolk straighten and Norfolk lean closer. Only Katherine, who was reaching for yet another handful of honeyed figs, was not hanging on every word.

"No, Your Highness." She almost left it at that, but some unseen force drove her forward. "I thought you might know."

"Me?" His face slackened into a perplexed question mark. "How would I know where that rascal has gone?" The king tossed a wrist to the honeyed figs, eyes twinkling as his fingers collided with Katherine's hand in the gold bowl. "Well, we shall all watch and listen, and try to reassure ourselves that he has come to no harm. Is that not correct, Norfolk?"

He jumped when his name was called. "Of course, Your Majesty."

"Well, Norfolk? Do you know where Hamilton is?" The king could barely hide his annoyance, and he concentrated instead on another fig.

Deanie bit her lip, resisting the urge to scream at the king. Why was he doing this? Everyone knew Kit had been taken to the Tower of London. Had the royal amusements grown so thin that the king was forced to resort to this callous behavior?

A steward entered the room and bowed to the king. "Your Highness, there is a missive just arrived for the duke of Suffolk."

"Ah, Charles." The king seemed to forget the previous conversation. "You may take the message. I assume it comes forth from that troubled household of yours."

"My household is surely troubled, Your Grace," Suffolk agreed as the servant handed him the note. For a brief moment his face changed, tightening into concern before he again relaxed into his usual contented half smile. "The trouble is now with the dairy cows, who seem to have gone on a rampage. All will be well soon, Your Highness." He folded the note and slipped it into his doublet.

"Very well." The king then remembered Deanie. "Good mistress, favor our ear with one of your Welsh songs."

She blinked as if he had asked her to do a handstand. Music. It had once been so vital to her, the most important thing in her life. Now it seemed a worthless substitute for real emotions. Until Kit, music had been her only passion. Had her life been that empty?

"Mistress Deanie." Suffolk raised his voice, not unkindly but to reach her. She had seemed lost in her own thoughts. "The king wishes for a song."

She turned to Suffolk and suddenly felt lost. She gripped her hands together to stop them from visibly trembling. What the hell was she doing, chatting away over honeyed figs while Kit was rotting in the Tower?

"I don't remember any songs," she said flatly.

"Come now," soothed Suffolk, urging her with a pointed glare. "I recall you singing a song about an addled mind."

"Yes!" The king clapped in agreement. "And about losing one's limbs. The words were most peculiar, but they pleased us."

The servant who had delivered the message to Suffolk returned with a familiar guitar. The back was pieced together with squares of wood, alternating light with dark to produce a strangely modern geometric pattern. Tied to the neck and base of the instrument was a sash, so it could be looped across her shoulders.

It was Kit's guitar.

"Where did this come from?" She stroked the wood gently, as if it were Kit himself.

"It was sent from Hampton," replied Norfolk, irritated by the king's lack of interest in his niece, who was examining the seeds of a half-eaten fig as if it held the mysteries of the universe.

Deanie sang the songs they requested—"Crazy" and "I

Fall to Pieces"—with less emotion than she used in ordering a pizza. But her audience did not seem to notice, and on the last verse the king's voice was raised with her, blending with a force that left the royal eyes damp with tears.

At last Suffolk had Deanie alone, cornered in one of the short corridors of Richmond.

"The note was from your cousin." He spoke quickly, without preamble or his usual flowery words. "He is being held but treated well."

"Where is he?" She wanted to grab him by the lapels, but he had no lapels. "When can we get him out?"

Suffolk grasped both her wrists in one of his large hands to prevent them from going about his neck. "He is being treated well," he repeated slowly. "He sends you his love."

"What? What does he think this is, a postcard from camp? Let me see the note."

"Nay," he replied, relieved to have her hands captive. "I have destroyed the note for obvious reasons."

"Goddamn it, Suffolk! Why did you do that?" Her eyes filled with hot tears, and she wanted to strike someone, but he gripped her wrists more firmly.

"The less you know, the better for your safety," Suffolk said with authority.

"Don't give me this 'Father Knows Best' stuff. Tell me where he is! In the Tower, right?"

"Calm yourself." He lowered his voice. "He wrote that he loves you above all else, Mistress Deanie. That is all a maid needs to know."

"Hell, I'm not a maid!" Suffolk flushed, but she continued, trying to sound convincing but not hysterical. "Please understand. Kit and I need to be together and to go to the maze at Hampton. In order to be together, he must be released from the Tower. Now, if you would simply tell me where he is, which part of the Tower, I will leave you alone."

"He wrote of the maze."

Deanie stared at him, not sure what to believe.

Suffolk dropped her hands and walked away, a clenched fist tapping against his other hand as he thought. "He told me to help you, to ignite small bundles of gunpowder while you are in the maze. He said you would know when to do it, and that—"

"He said that in the note?"

Suffolk nodded.

"That means he doesn't think he'll get out. He must be in the Tower." The feelings of blind panic she had been trying to crush began to surface again, and she took a deep breath.

"He wished me to reassure you," Suffolk continued. "Should he not return—those were his words—I am to care for you, and you are to receive all of the monies from his estate."

"I don't want anything from his estate." She felt as if the walls were closing in around her. "I want *him.*"

Suffolk opened his mouth, about to tell her that Kit himself did not know where he was being held. But the less she knew the better. And she couldn't ask the servant who'd delivered the message where he had come from, for it was simply left on the threshold, according to the staff. Let her believe he was in the Tower, and she was less likely to attempt something foolish.

"I have known Kit for a long time," he said gently. "Since he was a young man, all legs and fire and spirit. He came to court a youngster, and now he is one of the bravest and best men in England."

Deanie wiped her eyes with an inelegant hand, and he continued.

"I can truthfully say, Mistress Deanie, that he loves you a great deal. He wishes you to be together, but barring that happy possibility, he wishes you to be well alone. Few men love so much that they dare to envision their sweethearts without them." He lifted her chin. "I know I never have. So do as he requests; he risked much to send the missive to my hands. Trust him—and by proxy, me—and all may soon be well."

She was about to protest, to run straight to the Tower and

252

release Kit, but realized that she must find another way. Suffolk was doing his best, she knew that. So instead of kicking him in the shins and escaping, she gave him a genuine smile.

"Thank you. I'll try my best."

Somehow, neither of them truly believed her.

His head had finally stopped its ceaseless drumming.

The jailer had been considerate enough to provide a limitless supply of candles, which was another reason Kit believed he was not a prisoner of the king. Henry would never waste such a large store of tallow on a prisoner, no matter how favored he had once been.

Another fact that led him to believe he was being held by someone else was the king's recent behavior. He was certainly not angry at Kit, for the king let his rage be known whenever a subject displeased him. No, someone with a very good cook was holding him against his will.

He ran a hand over the new growth of beard, scratchy and uncomfortable, but certainly not intolerable enough to be called torture. His eyes watched the flame. He didn't even know what time of day it was; his dark, silent world gave no indication.

His thoughts turned to Deanie, wondering if Suffolk had received his note. If so, it was possible she knew by now that he was being treated well. He just wanted to get the hell out of there without placing her in danger.

Deanie.

How would she look in an evening gown? Not one of those stiff, corseted monstrosities the women wore at court. No.

He could envision her in something of satin, with a low-cut back, a Myrna Loy gown to show off her curves. No wooden headpiece, no layers and ties and leather bindings to hold a sleeve in place, but a delightfully machine-made dress.

And how would her legs look in flesh-colored hose? So far

he'd been the one to wear hose, and he grinned in the soft light, thinking of how his chums in the squadron would react if he asked them if his seams were straight.

Deanie's hair could fall freely to her shoulders, loose and dark and gleaming in the sun. He would show her London, or what was left of it. London would see her, and the grimy eyes of the shell-shocked East Enders would squint at the sight of his Deanie.

Maybe he could take her up in a plane, let her feel the thrill of flying in the clouds.

"Duke? Another meal for you." His eternally cheerful jailer rattled the door and pushed yet another feast into the room.

"Thank you," Kit said automatically. "Oh, wait."

He could hear the man pause.

"Did the message reach Suffolk?"

"I don't rightly know, Sir Duke." Kit could almost envision the man scratching his head. "I believe it did, for it was not returned."

"Thank you," Kit said again, not bothering to examine the irony of a prisoner thanking his jailer. "Oh, one more thing."

"Yes, Duke?"

He was almost afraid to ask. "Is my cousin, Mistress Deanie Bailey, also being held here?" He tried to make his tone conversational, so as not to insult the jailer, who seemed to have his own sense of honor and propriety.

"No! Do you think we'd keep a lady in here? I'm surprised, Sir Duke, that you would even think of it! Why, I never . . ." The man muttered to himself down the hallway.

That was the answer Kit had been hoping for. The man was not a good enough actor to have responded with such force unless it was the truth.

Ignoring the meal, which was rapidly growing cold, Kit settled upon the cot and, his hands linked behind his head, thought more about Deanie.

* * *

She had managed to avoid performing another song at dinner by pleading a headache, which was in fact the truth.

It was astounding how every meal of the king's was orchestrated with the precision of a theatrical performance and the solemnity of a religious rite. Even with but a few of his subjects to bear witness, the scores of servants wordlessly carried out their duties, from the royal napkin steward to the bearer of toothpicks. The king never thanked the silent army whose mission it was to keep apace with his every whim. Had he acknowledged each one, he would pass the day in a never-ending chain of thank-yous.

The advantage of such a small court was that each course was served with astounding speed. With so few distractions, the king ate quickly and greedily, ignoring the bits of food that flew from his mouth as he gnashed his way through each tier of the menu.

Finally it ended, and the women—Katherine and Deanie—were dismissed. Katherine seemed reluctant to leave, and she batted her lashes becomingly at the king. Upon second thought, the king asked Mistress Katherine to linger yet.

Before he could call her back, Deanie slipped quickly from the chamber. He had officially dismissed them, so she simply pretended not to notice Katherine's maneuver. Just as she left, she saw a decidedly smug expression on Norfolk's narrow face.

It was a relief to be alone, to walk through the halls without pretending restrained delight with court life. She was finally able to stop smiling. Her cheeks and lips ached with the artificial smiles she had flashed the king. He wasn't such a bad guy, she mused, rubbing her sore face. He just had no idea that a world existed beyond his own desires.

The hallways at Richmond were not only empty, but far more modest than those at Hampton. This was already an old place, built years ago, before the more modern ideas of airy, spacious architecture became popular. Before Henry, who embraced all things modern, came to the throne.

In a way, she liked Richmond better than Hampton. It was less imposing, more like a regular home than a self-conscious palace.

She strolled through the halls with a very twentieth-century need to unwind and just think. She racked her brain for a way to get to Kit, even just to see him. She *had* to free him, for she had no intention of attempting a journey back to her own time without him.

Then she saw a swish of fabric, green velvet, from the corner of her eye.

At first she thought of Hampton, and the similar experience of wandering the halls alone and being confronted by Surrey. That thought quickly evaporated: Surrey was still at Hampton. There was no one here to harm or even threaten her—except for Norfolk. And he had seemed more than content in the presence of the king and Katherine.

She entered the room where she had seen the green velvet, unquestionably the gown of a woman. The room was empty, with several small chairs and some papers on a window seat.

"Is anyone in here?"

For a few moments there was no response. Just as Deanie was about to leave, a tiny figure stepped from the shadows of a sideboard.

Deanie's first thought was that it was a midget, for she was dressed as a miniature adult. But it was a child, a little girl attired as formally as the highest-ranking courtier. On her head was a diminutive French hood, and her bodice was bound so tightly that it looked even more uncomfortable than usual. Her hands, dimpled and red as if she had tried to scrub them clean, were the only feature that seemed childish.

The little girl sank into a curtsy, her eyes pinned on Deanie's feet.

"Hi there," Deanie said, shifting into her coo-at-the-baby tone.

The girl looked up, and Deanie immediately realized who

it was. The red hair, the translucent eyebrows, the dark eyes—this was Princess Elizabeth.

Her face was grave, too pinched and worried for a child so young.

"I just had dinner with your father," Deanie said. The girl's face remained impassive.

"Are you Katherine Howard?" The princess' voice did not sound like a regular kid's. It was full of uncertain authority.

"Heck no," Deanie responded. "I'm Wilma Dean Bailey, but you can call me *Deanie*. All my friends do."

A dawning expression crossed her features. "I heard you sing before."

"Did you? Why, I don't believe I saw you."

A very tiny smile, small as the girl herself, curved her lips. "I was hiding," she whispered. Then she straightened. "You will not tell, will you?"

"Of course not." Deanie frowned. "I'm no stoolie."

"You are no what?"

"I mean I will not tell. I promise."

The princess seemed satisfied. She looked up at Deanie, her eyes glinting with the same unnerving intelligence as the king's. "Why are you so sad?"

Deanie was about to deny it, when the princess continued. "Your songs were all sad, nothing happy. I am only allowed to sing religious songs in Latin, or happy hunting songs. Why are you so sad?"

"Well, for one thing I don't know any Latin or happy hunting songs," she admitted. "But I suppose you're right. I am sad."

"Why?"

Deanie cleared her throat. "Because I miss someone."

The girl nodded eagerly. "I knew that was the cause! You sounded just like me." With the lightning-swift subject changes of all children, she pointed to the papers on the window seat. "I drew some pictures today."

"Did you? May I see them?"

The princess narrowed her eyes in speculation. "You are

257

just being nice because I am a princess." She spoke as if she knew it to be the truth but wanted someone to contradict it.

"Well, maybe that's part of the reason," Deanie admitted. "Mainly, I want to see your drawings because everyone else in this house is insufferably dull, and I'd rather draw with you than yawn with them."

Elizabeth's mouth dropped open, and then she clapped her childish hand over her mouth and giggled. It was the first truly natural gesture Deanie had seen her perform. She half skipped over to the window seat and grabbed her drawings.

When her back was turned, Deanie saw that the gown was frayed and much too small for a girl of Elizabeth's size. The back was stitched in delicate-yet-entirely-noticeable attempts to repair the garment; the thread was slightly darker and sewn in jagged patches. It was also obvious that the hem had been let down several times, then finally lengthened by a few inches of blue fabric. In an effort to make the repair job less apparent, as well as lengthen the sleeves, the same blue fabric circled her cuffs.

How could the princess be clothed in such threadbare gowns when her father spent a fortune on his embroidered undergarments alone?

She returned with her drawings and handed them shyly to Deanie.

"Let's get closer to the candle, so I can see them better," she muttered, glancing at the top picture.

Deanie had no idea what to expect. She imagined a real princess would draw the same sort of pictures other kids drew, of silly-faced dogs and smiling suns. She cleared her throat, ready to praise the imprecise lines of an elf or crude stick figures.

Instead she saw landscapes, beautifully rendered. "No way," Deanie exclaimed without thinking. She shuffled through the pile, but they were all of the same quality, exquisitely drawn with pen and ink. The details were astounding, every leaf and rock shaded as to appear three-dimensional. One of the drawings did indeed have an animal, but it was a very realistic rabbit peeking from beneath a fallen branch. Even the animal's fur, the differing textures in the fuzzy ears and the sleek back, was done so expertly that she could almost pet it.

"You did these?" Deanie realized her mouth must have been hanging open in stupid befuddlement. "These are amazing. I mean it—these are about the best drawings I've ever seen."

Elizabeth clapped delightedly and nodded, her face reddened with the unfamiliar pleasure of genuine praise.

"I did! I did draw them these past long days, when I have not been allowed to venture forth from this room. I did them from this window, looking down at the grounds through the glass." She peered critically at the one in Deanie's hand. "I saw the hare but a moment, yet I recalled him in most every feature. His nose looked wet." She crinkled her own nose in unconscious mimicry of the animal. "I did not know how to make his nose look wet in my drawing."

"Princess Elizabeth, you are a natural artist," Deanie marveled. Then she looked again at the girl, who was still appraising her own work. "What do you mean? Were you forced to stay inside, even during the beautiful weather?"

The girl straightened and said nothing, as if weighing all possible answers. When she faced Deanie directly, her expression was one of disarming honesty. "Yes. My father, the king, did return unexpectedly to Richmond. He forgot that I was here, and I have been banished to this room. He would not wish to see me. In this remote wing he is most unlikely to stumble upon me."

"That stinks," replied Deanie without thinking.

The princess looked shocked, as if she had rehearsed the reaction frequently. Then she began to giggle again, both hands clamped over her mouth.

"You're right, Mistress Deanie," she whispered. "I think it stinks too."

A large woman garbed in black suddenly appeared in the doorway. "Lady Elizabeth," the woman snapped, with a brief glare in Deanie's direction. "It is well past the hour of prayers and bedtime."

"Thank you, Lady Bryan," the little girl replied solemnly. "I will be there anon."

The woman left, and Deanie leaned closer. "Why didn't she call you *Princess Elizabeth?*"

"Because I have been all but disowned." She began to gather the pictures neatly, brushing off a speck of dried ink from one drawing. "My father had my mother beheaded. Then the next lady he married Queen Jane"—the girl made a sign of the cross—"tried to bring us together, but she died."

"Do you remember your mother at all?"

The child beamed. "I do! She was ever so lovely, with long dark hair all the way to her waist, and her eyes were brown—much as yours are. I remember her laughing all the time, and running after me in a garden. I know not which garden it was, but I know it was so because it is so clear in my mind."

Deanie reached out and touched Elizabeth's soft cheek, feeling the delicate skin only a child can have. At first the girl stiffened, unaccustomed to being caressed. Then her forehead creased, as if in deep thought. "I do remember my mother," she said emphatically.

"Your mother would be very proud of you, Princess Elizabeth."

"Do you think so?"

"I know so."

The girl stared at Deanie. Then, with a swift curtsy and a small smile, she began to leave.

"Oh, wait a minute, Princess."

She paused and faced Deanie, an inquiring expression on her face.

"May I please have a few of those drawings?"

For a moment she hesitated, then shrugged and handed

Deanie the whole stack. "They are for you, Mistress Deanie. Thank you for the praise."

Her back stiff, she left the room with regal bearing. Only when she reached the door did she turn back to Deanie, and she gave a childish wave of her hand before ducking through the door.

Deanie sat alone in the room for a long time, flipping slowly through the drawings, and thinking again of Kit.

Chapter 17

*T*HE KING SAW HER IMMEDIATELY, SEATED IN THE COURTYARD directly below his apartments. He hastened to dress and join her before the rest of the house stirred, before Norfolk could cast one of his disapproving grunts, before even Suffolk—beloved brother-in-law though he was—could overwhelm with his forceful presence.

He checked his appearance in the glass, his privy stewards clucking in pleasure at the sight of their master. He knew his looks were at their best this morn; he had consumed neither drink nor food to excess for these past few days. Henry may not be as handsome as Hamilton, but by God he was king, and that should count for something in the eyes of a maid.

A momentary frown crimped his forehead. Where *was* Hamilton? Subjects had disappeared from court before, certainly. In those unfortunate cases, Henry had known very well where they had vanished to: usually a remote corner of the Tower. Or the bottom of the Thames.

This was different. He liked Kit, enjoyed his company as much as his excellent sport. He sincerely hoped nothing had happened to his friend, and that he would soon return to court hale and healthy.

In the meantime he was more than aware of Hamilton's cousin. With Kit at court, she seemed to ignore all other men, including—most vexatiously—the king himself. Even as he prayed heartily for Hamilton's return, he prayed it would take but a few more days. He certainly wished no harm to befall Hamilton. But should divine providence keep Hamilton from court, well so be it. He would take it as a sign, a message from the Lord himself that Henry was to pass some time in the presence of the lonely Mistress Deanie.

Straightening his imposing shoulders, he tilted his head to observe his reflection in the hand mirror. In truth, it was becoming ever more difficult to appear the way he wished to look. His helpful tailors had broadened his back to make his waist appear more slender. And if the king tipped his head slightly to the side, the unsightly double chin, a recent acquisition, became all but invisible. He would tilt his head thusly when speaking to Mistress Deanie.

When his toilet was completed, he dismissed his servants and checked once more in the courtyard. She was still there, alone, sitting under a tree and drawing. What a fetching picture she made of herself, even in the Germanic gown. He had quite forgotten his own queen, the wife he was beginning to despise less the more time he spent away from her.

He made his way outside quickly. Just before he entered the courtyard, he made a swift inspection of his gold-hued doublet. It would never do to appear before a maid with bits of food flecked on one's doublet.

Deanie brushed a piece of grass from the red folds of her gown, awaiting the arrival of the king. She knew with absolute certainty that he would come lumbering out the door in a matter of minutes. All she needed was a little time alone with him, without Norfolk or even well-meaning

Suffolk. Perhaps she could straighten out this entire mess with a few well-chosen words.

Unfortunately, she wasn't exactly sure what she was going to say. She somehow needed to free Kit, reunite the little princess with her father, and convince the king to spare his wife.

The key to winning over the king was to bend with his moods. She couldn't exactly plan a speech without first discovering his humor. The drawings in her hand rattled as she looked them over once more. Her eyes took in the landscapes, the trees and the wet-nosed rabbit, but all she could really see was Kit.

Had it only been three days since they were together? She could recall every detail, the weight and warmth of his arm around her shoulder, the wistful expression on his face as he looked toward the night sky.

When she first heard that he was taken to the Tower, she was furious with herself for wasting that night. They had said virtually nothing to each other. For most of the time they hadn't even looked at each other, just stood side by side, or sat on the lawn touching hands.

Now she realized how perfect it had been. There was nothing they could say, no words that could convey how they had been feeling that night. Conversation would have been superfluous. And maybe, just maybe, it would have broken the enchantment.

He had to be safe and well. Surely she would feel it in her heart if he was not.

"Mistress Deanie!" The king limped toward her, waving a large hand as if she might not see him. Very unlikely that she could possibly miss his entrance. Not only were they the only two people in the yard, but the jewels of his doublet and round plumed hat caught the sun with the brilliance of a hundred flames.

She smiled and waved back, rising to her feet to drop into a curtsy as he approached. Only as she watched his difficulty in walking did she realize there was no chair or bench for him to sit upon. She herself had been on the grass. She had been used to sitting with Kit, who could spring to his feet and bring her with him.

"Your Majesty," she began. "Shall we go inside, or have someone fetch a chair?"

The king was delighted. He had half expected her to leave. It wasn't until she mentioned the chairs that he realized she meant to stay. With a gruff swat of his hand he gestured to the grass.

"Nay, Mistress Deanie. Whatever gives comfort enough to you will serve me as well." He took her hand. After a moment of hesitation, she realized he was assisting her back to her place on the grass.

Once she was again seated, he lowered himself beside her, his gouty joints creaking in protest. It was obvious the effort caused him a great deal of pain. His thin lips became almost invisible with the strain. But in a surprisingly short time, he was settled on the grass. His ulcerous leg was stretched to the side, as if bending it would be unbearable.

"I'm sorry, Your Highness. We should have called for chairs."

"Nonsense!" He grinned, a single feather from his hat dipping over his left eye. "It has been years since I have had the chance to sit upon the ground. As a boy I sat in this very yard, gazing at the heavens."

He was in an exceptionally good mood. They both knew it, and both suspected it had more than a little to do with springtime and romance. And the possibility of . . .

"Did you sleep well, Your Majesty?"

His eyes became almost comically heavy-lidded as he perused her. "Tolerably well, mistress. Tolerably well."

This was not going in the direction she had planned. She needed to change the topic; something neutral.

"Have you ever had a dog?"

The lascivious smirk fell from the royal visage like a loose brick. "A dog? Why, yes. I believe as a boy I did have a hound or two." Then he smiled, this time a sweet smile of childhood memories. "I loved one dog. His name was Lancelot, for he was brave and strong. That is the reason for the shameful number of dogs at court. Every year or two I issue a proclamation banishing all hounds, other than ladies' lapdogs, from Hampton and Whitehall and every other palace. Then I see a cur who reminds me of old Lancelot, and I forget all about the proclamation."

Okay Bailey, she thought. Now was her chance. "What a wonderful childhood you must have had, Your Majesty," she began.

"Yea, it was. My father was stern, but my mother was soft and kind."

"It's important for a child to feel loved by his or her parents, Your Highness."

He did not reply but raised a suspicious eyebrow.

"Could you tell me about your children?" Her voice was beginning to waver. "You have three, Your Majesty?"

"I have a son, Edward." The king kept his face bland, but his eyes betrayed his suspicions. He spoke carefully. "Edward is a fine son. Perhaps a trifle frail, so I keep him away from the diseases of court."

"Edward has sisters—"

"Mary is my eldest child," he cut her off. "She is a young woman now, and unfortunately follows her mother in temperament and looks."

"And where is she?"

"Mary is elsewhere," he said cryptically. "I see you have done some drawings, Mistress Deanie. May I see them?"

"I met your daughter Elizabeth, Your Highness. She is a wonderful child, bright and curious and full of . . ."

He raised his eyes to her slowly, and she faltered. Never had she seen an expression of such cool fury. She had gone too far too quickly. He began to heft himself up, and she reached out a hand and touched the sumptuous quilted satin of his sleeve.

"Please stay, Your Highness," she groveled. "Forgive me. I talk too much."

The king stopped and looked at her, as if pondering the worth of staying. Perhaps it was simply too much work to lift himself from the ground. Perhaps he wanted to regain his earlier good humor. Without saying a word, he lowered himself back onto the grass. But he did not speak to her.

Her upper lip was perspiring, even though it was cool in the yard. She had to be careful. There wouldn't be a second chance.

"What a lovely day it is, Your Majesty."

He remained silent.

"What is your favorite thing to do in weather like this, Your Highness?" She was beginning to sound like the hostess of a children's program. "I like to take long walks."

Again he remained stubbornly silent. He refused to look in her direction; instead he feigned great interest in the root of a tree that poked just above the surface of the lawn. With his jeweled fingers he poked and prodded at the root, digging away at the dirt, pulling the bark with his well-manicured nails.

She was about to give up when he spoke.

"I like to hunt."

"Oh, hunting?" She folded her hands over the drawings. "What do you like to hunt?"

Again there was a long pause before he answered. "All manner of game." His attack on the defenseless root seemed to let up. "I especially love to bring down a stag, or a wild boar. The bigger the beast, the greater the feeling of triumph. Your cousin is an excellent hunting companion."

"Kit?"

"Indeed." The king smiled and looked at Deanie. "He does remind me of myself in my youth. I watch him on a hunt, and wonder who is the less tamed, Hamilton or the beast." He chuckled. "Usually I vow it is Hamilton."

She had a hard time envisioning Kit as a feral hunter. Mostly she had seen his gentle side. Of course, he did what was expected of him in this time, and that meant hunting animals and jousting on horseback and even engaging in battle. It was also difficult to imagine him as a pilot, dashing to a plane when the alarm sounded, dressing for flight as he ran.

It hit her then: Kit had to leave with her. She did not think he could survive in this time. Deanie had upset the delicate balance he had been forced to maintain in order to endure the brutality of this existence. Already she had seen him falter, think too much instead of instinctively raising his sword.

She had eliminated the edge he had honed during the past decade.

The king was still speaking. Slowly, she turned her attention back to what he was saying.

". . . wherever he is. Norfolk claims to be searching, mistress. Do not worry, for we shall find your cousin. God's will, he will be well in body when we do."

"Wait a minute, Your Majesty. You mean you *really* have no idea where Kit is?"

"Isn't that what I just said?" He began to pluck at the root again. "Women. Every one is the same."

It took her a moment to process the information. The king, whatever faults he may have, had not imprisoned Kit. Was that good or bad? The bottom line was that Kit was still missing. He would not have left willingly.

She took a deep breath. So far this conversation had been a disaster, although at least she'd garnered some information on Kit.

"Well, Your Majesty. Not every woman is the same," she began coyly.

He stopped pulling on the tree root, which was now a pathetically frayed lump of wood. "Yes, mistress?"

"There is one woman who is devoted to her king beyond all else, who will do whatever her sovereign commands." She lowered her voice so that he had to lean close to catch her words.

"Is there?" The leer returned in full force.

"Yes. She is gentle and good, and dotes upon the king. Her days are spent anticipating his wishes."

He began to breathe loudly, and a slight wheezing sound whistled through his nose.

He could barely speak. "Yes?"

"And her name, Your Highness, is Anne of Cleves."

The king looked as if he had been jolted by a live wire. "Bloody hell!" He glared at Deanie and again began to rise to his feet. "This is turning out to be a day fraught with disappointment." He grunted as he stood heavily on his feet. "My hose are ruined," he accused both Deanie and the ground.

"I'm sorry, Your Highness, if my honesty disturbed you. But I—"

"Cease your prattle, mistress! My head pounds with your frivolous words," he sputtered. "By God, you have the ability to make Katherine Howard seem as learned as Erasmus himself."

Deanie stood up without his assistance, gathering the drawings. She bit her lip, aware that one of her unfortunate fits of laughter was about to overtake her. She concentrated on the drawings, busily arranging them in an imaginary order to keep herself from losing control. Something about the king of England, stomping about in baggy stockings, seemed howlingly funny.

"Well?" He planted his hands on his hips, towering over her like a malicious elm. "Have you nothing to say?"

She bit her lip harder and shook her head, silently willing him to leave. Now. Before she began to laugh.

"You tremble, Mistress Deanie. Do you fear your mighty king?"

Oh please, she prayed. Just leave. Take those baggy stockings and leave before . . .

"Look at me, mistress," he commanded.

She glanced up, and their eyes met. And she began to giggle. She saw an expression of incredulous wonder on his face before her vision was blurred with tears. The drawings fell from her grip and floated to the ground, and still she laughed.

And then something astounding happened.

The king began to laugh.

At first he simply stared at Mistress Deanie as if she had been stricken with an infectious illness. He watched her clutch at her drawings as they whirled to her feet, grasping at air. Then she laughed harder.

He suddenly remembered being in church as a child, and the old priest conducting the regal service belched. He too had been overcome with laughter, and his mother scowled, which made him laugh all the harder. As he began laughing with Mistress Deanie, all the weight and cares of the realm seemed insignificant. He was just a man, laughing in the springtime sun with a very pretty woman.

It felt wonderful.

Windows flew open as servants peered in stunned marvel at their king, laughing like a carefree schoolboy with Mistress Deanie. After they had recovered from their initial shock, they too smiled. No one had seen or heard the exchange that had led to the scene, but they enjoyed their king's happiness.

Finally their giggles faded, and both wiped their faces of tears.

"I'm so sorry," she gasped, clutching her aching sides. "I don't know why, but sometimes I lose control like that."

The king sniffed and shrugged, a smirk still on his face. "We have that in common, Mistress Deanie. Here." He bent down and retrieved the drawings, feeling relaxed and content. He glanced at the top paper, and the smile vanished from his face.

"Mistress Deanie, you have not been forthcoming. Not only do you excel in music, but you possess a most artistic hand." He shuffled through the drawings, nodding in approval.

"Oh, I didn't draw those," she admitted cautiously.

"You did not?" He continued looking at them. "Well then, who did?"

"Your daughter."

He stopped, his eyes narrowing. "Mary? Nay. She cannot render a landscape, or even a chair. I have seen her efforts." He shuddered at the thought.

"Elizabeth." Deanie swallowed, all sense of mirth gone from her voice. "Your daughter Elizabeth drew those. She was in her chamber upstairs."

He stared straight ahead, over the paper in his hands.

"She is very much like her father, Your Highness." He looked at her, not anger on his face but bewilderment. Deanie continued: "She has the eye of an artist, and the heart of a prince."

Without speaking, he straightened the drawings and put them under his arm. He crooked his other arm for Deanie to take, and she did. Together they walked back into the palace.

When they reached the door he finally spoke. "Thank you, Mistress Deanie." He touched her shoulder for a moment, staring at his own hand. "I believe I have found something most rare in a woman."

Deanie held her breath. "What is that?" she asked at last.

"A friend," he said simply. And he walked down the hallway, his daughter's drawings still under his arm.

She couldn't wait to speak to Suffolk.

"He's not in the Tower!" Deanie sideswiped the duke just after the midday meal, forcing him into an anteroom.

"Good God, woman!" he sputtered as she closed the door. "What ails you?"

"I spoke to the king this morning, and he has no idea where Kit is. Is that good or bad?"

Suffolk stroked his beard in thought. "I do not believe Norfolk has the power to act without the king's authority," he mused. "And I do not believe Norfolk would do this, not before his niece is secure on the throne."

"So where is he then?"

"I still believe him to be safely ensconced in the Tower," he said at last.

"How could he be in the Tower if the king did not put him there?"

"Ah, my dear. Sometimes the king, well, he occasionally forgets who is in the Tower. In truth, it is so confusing it would take a full-time minister simply to keep track of the occupants."

Deanie was stunned. "You're not kidding," she said, astounded. "He puts people in jail and doesn't remember? Isn't there someone who can remind him?"

"Indeed," Suffolk stated, neatly turning the subject. "Why, Countess Salisbury has languished there these past two years, and she's likely to remain there until she dies. Since she's well-nigh seventy years old and in ill health, she may not have long to wait."

"That is atrocious." Deanie was sickened, not only for the poor woman in the Tower but newly frightened for Kit. "What has this Salisbury woman done to be locked up for so long."

Suffolk seemed surprised. "Do you not know? She is a close relation to the king—a cousin, I believe. He fears there may be those who wish to usurp his crown and make her into a puppet queen. She has already seen the rest of her family executed or killed in battle."

She had seen cruelty in this time, instances of savage behavior—such as the ease with which Cromwell ordered Kit's beating. But somehow she had seen them as isolated incidents, not likely to occur again.

But she had been wrong. Kit had tried to tell her of the violence of court life, the dangers there. She hadn't understood, hadn't listened to his words. It had seemed so unbelievable that gentlemen in embroidered doublets could turn around and order a helpless woman to the Tower.

There was nothing to say, nothing to lessen the sick

feeling in her stomach. Now more than ever she wanted to leave this time. Kit had been right: Just about any place else was better than staying here.

There was a murmur of voices in the corridor. One of the king's stewards knocked once and opened the door.

"Mistress Deanie?" His face was mottled in panic. "Mistress, please come. We need your help."

The first thought that flashed through her mind was of Kit; that he had been found and he was hurt.

Suffolk stayed her with an outstretched hand. "What goes?"

The steward grimaced. "There are more than fifty members of the barber-surgeon guild below, and all wish an audience with Mistress Deanie."

"For crying out loud!" mumbled Deanie. "Don't they have anything better to do than shave my legs?"

"It appears not, mistress," said the duke, winking at her.

"All right. Tell them I'll be right down."

The grateful steward bowed and slipped out quickly, not wishing to give Deanie a chance to change her mind.

Resigned to her fate, she stepped to the window and stared down at the scores of burly men milling about in the courtyard. Suffolk stepped by her side and chuckled.

"They are a virtual army," he muttered, shaking his head in amusement.

Deanie was about to agree, when she stopped. "What did you say?"

"I said they are a virtual army," he repeated.

"An army," she said softly. "My own army . . ."

"Mistress Deanie," Suffolk warned, "I like not your tone."

She answered him with a beaming smile.

"Tell me what is churning in that mind of yours," ordered Suffolk.

But Deanie said nothing. She simply nodded at him and left the antechamber with an alarmingly light step.

After a brief pause, Suffolk began to follow her through the door. "I am getting too old for this," he mumbled to himself as he straightened his sword.

Before he could make it to the courtyard, he was stopped by Norfolk, who informed him that the king needed his counsel on urgent business. Suffolk had no choice but to go with Norfolk.

He was not particularly worried. After all, what harm could befall Mistress Deanie in the few short minutes during which he would be closeted with the king?

If he weren't so damned well fed and rested, he wouldn't be so damned annoyed.

"I will repeat my question," Kit said between clenched teeth. "Who is holding me?"

"Now now," soothed his tormentingly cheerful jailer. "How's about another slice of pheasant?"

"I do not want pheasant." Kit realized he was sounding like a petulant child. "I want to leave this place."

"Now why would you want to do that, Sir Duke? Is not the cooking to your liking? Is the wine off?"

"The cooking and the wine are more than agreeable."

"Why thank you, Duke. I will go and inform Cook, and pleased as Punch he will be, let me tell you."

"No!" Kit wiped a hand over his mouth in exasperation. "Please, just tell me where I am."

"You are in a lovely place, really."

A noise very much like a growl escaped Kit's throat, and he heard his jailer back away.

"Now, now, Sir Duke. Why would you want to leave here and go back to that nasty court?"

Kit was about to speak when something about the jailer's words made him halt. He bit back the venomous urge to shout. Instead, he softened his voice. "You do have a point there, my good man," he coaxed.

"Yes I do, Sir Duke. All those evil people, God help us,

running about, mucking about where they have no right. Yer better off here, that's what I say."

"I suppose you're right." Kit tried to keep his voice calm. "I am just concerned about my cousin."

"Mistress Deanie? Awe, don't you worry about her, Sir Duke. He'll watch out for her."

"He will, won't he?" Kit willed himself to relax. "He has always been a good friend to me."

"The flower of manhood he is!" The jailer stopped and sucked in his breath, as if he could suck back his words from the air. "By God, I had best see to my chores."

Kit sat heavily on the cot, fury surging through him. Now it all made sense, his well-meaning, confoundedly meddling friend. The flower of manhood.

Blast him to hell!

From below the cellar, the entire house was racked by a single bellowing voice.

"SUFFOLK! DAMN YOU, I'LL GET YOU FOR THIS!"

The servants, the kitchen staff, the stable boys and laundresses and gardeners all stopped, exchanged perplexed blinks, and returned to work.

It was always an adventure working in the household staff of Charles Brandon, the duke of Suffolk. Always an adventure indeed.

Chapter 18

THE PLAN WASN'T QUITE WORKED OUT YET. THERE WERE A few minor details missing, a very few trivial items that needed to be fine-tuned.

For one thing, Deanie had no idea where the Tower of London was located. Of course it was in London, and it was a tower. But that was all she knew.

Finding London was also something of a problem. The last time she was there it had been marked with reflecting road signs and tourist kiosks. She'd been lounging in the back of a large, American-style, air-conditioned bus, her headphones plugged into the rough tape of a new CD, and had paid absolutely no attention to landmarks or directions.

Once at the Tower, Deanie had no further strategy. That was it. She had an imprecise notion of storming through the Tower gates with a gang of barbers and exiting with an extra barber—namely Kit. If she could find that woman, the countess of Salisbury, she would grab her as well. Nothing mattered other than getting Kit out of there as soon as possible.

Assuming Deanie and her makeshift army of confused barbers could actually locate the right town and the right tower, finding Kit within the walls of said tower was also going to be rather exciting. She had convinced the barbers that she was going on a mission of mercy to shave and bleed some of the more unfortunate occupants of the Tower. They knew she had become a favorite of the king's and did not dare question her authority.

Deanie added an extra incentive: If they followed her occasionally strange-sounding orders, she would give them permission to shave her legs as much as they wished. She further promised to make hair-free legs en vogue at court, thereby providing them with an intriguing sideline.

"What if men decide to have their legs shaved as well?" The question came from a massive young man named Yerkel. He seemed to have no first name, no last name. Just *Yerkel.*

"Here, here!" shouted an enthusiastic barber with a disfiguring growth on the side of his face. "I will not shave a gentleman's limbs."

"No. I think you're all safe. I don't think men would like it." She tried to sound convincing, but she herself wasn't so sure. Men in 1540 did wear stockings, after all.

The trick was to persuade the barbers that going to the Tower had been their own idea, a guild-sponsored charity mission. After a few moments of heated debate, they agreed to allow Deanie to go with them.

Surprisingly, to the barbers, the Tower itself did not conjure frightening images, no apparitions of Vincent Price or looming shadows. Only recently had it been used as Henry's jail. Before, it had simply been a royal residence, like Nonesuch or Richmond. Since it was much older—it had already been standing for hundreds of years—the building was well fortified from the days of ever-changing kings and hostile invasions. After the more recent imprisonments of Anne Boleyn, Thomas More, and a handful of other executed nobles, it was just beginning to garner its sinister reputation.

They had left immediately, the barbers on their mounts and Deanie on Fancy, the same horse she'd ridden weeks earlier from Hampton. She didn't want to wait a minute for Suffolk to follow, or for anyone else to discover her plan. Even running back into the palace to change into more suitable riding attire was out of the question; she surely would have been stopped.

They were but a few miles from London, continuing on the muddy Thames-side path that traveled from Hampton to Richmond.

She now understood why Suffolk had called the road dangerous. Even in the full sun of a spring afternoon, she caught sight of half a dozen undesirable, suspicious-looking characters, all of whom seemed capable of the most vile of crimes. Only when the potential felons seemed to be following at an alarmingly close pace did she realize they were reinforcements for her army. The extra barbers joined them on the road, casting curious glances at her ankle when the skirt of her red velvet gown became caught on the saddle.

London was still nowhere in sight, or even on the horizon. She felt as if they had been traveling for hours. Even as they entered a village, there were no indications that the great metropolis of London was near.

The village was sprawling, hundreds of half-timber houses and single-story cottages sprinkled along a gentle rise. Some of the homes boasted glass windows and brick chimneys; others had nothing but oiled linen covering the windows.

The more modest dwellings had no chimneys at all. Instead they had gaping holes in the roofs. Since it was now spring, most of the roof holes were covered with lengths of thatch or wooden boards or more oiled linen, anything else that might keep out the rain.

Cattle meandered at a leisurely pace through the muddy

streets, making them more evil smelling than even the Thames-side road. Nothing was paved, and the streets were dangerously slick with animal excrement, rotting garbage, used bathwater, and the tossed-out remains of household privies.

The buildings became progressively larger and more impressive, the gardens smaller as the houses were packed closely along the streets both broad and narrow. There seemed to be no plan to the village, no sense of zoning commercial buildings from the residential ones.

She caught sight of a wide bridge spanning the river. The amazing thing about the bridge was that it was an actual street, boasting two parallel rows of houses, some as tall as three stories. They were pointed and spiraled, triangular and square.

A chiming in the distance signaled the hour of two. Deanie turned to Yerkel, taking a deep breath through her mouth to avoid the surrounding stench. She had become used to the odors of the court, but this was another level of stink she could never have imagined.

"Where are we?"

Yerkel, whose single expression seemed to be one of bland resignation, lifted his blond eyebrows. "We are in London, Mistress Deanie."

Deanie was about to respond, but instead held her tongue. What had she been expecting? Piccadilly Circus with candles? Signs pointing the way to Heathrow?

At once a vile gust of wind blasted past them. Deanie gagged. Yerkel gazed calmy as she struggled against the urge to wretch.

"Yonder are the tanners," he explained with the air of a bored tour guide. "The fishmongers and the butchers ply their trades together, so their smells do not poison all of London. The bear-baiting pits lay there as well, if you enjoy the sport. So are the baths, the stews, and so forth."

He smiled in benign contentment.

"Where is the Tower?"

Without speaking, he nodded in the direction of a brick structure.

While she was instantly relieved that Kit was not imprisoned in a more horrifying building, it was something of a disappointment. She had been expecting a dramatic Gothic castle, black and sooty, covered with chains and the remains of tortured victims, faces contorted in silent screams of eternal agony.

Instead it was almost cheerful, the gray bricks edged with lighter trim, impressive turrets on every corner. The clustered towers made the compound resemble a Disney creation.

The only hint of foreboding was the well-armed guards standing with rigid authority at the gate. They held staffs much like those of guards at Hampton, and their determined expressions appeared even more fierce because of the iron helmets worn low on their foreheads.

The closer they got, the less cheerful the Tower appeared. Most of the expansive windows were covered with spiked bars. They rode over a small arched bridge to the main entrance. From that angle Deanie could see the river entrance, the so-called Traitor's Gate, through which so many of Henry's enemies had made their one-way journey.

The large guard, standing with his muscled legs apart, did not seem to notice Deanie and the barbers. He did not seem to move a muscle, not even to blink.

"Hey," Deanie called as her horse broke away from the pack. The barbers remained a few feet behind in a shifting cluster. The guard gave no response to her greeting. "Good day," she tried again. "Um, we've come here to shave the prisoners."

With that statement the guard's steel-blue eyes slid to her face. Still he remained silent, impassive as a log.

"You see, we're all here to make the prisoners a bit more

comfortable. It's the little touches that add up." What was she saying? Next she'd go on about a chocolate on the pillow and a complimentary Continental breakfast.

Although it seemed impossible, the guard appeared even more solid than a few minutes earlier.

She heard the clip-clop of hooves behind her and turned to see Yerkel, his face partially obscured by the cowl of his cloak, approach on his oversized horse. She tried to gesture him back to the rear. The last thing she needed was Yerkel's brooding presence by her side.

"Good day, Robert," Yerkel said to the guard.

"Good day to you as well, Yerkel," the guard muttered without looking up.

"You two know each other?"

Yerkel said nothing, but the guard nodded, a gesture so slight she would have missed it had she not been alert.

"Yerkel," she whispered. "Can you get us inside? Bribe him, threaten, promise him just about anything—just let us get inside."

Yerkel remained silent, but he dismounted from his horse and walked over to the guard. They exchanged a few words, a very few words, and the guard's eyes widened, and he looked Deanie up and down. Finally he nodded once and called to someone inside the gates. The man inside called to another unseen person, their shouts echoing against the brick walls.

"What did you tell him?" Deanie hissed to Yerkel, who was motioning to the other barbers to dismount.

Yerkel did not respond. Instead he patted his horse and began to walk through the open gates.

"Please, what did you say? It had to have been a threat, perhaps a dire warning. Did you threaten to fight with him? Please, Yerkel."

He stopped, his massive shoulders straight, his rounded blond head still. "The truth?" His tone was ominous, and Deanie was again reminded what a barbaric age this was.

She nodded, bracing herself for the savage warning Yerkel must have imposed.

"I told Richard that should he allow us to pass within the Tower gates to shave some of the prisoners, we will divide with him any coins we are given."

"That's it?" She was unreasonably let down. "You guys promised to share the tip?"

"That was not all." Yerkel's voice took on a menacing edge.

Her eyes widened. She needed to know what bloodthirsty method Yerkel had employed to gain entry. She may need the technique later.

"I told him that should he allow us to pass unhindered, I will ask Mother to make a beef pudding."

"Mother?"

"Richard is my older brother," he concluded, nodding to his sibling as they passed through the gates.

"Oh." She looked over at the guard, trying to imagine a large, doting mother silently stirring a kettle. "Can you ask him where the duke of Hamilton is?"

Yerkel shrugged, handing Deanie the reins to his horse, and returned to his brother. After a few more brief words, Yerkel walked back to Deanie.

"My brother says the duke of Hamilton is most likely at court with the king or at his own estate, Manor Hamilton."

"No, no," Deanie corrected. "Tell him it's perfectly all right, we know Kit's in here."

"My brother says he is not."

"No offense," she said, studying Richard's solid and unyielding form. "But is it possible that he just doesn't have everyone's name straightened out?"

Yerkel gave a half shrug of acknowledgment. "It is possible."

"Well, then." She sighed. "I guess it's about time for us to begin shaving the prisoners."

"Only their faces," he warned. "I will not shave the leg of a man, or the arm either."

And with the limb issue settled to Yerkel's satisfaction, they began searching for Kit.

"Hamilton! God's blood, move that carcass of yours!"

Kit jumped from the cot at the sound of the voice, the clattering of a sidearm becoming louder as Suffolk approached.

"So has he told you, Suffolk?" Kit warned. "Has my jailer told you that I intend to kill you? I shall enjoy every moment, you black-hearted whoreson."

"Hold, Kit. We do not have time for this." The rusty lock clicked open and light flooded the cell. "Mistress Deanie's in the Tower."

"What happened?" His anger vanished as he was released from the room. He bolted down the hall with Suffolk, paying little attention to the stone corridor or the startled servants.

"I must apologize, my friend," Suffolk panted. "I thought to only help you, the both of you."

"Tell me, what happened?"

"I took you here, to my own estate, as I garner you have deduced by now. The rumors were running thick and fast that you would attend Cromwell in the Tower. I wanted to remove you from danger, and had to move quickly, while the king was yet away at Richmond."

"Did Deanie know of this?"

"Nay. I underestimated her, Kit. I told her naught of my plan, feeling she would be safer if she acted the part of the grieving cousin."

"Poor Deanie," he mumbled, squinting against the unaccustomed sun. "The Tower, Charles. Tell me how she was arrested, and why." He tried to keep the dread from his voice, tried to remain calm.

"Oh, she was not arrested."

Kit stopped, pulling Suffolk to an abrupt halt with him. "What?"

"She stormed the Tower, Kit. Entered on her own free will with a pack of barbers, intending to free you."

"She broke *into* the Tower? That ridiculous, empty-headed . . ."

"Here's your mount. Forgive me, Hamilton. I did what I thought was best."

Kit, his harsh features a mask of intensity, paused and smiled at Suffolk, a brief, fleeting smile. "I know that, friend. Were the positions reversed, I daresay we would be galloping away from my own estate, at this very moment."

Together, with their hastily banded group of men, they raced to the Tower of London.

They had shaved at least two dozen men, some less alert than others. Some did not even appear to realize they were being tended to. One fought back with blind fear when he saw Yerkel approach with a glinting straight razor. Only later, when he had been calmed, did he understand he was not to be tortured or executed.

She could not believe the conditions these men were forced to endure. Although a few of the chambers were fairly well furnished, she quickly realized those were mainly the newcomers. By the time the days had stretched into weeks, and the months to years, the once-noble courtiers became forgotten by all, including their own families. Life ground on outside the Tower walls, while the captive inhabitants were forced to endure the cruel boredom of imprisonment.

Every door held the possibility of Kit. She would hold her breath as Richard, watching them with unflattering intensity, allowed them into the chambers.

She was beginning to give up when Richard led them to a corner chamber. The key to this room was more ornate, the door itself was more massive.

This might be it.

The door swung open with a heavy thud, and Deanie entered. There was but little light in the dim chamber. In the center of the cell was an oversized desk covered with papers.

"Kit?"

Her voice bounced off the stone walls, sounding hollow and unnatural. From a darkened corner came a low chuckle, mirth without humor.

"Who is it?" Her question was not answered. Instead, the man laughed some more.

"Mistress Deanie." The man emerged from the shadows, and Deanie instinctively stepped back. "How very kind of you to visit. Forgive my squalid lodgings."

"Cromwell."

"Indeed."

She could see him more clearly now. He still wore the elegant clothing of his recent office, but the fur collar and cuffs were matted, and the cloak had dark patches of soil and grease. Although he was not wearing a hat, his dark hair clung to his round head as if it were still tamped down by a fashionable bonnet.

"I'm sorry," she mumbled. The barbers did not enter the cell, but the guards watched warily. She began to leave, moving backward as if not comfortable turning her back on the prisoner.

"What brings you to the Tower?" he asked mildly. "You have not been arrested."

"I was just leaving."

"I see. You were simply walking through the pleasant Tower corridors, and decided to pay an old friend a visit."

She had reached the door, about to turn and flee.

"Wait." His voice was less a command than a plea. She paused, comforted by the sight of the barbers, who were discussing which level to enter next.

"How fares the queen?"

Deanie squinted, wondering what game Cromwell was playing.

"Of all the things I have done, I regret that the most." He seemed to be talking to himself. "My intention was not to deceive the king, nor to harm an innocent from Cleves. I thought they would find a fair measure of happiness."

Cromwell moved toward the desk piled with papers. "He makes me work yet, forces me to labor for the annulment. There are indeed grounds for this annulment, real ones. It is the last thing I will do for him. I hope that one day he will recall my toil, even in here."

He seemed lost in his own world, as if Deanie had vanished. She made another movement to leave. His eyes, suddenly clear, focused on her once again.

"Tell her to agree," he said softly.

"Tell who to agree to what?" She was torn between wanting to leave and wanting to know what he was talking about.

"The queen. I am making provisions for her well-being. Tell her not to quarrel, not to demand more. There will be humiliation, of course, but better humiliation alive than pride dead. The king will want this done with, and will not stop to think about how generous he is being with Queen Anne. By the time he does know, he will not change the settlement. He will have been complimented on his kindness, a thing he relishes."

Deanie watched his face. Gone was the ruthless ambition, the constant drive she had seen before. Now he was calm, resigned.

"I'll tell her," Deanie said.

"Thank you."

Again she started to leave. She could feel the heat of his stare on her back. Without turning, she spoke. "Why were you so cruel to me and Kit?"

"Mistress?" His voice was incredulous, and she spun to face him.

"Why did you try to kill him? Why did you want to see us apart?"

Cromwell remained still for a moment, weighing her words. "It was not my intention to be cruel." He glanced back to his desk. "I did what I felt was best for the king. He did not want the Cleves union. I thought to offer him a choice. But you, the two of you, would not allow it." Then he shrugged. "It was too late. I did not know it, but it was already too late for me."

"Is he here, in the Tower?"

"Hamilton?" Cromwell seemed surprised. "Nay. Not as I know."

She grappled for something to say but could think of nothing.

"I did my best." Cromwell frowned and plucked at his cuffs. "Always I did my best for the king. I learned from Wolsey how to bend the law to suit a royal whim. It seems I neglected to follow Wolsey's last lesson, the most important one. I did not learn from his fall. I thought I would be different, but just as Cromwell replaced Wolsey, Norfolk will replace Cromwell. Not for long. Norfolk is not clever enough to keep apace. His nobility will prohibit his success."

It was time to leave. The guard slowly closed the door, and Cromwell, still staring at his desk, made no notice.

"Mistress Deanie," he said.

The door was almost closed, and she halted the guard's arm on the lock.

"Yes?"

Cromwell cleared his throat, as if deciding whether or not to speak. "Watch yourself, mistress. You and Hamilton. Get yourselves as far from this shore as you can. Go now. Go far, and do not delay."

The heavy door swung shut. The barbers and the guard said nothing but exchanged curious looks over Deanie's head.

"I don't think Kit's here," she said to herself, rubbing a tired hand over her eyes. "Do you want to call it quits?"

Yerkel shifted his leather satchel to the other hand, his gaze involuntarily sliding down her leg.

"I am not tired. Are you men tired?"

"I am not tired," seconded the barber with the facial growth.

"Hell," she muttered. "I suppose I'm going to have my legs shaved again."

Yerkel thought for a moment. "Perhaps we should give some of the prisoners a healthful bleeding. Then we can shave your legs." He blushed when he said the word *legs*.

A new guard suddenly bustled into the hall, breathing hard from climbing up the steps. He bowed to Yerkel's brother. "Sir, below are two dukes. They have men, and wish to gain entry."

The guards discussed the situation, but Deanie paid no attention. She was bone-tired, depressed after seeing the prisoners—most of whom seemed to have done nothing more serious than be born into the wrong family—and needed to think.

If Kit was not in the Tower, where the hell could he be?

"I have never liked this place," Suffolk mumbled. He sniffed with distaste as a guard held them at the gates, waiting for an answer to their request to enter. "Even when the king and I were boys, and the Tower was a place where sovereigns awaited their coronation, it made me uneasy."

"Perhaps it was the tale of the lost princes." Kit tried to peer beyond the guard, but he could see nothing.

"Perhaps. The king's father spoke often of the two princes, murdered by their uncle."

"Who was in turn murdered by the king's father," Kit added distractedly.

"Watch your step, Hamilton," Suffolk warned. "You are my friend, but above all I serve the king. Richard fell in battle; there was no murder. My own father died on Bosworth Field."

"I apologize."

Suffolk said nothing. He knew the king's faults, knew the thorns in the Tudor dynasty better than anyone. But he would not hear a word raised against the Tudors, would not allow disparaging comments to be uttered in his presence. Not of serious matters. To Suffolk as well as to the world, such was the stuff of treason.

"Damn it, where is she?" Kit spat.

The gate opened, and a dusty group of men leading their horses began to exit. Kit passed an impatient hand over his face, surprised by the full beard he had acquired. He had forgotten. How long had it been since he had . . .

He saw a flash of red in the center of the passing men.

Without seeing more, without even seeing a face or a form, he knew who it was.

"Deanie!" He cupped his hands over his mouth so his voice would carry.

The flash of red stopped. The clatter of horses' hooves blanked the sound of a single voice, and the flash of red continued.

"DEANIE!"

This time she handed the reins of her horse to a hulking blond youth.

"Kit?" Her call was distant, and she was looking about.

He charged toward her, brushing past startled barbers and their horses.

She seemed so small, her back turned, calling his name in the wrong direction. Had she always been so small? In the red velvet German gown, the sleeves tightly laced, she seemed like a doll, a dash of brilliant color in a swirling beige world.

His arms gripped her shoulders, and even under the layers of fabric he could feel her shoulder blades. Then he turned her around, and she faced him.

Kit. Her mouth formed his name, but no noise came out.

His hair was dark and tossled, and his face was covered with a fierce beard, but his eyes, green slivered with brown, seemed lit with an inner fire. She reached up and threw her arms about his neck, her own eyes closed against the sudden rush of tears.

Just to feel him, the iron grip as he lifted her off the ground, his long fingers splayed against her back and shoulders, caused her head to spin. His familiar scent, the soft bristle of his beard against her face. She swallowed, inhaling against the crook of his neck, feeling his warm breath as he kissed her temple.

"I was so afraid I'd never see you again," she cried. That had been her fear, unspoken, silent. She had wondered if she would ever feel his touch. Ever hear his rich voice . . .

"Deanie." His tone was tight, warring with the overwhelming desire to hold her forever.

She felt herself sag against him. Her relief was crushing, almost painful.

Then his mouth was on hers, hot and demanding and shattering. Her hand, which had been clutching at his powerful back, clenched into a fist, then, ever so slowly, unfolded.

There was a noise, like buzzing in her ears. He pulled away from her mouth, cradling her head with a broad hand. Their eyes met, focused only on each other, and for the first time in days, he grinned. She stared at his mouth, the lips that had just left hers. His impossibly white teeth, the one crooked bottom tooth.

Someone whispered, a distant sound, and another cleared his throat, a faraway shuffling. The buzzing she had heard was the hiss of conversation.

She blinked. Only then, as she peered past Kit's shoulder, did she realize they were surrounded by dozens of onlookers: horses, barbers, guards, tradesmen with carts, curious housewives.

"Many pardons." She recognized the voice as Yerkel's. "But would the duke be wanting a shave?"

Deanie ran a finger over his jaw, the lush beard. It made him look dangerous, a ruthless pirate. He caught her hand and kissed it, closing his eyes as he did.

There was a smattering of laughter. Kit opened his eyes

and raised an eyebrow in the direction of the duke of Suffolk.

"What did you say?" he asked, but his eyes had returned to Deanie.

"I simply noted that should they wish to give you a shave at this very moment, you would end up bald as Caesar," answered Suffolk with a good-natured chortle.

"Caesar?" Deanie smiled up at Kit. "The salad guy?"

The onlookers watched in wonder as the pair managed to laugh even as they kissed.

Chapter 19

*E*VERYONE THOUGHT THEY WERE MAD.

Deanie and Kit had been together a scant few minutes when they proclaimed a driving need to journey to Hampton.

"Hampton?" Suffolk spit out a mouthful of ale. The guards, upon realizing the exact identities of the august dukes, had produced ale, cheese, and bread for all to partake of before they left the Tower. The three sat on a low fence, their makeshift bench. Deanie nibbled guiltily at the coarse bread, wondering if their impromptu picnic would mean hunger for some of the prisoners.

She had not been able to stop looking at Kit, at his sure and solid movements, the protective arm he would drape around her shoulder. Now that they were together, and it felt so very right, an extraordinary sense of belated terror made her knees weak.

They had come so close to losing each other. Had she stayed within the Tower gates but a few extra moments, if she had left through the side gate as they had originally planned, they would have missed each other.

The bread was hard to swallow.

Kit and Suffolk were still debating the matter of going to Hampton.

"Richmond is closer by miles," Suffolk emphatically pointed out. "And the king wishes to see you, Kit. He has been sore put to discover your whereabouts."

"I am flattered. But we need to travel to Hampton, and we need to get there before nightfall."

"Before nightfall! Already it is well past the hour of four."

Deanie leaned closer to the conversation. Although she addressed both, she was clearly speaking to Kit. "The sun sets at about six, right?"

"Later." Kit shifted, pulling her closer, her shoulder pressed to his chest. A delicious thrill ran through her at his touch. She wondered, distractedly, if it would always be like this, if she would always take such delight in his nearness. He spoke, and she felt his voice rumbling against her. "It is spring, so the sun stays up longer. We have until seven, perhaps later."

Suffolk made a fist in frustration. "You will not be dissuaded, then." Kit and Deanie, in perfect unison, shook their heads. "I will go ask the guard where a boatswain may be had." He stalked off, muttering under his breath as he took a sip of ale.

After days of uncertainty and tormenting anxiety, Kit and Deanie were finally alone.

For a moment she did nothing but relax in the circle of his arms, unconsciously falling into the rhythm of his breathing. There were some things she wanted to say. She needed to tell him how she had felt without him, how her life before all of this meant nothing to her now. All she needed was Kit. He was all that mattered.

She was safe here. She sighed, drowsiness overtaking her. It had been impossible to sleep before she found Kit. Now she was safe.

His hold on her tightened as her eyes fluttered shut. Gently he kissed her forehead. Should he tell her now? He wondered, watching as she drifted off to sleep.

He had done much thinking in his jail cell; there had been little else to occupy his time. Deanie had been the center of his swirling thoughts. Wherever they went, no matter where they eventually settled, he hoped they would be together. Of course he would give her time alone, for she had forged a life for herself, just as he had forged one in this century. It would take some adjusting. Yet he knew they could make a go of it, wherever they were.

One of the barbers began to approach Kit, offering to give him a shave. But the barber halted, transfixed by the tender expression on the duke's strong face. His harsh features softened as he stared down at the woman in his arms.

They would speak later, Kit thought, noticing the dark smudges of gray under her eyes. She could use a nap, no matter how brief. A slight smile of recognition lifted the corners of Kit's mouth, for he too had been unable to sleep.

Then the barber heard the duke speak in a low, rasping voice: "My love."

And the barber wisely decided to choose another occasion to ask the duke of Hamilton if he would like a shave.

She had a dream she was gliding.

There were splashy water sounds in the distance, but she felt no urgent need to wake up. The sun warmed her limbs, and she took a deep breath, contented and lethargic.

Then, rudely, something cold and wet dripped on her face. With a gasp she sat up.

"The boat! Don't rock the boat!"

Shielding her eyes, she saw Kit, working a clumsy pair of oars. His doublet was removed, and the white linen sleeves of his shirt were rolled above his elbows, exposing the corded muscles of his forearms.

"How long have I been asleep?" Her eyes focused on the bare throat revealed by his open collar. His skin, flushed with the exertion of rowing, gleamed through the nearly transparent shirt.

He grinned, looking very much like a pirate with brilliant teeth set against a black beard. Without thinking, she reached out and touched the hollow of his throat, her thumb feeling the throbbing pulse there. His grin vanished slowly, and he took a deep breath, leaning toward her as the oars rose above the water.

"Faster, Hamilton!"

Deanie jumped. Just behind her, lounging on the opposite end of the rowboat, was a much contented Suffolk. He still held a mug of ale in his grip, while the other hand dragged languidly in the water.

"You said you needs be there before sundown," Suffolk chastised. "Unless you row faster, we will miss it altogether. The sun lowers even now."

Kit grunted in reluctant acknowledgment and began to row harder, harder still.

"You're a big help," Deanie said to Suffolk. With a smile and a guiltless shrug, he took another swallow of ale. "The boat would hold but three. Hamilton said he would row if I but curbed my tongue so you could sleep. I did, as you can see. And you, Mistress Deanie, were drooling."

She clapped her hand over her mouth, and both Suffolk and Kit laughed.

"Be kind, Suffolk. I have seen you do far worse in your sleep, and even more atrocious deeds while awake," Kit said, winking at a mortified Deanie.

"Aye, it is true. There! I see Hampton on the rise! God's blood, Hamilton, I believe we will make it."

Deanie reluctantly pulled her gaze beyond Kit. And as Suffolk had said, Hampton Court Palace, its splendor bathed in the ethereal light of an afternoon sun, was in view. The twisting brick chimneys seemed to glow in the springtime warmth.

"You have the bottle?" Kit asked her, glancing over his shoulder to guide the boat.

"Not anymore. It is empty," Suffolk announced with sadness.

"Not that bottle." Kit shook his head in amused resignation.

Deanie flashed a smile at Suffolk and turned to Kit, her tone more serious. "Last time I checked it was in my chamber at Hampton. It should still be there."

He nodded once and returned to the business of moving the oars. Deanie was astounded at his stamina, at the strength it took to row the boat and its three adult passengers upstream the many miles to Hampton. He was only slightly out of breath, and Deanie could see that the shoulder wounded by Cromwell's men seemed to be giving him some trouble. He favored the other arm, and he rotated the painful shoulder as if trying to work away the stiffness.

"Suffolk, you know what to do about the gunpowder?"

"Why do you think I have had to quaff so much ale?" Suffolk muttered, shaking his head in disbelief. "Yes, my brain-addled friend. You will find two dozen bundles of gunpowder and wadding placed about the maze. I will, if given but another mug of this inferior brew, touch off the lights for you, and trust myself not to blow us all to the heavens."

Then he paused, and an entirely different expression passed over his face. He seemed able to shake off the effects of drink like a cloak. He grew somber, staring into his earthenware mug. "I warn you, if the king is in residence, I will not do this thing for fear of harming him."

"Oh, he won't be there," Deanie said. "I know he wasn't planning to return as long as Queen Anne remains."

Suffolk seemed satisfied, carefully studying the empty mug as Kit steered the boat to one of the smaller docks. A man at the dock grabbed the ropes, and Kit stood up, pulling on his doublet as he took her hand.

"What, Hamilton? Will you not assist me?" Suffolk rose unsteadily to his feet.

"How much did he have to drink?" whispered Deanie.

"I thought not much," he said as he lifted her over the water and placed her on land. "I did not count. I was too busy."

"Rowing?"

"No." He winced as Suffolk staggered through the water, headless that it was up to his waist. "I was busy watching you drool."

She would have responded, but they didn't have time. The sun was beginning to sink at an alarmingly fast rate.

"I'll run to get the bottle," she said, picking up the heavy hem of her gown. He nodded.

"I will get the fireworks ready." He suddenly turned to her. "We're a little early for your Fourth of July celebration."

"It's the middle of June." She smiled, pushing a lock of hair from his forehead. "We have a couple of weeks to go."

"More like a couple of centuries," he mumbled, more to himself than to her. His eyes were focused on the maze just beyond, and the burlap bundles Suffolk was ordering a perplexed gardener to arrange.

"I'll be right back," she said, touching his arm.

He seemed to be lost in his own thoughts, staring ahead. Abruptly he grabbed Deanie's wrist. "It's going to work, you know," he said. "I can feel it. It's the same way I felt before, when I first came here. That day I thought I was experiencing a premonition of my own death, but it was the journey here I was anticipating."

With a shake of his head, as if to dislodge his tumbled thoughts, he gave her hand a squeeze. "We'd best get on with this."

She was reluctant to leave his side. "I'm frightened," she murmured. It was as if a knowing breeze coursed through her; she had never said those words before. In all the triumphs she had managed in her life, the setbacks and the roller-coaster panics, she had never uttered those words.

She was scared to death.

Instead of coddling her, or calming her rampaging fears, he simply smiled. It was a sweet, sad smile. "I am too, my love," he breathed. "You had best get the bottle." Then he left to assist a badly reeling Suffolk, who was unintentionally dripping ale on the gunpowder bundles.

Hefting the weighty velvet hem above her ankles, she ran to the palace. Part of her wanted to see Anne of Cleves one last time. The more sensible part realized she could do little to help her. She had already told Suffolk of Cromwell's advice to follow the king's whims. Seeing the queen would not help anyone.

The halls were virtually empty. Since the king was now lodged at Richmond, most of the more fashionable and ambitious courtiers had already begun the laborous shift to Richmond. It was much work, sending servants and lesser nobles ahead, folding rich clothes into the dome-lidded trunks. But to the courtiers, it was well worth the effort.

The bottle was right where she'd left it. She grabbed the neck and paused, startled by a peculiar sense of having her middle cinched by a wide band. If all went as planned, this was the last she would see of this century.

There was a pang in her throat, an undefined longing. She placed her hand over the low square neck of her gown and felt the pounding of her heart. Why did she have such terrible feelings of regret?

Kit.

It was because she associated this era—the smells and sounds and fingertip sensations—with one man. Without him it would have been simply a curious journey. It would have been like a well-designed historical theme park.

But it was here, where violence and death and inscrutable absolutes were everyday occurrences, where she met Kit. How strange, she thought with a smile, that a place ebbing with such misery should bring her the one true joy of her life.

She regretted leaving because she knew she would soon feel nostalgic. Kit would be at her side, his arms about her, and they would talk of this time, in the hushed whispers of a shared experience. These would always be their magical days of courtship.

Without a second glance, she left the room. The seeds of her future were here. But the reality of her future was just beyond eyeshot, in a black beard and dusty doublet.

It was time to begin her future.

Had they planned for days, it could not have been more perfect.

She reached his side, breathing hard through her mouth. Panting, she simply held the bottle up. He ran his knuckles over her flushed cheek and smiled.

The preparations were completed. He reached out his hand to Suffolk, fumbling for words.

"I . . . we both thank you," he said at last. "We will be gone from this place, yet we will always remember you."

Suffolk grunted. "I understand not where you go. I only hope you will achieve the happiness that so eluded you here."

She almost spoke, wondering how much Kit had told him. He seemed to understand precisely what was going to occur within the maze.

Suffolk nodded as if they were attempting a risky but entirely normal sea crossing. How could such a pragmatic man believe in miracles? Then it occurred to her that everyone here, with the exception of Kit and herself, had been raised with a sincere believe in witchcraft and magic, in fairies and worlds beyond reason.

The funny thing was, they had been right.

"Please, light them when I tell you." Kit's hand gripped hers as he spoke to Suffolk, one hand holding the future as he spoke to the past.

"Oh, and remember to tell Queen Anne to do as the king

requests. Cromwell has set it up so that, well . . . I told you." She smiled at Suffolk. "And please watch after Princess Elizabeth. She is so little, and needs—"

Kit's hand clamped over her mouth, and they all laughed.

"It's time," Kit said, but they all knew it even without his words.

The two of them walked into the maze, slowly, deliberately.

A lone voice pierced the air.

"Hamilton!" It was a growl of impotent fury.

"Goddamn," Kit grumbled. "It's Surrey."

They did not halt. Instead they walked faster, but Kit's hand rested on the hilt of his sword.

"Suffolk! Now!" Kit shouted as they picked up their pace. They were not in the exact spot they needed to be but hoped that by the time they reached the center the bundles of gunpowder would be set.

"Hamilton!" Surrey, his pale face a mask of fury, charged after them into the maze.

"Faster, love." Kit handed her the bottle so he could grab her arm, half dragging and half carrying her to the center. Her feet skimmed the gravel path as she struggled to hold the bottle.

The headdress, a small French hood, caught on a branch. Although her hair was ripped from her scalp, bringing tears to her eyes, she said nothing as her head snapped back for a moment. The headpiece, with a clump of chestnut hair, was left dangling in the shrubbery.

The first explosion of powder boomed, and she gasped.

"We're almost there," he breathed, covering her face with his open hand as a shower of gravel rained down. "Damn, what did he put in those packets?"

Another explosion tore through the air. They had reached the center of the maze, and she threw her arms about his waist.

Lifting the bottle from her hand, he wrapped his other arm around her shoulders. Two more bursts of gunpowder discharged some rocks, and Deanie closed her eyes, burying her face against his doublet. His heart thundered wildly against her ear, as loud and fierce as the explosions beyond the maze.

Shielding his eyes from the sprinkling of dust and rocks, he then held the bottle high over their heads.

Immediately, the ground began to tremble, from far more than the concussion of the explosives. A hum vibrated, low and mournful, rattling both of them to the core.

She opened her eyes and saw the cobalt-blue light dart from the bottle, causing brilliant lines to bounce in angles all about them.

"HAMILTON!" Surrey's voice peeled over the layers of explosions.

"For Christ's sake!" Kit swore. His tone was pure annoyance, as if an irritating gnat had disturbed their privacy.

Surrey stood less than six feet away, his sword pointed at them, his mouth open in an exaggerated expression of confusion. Then he closed his jaw and glared at Kit. Slowly, deliberately, he approached, the tip of his weapon directed at Kit's throat.

Kit reached for Deanie's hand and raised it carefully, not wishing to disturb the laserlike beams. He slipped the bottle into her hands, wrapping her trembling fingers around the neck of the bottle.

Deanie blinked, looking up at Kit. He cautiously dislodged her arm from his waist and drew his own sword.

"No, Kit! Not now!"

But Surrey had already lunged. Kit pushed her out of the way and countered Surrey's sword.

Frantic, she tried to keep the bottle above Kit's head, to maintain the pulsating prism that was flashing more violently now. Four more explosions rattled her very teeth, and still she stayed at his side.

Surrey slashed the air, attacking the spots that seemed to dance before his eyes with a frenzied passion. Kit moved Deanie out of the way, his arm scooting her into the center of a tender bush. From the corner of her eye she saw the lash of Surrey's sword, and a bright line of crimson mark the top of Kit's arm. The black doublet and white shirt underneath shredded, hanging from the tip of Surrey's blade.

The bottle was hot, and Deanie struggled to get back to Kit, who was countering Surrey with one arm while trying to protect Deanie with the other.

There was a terrific roar. Deanie clutched at Kit and she saw his gaze, those strangely colored hazel eyes, flick to hers. An emotion passed through his eyes, even as she saw Surrey's merciless sword fly before him. Then his arm, bloodied, fell limp and his weapon clattered to the ground.

She recognized the expression on his face. Pain? Regret? No. It was farewell.

She screamed his name, but the roar continued, rampaging and unstoppable.

The bottle slipped to the ground, and suddenly everything was dark.

Suffolk arranged the last of the bundles, wondering when all the ducks and quails he had just sent flying would finally return.

A figure in a rich blue cloak ran toward the maze waving a piece of paper. With annoyance, Suffolk realized it was Norfolk. He wished he had consumed more ale that afternoon, for facing Norfolk while sober was more than he could bear.

"I have it! I have it!" Norfolk's thin face was animated, his eyes glistening in triumph.

"What do you have, Norfolk?" muttered Suffolk. "A soul? I think not. What you do have is a demented son who just this minute chased Hamilton and Mistress Deanie into the center of the maze."

Norfolk swished a hand, dismissing Suffolk's information with annoyance. "It matters not. What is in my hands is a warrant for the arrest of one Christopher Neville, duke of Hamilton, and his kinswoman Mistress Deanie Bailey."

"On what charges?" Suffolk snatched the document from Norfolk's slender fingers.

"Treason."

"Nay! It is impossible!" Suffolk scanned the parchment. It was genuine, right down to Henry's seal.

With that, Norfolk plucked something from his cloak. It was a strange sort of book, narrow, with glossy paper and color and tiny words.

A Tourist's Guide to Hampton Court Palace.

"This book tells of the death of our sovereign." Norfolk sniffed in self-righteous pleasure. "The name in the book belongs to Deanie Bailey. They worked in consort to end our glorious king's reign through witchcraft. A woman alone could not do this." Then Norfolk's eyes narrowed. "And what of you, my duke of Suffolk? What brings you to this place, with fire and explosion?"

Calmly, Suffolk paged through the booklet, pausing once at a picture of himself, grizzled and old. There was also the wedding portrait of Mary Tudor and Suffolk, both flush with youth and love, her small hand resting in his. There were dates, but he did not want to look. He did not want to know.

So this was their magic, he wondered silently. He hoped with all his heart they had returned home. They were not guilty of treason. If anything, they were guilty of but one offense: Love.

His movements smooth, he watched Norfolk frown at the sod clumps that now pitted the lawn. While Norfolk scowled, Suffolk, gentle as a mother with a baby, reached for another taper. Smiling, he slipped the booklet under the final bundle and lit it.

He escorted Norfolk several yards away, musing on the implications of the arrest warrant, when the explosion shattered the fragile calm.

"What! What!" Norfolk sputtered, his face mottled and red. Then he leveled his malicious gaze at Suffolk. "Where is it? Where is my book? The king has not yet seen it, you villain. This is the proof of their treason! Henry signed the warrant based on my word! I told him it also saw an early death for Edward, the prince of Wales. He will never believe me without the proof."

Smiling, Suffolk pointed to the air, silencing Norfolk in midsputter. Tiny pieces of blackened, charred paper twirled to the ground.

"Come, Norfolk. Let us drink to a prosperous future."

Norfolk stamped on the ground, unable to articulate the furious words that shattered his well-practiced veneer.

Suffolk laughed and walked away. "I shall presently remove myself from the scene of the next explosion. From the blood in your face, Norfolk, it will be your head, and it will be very messy indeed. Good day."

And with that Suffolk left in search of friendly companionship and a cool draught of ale.

Something was scratching her face.

Deanie tried to open her eyes, but twigs and sharp leaves made her close them again. She tried to move her legs and arms. They were pinned in a spiraling grip, one hand raised over her head, the other straight back. Her feet did not even touch the ground.

"Kit," she moaned, feeling herself slip. The red velvet gown began to tear, slowly, steadily, as she sank down.

Then she realized what was happening. She was inside one of the bushes, the thick, impassable walls of the Hampton Court maze surrounding her. This was no young shrub but a plant decades old. Centuries old.

"Deanie, where are you?" A man was calling her. Kit?

"I'm over here! Thank God!" Squirming, she managed to free a hand and waved it frantically. Now she could see a little, and the shadow of a man holding a sword approached.

With a thrust, he plunged it into the shrubbery.

"Kit! Help! Surrey's here and he's trying to kill me!"

Someone laughed. A male voice. Familiar.

It was not Kit.

It was Nathan Burns, her video director. She had not seen the shadow of a sword; it was his stupid riding crop.

The laughing stopped. "You are in the bushes. How the hell did you get up there?"

His words sounded strange, hard edged and unpleasant. Had he always spoken like that?"

"Please help me," she pleaded. "I am looking for someone. Kit, the duke of Hamilton."

"Very funny, Deanie. Your British accent is as phony as a rubber crutch." Then he became angry; he had meant to say *funny as a rubber crutch.*

His face reddened. "First you blow the shoot, now you're hanging in the center of a very valuable landmark. Did you think we would cut you down? Damn it. And you have a concert in two hours. Wembley is sold out."

"Kit," she whispered. "Oh dear God."

"What the hell is that thing you're wearing? It's all wrong! Completely inaccurate. Goddamn, Deanie. Are you trying to screw up my life?"

Much to Nathan Burns's surprise, Deanie began to cry. He had never seen her so much as whimper, never seen her behave the way those other female singers did. Now she was sobbing, crying her heart out.

"Do you have a broken bone?" He didn't know what else to ask. Some Tudor Babes, the extras from the video, had arrived, along with the costume mistress and a cameraman, all staring up at a splotch of red hanging a dozen feet over their heads.

"Kit," she murmured. "He's gone. Dear God, he didn't make it." They heard a sharp intake of breath, and her cries became hysterical.

"I think she wants her cat," hissed Monica.

Nathan snapped his fingers, and a production assistant, a clipboard tucked under his arm, stepped to his side. Without looking at his underling, his eyes still focused overhead, Nathan ticked off his orders.

"I want a ladder and a gardener. A first aid kit and a medic. Go into my case and get the prescription of Valium. Call Wembley and stall them."

Monica the video extra whispered something, and Nathan nodded.

"Oh, and find a cat."

"A cat?"

The production assistant ran off, hoping he could find his way through the maze.

The costume director, her eyes peering through thick glasses, shook her head. "That is not the gown she was wearing a few minutes ago," she complained. "What's wrong? My work isn't good enough for this video?"

"Thelma, the costume is the least of our problems," Nathan ground out. "The costar of this video is at this moment perched in a bush crying for her kitty-cat. She seems to think this is the road show of the Frances Farmer story. Bucky Lee Denton has just been taken to the hospital with an infection of his latest hair-transplant operation. We have lost the light, and the weather reports predict rain for the next ten days. This whole video is about to self-destruct. Frankly, Thelma, if I were you I would be rather pleased that she is *not* wearing one of your creations."

The costume director thought about it for a few moments, then shrugged.

A red-faced worker with a gray cap that made him resemble an old train engineer entered the maze, an aluminum expandable ladder over his shoulder.

The gardener arrived next, his face twitching in anger. They should never have allowed these hillbillies on the palace grounds! The woman would have to be cut down. The maze had survived two world wars, a civil war, and countless bungling gardeners. But never—never—could it survive a video shoot.

After almost an hour of strategic sawing, with heated debates over which branch would cause the least amount of damage to the plant, Deanie was lowered to the ground. Her face and arms were scratched, her gown shredded and caked with sap and twigs and muddy leaves.

The worker had a unique expression on his face.

"What's wrong, mate?" asked the other gardener.

"That woman, she smells to high heaven. I work with fertilizer and every organic slime known to man." He shuddered. "She smells worse than a three-month-old compost pile."

The costume director approached the dazed and still sobbing country star. Her curiosity about the clothing overcame the nausea from the stench.

"This gown," she said, breathing through her mouth. "It's exquisite. That's real gold thread! And it's hand-sewn! I've only seen the likes in a museum!"

"Her hair is filthy, as if it hadn't been washed in weeks," growled the makeup woman, who had personally combed out Deanie's hair just that morning. "And it's grown. It was just at her shoulders this morning; now it's longer by several inches."

Nathan crinkled his nose in distaste. "Get her back to the Dorchester. She needs a good scrub and a change of clothing."

Numbly, Deanie Bailey was led back to her bus, her eyes unseeing, her hands trembling.

The same vehicle she had traveled in a lifetime ago.

Stanley cursed the entire American crew of the video.

His car, several years old and several payments late, was parked in the Hampton Court lot. He watched the commotion with a sense of joy. He had his paycheck in hand. The rest of the project could go to hell in a handcart for all he cared.

Opening the door, he thought about the star of the video.

She was a bit of all right, that's for sure. The only pleasant aspect of the work had been meeting her, exchanging a few words with a genuine American recording artist.

The keys dangled in the ignition. He reached for them, when someone began to stagger across the parking lot.

The lights illuminated the limping man. He seemed to be another extra just like himself, but his costume was all wrong. It was early Tudor, not Elizabethan. No wonder he had been sacked, poor sod.

Then Stanley noticed that the man's arm was bleeding, and he seemed to be in some sort of shock.

"Damn," Stanley spat. Then he stepped out of his car. "Hey, man. Need a ride?"

The man spun about and faced him, and Stanley's breath caught in his throat. Not only was the guy massively built, but he had a wild look in his eyes.

"Aye," the man said, still clutching his bleeding shoulder.

Stanley swallowed, wondering if he had made a mistake. But the man wore a costume, filthy though it was. He was an actor just like himself. As the man approached, Stanley eyed his movements: graceful, athletic. This was a physical actor, not one of those introspective soliloquy types. Then he realized who the man probably was.

Poor chap, he said to himself. *He must be from that troop out of Durham.* They had folded and left the actors without money, stranded them without notice.

The guy got closer, and Stanley unconsciously stood straighter. There was a nobility about the stranger that made Stanley want to behave.

He held the door open, and the man slid in, as if used to having doors held for him, wincing in pain. "We'll get that stitched up in a jiffy," Stanley said. To his own surprise, he heard himself add, "Then you're welcome to stay in my flat."

The stranger looked at Stanley. There was an expression of overwhelming anguish in his eyes, more than just the result of a physical injury. The man did not speak but nodded once.

Together, they drove out of the parking lot, tires crunching on the gravel.

Moments after they had left, Wilma Dean Bailey boarded the large bus. She seemed incapable of speaking, and in spite of being forced to swallow two Valium, she was clearly on the edge of some sort of hysterical fit.

The bus headed for the Dorchester Hotel.

Aboard the bus, Nathan Burns made a series of calls, the first of which cancelled that evening's show at Wembley Arena. The second cancelled his contract with the record company.

This would be the last music video of his career, and he intended to get very, very drunk that night.

Chapter 20

LORNA DUNE BAILEY PACED HER DAUGHTER'S LIVING ROOM, her thin arms folded over her chest as if warding off a chill. She automatically reached for another cigarette, fumbling through her large canvas purse, the green plastic lighter clicking against the clasp. She paused, glancing down at an ashtray already filled with the crisscrossed remains of cigarettes. Each had puckered lipstick marks on the tips, wrinkled and red and in Lorna's unique coral shade.

She shoved the nearly empty pack and plastic lighter back into her purse, disgusted with herself. It was a filthy habit, one she had never even contemplated until Deanie returned from England.

That's when all the trouble began.

Lorna began pacing again, her movements jerky and distracted. Upstairs, her daughter was speaking with the psychiatrist. Lorna had protested when everyone said her daughter needed a shrink.

"All she needs is a rest," Lorna had insisted when her daughter returned from England. But Deanie had refused to rest. Instead she did nothing but write and record her songs, all by herself in her basement studio. Before England, she used to love working with other musicians. Now all she wanted was to be alone with herself and an old guitar she'd paid way too much for at an auction.

Finally her record label, worried about her increasingly reclusive behavior, had insisted she get professional help, as had her manager and even a few newspaper columnists. In the end Lorna agreed. Deanie had been hanging about the house ever since, not really caring about anything except her songs. Even the expensive house calls from that lady psychiatrist didn't seem to matter.

A door upstairs creaked open, and soon the elegant Dr. Mathilda Howler descended the carpeted staircase. Deanie had laughed when she heard her psychiatrist's name. She had laughed a lot in the past months, but it was never with humor.

"How is she?" Lorna tried to keep her voice low, yet a high pitch had crept in, unwelcome and naked.

The psychiatrist shook her head, her well-lacquered hair remaining firmly in place. "Mrs. Bailey, your daughter is a most unusual case. I see many music industry professionals in my practice. There are usually warning signs, or some form of substance abuse before this sort of thing happens."

"Did you find out what set her off this time?" Lorna's hands were twitching for a cigarette.

The doctor shrugged in confusion. "She says it was a book, a history book."

"On old England?" Lorna closed her eyes in resigned exhaustion. "She's become obsessed with this duke from the court of Henry VIII. She was real quiet-like, staring at all these old paintings in a book, until she saw something about this fellow named Hamilton. It had two dates. One was 1516 with a question mark, as if they weren't real sure that's when he was born; and the other date was 1540. She tore through books, spent a fortune buying out a store, looking for different dates. But they all said either 1516 or 1517, and the last date is always 1540. Always 1540."

"I know I've asked you this before, Mrs. Bailey, but is there any way she could have become something of an expert on the Tudor monarchs? She is extremely knowledgeable."

Lorna's laugh was a dry bark. "Deanie! Ha, that's a joke! No, Dr. Howler. Deanie was no scholar—ever."

The psychiatrist frowned, marring her excellent makeup foundation for a brief moment. "Deanie seems to be quite upset over a picture book on the RAF."

"The what?"

"The Royal Air Force, over in England. It was a book from the Time-Life series about the Battle of Britain during World War II, the young pilots who fought the Luftwaffe, you know."

Lorna nodded, not quite sure what the doctor was talking about. "Well, what about the book? Did she say?"

"It's the photograph of a young man, quite handsome in fact. Black and white, of course. He's reading a book and holding a chipped mug of tea. His eyes are tired— extraordinary eyes, even in black and white. He's still wearing his flight jacket, and according to the caption he had just returned from a mission. Oh, and he was lost the following week, in September of 1940."

"So?"

"This is the confusing part, Mrs. Bailey. Your daughter insists he is the duke from Tudor England. She swears up and down that they are the same person. She's cut out the photograph and put it in a frame."

"So she's crazy then," Lorna muttered to herself. "I knew I should have changed her name. Did you know that? She was named after the Natalie Wood character from *Splendor in the Grass.* I didn't know then she ends up in a looney bin."

The doctor cringed, and Lorna waved a hand.

"Sorry. You know what I mean."

"Your daughter is not insane, Mrs. Bailey. She is fully aware of her surroundings, of her career, of you."

Lorna nodded. "Yes. But she also seems so distant, so remote. We were always real close, but now I can't understand her at all."

"I understand," agreed Dr. Howler. "In some respects, she has a clear vision of her life. In others, well, she's simply delusional, and we do hope we can reverse the problem."

"When will she be all right?"

The doctor took a deep breath. "There is no way to tell. A great deal depends on her own will. She is not suicidal, nor will she harm others. I believe she is suffering from a great sense of loss."

The doctor then paused, as if trying to formulate a way to phrase her next words.

"She is grieving, Mrs. Bailey, mourning the loss of a man who never existed, or if he did, she could never have possibly met. I believe the seed of this delusion was planted in England. She met a gentleman there who related a tale of grand passion and a dead pilot. His parents, as I understand, were deeply in love. Deanie's mind, already fragile, created her own grand passion, a perfect love that could never be destroyed, simply because it was never real."

"No offense, Doctor, but you're not making a heck of a lot of sense to me right now."

The psychiatrist folded her hands before speaking. "From her background—her childhood and her unstable relationships with men—I believe she created this fantasy to make up for the lack of a loving male figure."

"I don't understand."

"There were no good men in her life, Mrs. Bailey." The doctor tried to be gentle. "She never knew her father—through no fault of yours, I hasten to add."

Still Lorna swallowed, remembering her daughter as a beautiful, dark-haired child, sitting at home the night of the daddy-daughter dinner dance at school. She never complained, not then. The doctor continued.

"As an adult, she has made a success of her life in all areas except for one—namely, romance. She is becoming well known, she is physically beautiful and talented . . . and very, very lonely."

"What should we do?"

"I have discussed her case with some of my colleagues—strictly in confidence, of course. We believe she needs to go through the same process as a widow."

Lorna was about to protest, but Dr. Howler held up a firm hand to stop her. "Listen to me, Mrs. Bailey. Your daughter needs to mourn. She is a creative, intelligent woman who has been able to invent a man who is completely real to her. What she feels is a genuine loss. There is an emptiness in her life that is no less painful simply because the man who once filled it never existed. Let her mourn and experience her grief. Do not judge her, just help her. Listen to what she says, be sympathetic. Time will heal this."

"Good grief," Lorna spat. "My little girl has lost a pretend boyfriend, and we're supposed to feel sorry for her? I'll tell you what: She's made too much money, that's what her problem is. I was a single mother and I worked sixteen hours a day at the truck stop just to keep food on the table and . . ." She stopped, aware that she was shouting.

Dr. Howler gave Lorna an appraising, professional look, narrowing her eyes as if observing a specimen. Lorna grew quiet, then said, "What about her career? She hasn't expressed an interest in performing for over four months. She's writing songs like crazy, the best stuff she's ever done—at least that's what her producer is saying. They're about to release her album, and she needs to back it up with a major tour. If she doesn't hurry, she'll never get another chance. Her duet with Bucky Lee Denton is hot, and—"

"She will perform when she is ready," Dr. Howler replied frostily. "We cannot rush the process. Grief is a very personal thing. Everyone has their own schedule."

Lorna nodded.

"I will prescribe a mild sedative for when she needs to

sleep. Part of her problem is sleep deprivation. I will return tomorrow. Good day, Mrs. Bailey."

With that, the doctor gave a brittle smile, collected her bag, and walked out the front door. Lorna fell into a leather chair and looked at the mantel, the music awards twinkling in the afternoon light. With a defiant glance in the direction of the ashtray, she lit a cigarette.

It tasted damn good.

Chapter 21

*F*OR THE FIRST TIME IN HER ENTIRE CAREER, DEANIE BAILEY was paralyzed with stage fright. The sounds of the audience filtered backstage, a deafening, distorted neon nightmare. Thousands of voices roared across the arena, calling to her as one giant beast.

"Dean-ie! Dean-ie!"

Their voices grew louder. The stomping and clapping seemed to march up her spine.

As a show-business veteran with years of hard-won experience, Deanie did the logical thing when faced with such a reception: She decided to flee.

"Now, now," shouted Nathan Burns, gripping the arm of her sequined gown. "They are all calling you because they like you, Deanie. Not because they wish to harm you. In fact . . ."

Deanie tuned him out. After his lengthy stay at the Betty Ford Clinic and extensive psychotherapy, she was now witnessing the dawn of a kinder, gentler Nathan Burns, full of New-Age wisdom and homilies.

He no longer wore an Erich von Stroheim costume, instead opting for more of a love-beads and tie-dyed look. He was universally acknowledged to be more than a little unstable. But since her decision to return to the stage, he was the only one who seemed to understand her. He had been drunk and crazy, she had only been crazy, and together they had reached an unspoken agreement: They were allowed to wig out, but only in each other's company.

"Do I look all right?" She tugged at the midnight-blue gown, sleek as if the silk had been poured on. It was over a year since she'd faced an audience, and her heart was pounding in unison with the audience's chants.

"You look incredible, Deanie. And as your new manager, I must say this was a brilliant move on your part to open your world tour at Wembley. You're a star now, ever since that Bucky Lee duet. Those last four hits of yours have left poor old Bucky Lee green with envy."

The crowd stomped even louder, vibrating the backstage area with terrifying thunder.

"They've forgiven you for your nervous breakdown, my dear." Nathan continued as if the crowd had been a faint murmur. "I believe you knocked Princess Diana off the front page of the *Mirror.*"

"Poor thing." Deanie grinned. The lights dimmed, and the audience hushed as one, as if a soft blanket had silenced them, row by row.

Her name was announced, strange-sounding as if it belonged to someone else, echoing in the vastness of the arena. The spotlights darted as her band took the stage, and for a moment she thought of other darting blue lights, pulsating in a prism.

Not now. She couldn't think of him now.

Nathan gave her a gentle shove. She walked across the stage.

Was this real? The stadium vibrated with shouts, her name reverberating to the rafters with inarticulate and furious cheers. The white-hot lights blinded her, and she stopped, shaken.

What was wrong? She had played hundreds of gigs, thousands of them.

But that was before. Before the thought of an empty hotel room at the end of a performance could cause her knees to buckle. Before she realized the adoration of an audience was a mechanical, hollow parody of real love. Before Kit.

The bass player handed her the guitar, and she looped the strap over her shoulder. Then all was silent. Thousands of people, on the edge of their seats, peered at every move she made. She could hear the vague whir of the cameras.

"Hey," she said, mentally kicking herself for sounding so frightened. "Um, it's great to be back here in England."

Wild applause, more hoots.

"Um, some of my best friends are English," she added. The audience went nuts, leaping to their feet and cheering.

In her mind, she thought: *My best friend is English.*

Then, without waiting, she nodded to the band. With the resounding hum of her guitar, they began the performance.

And it was extraordinary. It was as if she had always played to a house of forty thousand. The songs felt right, her voice had never sounded better. The band played brilliantly, not just hitting the notes but putting character into every phrase, subtle nuances that could never be taught but must be felt. They seemed incapable of blundering, and every note was unadulterated magic.

Then something strange happened.

She paused between songs, reaching for a glass of water on a stool. As she sipped, her eyes wandered to the audience, where a beam of light traced back and forth with frenzied precision. She saw the usual sights from the stage: the eyeglasses reflecting their piercing glare, stray glitters of jewelry, rolled-up programs being used as fans, random flashes of movement.

And off to the side she saw Kit.

Choking on the water, she gasped. The bass player

reached over and slapped her on the back, but still she coughed.

"Don't drink the water here!" someone in the audience shouted. "It's not safe!"

Oh dear God, she thought. She was going to wig out right on stage.

She looked back to where she saw the man earlier, and he was gone. No one was there. She had imagined it all, just as Dr. Howler had said she imagined Kit.

"My next song," she said, leaning into the microphone, "seems appropriate. Hope you all agree."

She then performed the most perfect rendition of Patsy Cline's "Crazy" that anyone had ever heard.

The show lasted another two hours, passing in a complete white-hot blur. Time seemed meaningless as the songs and audience became one. Three encores later, when she finally left the stage, the audience and Deanie and her band were exhausted, limp with relief and deliriously happy.

Nathan presented her with a sloppy, alarmingly friendly kiss. The record company executives declared this would be her next album; the performance had been recorded for the purpose.

Anonymous hands clapped her back, sending the remaining sequins on her costume scattering to the floor. She signed every bit of paper shoved into her face by autograph hounds. The flashing lights made her dizzy, spots dancing before her eyes. Nathan fielded questions, requests, demands. Everyone was ecstatic.

A panic began to rise in her throat at the frenzy. And she had to be alone.

Her dressing room backstage was thick with flowers, some still boxed, others in massive arrangements. The sounds of the audience leaving the arena were mercifully muffled; distant laughs and shouts and the grating scrape of garbage cans as the crew cleaned up.

Nathan followed her into the room, beaming, holding a bottle of champagne and a single flute.

"Here, Deanie," he said, popping the cork. "This is for you."

Sighing with exhaustion, she accepted the glass and watched the bubbles float to the top. Some seemed to swirl like propellers, twisting their way through the pale froth. Propellers reminded her of Kit, his love of flying, the way he . . .

Stop! She was not to think of him. Dr. Howler explained how the mind could do astounding things, such as allow people to walk over hot coals without being burned, or cure an incurable illness. In her case, she was cured ever so briefly of loneliness.

Then what about her knowledge of Tudor England, and the very real duke of Hamilton, and the photograph of the RAF pilot that sat at that very moment on her dressing-room table?

Dr. Howler had an explanation for that as well. Somehow, during Deanie's trip to England, she had come in contact with the information. It was completely logical: She was at Hampton Court filming a video, she had taken a tour of the palace and even purchased a guide booklet. She had met a man named Neville Williamson who provided a charming, magical tale of pure love.

Under the stress of the filming and her first big chance, combined with the very real career threat posed by Bucky Lee Denton, she had retreated into a world of her own, a time and place where she would feel more in control.

Then she had invented Kit, her dashingly handsome duke. He became her fantasy hero, rescuing her from danger as no flesh-and-blood man ever had. Deanie's imagination had endowed the fictitious Kit with all the qualities she had desired in a man, and even a few irritating ones just to add a theatrical dash of realism.

And then she saw the photograph of the equally handsome—and dead—RAF pilot, and somehow she combined the two fantasies. A brief glimpse of a forgotten pilot, and her mind took off.

Deanie grasped the champagne flute with firm hands and took a swig, downing half the contents in a single swallow.

But Dr. Howler's fine logic had not been able to explain the clothing she was wearing when they cut her from the maze, or how her hair could have grown by inches in a single afternoon.

Or how she could recall every detail of her imaginary Kit, from his strong arms that could suddenly turn gentle to his crooked bottom tooth. She could still feel the texture of his hair, the few gray strands only visible in the sun.

Could anyone imagine the wondrous man who was Kit?

There was a sharp knock on the door, and she jumped, the straggling blue sequins on her gown rattling with the movement.

"Come in," she said, not really meaning it.

A polite guard poked his head into her dressing room, sniffing at the overpowering scent of flowers.

"Excuse me, Miss Bailey, but there is someone here to see you. Says he is a very old friend of yours."

Deanie sighed and took another sip of champagne. The last thing she needed was to make small talk with someone she knew from her past, probably high school.

Nathan glanced at her, then shook his head toward the guard. "No, sorry. It's out of the question. Tell them she's too exhausted, but if they leave their name and address we'll make sure to send a personally autographed picture."

"All right," said the guard. "Oh, wait a minute. He wanted me to give this to her. Said she would know what it meant."

Nathan shook his head even as Deanie shrugged weakly and reached for the envelope.

"Thank you." She smiled to the guard.

Something in her stomach lurched as she touched the envelope. Her name was written in a strong, bold hand across the top.

"Mistress Deanie."

Nathan was beginning to chatter about the flowers, but all

she could hear was the blood whooshing through her ears. Her fingers trembling, she eased open the paper.

Inside was a small square of whitish cloth. She knew what it was before she turned it over. It was a clumsy attempt at needlepoint, speckled with brown spots that resembled blood. To most people it was just an amateurish depiction of a blob with wings, a bug or a bird.

Or an airplane.

She gasped and rose to her feet, sending the crystal flute crashing to the floor.

"Christ, Deanie! That's Dom you've just spilled, not André. A few months ago I would have licked it off the floor, glass and all." Nathan then looked at her, her pale face and white lips. "What's wrong?"

Her mouth worked, but no sound escaped. Then she croaked, "Guard." Softly at first, then louder. "Guard!"

The guard returned. "Yes, Miss Bailey?"

"Please, please send him in," she rasped, her voice dry. The guard nodded and left, closing the door.

Deanie's knees gave way, and she felt behind her, blindly grabbing a chair.

This was impossible, she said to herself, sinking into the hard folding chair. Kit never existed. She imagined it all.

There was a single knock on the door, and Deanie turned. Her heart literally stopped; she felt her entire being pause, as if waiting to decide whether or not to continue existing.

Slowly the door opened.

And there he stood.

A small sound came from her throat as she saw him, her heart now pounding so loudly she thought it would shatter her soul.

"Kit," she breathed.

He stepped through the door, his very presence resounding in every corner of the room, filling the empty spaces with his vitality. He was her Kit, his shoulders broad, his stance solid and proud.

Instead of a plain black doublet he wore a tweed sports

jacket with khaki slacks and a slightly rumpled button-down shirt. She saw him take a deep breath as he stared at her, the incandescent depths of his eyes searing through her.

"I thought you were dead," she said, her voice cracking into a sob.

"So did I," he whispered, his throat working, his jaw tight with emotion.

Nathan Burns emerged from the foliage of a horseshoe-shaped arrangement. "Goddamn, they must have thought this was a horse race," he muttered to himself. Then he looked up at Deanie. "Should this stuff be divided between a children's hospital and nursing home? The usual?"

Deanie did not respond; her eyes were locked on the tall dark-haired man in the doorway. Nathan looked between the two, and an uncomfortable feeling prickled his thick skin.

"What happened?" She spoke as if in a trance, and only to the stranger. Nathan frowned. It was as if he didn't exist.

"We were separated in the maze, Deanie, but we did travel together. It worked." Kit's words were terse, his teeth clenched.

"Why . . . where . . ." She closed her eyes, unable to think clearly with him so near. His shirt was open at the throat, and she saw his sun-darkened skin, the sprinkling of dark hair she knew was just under the cloth. How well she knew the feel and scent of him, the muscles on his chest.

She folded her arms and opened her eyes. "Where have you been? Why didn't you let me know? Oh Kit, I thought . . ."

"Shh." His voice was deep, resonant. He reached toward her, his long, strong fingers open, then pulled back. The gesture was so swift she thought she had imagined it.

"I tried, Deanie." His accent was still bent by archaic vowels, intonations that had been lost for centuries. "I tried to reach you at your hotel, before you left England. But they would not let me. I cannot say that I blame them."

Then he smiled, and she felt as if the wind had been

knocked from her chest. His smile, the crooked bottom tooth, the cheeks kissed with his glorious dimples, elongated, strong. His eyes crinkled at the corners.

"They did not truly think me mad until I expressed a rather firm desire to see you." Distractedly, he pushed a wayward thatch of hair from his forehead. "You see, the mere utterance of your name transformed me from a rather pathetic out-of-work actor into a dangerous stalker."

Her mouth dropped open, and he continued. "I tried to find you, but London had changed so—more in the last fifty years than in the previous five centuries."

Nathan Burns snorted, but they ignored him.

"Oh, Kit. No one told me. Then what happened?"

"Well, when I tried to find you, I must have seemed a bit disoriented. So they put me into a very nice suite. I believe they called it a ward." He gave a small chuckle, but it was painful, bitter. "I shared the ward with a fascinating young man who firmly believed he was Bette Davis."

"Bette Davis?"

"He was quite good, actually. But the poor chap tended to refer to her later films, always reminding me to 'fasten your seat belts, it's going to be a bumpy night,' whatever the bloody hell that was supposed to mean. Then he'd puff on imaginary cigarettes, proclaiming the place a dump."

"Oh," she said, stunned.

"Yes, well. They gave me some marvelous medication and took copious notes whenever I babbled, which was often. They interrogated me, asked me questions I couldn't possibly know the answer to, like the first moon walk, for Christ's sake, or Jodie Foster."

"Kit."

He straightened. "You were wonderful tonight, Deanie. When I met you before, I had no idea . . . well. I didn't understand. You tried to tell me about all this." His hand opened and quickly closed. "I didn't understand."

She said nothing. A thousand thoughts tumbled through her mind, but she said nothing.

"Well, once again I seem to be babbling," he said, as a strange, hooded expression crossed his features. "I'll not keep you any longer, Deanie. You have all of this—you don't need me puttering about as a reminder of a time when you almost met with disaster. I shall let you go to be embraced by, well, your fans."

He gave her a curt nod and turned, reaching for the doorknob.

"Kit!"

He paused, his back toward her.

The finely tailored sports coat seemed to expand as he drew in a deep breath. "Yes?" He still did not face her.

"Where are you going? Where are you staying?"

The dark head, a mass of glossy, unruly waves, dropped forward, as if he had suddenly become very tired.

"I am going to my sister's." His voice was flat. "She's Lady Carolyn Deighton now, and a bit long in the tooth to be called *Sis*. She's well into her eighties."

Nathan Burns knocked his head on the closet as he glanced up.

Deanie still could not speak.

Kit cleared his throat, as if deciding whether or not to continue. "It's my birthday today," he said at last.

"Oh, Kit." Her voice was soft.

"I'm four hundred and seventy-nine."

"Happy birthday," and he heard the warm smile in her voice.

"Of course, depending on how you look at it, I could be seventy-nine." He then turned around. "Or thirty-five."

Their eyes met as if for the first time. There was a clarity there, an understanding that reached across the room, palpable as a caress.

"Okay, buddy," said Nathan, his face set in an annoyed scowl. "Let's get out of here now. I know enough about drugs and booze to see an abuser."

Deanie reached for the bottle of champagne for something to hold on to, anything at all. "Stop, Nathan," she ordered.

Nathan ignored her and placed his hand on Kit's broad back. He paused, startled by the strength he felt under the tweed.

Kit did not move.

His eyes had wandered to Deanie's hand, now gripping the neck of the bottle, her knuckles white as her face. That was not what he was focused on; it was a black-and-white image in a silver picture frame. Of a young World War II pilot clutching a mug of tea, his eyes weary and wary.

"Deanie," he said huskily. "My love."

The heavy bottle of Dom clattered to the floor, and Deanie threw herself into his arms, waiting and warm.

Her hands clutched at his back as she inhaled his scent, more potent than any substance on earth, clean and male. His hands raked through her hair and he gently pulled her head back, hungry for a look at her face.

His expression as his eyes took her in was shattering in its focused intensity. All pride and common sense had been replaced by ragged desire. Shakily, her thumb traced his lower lip, tenuous, frightened he would again vanish, that she would again suffer the barren longing of his absence.

But he was real and solid, his heart pounding against her breasts as if proclaiming his existence.

She tried to speak but was silenced by her emotions, the rampaging surge of passion and unmatched joy and, above all, love, pure and intoxicating.

Tears fell hot and heavy onto his shirt, and she pressed herself to him, his powerful arms embracing her as if their lives depended upon it.

Her mind was reeling. Could this be happening? Had she finally gone completely insane?

He spoke: "If this is madness, may it never cease." His mouth descended upon hers, savagely, with a thirst born of anguish and longing and love.

In a distant corner of the room, Nathan Burns was on his

hands and knees, gingerly tasting a splash of long-forgotten champagne.

The breakfast tray was shoved next to the door, untouched save for the empty coffee cups. Only the single red rose had been moved, and it rested on top of a folded linen napkin.

The sheets on the bed were twisted and gnarled. Two oversized pillows, complete with the embroidered Dorchester Hotel emblem on the soft linen, lay mysteriously on the floor in the center of the room.

Deanie sighed and leaned against Kit's chest, her eyes closed in contentment. She wore a plush hotel robe, he wore a single sheet.

"I still feel as if I'm in a dream," she mumbled, planting a kiss on his chest.

"This is better." She felt him swallow. "In my dreams I never imagined running water and an indoor toilet."

"How romantic."

He laughed, then grew silent. She felt his arm become tense about her shoulder and, curious, she glanced up.

There were comb marks in his hair from the shower, and he was staring down, long dark lashes shuttering his eyes.

"Do you know what happened back there?"

He didn't have to explain his meaning. She fully understood his soft words.

"I've read dozens of books, Kit. I was searching for you, looking for you in those dry history books." She was unable to keep herself from shivering, and he smiled tenderly, rubbing his thumb slowly on her shoulder.

"You saved her life, you know. Anne of Cleves would have been beheaded, but you saved her." His voice was full of wonderment.

"Do you really think so?"

"I am sure of it, love. Cromwell would have been forced into having her executed, and Henry would have agreed. And Anne lived in splendor at Richmond as the king's honorary sister. Of all Henry's wives, she was the most fortunate. And she had you to thank, Deanie."

"But poor Katherine Howard." Deanie sighed. "She may have been annoying, but she didn't deserve to be beheaded. She was a giggling teenager who should have been grounded, not a queen. She was used by her uncle."

"Everyone was used, Deanie. It still occurs, but on a less-than-grand scale." There was an astringent edge to his voice. He took a deep breath. "Poor Surrey, Norfolk's son. He was eventually executed as well, another victim of the most esteemed duke of Norfolk. The only thing that kept Norfolk's scrawny neck from the block was Henry's death."

They were both silent for a moment, trying to make sense of the waste of lives and talent so many centuries earlier.

"At least Suffolk did well," Deanie said thoughtfully. "I mean, when he died it seems Henry really grieved."

"He did, I think. By that time Henry was such an old man—Katherine's betrayal did it to him, Deanie. He wanted to love and be loved so badly that it killed him, killed the great Henry of England."

"I read about Suffolk's granddaughter, Lady Jane Grey. At least he never knew about it, that his granddaughter was beheaded because of a plot to put her on the throne. Another innocent, I suppose. Like Katherine and Surrey, she was used. Used to death."

Deanie suddenly remembered the feel of Suffolk's rough hands on hers, his scratchy beard when he would kiss her on the cheek like a favorite uncle. "I liked him," she said at last.

"And he liked you, Deanie. Enough to risk hiding me, incurring both my wrath and that of the king. He did that for you as much as for me."

"He was an overgrown romantic." She smiled. Then she grew serious. "What do you think of Cromwell's end? I mean, he was nasty enough, but I still can't believe he was beheaded. I really didn't think the king would do that to Cromwell. I thought he'd just rot in the Tower."

Kit shook his head. "And he was executed on the same day Henry married Katherine. That should have been an omen. Someone should have noticed the gross crassness of the timing. Have you read some of the letters Cromwell wrote to Henry, begging for his life? My shoulder still bothers me, and I would have liked to see him punished. But those letters, Deanie. They must be the most pathetic words ever written."

"Do you think Henry ever saw them?"

"No. I don't think Norfolk allowed it, all in the name of dispatching his own duties."

"Oh, Kit."

Then he planted a kiss on her head. "Little Elizabeth turned out rather nicely, though."

"She did, didn't she?" Deanie found it hard to believe that the same small girl who drew a wet-nosed bunny became arguably the greatest monarch England ever knew.

Together they rested in comfortable silence. She was about to suggest they order lunch, or at least poke at the long-cold breakfast tray, when the expression on his face suddenly altered. It was as if a tide had shifted, inevitable, unstoppable.

"Kit, what's wrong?"

His gaze was straight ahead, as if he was unable to see the room. Then he looked at her, a sadness darkening his eyes.

"I have to leave," he said.

"What?" Raw panic made her tense up, and her hands clenched convulsively. "Are you joking? All of a sudden you have to leave?"

"No, Deanie. Please, you must listen to me."

She straightened, her back rigid, as he sat up and pulled on his khaki slacks. For long moments they said nothing, but were aware of each other's every movement.

"This thing that happened to us, this journey," he began, then halted. "Deanie, I need to find my own way."

"What do you mean?"

"I refuse to become an albatross about your neck, weigh-

329

ing you down. No, listen." He placed a finger over her lips. "Please listen."

She nodded, unable to keep the sudden tears from her eyes.

Then he spoke. "Deanie, everything I know, everything I have ever known, is gone. Yes, my sister still lives, and thank God you are well, but everything else has vanished. I grew up in a vastly different world. I'm not sure if I can explain it properly, but it is as if every single value I believed in has now been proven false."

"Do you mean from Henry's time, or from 1940?"

"Both." He looked up at the ceiling, as if the answers would be there. "I managed to adjust once to a new time. It was more than difficult, at times it was hellish, as you well know. But to be forced to adjust again, to rethink my entire existence beyond this room, where I fit in and how I came to be here, it has exhausted my resources. Deanie, I am not yet whole."

"But can't I help you?" She reached for his hand, and he took it. "You helped me, Kit. I wouldn't be alive if it hadn't been for you. Let me help you."

"No, Deanie." Without looking at her, he brushed his lips over her knuckles. "You have no idea how you have helped me, just by being alive. Your existence is what has kept me sane, given me a reason to even try to do this thing."

"I'm still confused," she admitted.

"You have a life, Deanie. A rare, unique talent. You are magnificent—no, listen. I do not want to touch that part of your life."

"But it means nothing without you!" Her voice was a cry.

"But it must! Don't you see? We need to be strong alone before we can be together. You have done that; last night you proved it. Now it's my turn."

"How can you say you are not strong? After all of the accomplishments . . ." Her voice trailed off.

Kit laughed then and pulled her close. "I think you are beginning to understand, my love. I need to find a purpose in this time, a meaningful life. Think of my resumé, Deanie. I'm university-educated; that's good enough. I can fly a vintage airplane and drop bombs on Berlin, which was useful in its day but hardly a worthwhile career at this point. And I am perhaps the finest tournament jouster in the land. Nay, excuse me, no—in the world. Unfortunately, there have not been jousts, real jousts, in about four centuries.

"What else can I do? At the risk of boasting, I am fully able to put down border uprisings in Scotland and have foiled several pretenders in their efforts to take the crown from Henry. I am courteous, courtly, proficient in both the long bow and short—"

Deanie reached up and silenced him with a kiss.

"I understand," she murmured.

"In short," he concluded, "I have not yet found a useful purpose. I am nothing more than a walking anachronism, a breathing sideshow curiosity." He fell back against the pillows. "I would make a perfect addition to the House of Windsor, but alas, there are no vacancies."

"Kit, I'm not sure if I can live without you," she said, pulling the robe tightly around her.

A ghost of a smile flickered on his lips. "Oh, but you won't have to. Not for long, anyway. Deanie, I just need time—a few weeks, a few months. Before last night, before we were together, I didn't know if I could find the strength to continue. But now, my God, Deanie. Now that I know you will be here, I feel I can do anything."

"Kit," she breathed. "Anything?"

"Anything," he repeated. But the word was muffled when his lips touched hers with a glorious promise of the future, of the yet-untasted joys that would soon be theirs.

Epilogue

DEANIE BAILEY TIGHTENED THE BELT OF HER TRENCHCOAT against the early spring chill. There were few tourists this time of year at Hampton Court Palace. It was still too early for the rows of plush buses to be parked in the lot, for the dozens of travelers to wander the grounds plugged into electronic tour tapes.

The wind whipped her hair, and she closed her eyes to meet the misty spray of rain. This was a lonely place, a place to revel in melancholy thoughts and dark dreams.

After watching the horizon for a few moments, she eased herself onto a damp stone bench, her rear end feeling the cold even through her coat and jeans. It was strange to be back after so long, after all that had happened.

The scene was tranquil, deceptively so. With such a pastoral landscape, it was almost impossible to imagine anything but gentle movements, quiet encounters with oil-painting figures.

Dr. Howler told her she had imagined it all. Deanie had

no proof to convince her otherwise. Even the very real appearance of Kit was easily explained.

"You see, there is a perfectly logical reason for your new romance," the doctor had intoned, tapping her pencil on a stack of notes concerning Deanie's case. "You were in London right before your episode."

"Episode" was the psychological term for her nervous breakdown.

"You caught a glimpse of Christopher Neville from the window of your bus, or perhaps as you checked into the Dorchester. Subconsciously, your desire for a relationship caused your mind to file away the details of Mr. Neville. Then you saw the photograph of the pilot, who does indeed bear an uncanny resemblance to Mr. Neville, and your mind developed the elaborate fantasy."

"But what about his name, and that he was searching for me? Dr. Howler, you can't tell me that was pure coincidence."

"Ah, but it was. You see, without the very successful treatment you have completed with me and my staff, the two of you would never have found each other." A smile of professional triumph had crossed the doctor's face. "The only mystery here is mutual attraction. When he saw you in London, something clicked within his head as well. We can analyze many things, Miss Bailey. For hundreds of years science has tried to understand what causes sexual attraction in the human species, but there are no definitive answers, just tantalizing hints."

Then a softness had passed over Dr. Howler's very professional face, and all elements of science and logic seemed to vanish. "Perhaps some things are best left a divine mystery, Miss Bailey. And perhaps grand passions and romance—the greatest mysteries of all—should remain just that."

Dr. Howler had then straightened, as if embarrassed by showing a more human side, and slipped her pencil into the pocket of her white jacket. That had been her last session with Dr. Howler.

Deanie rubbed her eyes, bringing her thoughts back to the present. The chill in the air seemed to grow by the minute, a dampness unique to England.

A hand grasped her arm.

She jumped, startled for the briefest of moments.

"Did you see this?" He blinked against the light rain, holding the latest London tabloid for her perusal.

She glanced down and began to giggle. "They say I've married Aaron Neville." She turned her gaze up to meet his face.

"Aaron Neville, Christopher Neville—what's the difference?"

He settled beside her on the bench, his forearms resting on his thighs as he read the paper. His thick green Irish sweater and knee-high Wellingtons seemed more natural than doublet and hose, and he shook his head at the content of the paper.

"It says here that I dated Julia Roberts before I married you. Funny, I can't seem to recall that." With his hair cropped shorter, his eyes were far more startling, the planes of his face more apparent. There was a faint hint of whiskers about his jaw as his eyes narrowed while reading the paper.

"Sure, Kit. You dated Julia right before I had that fling with Elvis."

"Oh, that one." He grinned.

"Yeah, that one."

For a few moments they sat in silence, watching a bird plunder the soil for a worm.

"It seems so long ago," she breathed, watching her words puff in the cold air.

"It was."

The rain began to pelt down in earnest. He placed the newspaper on his lap and shook out the raincoat that had been tossed over his shoulder. Sighing, she leaned into the circle of his arms as he held the coat tentlike over her head. They huddled in silence, her face resting against the scratchy wool of his sweater, his cheek on her damp hair.

"I sometimes wish we could have done more," she said softly.

"Perhaps we could have," he murmured. "But we probably would not have made it back. We would be footnotes to Henry's long reign, very dead and very forgotten."

"We're still footnotes, and we're still forgotten." She smiled.

"True. But at least we're alive forgotten footnotes." He chuckled, brushing his lips against her hair.

"Do you miss anything from back then?"

"A few things," he admitted. "There are mornings I wake up and think to myself, What a perfect day for a joust. Or, What will the king require of me today? It's very strange, Deanie, not to be dictated by some all-powerful being."

A burst of thunder clapped in the distance, and he pulled her closer under the raincoat.

"That was Henry." She looked up as the lightning zigzagged through the sky. "He demands another platter of doughnuts."

Kit laughed, his eyes crinkling as the rain dampened his hair.

"We should leave now, love. Neville Williamson and his wife are holding tea for us; we should at least arrive on time. And we promised your mother we'd ring her this evening." Kit took a deep breath and glanced over her head at the maze, barely visible in the misty distance. "I think we've seen all there is to see."

"I suppose." Then she reached for his hand. "Have you made a decision yet?"

"Yes, I believe I have."

"Well? Tell me, Kit, are you going to sell? That's a heck of a lot of money they offered. I mean, how many fledgling airlines are the center of an international bidding war?"

"Not many, I imagine." He raised an eyebrow, unable to keep the smile from his face. "But then how many airlines are composed completely of vintage propeller planes?"

"It's the service everyone goes nuts over, Kit. It was brilliant of you to think of it: the old decor, the outfits worn by the flight attendants, jazz and old radio shows on the headphones, the antique magazines offered in-flight, those great old movies."

"Shush." He placed his hand over her mouth. "Don't tell me what happens at the end of *Casablanca*. Every time I almost reach the end, some pesky phone call interrupts."

"Pesky? Like British Airways doubling their offer? So you haven't told me, Kit: Are you going to sell?"

He paused and rotated his shoulder, feeling the ache of the old wound in the English dampness. "I've been thinking, Deanie. I have no real desire to sell. There's nothing quite like flying your own plane, and I don't believe I could give that up. Certainly not now, maybe never. But here in England, where the taxes are brutal and available land is so limited, it would be almost impossible for the airline to grow." His thumb traced over her hand as he spoke. "How about if I move the operation to the United States?"

"Really?" The excitement made her voice shrill.

"Someplace with lots of land nearby, so Monarch Air could expand. Perhaps someplace in the South. It might take awhile, with rough going at first, but we've been through worse. I have my eye on a bit of land outside of Nashville and—"

The rest of his words were cut off by her lips on his, as the black raincoat slipped off their shoulders and landed in the dirt, forgotten and muddied. At first he laughed at her response, but the laughter died in his throat, replaced by fierce desire, overwhelming passion for the woman in his arms.

His fingers combed through her hair, droplets of water drizzling from the ends as their embrace became tighter, their kiss deeper. She noticed the scratchy feel of his whiskers and the soft fullness of his lower lip, and it didn't matter where they were or when they were. It only mattered that they were together.

"A-hem," came an embarrassed voice.

In her haze Deanie did not respond, and Kit, only half aware of the intrusion, chose to ignore it.

"A-hem, a-hem."

Completing one last kiss, Kit raised his eyebrows, glancing at the red-faced gardener standing under a large black umbrella.

"Excuse me, sir," he said discreetly. "A-hem, and ma'am. The grounds are closing. You'd best be off, and get out of them wet clothes."

Deanie giggled, her hands dropping to Kit's chest, her eyes still steady upon his face.

The gardener cringed. "That's not what I meant."

Kit held up a hand. "Please, don't worry. We'll be off."

The gardener seemed reluctant to leave them alone. Kit gave Deanie's shoulder a light squeeze and scooped up his soggy raincoat.

"You should come back later in the spring," said the gardener, struggling for something to say. "It's lovely then, it is. Magical, almost."

The ghost of a smile traced Deanie's lips. "We know," she whispered, ducking under Kit's arm. "It's pure magic."

Together they walked back to the parking lot, the gardener holding the umbrella over their heads, chattering about the flora and fauna of Hampton Court.

But Kit and Deanie said nothing. For as magical, as glorious as the garden was in the spring, they alone knew the most magical thing of all is love.

Author's Note

The Hampton Court maze was not actually created until the reign of William and Mary, more than a hundred years after Kit and Deanie and, incidentally, Henry VIII. Anne Boleyn's family home, Hever Castle, did have a maze, however. Perhaps Henry wooed his vivacious ill-fated second wife there. Only they know for sure.

Anne of Cleves never did return to her homeland. She was granted the palace of Richmond upon the annulment of her marriage, as well as the extraordinary sum of four thousand pounds a year. Henry threw in the title of his "Honorary Sister," as well as the manor of Betchingly and his reviled late wife's Hever Castle. Her brother the duke of Cleves breathed a sigh of relief and admitted that he was "glad his sister had fared no worse."

Anne became something of a fashion trendsetter, and her unique position as a self-sufficient woman at court gave her a delightful sense of freedom. Although she never remarried, she remained good friends with Henry and his eldest daughter, Mary.

And after the annulment, Henry allowed Anne to become a mother figure to his little red-haired daughter, Princess Elizabeth.